THE KNOCKOUT RULE

Take a right hook to the heart with heavyweight boxer Brick Kramarov as he falls for the last person he ever expected: a woman who avoids boxing like the plague...

Praise for Kelly Siskind's Showmen series

"This is a must read!" ~ *USA Today* bestselling author Jennifer Blackwood on New Orleans Rush

"This is not your ordinary love story. It's *extraordinary*." ~ Bookgasms Book blog on New Orleans Rush

"Siskind is a **master at creating characters with heart that you fall in love with** while they're falling in love with each other." ~ author Jen DeLuca on Don't Go Stealing My Heart

"**The writing is delicious** and Kelly's voice is vibrant." ~ author Mary Ann Marlowe on The Beat Match

“There's only one way to review this...by yelling it from the rooftops about **how awesome it is!**” ~ Red Reader on The Knockout Rule

This book is a work of fiction. Names, characters, places, and incidents are the product of the author's imagination or are used fictitiously. Any resemblance to actual events, locales, or persons, living or dead, is coincidental.

First edition: CD Books February 2021

The author is not responsible for websites (or their content) that are not owned by the author.

ISBN 978-1-988937-15-1 (ebook edition)

ISBN 978-1-988937-16-8 (paperback)

Created with Vellum

ALSO BY KELLY SISKIND

Chasing Crazy

Showmen Series:

New Orleans Rush

Don't Go Stealing My Heart

The Beat Match

The Knockout Rule

Over the Top Series:

My Perfect Mistake

A Fine Mess

Hooked on Trouble

One Wild Wish Series:

He's Going Down

Off-Limits Crush

36 Hour Date

Visit Kelly's website and join her newsletter for great giveaways and never miss an update!

www.kellysiskind.com

THE KNOCKOUT RULE

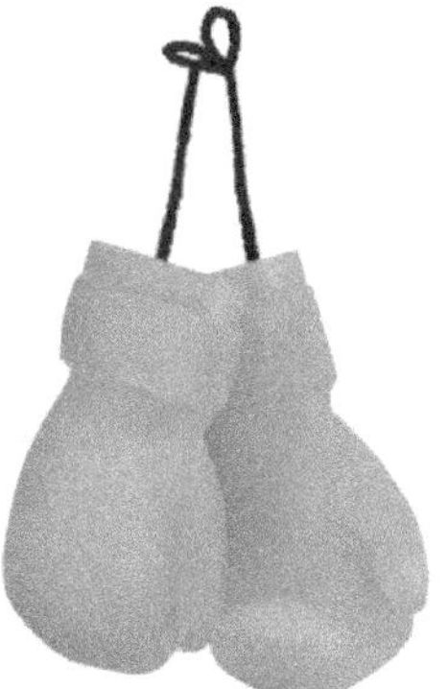

1

Isla loved having her hands on athletic bodies. Soccer players. Basketball players. Baseball players. The sport didn't matter, as long as none of them were boxers. Their bodies mattered, and Álvaro Garza's strong physique had her undivided attention. He was six-feet-two-inches of sculpted muscle, fine-tuned to be the best, and he wasn't giving her an inch.

"You can go harder," he said while lying face-down on her treatment table. "I'm not made of glass."

Isla pressed her thumbs into his hamstring, working into his biceps femoris. He grunted but didn't relax into the deep tissue work. This was her first session with the center fielder, soon to be Rookie of the Year, and she planned to rock his physiotherapy world. If she didn't, starting her fledgling business would be an uphill climb. Of the Everest variety.

Time for some active release treatment. Flexing his knee so his ankle could rest on her shoulder, she put her fist against his hamstring, ready to apply pressure. "Extend your knee as I work. If I go too deep, tell me."

"No pain, no gain."

Typical athlete. "Some pain is good, too much is bad. This only works if we communicate."

"Then go deeper." His tone was flippant. Even worse, he went slack and closed his eyes, like he was verging on a nap.

Not the relaxation she was after.

Álvaro may have been there for a free session to test her services prior to her opening, but she'd been through this before—the arrogance and snap judgments. Álvaro's last physiotherapist had been a man. Many athletes didn't believe a woman had the strength to work their muscles.

She dug her fist deeper as he extended his knee.

He flinched. "Fuck. *No.* Not that deep."

Gotta love making grown men weep. And proving a point. "That's what she said."

Álvaro laughed, short and abrupt, then he narrowed his eyes. "You're stronger than you look."

"You're as judgmental as you look."

Another laugh, this one loose and charming. "Strong *and* a ball buster. Where have you been all my life, Isla Slade?"

She'd been eyeballs deep in textbooks and classes, while inhaling take-out food on the fly. Lately, she'd also been inhaling details about Álvaro, like his enjoyment of dirty jokes and straight talk. She was seven weeks from opening her practice. All intel uncovered was crucial. "Are you flirting with me, Mr. Garza?"

"If you have to ask, I'm not doing a good job."

"I don't date athletes, or clients, and you're too young for me." Best to get the fine print out of the way, especially since she needed his business.

Snagging Álvaro Garza as her first client would be huge. A triumph that would draw other athletes to her soon-to-be opened doors. Proof she'd made the right choice leaving the security of an established practice. This whole business ownership thing was no joke. Her bank account was draining fast. Building out her office space had been fraught with obstacles. And failure wasn't an option. It would mean loss of independence when she'd worked so hard to support herself. But as the poet Ramona Estle wrote:

"cocoons are
dark
cramped
uncomfortable spaces
don't expect yours
to be gilded"

Isla was in her new cocoon now. A slightly terrifying place that might crush her, but change often came with risk.

She gradually increased pressure to Álvaro's muscle.

His come-hither smile widened as she worked. "At least I can enjoy the scenery while you...*shit*."

She eased up slightly. "There's nothing pretty about watching me shit, hot shot."

Another laugh. A bead of perspiration appeared on his temple. "That's good. Hamstring's tight as a motherfucker, but yeah."

They progressed from active release therapy to exercises in Isla's almost-finished, state-of-the-art mini gym. This physio session was preventative. Work to build-up Álvaro's chronically strained hamstring muscles. Her favorite part of physiotherapy: strengthening the body, protecting it from the wear and tear of aggressive sports. Not infallible, but if it wasn't enough, if a sprain or fall put a client on the injured list, she'd be there to walk them through the steps toward recovery.

She focused on her A-list client and guided Álvaro through his session. They started with "good mornings," adding a low-weighted barbell to his upper back, followed by a series of single-leg deadlifts, then leg curls on the floor, rolling the stability ball with his feet. She owed her father a kidney for sending Álvaro her way. And for fixing her leaky faucet this week. And for buying her the gym equipment, always wanting to help, to buy, to cheer her on. The one constant in her corner.

Watching Swinging Graham Slade get his face bloodied as he'd earned his heavyweight titles had been on the devastating side of stressful growing up, but he'd also been the man who'd shown up at school band concerts and dance recitals and spelling bees, his piercing whistle overshadowing her mother's usual no-shows.

There was no repaying her father for all he'd done.

After the session, Álvaro leaned on her reception counter, filling out his paperwork, because she'd nailed his therapy. "I'll send you a proposed schedule," she said. "We'll start at the end of next month, after I open. Let me know if anything conflicts."

"Will do. And can I pass your name to Mark Lawson? He's looking for a change."

The pitcher? Could this day get any freaking better? "Yeah, sure. Of course."

If she were alone, she'd do a celebration dance and knock out embarrassing dance moves. Instead she did an internal happy dance while smiling at the polished stone and natural wood in her sleek space. A trickling fountain would be installed in a few weeks, after the painting was finished. The contemporary design pushed her budget to its limit, but she wanted the space to exude relaxing calm and a healing atmosphere.

"Well, hello there, handsome." Heather swept into the small office, ogling Álvaro's defined legs and cute behind. So much for a healing atmosphere.

He placed his pen down and gave Heather a flirty wink. "I can't handle this much beauty in one place."

Isla cringed. "Seriously?"

Álvaro gave a sheepish shrug. "Too much?"

"Heather's the one who's too much," Isla said. "And you should save it for the groupies. What do they call those in baseball? Bat Bunnies?"

"I prefer Ball Handlers."

Isla snorted. "Let's pretend I didn't ask. Don't forget to do those hamstring stretches at least once a day. And have fun at your niece's birthday bash. I want all the gory bouncy-castle details next time I see you."

"Yes, ma'am."

He bowed to Heather, who fake fainted. Laughter trailed Álvaro out the door as Heather picked herself up off the floor. "How do you work with these fine male specimens and not drool all over them?"

"My salivary glands are on hiatus while at work."

"My salivary glands want to meet that man's rock-hard calves and full lips in a dark alley."

No doubt Álvaro was pretty, but Isla never crossed those professional boundaries. When she worked, she saw bones and muscles and joints, not rock-hard calves and full lips. "He probably wouldn't mind, but keep it PG-13 in the office or I'll have to ban you from visits."

Heather riffled through her oversized purse and lifted out a flask and two shot glasses. "No, you won't. If Mr. Rock-Hard Calves hired you, which I assume he did, we're celebrating. If he didn't, we're commiserating."

She grinned. "We're celebrating." And she could always count on Heather to bring the party with her.

The first day they'd met, both of them barista babes at the short-lived Bean and Babes—a Hooters-style shop for the coffee-addicted hipster set—Heather had handed her a note scrawled on a Just Say No to Drugs flyer:

Meet me at the Rusted Wheel for cheap liquor after our shift so we can bitch about the douche with the sweater vest who keeps hitting on you.

This message will self-destruct in sixty seconds.

Your new best friend,
Heather

Isla had read the note twice. Egyptian hieroglyphs were easier to decipher than Heather's handwriting, but the huge swell of Isla's heart had turned her eyes watery. Heather hadn't known Isla's mother had left the month prior, gallivanting off with some man, freed by Isla's college start and unable to handle her husband's boxing lifestyle. She hadn't known Isla had practically been sleepwalking through her days since then, struggling to make friends at school. Only that morning Isla had been sad and hiccupy, feeling out of depth in the bustling campus teeming with laughing students, all strolling in groups, instant bonds forged at drunken frat parties and whip-smart debates.

One scrawled letter later, she had a friend.

Present-day Heather pressed a shot glass into her cleavage and handed the other glass to Isla, a mischievous smile in place. "Boob shots for my Bean and Babes graduate."

When you find your people, hold them close. And do boob shots.

"If that's Goldschläger," Isla said, "I'll spit it up on you."

"Of course it's not Goldschläger."

Shots filled, Isla leaned forward, laughing as she suctioned her lips around the glass in Heather's cleavage. She slung it back. Of course it *was* Goldschläger. Grimacing, she wiped her mouth on the back of her hand. "They could use that to disinfect sewage tanks."

"Such a baby."

"Says the woman who cries bloody murder at the sight of a teeny, tiny spider."

"Arachnophobia is a real thing."

"So is Goldschläger-phobia."

Heather laughed and did her shot, blonde hair flying with dramatic flair. She smacked her lips and took in the almost-finished office. "Can't believe you actually did this."

Isla couldn't believe it either. Setting her own hours had been a lure—the freedom to come and go without answering to anyone but her neurotic, workaholic self. But the true draw had been her client control. She'd also be the one paying bills and balancing accounts, or *not* paying bills if clients dwindled. *Cue nervous butterflies.* Advertising and promotion wouldn't happen on their own. But one pro outweighed all the cons you could toss at her face: at Phoenix Physiotherapy, not one boxer would walk through her door.

The front door opened, a gust of wind blowing in with Isla's towering father.

Amendment: no boxers *except* her father would walk through her door.

Swinging Graham Slade kissed his daughter's cheek and tipped his head to Heather. "Been a while. How goes the food styling world?"

"Unlike Isla, I don't get to put my hands on handsome men all day, but I get by."

He nodded. "Probably safer for everyone."

"I'm offended, Mr. Slade."

"No, you're not." His tone was playful, but his scarred and battered face was as intense as ever.

To anyone else, that hard look would send their pulse rocketing, but to Isla—and Heather, thanks to the endless hours they'd spent together—Graham Slade's face was just his face. His I'll-beat-you-into-a-pulp expression was the same as his tickle-his-daughter expression and his celebrate-a-boxing-victory expression. Swinging Slade's hard features, with his slight sneer and broken-too-many-times nose, was a comfort.

"You have a minute to talk?" he asked Isla.

"You'll have to ask Heather, since she just dropped by."

He looked at Heather but didn't speak.

Heather blew him a kiss. "Your broody looks don't scare me. Lucky for you, my work here is done and I have a craving for those deep-fried pickles at the Pink Hen." She returned the flask to her purse but left the shot glasses on Isla's counter. "You'll need these on opening day, and for when you sign up for the Blossom dating app."

Her dad scowled. "Internet dating is dangerous."

Possibly, but more to the point, it was impractical. Dating would require extra hours to be added to Isla's days. "Ignore Heather. She knows not of what she speaks."

Heather scoffed. "Untrue. I'm proactive. This isn't *Jumanji*. Men won't pop out of those books you read."

"Stop mothering me."

"I love you, too," Heather said sweetly. With a wave of her fingers, she was gone.

Isla's father didn't mention online dating again, thank God. He breathed loudly, a slight wheeze through his nostrils, like each inhale was sucked through a partly clogged straw.

"You wanted to talk?" she asked.

"I need a favor."

It was a simple request, but he glided his thick thumb over

his fisted knuckles, his square jaw pulsed, and he avoided eye contact. There were only a few instances when Swinging Graham Slade had exhibited those habits all at once, and Isla remembered each of those devastating moments Swarovski-crystal clearly:

The time he'd told her Mr. Zucchini, her beloved turtle, had been crushed by his truck.

The time he'd told her, after promising he'd retire and give his battered body the rest it deserved, he was returning to the boxing ring.

The time he'd explained her mother had left them for another man.

Isla lifted her hand to tug on a lock of her long hair, only to remember she'd chopped it last month. A bold gesture. A new look for her new life.

"we are everything
and nothing
and nothing
we have
is ours"

The amazing poet, Ramona Estle, hadn't been discussing hair, per se, but the sentiment of not clinging to possessions had struck a chord. At least, that was Isla's interpretation. The writer's passages in general spoke to Isla, with their pared-down formatting, lack of punctuation, and insightful messages. She'd stumbled upon the woman's work a couple years ago on social media, quickly becoming addicted to her soulful wisdom.

Now Isla had killer shoulder-length hair. *Thank you, Ms. Estle.*

Her waves were still deep chestnut, but with that funky

balayage treatment—caramel streaks that screamed *I'm-effortless-and-cool-and-spend-my-free-time-sunning-in-the-sand.* Isla spent her free time reading anatomy books, absorbing Ramona Estle's words, and staring at spreadsheets for her fledgling business, but no one needed to know the banality of her existence. What *Isla* needed to know was why her non-twitchy father was acting twitchy.

Unwilling to twist her fresh-start hair, she fisted her hands. When that didn't calm her, she crossed her arms. "What kind of favor do you need?"

"An important one." More jaw bunching. Brown eyes skittering.

He could ask anything, really, and she'd say yes. This was the man who'd been her emotional support when her mother had left them. He'd picked her up when past boyfriends had let her fall. He'd called in a favor to his old sports agent and had sent Álvaro her way. He'd even given Isla start-up money, when he was struggling to run his own boxing gym.

"Name it and it's done," she said.

He met her eyes. "The contender for the heavyweight belt broke his wrist and they've asked my guy, Brick Kramarov, to step in. They've spent too much on advertising to change the event date, so I'm going to Vegas with him. They also want a longer lead-up than usual—bigger media circus to make up for the last-minute fight change. I'll be there for six weeks."

As long as he wasn't the one in the ring, she didn't care who he trained or where he lived temporarily. "So, you need what? Me to polish the Ferrari you refuse to sell? Housesit the mansion you also refuse to sell?"

"I earned that stuff. Blood, sweat, and—"

"Punches. Yeah, I know. But you wouldn't struggle with the gym if you sold some of your stuff."

"I actually did sell the Ferrari," he mumbled.

She tugged on her ear. "I'm sorry. It sounded like you said you sold the Ferrari you bought with your first winnings, the car you told me you'd rather be buried in than give up."

Graham Slade's dark eyes shifted to her exercise area, over the fancy equipment he'd helped her buy, refusing the repayment plan she'd offered.

Awareness dawning, she sucked in a breath. "You sold the Ferrari to help pay for my business."

It wasn't a question. The shocking fact was written all over his nonplussed shrug, and she couldn't wrap her brain around it. A sale that large would've funded his parched bank account, but he wouldn't have done it for himself. He'd been faced with bankruptcy in the past. She'd urged him repeatedly to liquidate his assets, sell one of his five luxury cars, his mansion, his excessive collection of sports memorabilia—Swinging Graham Slade could also be called Spendthrift Slade.

His infuriating replies had always been the same: "None of my stuff gets sold. I'll figure something out."

His money-scraping efforts had always been successful—a TV appearance, that horrid toilet plunger infomercial, exhibition fights with B-list celebrities—but she'd never understood the *why* of it. Why that stuff had meant so much to him. Proof of what he'd accomplished? Evidence that, although it had cost him his wife, boxing hadn't left him empty-handed?

There was no knowing with Graham Slade. His emotions were as toughened as his fists. But this? Selling his favorite luxury car for her?

She swallowed past the lump in her throat. "Tell me about that favor."

She hoped it was a big one, something huge she could use to show him how appreciative she was. How much she loved him.

He passed his hand over his mouth. "I need you to come to

Vegas with me and work with Brick Kramarov leading up to his fight."

She laughed. "No, really. What do you need?"

Through the years, their fights over boxing had been epic. She'd never told him how deeply boxing had scarred her, but she'd ranted plenty about men and women ruining their bodies, while their loved ones watched in resigned acceptance. Tears had been shed on the topic. Silent treatments earned. The man must have developed a sense of humor.

He didn't crack a smile, though. "I need you to come to Vegas with me," he said again, "and work with Brick Kramarov leading up to his fight."

She didn't laugh this time. "You can't be serious."

"Since when do I joke about boxing?"

Joking in general wasn't his forte. Neither was asking for favors, but this was too much. "My business opens in seven weeks. Renovations aren't finished. I need to be here."

"I have a guy who can oversee the renovation work, and you've told me how on top of the other business stuff you are. That you mainly have online things to organize. You'll be back for the opening."

"*I* need to oversee the work, and I actually have a life that can't be upended." Sort of. Not really. Definitely *not* the point. Her mental health was the point. "I can't," she said again, a cold sweat slicking the back of her neck.

"I need you, Isla. It's only six weeks. And Brick is a good guy."

Brick could be a saint for all she cared. Although she'd never visited her father at his training gym, she'd glimpsed a few interviews of his fighter while watching sports networks. Brick was a hulking boxer. Russian-American with buzzed hair, insane bone structure, and piercing gray eyes—hotter than any man had a right to be—with a vocabulary limited to *bust 'em up*, *gonna beat his head in*, and *Brick Smash*. Not that his looks or intelligence mattered. Shutting herself off from boxing mattered.

During her father's boxing career, Isla's nights had been sleepless and anxiety ridden. Sweaty and terrified, she'd wake from nightmares, her mind filled with images of his punched skull rupturing and brain exploding. She'd overheard so many devastating phone calls, had endured so many hospital visits. Face fractures. Nerve damage. She'd lived with dark circles under her eyes and fear in her heart.

Then the panic attacks had set in.

She'd hidden them from her father, Heather, everyone. She'd briefly sought therapy on her own. The therapist had been more intrusive than helpful, so Isla had consulted the internet instead, used techniques to help her cope. When Swinging Graham Slade had finally retired, the attacks had dwindled and ceased.

Until her first physio gig.

Her boss had been gleeful when he'd learned her last name, quickly using her as a draw to lure boxers to their clinic for treatment. A parade of fighters, all caring more about a win than the damage they were doing to their brains and bodies. The worry on their partners' faces had hooked into her heart. Her nightmares had returned. Different faces, the same agonizing fear. More panic attacks. She'd quit her job, found another. Her last name had followed again, bait used to build another boss's client list. Her self-taught therapy techniques no longer eased her anxiety.

Opening her own practice had been the only answer. The work helped her focus. Boxing clients would be a non-issue. And her mind had finally begun to settle.

Now her father was asking for the impossible.

"Do you know how hard this would be for me? How much I

hated watching you box? Being around the sport brings it all back."

Her dad didn't reply. He stared at her, unblinking, and she shrunk two inches. Swinging Graham Slade had one hell of a stare. When watching his boxing matches, she'd swear he'd just look at his opponents until the men hit the mat.

"Isn't there another favor you need?" She hated the desperation in her voice. "It's not like I'm the only physiotherapist you can hire." She felt herself caving, though, unsure how to say no when she owed him so much.

He scrubbed his chin with those thick, callused fingers. "I need someone I trust on this, and you're the best at what you do."

"I don't treat boxers."

"You treat athletes. Boxers are athletes."

"Boxers are adrenaline junkies, too stupid to realize they're killing themselves, one ridiculous round at a time."

Her father's hard-knocks face flinched. A minuscule wince. Enough to have her regretting her words. It was a familiar fight, but guilt pressed on her lungs.

"I'm sorry. You're not stupid. I just wish..." He hadn't boxed for so long. That his body didn't ache and pain him constantly these days. That she was strong enough to do this for him, without worrying about falling apart. To this day, she lived with an undercurrent of fear, wondering if the worst of boxing had yet to rear its dangerous head: long-term effects on the brain that developed as fighters aged. "I just wish you'd made different choices."

He focused on the floor so long her insides twisted. Nervous tics aside, his evasive behavior was unsettling. Selling his car, acting fidgety, stalling—this wasn't the indomitable man she knew. "Why does it feel like there's something you're not telling me? Is something wrong?"

When he finally looked up, tears shimmered in his eyes. "I didn't want you to worry."

Whatever worry he'd hoped to curb was on red alert now. "Dad, you're scaring me."

He placed his hands on her cheeks and blew out a rough breath. "I have Parkinson's, Princess."

2

When Isla was a kid, Swinging Graham Slade would lift her up like she weighed nothing and deposit her on his shoulders. She'd dangle her legs in front of his chest and grip his ears, one of them deformed into a "cauliflower ear," thanks to repeated hits to the appendage. She'd hum while exploring the rough cartilage, fascinated by the deformity. He'd go about his business, brushing his teeth, making breakfast, pretending he didn't have a seven-year-old hooked around his neck. Isla's mother would yell and glare at him. Isla would preen.

On her father's shoulders, she floated above the stress of homework, above her temperamental mother and the mean classmates who told Isla her hair was too frizzy, her scrawny body too small. On Swinging Graham Slade's shoulders, nothing could touch her.

She wished she could climb up there now.

Trembling, she pressed her fingers to her mouth. "No."

Her father's weary sigh seemed dredged from his bones. "I'm sorry, Princess."

Sorry didn't cut it. This was not okay. *She* was not okay.

"Maybe they're wrong? Maybe you're not eating right. You quit drinking those smoothies when I moved out. Maybe you just..." Got hit one time too many in the head.

The terrifying facts were etched in her brain, thanks to her research when pleading for him to retire. A boxing blow to the head was akin to being struck by a thirteen-pound boulder traveling at twenty miles per hour. Brain lesions and large blood clots were all in a day's work. If internal bleeding and damaged organs were your jam, bring on the boxing! Retinal detachment and hemorrhage? Always on the menu if you got hit just right.

She'd once made a PowerPoint presentation about it for him, including a slide of a cartoon man holding his mangled brain in his hand. Graham Slade had looked at her and simply said, "I know the risks, Princess."

Now she'd have to watch this larger-than-life man wither before her eyes.

Had it already begun? When doing her thorough PowerPoint presentations, she'd researched Parkinson's and Alzheimer symptoms—diseases more likely to affect boxers. His face had never been expressive, but it's possible his features had stiffened. It was a symptom. As were stooped posture, tremors, loss of movement, speech changes, sleep disorders, chewing problems... "What can I do? When's your next doctor's appointment? When did you find out?"

She'd do more research. Watch his diet. Maybe move back home.

"I've known two years, and all I need—"

"Two *years*?" Forget moving back home. She wanted to throttle him. "How could you keep this from me?"

"This isn't your burden to carry."

A maniacal laugh erupted from her. "Oh, so when you get

dementia or lose motor function, you think I won't notice? That it won't affect my life?"

His Adam's apple moved slowly down his neck. Trouble swallowing? Another symptom? How many signs had she missed these past two years? How many would she obsess over now? She pictured every future interaction with him overshadowed, their easy closeness usurped by *this*: her constant assessment of him, analyzing, worrying.

"I didn't tell you because of how it *would* affect your life," he said.

She deflated, her whole body turning heavy. She wanted to slip to the ground, curl into the tightest ball, hide in the tightest space. Hide from this diagnosis. Tears stung her eyes and burned her throat.

"We caught it early." Her father's voice gentled, going soft. "So far my symptoms have been the non-motor kind. I'm doing well."

"Okay, good. That's good." She fought the tears and stood taller. It was her turn to be his rock. She would not falter. "But you must be worried about this trip. Is that why you want me to come?"

She'd pack tonight, her boxing-triggered panic attacks be damned. She'd care for him, ease his discomfort any way she could. Parkinson's patients lived long these days. His quality of life would decline, but they'd make adjustments. She'd be there for him every step of the way. "I assume Brick's been understanding, giving you time to take care of yourself?"

He ticked up his chin. "Brick doesn't know. No one knows. Only me, my doctor, and now you."

Another delirious laugh threatened. "Of course no one knows."

She could add Stubborn-Ass Slade to his list of nicknames.

She leaned against the counter to catch her breath. Just

when life was looking up—new business, new client, new hair, *no boxing*—she got slammed with a sucker punch. "What do you need?"

"With this fight looming, Brick needs strength on his team. If they learn about my Parkinson's, his manager will fire me, worried my illness will get into Brick's head. He's not wrong, but I'm strong enough, and Brick needs me to win. Problem is I've been more tired during the day, having nausea. I'll need to take breaks. If I say I'm taking that time to be with you, they won't question me."

"So you don't want me because my work is good. I'm your alibi." His enabler—a fact that stung.

"No." He frowned. "I mean, partly. But you're a brilliant physio. You'll make a big difference in Brick's training."

His confidence in her skills mollified her *slightly*, but she was still mad. He clearly needed to destress, have supports around him, but boxing, as usual, took priority. "Why do you even care about Brick's win when you're fighting a disease? Why can't you just rest for once in your life?"

He flattened his lips. "If I rest, I die."

She clutched her stomach, too winded to reply, and a thousand *ifs* clogged her throat.

If he'd retired when she'd begged, maybe they wouldn't be here now. *If* she'd pushed harder, he might be healthier.

"What if you get worse?" she said, her voice suddenly small. "What if the stress advances the Parkinson's faster?"

He gripped her shoulders, two huge hands keeping her from falling apart. "I don't ask much of you, Isla, but I'm asking this. I need you in Vegas for the training camp. I need you to help me deflect questions because this is how I fight. By not backing down when I'm thrown a punch. And the publicity will be amazing for your business."

The last thing she wanted was boxing publicity. Still, how

could she say no? "Six weeks, and not a moment longer. And when we're back here, I'm going to all your doctor appointments. You'll listen to my diet advice and not push yourself as hard."

His twitchiness subsided, and he tugged on a lock of her newly cropped hair. "I like this, by the way. Not sure I told you."

Expert topic-changer. She sniffed and wiped her wet eyes. "On top of not pushing yourself so hard, after this fight, please consider announcing your illness."

"I'll pick you up next week." He pulled out his phone, ignoring her demands. "Brick's manager has a private jet. It's a sweet ride and Vegas is nice this time of year. Way warmer than Chicago."

She didn't care about some fancy jet and balmy weather. She cared about helping her father navigate this new, daunting stage of his life. At least new to *her*.

He kissed her cheek, his phone pressed to his cauliflower ear, his growly voice talking to someone about schedules and televised training.

He still seemed so formidable. Healthy. A sign he was one of the strong ones. His illness wouldn't define him, not under her watch. She'd micromanage the hell out of him. Make schedules, assure he had adequate rest. She'd use the next six weeks to work on him, convince him to use his illness for good. He was a boxing legend, after all. The heavyweight champ for over four years. Maybe together they could convince the World Boxing Association to wake up and make changes to better protect its athletes.

She nodded to herself, refusing to fall apart. She was a strong, competent entrepreneur. Would be one shortly, at least, with Álvaro front and center on her patient list. And she'd prepared herself to deal with her father's inevitable health issues. Those PowerPoint presentations hadn't been for nothing.

She'd just keep an emotional distance from Brick Smash Kramarov. They wouldn't become friends. There would be no connection beyond work, no panic attacks. He wouldn't affect her like the boxers at her previous physio jobs. Easy, considering the last thing she recalled hearing the brute say to an interviewer was, "Gonna bust him up so bad, he ain't gonna be able to eat through a straw."

3

Eliza tugged on Eric's sleeve, her adorable face scrunched up. "I can't find Mr. Squish-A-Lot, and I can't start the tea party without him. Everything's gonna get cold, and Mrs. Nutter and Mr. Green and Miss Candy Cane are gonna raise a fuss."

And Eric's studying would go the way of the West African Black Rhinoceros.

He closed his Latin textbook and blinked hard. So easy to get lost in his studies, his mind filled with verb conjugations, tangled masculine and feminine nouns, the unlocking of words once spoken on every tongue. So absorbing he could forget his seven-year-old niece was setting up a tea party beside him.

He brushed the brown curls off Eliza's puckered forehead. "I saw Mr. Squish-A-Lot in the bathroom. Probably got lost and forgot about the tea party. Should we send out a search party?"

Her eyes widened, bright with a new mission. "I'll get my search party hat! We'll use Whit to sniff him out."

It was impossible for anything to get lost in their cramped house, but Eliza was always up for a game. She bounded off, almost falling as she skidded around the living room's corner. Eric's bulldog, Whit, scrambled to his feet and scampered after her. His favorite human.

Chuckling, Eric unfolded his legs and stood, groaning at the stiffness in his joints. This morning's run and workout had been brutal. Hard, but invigorating. His hour of studying had been equally challenging. Maybe he'd earn a heavyweight belt for mastering dead languages, too.

Asher bounced into the room, his fists up as he punched at Eric's calves. "*Brick Smash! Brick Smash!* Gonna beat your stupid head in."

Goddamn it. How could twin seven-year-olds be so different? He grabbed the scrawny kid by his shoulders, lifted him until they were eye to eye. "What did I say about talking like that? Words are a resource. Don't waste them with meanness or thoughtlessness or..." He trailed off, waiting for Asher to fill in the blank.

Asher turned boneless in his grip, head lolling back with a theatrical sigh. "Or people'll treat me with meanness and thoughtess—"

"Thought*less*ness."

"Thought-*less-ness*, but"—he snapped his head up, fierce eyes challenging—"your big face is always on the TV, yelling *Brick Smash* and growling, and people are always nice to you. Giving you stuff. I want fancy stuff."

Eric had happily sold that fancy stuff to pay for his mother's dental care and to keep Eliza's asthma in check. And Asher was wrong about people being nice to his uncle. Boxing fans wanted a piece of him. Promoters and managers used him to fatten their wallets. His PR handler was some kind of evil wizard, having turned Eric Kramarovsky, a quiet Jewish boy who loved to read and study, into an alternate version of himself: Brick Kramarov, illiterate brute with a loud mouth and big fists. A far cry from the linguistics student who got off on words and meanings hidden in language. But smarts didn't fill seats, as they often told him, and Eric would sell his soul if it meant supporting his family.

His mother came in from the kitchen, tea towel over her shoulder. "Listen to your uncle, Asher. No more Brick Smash nonsense. And you," she said to Eric, her Russian accent less pronounced when laying down the law. "Breakfast is ready. You must eat before you go."

He put Asher down and ruffled his hair, then nodded to his mother. "I'll be in after I help Eliza hunt for Mr. Squish-A-Lot."

She reached up and patted Eric's cheek. "*Moy horoshiy mal'chik.*"

He hadn't always been her good boy, not when they'd first moved to the United States and he'd been bullied and lonely.

"*Tvoy yedinstvenney mal'chik.*" *I'm your only boy*, he replied in Russian. His usual retort.

She swatted him with her tea towel. "*I ya tvoya yedinstvennaya mama.*"

Yeah, she was his only mother, and he was lucky for it.

When she spoke in English, her accent thick with her history, words like listen sounded like *leesten*, walk sounded like *valk*, and she often skipped articles like *a* and *the*—giving her vocabulary a childish lilt. In Russian, she was fluent and no nonsense. Using either language, she was the strong woman who'd given up everything so her kids could live the supposed American Dream. He knew better than to let breakfast get cold.

Eric kissed her cheek. "I'll be in soon. Don't clean anything. That's my job."

She mumbled about doing whatever she pleased.

An hour later, Mr. Squish-A-Lot had been found, Eric had inhaled five poached eggs, two slices of toast, a bowl of yogurt and fruit, his niece and nephew had fought and made up *twice*, and Whit had licked up a pile of fallen porridge from the floor.

"Your car is here," his mother called as he packed the last of his books. Upping his boxing training didn't mean he'd let his mind go soft.

"The Brute Philosopher." Rosa leaned on the door frame to his room, his sister's blue eyes traveling over his textbooks.

"I don't study philosophy."

"Sorry, *Mr. PhD*. The Brute Linguist."

He wasn't studying for his PhD either, but Rosa was kidding, and he should be used to the teasing. *Should* being the key word. Everyone he met misjudged and misunderstood him, but comments like "brute" brought more irritation lately.

"You're taking Whit with you?" She sat on his bed and massaged the dog's wrinkled neck.

Eric stuffed the last of his clothing in a bag, glad for the benign topic. "Hotel tried to say no, but they gave in."

"No one says no to Brick Kramarov."

Another joke about his fighting alter ego, and he yanked his zipper closed harder than intended. He loved that Rosa still had the energy to tease him. Before her pregnancy with the twins at nineteen and her failed marriage, she'd made it her job to mock him, teasing how he slurped his soup, rolling her eyes at the chunky gold chain he'd worn daily, because he'd mistakenly thought it was cool. She'd talk a mile a minute, imitating his deep voice, pretending to box, until their mother had tears streaming down her cheeks.

She'd also been incredibly ambitious, had dreamed of becoming a lawyer, fighting for justice and standing up for the little guy. Now she talked about play dates and hollered at her kids to do their homework, while working part-time as a receptionist.

As much as he'd grown to hate any teasing related to his

boxing persona, he didn't have the heart to come down on Rosa about it. "I left you something for while I'm away. Check your bank account."

Her eyes turned soft. "What did you do?"

"Got my advance for the fight, deposited the excess. It's just the start, Rosa. If I win this match, everything will change."

He'd send Rosa to college to study whatever she wanted. His mother would quit her food packing job at that awful factory. He'd hire a cook and cleaner, force his mother to rest for once in her life. He'd buy them a bigger house, make sure Eliza and Asher never had to worry about affording school or covering medical care.

"You just go have fun," Rosa said. "Get out while you're in Vegas."

He wouldn't do much except train, but he nodded as they both stood. "Read to the kids every night for me. I'll miss that."

More than a head shorter than him, she gripped his shoulders. "*You* don't get hurt. You be careful and come back to us in one piece."

He loved her like this. Strong, so much like their mother. "Stop being so nice. It's freaking me out."

She laughed and punched his arm.

Eric whistled for Whit. The dog jumped off the bed, trailing after him, both of them walking with purpose. Next time Eric stepped inside this house, it would be to put a For Sale sign on the property and tell Rosa she could have whatever future she wanted.

ERIC'S TAXI pulled onto the tarmac, close to Preston's private jet. His manager was on his phone as usual, the thing practically an extra appendage, and waved vaguely at Eric. By the time Eric's bags were unloaded and Whit was sitting happily at his feet, Preston stashed his cell in his expensive suit pocket, grinning his world-conqueror grin. "Guess who's considering offering you a killer endorsement deal?"

The best offer he'd had to date was from a used car dealership. It had entailed Eric wearing a barbarian costume. "It better not involve a ridiculous outfit."

"That's not a guess."

"Ask Whit. He enjoys your guessing games more than I do."

Whit made his usual wheezy, snorty sounds.

Preston wrinkled his nose. "I'll never understand the bulldog thing. And since you're no fun, the answer is Big Dipper Athletics."

BDA wasn't Nike or Reebok, but they were no joke. "How serious are they?"

"If you win this match, they'll be begging on their knees."

When he won this match.

He was an underdog. It was no secret. Telecasters blasted his stats all over social media, a different song than those gossip mongers used to sing.

He'd been a golden boy once, on the cusp of greatness, before he'd fractured the metacarpal bones in his hand. Everyone had written him off. Preston had told him to find a new gig. Then his mother had lost her factory job for a few months, thanks to a dip in the economy. She'd needed dental work. Eliza's asthmatic bronchitis had ended in a pile of medical bills. He hadn't weighed his options. He may love linguistics, but it didn't pay the bills. Boxing was his ticket, his fastest way to a decent paycheck.

So he'd hired Swinging Graham Slade to train him. They'd developed an intense schedule that'd left no room for studying or socializing. Hard core physiotherapy. Strict sleep guidelines and a stricter diet, everything in his life measured and planned, all with one end goal: get back into fighting shape and support his family.

Three years later, at age twenty-seven, Eric had defied the odds. His body pained him most days, but he was a contender for the heavyweight champion, his recovery story part of why they'd asked him to fight. Along with the ridiculous Brick Smash image his PR team had concocted. *And* the fact that the first three guys they'd asked couldn't do the short notice and balked at the shitty contract.

"Tell them the match is mine," Eric said. Failure wasn't in his vocabulary, unless he said it in Latin or French or Japanese. But he suddenly thought about stuffed animal hunting with Eliza, running around the backyard with Asher, cleaning with his mother in the kitchen. All mundane, ordinary things, but a pang went through him. Like he didn't want to leave.

He shook his head, unsure why he was feeling sentimental.

Preston clapped him on the back. "That's my guy. And FYI: there's been a switch in physiotherapists. Slade's daughter is coming on board for the fight."

Unease curled through Eric's stomach. Preston slipped that nugget in like it was no big deal, but change before a fight this big wasn't cool. "I'm used to Gilpin. He knows my body and what I need."

"I hear you, but Slade pushed for this. Figured having him was more important than having Gilpin."

That kind of nepotism didn't sound like the Graham Slade Eric knew. Slade was all business, always making the best decisions for Eric's career. He'd never even mentioned his daughter's job, let alone suggested she work on him. "Did he actually say he wouldn't coach me unless we hired her?"

"You pay me to manage you, so let me do my job. There's no need for you to stress about the details."

The vague answer didn't settle his agitation. "Is she good?"

"Great, as far as I've heard. And she's hot."

Eric wouldn't know. Graham's daughter had never shown her face at training sessions or fights. "Doubt Slade wants a player like you ogling his daughter."

"First, maybe I'm tired of playing the field. Kind of like the idea of settling down, so don't go spreading rumors. And Slade went out of his way to tell me about her. He actually suggested I ask her out." He shrugged. "No harm testing the waters."

Preston changing his womanizing ways was a surprise, but the man had a heart of gold. When Eric had asked him to help with his mother's dental care, before Eric had recovered enough to fight again, he'd loaned him the money, no questions asked. He never missed the twins' birthday parties. Kind-hearted or not, he still blew through women like a fickle, careless wind.

"Tread lightly," Eric said, slightly envious of having a dating prospect. The void of not having someone in his life, a woman to love and spoil, frustrated him at times. None of it was possible with his insane schedule. Now more than ever. "And I'm not one hundred percent sold on her as my physio. If she's not strong enough, I'll have words with Slade."

"If you're unhappy, *I'll* have words with Slade. For now we're on the yellow 'Brick' road. Nothing but gold paving ahead of you, man. So let's board my very exclusive, very posh jet. They should be here shortly."

Eric grunted, irritated *again* at being called Brick. A knucklehead image he was stuck with if he wanted this title.

He knelt and gave Whit a rub. "What say you, Walt Whitman? You okay with a new woman working on me?"

Whit gave a slobbery snort of happiness. Eric grudgingly

agreed. He owed Graham Slade a lot. That man was a big part of why he'd recovered as quickly and efficiently as he had. Eric would oblige his wishes, as long as his daughter was a good physiotherapist and didn't add more stress to their training. He also hoped Preston didn't make things awkward by asking her out.

4

Isla hadn't been on a private jet in years. Not since her father's heyday, when managers and promoters had showered him with riches. Penthouse suites. Expensive champagne. Steaks the size of California. When Swinging Graham Slade had been golden, the world had been his oyster. When his shine had dulled, he'd become an in-debt trainer, unwilling to part with his material possessions. Unless he was helping his entrepreneurial daughter, apparently.

"Told you the ride was sweet," her father said, his appreciative gaze on the private jet.

"Told you I don't care."

The second their driver left to carry their bags to the plane, she swiveled in the back of the car and studied her father's stony profile. "Have you talked to your doctor about zantamide? If your symptoms worsen, an article said taking it with sefadopa can help decrease or eliminate symptoms for longer periods."

Jaw clenched, he faced her. "No medicine talk, Isla. No talk about symptoms or treatments. Don't even ask me how I'm feeling. I've been dealing with this for two years on my own and have been doing fine. We can talk about stuff after the fight when we're home. Until then, not a word." He reached for the door but turned back. "You're a hurricane. So strong and determined. When you want something, nothing gets in your way. Makes me proud to be your father, but now's not the time."

He pushed out of the car, and she fought the angry retort on the tip of her tongue. She wanted to call after him, give him a piece of her mind for keeping her in the dark so long, forcing her acquiescence now. She wanted to scream at Brick and Preston and the entire world of boxing. Those people didn't give a damn about her father. If they learned he was sick, he'd be tossed to the curb like yesterday's garbage. And here she was, about to make nice with the enemy, all because her father couldn't let himself rest.

She breathed deep and remembered one of her favorite Ramona Estle quotes:

"be a snowflake
my mother whispered
my father, stern
be a blizzard"

Isla was okay being a blizzard made up of millions of quiet snowflakes. It meant she had the power to affect her stubborn-ass father. Control she'd wield after the fight. For now, she'd suffer through this job, put her hurricane and blizzard tendencies on lockdown, and do excellent physiotherapy work.

Body stiff with agitation, she left the car and marched toward the plane. The stewardess greeted her with a wide smile. Isla forced a half-hearted nod. The luxurious black-and-white interior had seating for eight, with plush armchairs arranged in isolated groups of twos that faced each other. Her father was talking with Preston in the grouping closest to the front, the big men sprawled in their seats. Brick was probably in the back, behind the dividing curtain: the king of this castle.

She wanted to plop down in one of the seats, close her eyes and pretend she was flying to some Caribbean vacation, but there was no point delaying the inevitable. She'd use the flight to have Brick fill out forms, answer her introductory questions. Being a good physiotherapist meant being a detective of sorts, figuring out which treatments would serve her clients best. The familiar work would calm her irritation.

Briefcase satchel hung over her shoulder, she passed her father's seat and aimed for the curtain, but Preston stood and maneuvered in her way. "We've never officially met. I'm Preston, Brick's manager."

Her strained smile felt plastic. "I know who you are."

He didn't move. She tried to relax, but her body felt brittle.

"Your father talks about you all the time. We're thrilled to have you on our team." His gaze dipped down to her T-shirt and jeans. She hadn't dressed nice for the flight. No point when she wasn't there to impress. Preston's nostrils still gave a slight flare. "I'm hoping we can spend some time together. Maybe grab a drink in Vegas."

Preston was attractive. The type of handsome that graced a Fashion Week runway: hair perfectly coiffed, thick eyelashes, brown eyes with a hint of gold, and an aquiline nose suited to a Roman statue. Good looking or not, his timing couldn't be worse. "I'll be busy in Vegas."

Instead of backing off, Preston's grin grew. "Then it's a good thing we have the next few hours together. We can sit and chat."

It was an innocent suggestion, but there was a predatory gleam in Preston's eyes. Today of all days, she'd rather eject herself from the plane than flirt with a boxing manager. "Are you actually hitting on me in front of my father, who happens to be the former heavyweight champ of the world?" She turned to share a laugh with her father over this idiocy, nip this flirty situation in the bud.

Her father shrugged. "You were talking about internet dating. It's not safe, and Preston is good people."

Seriously? Not only was he forcing her to live and breathe boxing again, now he was setting her up with a man cemented in the industry?

"We will be having words," she told her father, then turned to Preston, attempting to control her temper. "You may be the nicest guy on the planet, but I'm not in the mood. If you insist on flirting with me, I'd suggest you keep a parachute close."

So much for temper control.

Embarrassed by her outburst, she shuffled past him, moving toward the back of the plane.

Preston's low chuckle followed her. "You're right, Graham. She's feisty. I like her."

Her steps faltered, aggravation burning a path up her chest. Honestly, what had her father been thinking, playing matchmaker with a guy like Preston? Had he never noticed her dating history? Although it had been a while, she'd only ever dated men with intellectual leanings. The bearded sort with crinkly eyes and deep thoughts. Nothing about Preston was her type.

Freshly irked, she pushed into the plane's back section and stopped short.

Instead of groups of seats, large white couches filled both sides, with a giant man sitting on the sectional at the right. Brick's massive shoulders were hunched slightly as he frowned at his phone, his muscled forearms planted on his knees. He was wearing earbuds and hadn't noticed her, but the dog at his feet watched her, a symphony of snorts and grunts coming from the bulldog's drooly mouth.

"Stupid technology," Brick mumbled, his frown sinking deeper.

The guy seemed inept with his phone, which wasn't a surprise. He probably had an IT underling on payroll to do his computer/phone work when at home, another servant to tie his shoes, one to blow his nose and fan his face.

He also had a trainer who ignored his own health to cater to this hulking man's needs.

Her thin hold on her emotions threatened to snap.

His dog pushed to its stubby legs and waddled over to Isla, slobbery face turned up to investigate. She petted his thick head. With the snorty noises and horrific underbite, this pet wouldn't win any doggy pageants.

"His name's Whit."

Brick's voice was rough and low, and Isla released a startled laugh. For a boxer who didn't seem to have much *wit* in interviews, it wasn't surprising he'd buy it in the form of a snorty pet. Even funnier was the dog's name tag, which read *Whit*. He hadn't even spelled the name correctly.

"Do you have a cat called Smart?" she asked, then winced at her blunt sarcasm, unsure when she'd become this girl. Judgmental. Rude. Unacceptably unprofessional. She was just so on edge, worried about her father, annoyed with him for playing matchmaker.

She met Brick's eyes, which were coolly assessing.

The intensity of his gray eyes had been impossible to miss in TV interviews, bold and magnetic against his fair complexion. Up close, under his scrutiny, she felt skewered in place.

The guy didn't even blink. "No cat named Smart. Just Whit here."

"Well, he's...cute." He was the furthest thing from cute, and her tone still held an edge. She was clearly in no shape to be meeting a new client. Not today, with her frazzled state. And why was Brick's stare so intense? Couldn't he look somewhere else?

Those stormy eyes narrowed, assessing her, then he clicked his tongue. Whit returned to his master. "My name's—"

"Brick. Yeah, I know," she said quickly, feeling nervous and uncomfortable. "That *Brick Smash* tagline is quite something."

He fisted his phone and crossed his arms. "Like that line, do you?"

"It's very Neanderthal." As were the size of his biceps. Grotesquely masculine. The sight of his perfectly sculpted body made her already primed anger flare. Why a man worked to be in such good shape, only to invite trauma was beyond her. "I'm sure the name strikes fear in your opponents."

She meant to say that lightly, with a smile. Instead it had come out harsh, no smile to be found. She really was being bitchy, judging his intelligence before having a real conversation with the guy. She hated feeling off-kilter, but everything was bubbling under her skin, including her father's demand to not talk about his illness. And being around a boxer again was making her slightly queasy.

Taking a breath, she tried to find her Zen. "I'm Isla, your physiotherapist for the next six weeks. I'm also Graham Slade's daughter, which I'm sure you know."

Brick's unrelenting stare had her feeling like a rookie physiotherapist, shaky and out of her depth. Mentally shirking her discomfort, she sat next to him and gathered papers from her satchel. "I have forms for you to fill out, basics to help me assess what treatments you need, how to help your body perform optimally during training. If you need help filling anything out, just holler."

"Because I'm an idiot who can't do it on my own?"

She froze, attention glued to the papers in her hands. There had been no joking in his tone. He'd sounded downright angry. Which she kind of deserved.

She looked up slowly. "Sorry if I came across as judgmental. It's been a challenging day." Week. Month. Life. "Just offering you help if you need it."

Brick raised his phone, his expression bland. "I've got this for when I have trouble spelling my name, so I'm good."

Definitely angry, and remorse hardened her stomach. It would take more than an apology to overturn her nasty first impression, and today wasn't the day to dig deep. She was too annoyed with...everything. She wanted to be at home, working on her business. She needed to find the inner strength to help her father deal with his health issues. And here she was, with an oversized brute, who reminded her too much of how strong and healthy her father had been, before boxing had beaten him down.

She left the forms in a pile and stood. "If you need me, I'll be up front. We'll start sessions tomorrow."

His dog chuffed, but Brick didn't reply. He just watched her with those unwavering eyes.

She'd try for a fresh start tomorrow, tame her inner hurricane and build their trust in the gym. She'd still keep her walls up, fortifications to stave off emotional setbacks like she'd suffered at her past physiotherapy jobs, but she'd find a way to be nicer.

As she neared the curtain, she heard a murmur from behind. Something not in English? Asian sounding? Whatever the language, the tone certainly hadn't been polite. She glanced back, but Brick's eyes were closed and his earbuds were in. She must be hearing things on this fun-filled morning.

Back in her seat, she clicked on her seat belt, closed her

eyes, and somehow managed to lower her tense shoulders during takeoff. When the plane leveled, the sound of ice clinking into a glass had her cracking one eye open. Preston was, thankfully, still sitting opposite her father, but he raised his cocktail glass and winked at her. *Ugh.*

The stewardess rolled her cart toward Isla. "Can I get you a drink? Champagne? Cosmo? Whiskey sour?"

"Whiskey sour, hold the sour."

She arched a manicured eyebrow. "That kind of day, huh?"

"You have no idea." She could still feel Preston looking her way and hated that her father had had the nerve to play cupid with a guy she'd have to see regularly. "Make it a double, on the rocks."

"Coming right up."

Glass in hand, Isla sipped her drink, enjoying the burn of the alcohol slipping down her throat. Until Preston appeared at her side, grinning. He must have taken her drinking as a sign to socialize when all she craved was peace.

"May I?" He tipped his chin toward the empty seat opposite her.

She wanted to tell him to give it a rest but felt badly for how hard she'd shut him down before. If her father said Preston was a decent guy, she had no doubt he was kind.

"The seat's all yours." It was his plane, after all.

He made himself at home and sipped the amber liquid in his glass. "How'd it go with Brick?"

Awkward and unprofessional. "Good. We'll start on therapy tomorrow."

He settled deeper into his chair. "It's a tough job, physiotherapy. How'd you get into it?"

"I was angry."

Preston cocked his head and waited. "Care to elaborate?"

The rumbling jet drowned her heavy sigh. The odds of

Preston understanding how her father's career had affected her was slim to none, but the need to speak up surged. She couldn't talk about her father's illness, mention anything about his health *today*, but she could talk about their past.

She glanced at her father. He was asleep. The man had a talent for passing out anytime, anywhere. Still, she kept her voice low. "I grew up watching my father get his face pounded in, saw how it affected his health and body. Recovery got harder every time. He lived in pain, and it was tough on my mother. Boxing tore down his body and his marriage, and all I wanted to do was fix him somehow. Help him any way I could."

"So you devoted your life to helping boxers like him stay in better shape."

"No." She was about to say she didn't treat boxers, but that would lead to questions about why she was on this trip. "It's not about staying in shape. It's about building their defenses, giving them better tools when faced with injury. I educate athletes as much as help them. *All* athletes. Even if it means helping them make tough choices."

He leaned back and regarded her. "Wow."

She narrowed her eyes at him. "Wow, what?"

"Not many people I meet are passionate about their work, but you..." He tilted his head with interest again. "It's refreshing."

Talking to Preston was easier than she'd expected, aided by her non-sour whiskey, no doubt. But she glanced at the closed curtain, hating how she'd left things with Brick. For a woman who tried to build athletes up, she'd done a miserable job of it with him.

"Brick is lucky to have you on board," Preston said, drawing her attention back. "As am I." He unleashed a megawatt grin.

Again with the flirting. "What about you? Do you love your job?"

"I love my clients."

"All of them?"

He tapped his finger against his glass. The large ring on his pinky clinked against the crystal. "*Now*, yes. When I started out, I couldn't be choosy. Money talks, and I like nice things." His gaze roamed around his luxurious jet. "After business took off, I cut some clients. Now I only sign those I'd be happy spending a night drinking with."

"A night drinking." She whistled. "Those are some high standards."

He unleashed another devilish smirk. "How about I show you just how high my standards are? Have dinner with me in Vegas."

Preston didn't give up easily, and no part of Isla perked up at the offer. He was nice enough, but you couldn't force chemistry. And part of his life revolved around boxing. "Thanks, but the answer's still no."

He sipped his drink, a wrinkle sinking between his brows. "Your father said you're doing online dating. Is that why? You've met someone?"

She wanted to throttle her father again for gossiping about her, but the online dating excuse was an easy out. A way to shake Preston and leave his ego intact, especially since they'd be spending plenty of time together over the coming weeks. After the way she'd treated Brick, she didn't need more awkwardness. "I actually did. Never thought I'd do the internet dating thing, but...when in Rome."

She wasn't in Rome. She had no clue why she'd said that nonsense. She certainly hadn't set up an online dating account, let alone found a match.

Preston leaned forward, eager again. "Guess we'll see how that plays out, won't we?"

The cocky glint in his eye was trouble. She should disabuse

him of his hope, drill home that she preferred for their relationship to stay professional, but she was still unsettled by her botched start with Brick. Something about their interaction —his reaction to her sarcasm—felt off.

"About Brick," she said. "Does he usually get upset if people joke about his intelligence?"

Preston squinted. "Like how smart he is? No. If anything, he gets pissed they think he's dumb. But promoters gotta promote, and brute boxers sell."

"What do you mean *how* smart he is?" By intelligence, she'd meant *lack* of smarts, not an abundance of brains.

"Doesn't your dad talk about him?"

"I don't talk to my dad about boxing."

Preston frowned but thankfully stuck to the subject at hand. "Brick's the most intelligent person I've ever met. Takes all these linguistics courses, speaks eight languages, reads the kinds of books that put me to sleep in three seconds." He let out a self-deprecating laugh. "No clue why he bothers with all that stuff, but the guy's impressive."

Preston's honesty was surprising and sweet, and Isla's attention shifted back to the curtain separating them from Brick.

Brick had shut down the second she'd asked if he had a cat named Smart. He'd then played the role of dumb jock, saying he'd use his phone to spell his name, storminess in his gray eyes. Jesus, she'd royally messed this up, and his team certainly earned their paychecks, building him into an illiterate brute. An image she'd happily accepted. Now she had more to atone for than her rudeness.

5

Isla glanced at her bedside clock, then back at her laptop, her fingers frozen on the keyboard. She had to meet Brick in twenty minutes. She wasn't sure if she was more unnerved by that impending meeting or the dating profile she was about to put live. Telling Preston she'd met someone online would hopefully shake his advances, but if she wanted her father to quit playing cupid, a man in the flesh would be needed. She was even a little excited to flex her atrophied flirting muscles.

Heather's chiding about men not popping out of books like *Jumanji* had hit its mark. Isla missed dating and had put zero effort into meeting someone. She missed having a warm body beside her. A partner who understood why she preferred reading poetry over binging Netflix. Someone she could spoil and love. A confidant to discuss her complicated feelings surrounding her father: how much she loved him, her fear for the future, how she wanted their time together to be upbeat and positive, because he really was doing well, working, living, being his usual stubborn self.

The best way to meet someone special was to hop into the

dating pool. The distraction would also make it easier to give her father the space he wanted, and being here, away from her fledgling business, she actually had the time to chat online. A first for her in a long while. Still, taking the final step wasn't easy.

She picked up her phone and called Heather.

Her best friend, who'd be none too pleased about the early wake-up call, answered after four rings. "Why are you calling me at kill-your-best-friend o'clock?"

Isla smiled. "Brick has an insane workout schedule and does two physio sessions a day."

"I still have no clue why you agreed to this." Heather's voice was rough with sleep. A yawn carried through the line. "Your business opens in less than two months."

"I told you, I couldn't say no to my father. He paid for my gym equipment." It wasn't a complete lie. She owed him for that generosity and so much more. But she didn't breathe a word about his Parkinson's. If she broached the topic, voiced how stressed she was this soon after learning about his illness, she wasn't sure she'd be strong enough to bottle it back up and be the positive support he needed.

"Yeah, well, I still think you're nuts," Heather said. "And I'm exhausted. Call me later."

"Tell me again why downloading this dating app is a good idea?"

A muffled crash sounded. "I am no longer tired. Please let me vet your profile."

"Not in this lifetime. I'm just nervous to put it live."

"What picture did you use?"

Isla glanced at her profile page. "The one you took this year, when I decided to open my practice, and we went out dancing."

Isla's hair was still long in the shot, her smile a bit sloppy from a couple of celebratory drinks, but it wasn't one of those filtered images that didn't look like her. Her description was accurate, too. The first line read: *I love poetry.*

"I approve," Heather said. "And dating online is no big deal. There's no commitment. You don't have to chat or agree to meet someone unless you want to. And you're obviously curious to try, or you wouldn't have ruined my sleep."

An excellent point. She'd just needed that extra push.

She also needed to get her butt in gear.

Adding tardy to her list of misdeeds with Brick was not on today's to-do list. She'd already thought about him too much since yesterday's revelation, wondering which languages he spoke, if he was planning to do a PhD, why he'd ever agreed to hide his intelligence. Along with those questions came snapshots of his elegant bone structure, the intensity in his piercing eyes, the huge breadth of his wide shoulders.

If a picture of him popped up on the dating app, she'd swipe right so hard, she'd send her phone flying.

"I'm hanging up now," Heather said, her voice groggy again.

The phone went dead, and Isla gave herself a mental slap. Thinking about Brick—a freaking boxer—in any way but professional wasn't cool.

She quickly added "I hate boxing" to her profile and published it. That was one daunting prospect conquered. With the app on her phone, she'd hear a few cute buzzing chimes when she had a match. Her mood lifted at the prospect. If her father's Preston setup haphazardly resulted in her finding a nice man who hated boxing, she'd have to thank him.

She hurried to the elevator, tapping her heel when it made two stops before the main floor. The hotel was typical Vegas, flashy and busy, filled with people parked at slot machines and poker tables, chips slipping through their greedy fingers. Even at this early hour, the desperate were out, betting it all on Lady Luck.

The lobby's towering ceiling accented with blown-glass chandeliers gave her a reprieve from the casino's smoke-tinged air, but she hurried through, a woman on a mission.

She'd apologize to Brick the second she walked in, admit how bad her day had been yesterday. What she wouldn't do was ask him which languages he spoke and how playing the role of dumb brute made him feel, her curiosity be damned. Protecting her mental health and keeping her distance from boxers was more important than untangling his interesting story.

She stopped at the gym entrance and smiled at the security detail at the door.

"Name and ID, please," the guard said.

"Isla Slade. Physiotherapist for Brick Kramarov." She fished her ID from her wallet and handed it over.

The guard accepted it but didn't glance at the clipboard in his hand. "You're Swinging Graham Slade's daughter, aren't you? Man, that guy was a legend."

She pursed her lips. "He still is."

Ignoring her hard tone, he beamed. "That fight with him and Hector Narvarez? Totally insane. Your dad took a crazy beating. But, man, that knockout at the end? One of the best fights I've ever seen."

She'd never forget that harrowing match. Every time Hector's punches had landed on her dad's ribs, she'd flinched, feeling the sharp pain in *her* body.

She'd just turned thirteen, had seen his fights before, live and on TV. But her parents had fought that morning, louder and uglier than in the past. Her mother had screamed about hating boxing and all of Dad's stupid cars and his ugly scarred face. He'd answered with harsh rebuttals, ranting that she was cold and heartless and a bad mother.

"Fuck you and her," had been her mother's final reply.

She'd stormed out of their room, right into Isla, who'd been eavesdropping around the corner. Her mother hadn't apologized. No tearful excuses offered for the disgusted curse. She'd simply glared at Isla as though she'd been the cause of their fight, the child she hadn't wanted. The kid who'd kept her chained to a man she'd grown to detest.

Her mother hadn't returned until late that night, leaving Isla to order pizza and watch her father's fight alone. Hector Narvarez had laid into Swinging Graham Slade. Punches to his face, hard jabs to his nose. She'd pictured her father hitting the mat, not moving, leaving her with a mother who didn't want her. She'd pictured the casket, the funeral, earth shoveled into his grave until her heart was beating so fast she couldn't draw in enough air to breathe.

Hector may have hit the mat at the end of that fight, but her father had landed in the hospital, with a punctured lung and nerve damage to his right eye.

And Isla had suffered her first panic attack.

She clutched her chest now, feeling the sudden rush of her heart, those memories too damn vivid.

"Can I get in?" She nodded at the door, desperate to get away from this security guy and those memories.

"Yeah, of course. Have a great day." He handed her ID back.

Without looking at him, she hurried into the private gym Brick's team had rented and rested her back on the closed door. She shut her eyes and breathed, counting slowly from one to ten. Pressed her hand to her stomach, focused on the air filling her belly like a balloon.

Inflate, deflate.

I am here. I am fine. Nothing bad is happening.

She dug her feet harder into the floor, the solid foundation grounding her. Her breathing became easier. Her lungs expanded wider.

"You okay?"

Isla snapped her eyes wide. Brick was in the middle of the room, watching her intently. He was in a tank top and shorts, every muscle in his massive body glistening with sweat. Her heart resumed warp speed. "I'm fine." But she sounded curt again. The opposite of her planned apology.

He dragged his forearm across his sweaty forehead. "You don't look fine."

The last thing she needed was to acknowledge how messed up she was to her client. She may not have wanted to treat Brick, but she couldn't have a chink in her reputation. Not when starting her practice.

"Did you get the paperwork done?" She couldn't tell if the question had come out as a challenge. That slight panic attack was still lingering, her nerves shot to hell.

His lips flattened. "You mean did I manage that tough work on my own?"

Yep. She'd been challenging. Constantly sticking her foot in it with this guy. "I didn't mean *on your own* like I thought you needed help. You clearly didn't. The questions were straightforward. Not that the difficulty matters. I'm sure you'd have been fine with harder questions. You're just busy with training and getting settled, and you have that dog, and I..." Needed to shut the hell up. "Where are the forms?"

Embarrassed by her motor mouth, she dropped her gaze from his intense stare to his neck. His tendons flexed, sweat dripping down the strong cords. She watched the moisture slide over his collarbone until it dipped under the damp cotton of his tank top. The thin fabric clung to his body, outlining his defined pecs and a hint of his abdominals. Hard ridges that made her mouth go dry.

She needed to get a grip. Brick was no more fit than most of her clients. Abs were just muscles that formed a wall of protection for the viscera and helped maintain erect posture. But now she was thinking about erect things. Defined hip bones. Impossibly strong thighs. If one of those powerful legs pressed between hers, lifted her up, rubbed just enough...

"On the treatment table," he said.

"What?" Heat bloomed in her lower belly as her heart resumed racing.

He squinted at her. "The forms—they're on the treatment table."

She wanted *him* on that treatment table, in a non-professional manner, and she had no clue why. Attraction never blindsided her like this, not when treating clients. She walked into meetings with her physiotherapy hat on. Not her come-hither hat. That slight panic had muddled her brain.

Flustered, she walked over to the table and almost stumbled over a dog. "Jesus."

"His name's Whit, not Jesus."

Right. Whit. She'd made that crack on the plane, asking if he'd had a cat called Smart. She'd also assumed he'd misspelled the dog's name. Now she'd bet it had another deeper meaning. "Does he go everywhere with you?"

He eyed the wrinkly bulldog with adoration, his moodiness dissipating. "As much as possible."

He clearly loved the ugly mutt. Pretending to be a dog person might be a step forward, a way to thaw the ice between them. She squatted down and gave Whit a pet. The pup chuffed and leaned into her hand. Isla hadn't spent much time around pets. Neither of her parents had cared to take on the responsibility, and she'd been happier reading than cleaning up dog poop.

She stroked Whit's thick neck, the heat and solidness of him grounding her more than her breathing exercises had. He leaned harder into the touch, like he wanted to absorb more of her tension. The nicest warmth spread up her arm.

"He's good at calming me down, too," Brick said, his voice closer than expected.

The sprawling room had a full gym, including assorted physiotherapy equipment, two treatment tables, a stretching area, and boxing accoutrement. The space was huge, but Brick had moved closer, *too* close, the air around her condensing with his body heat.

She stood and walked briskly to the treatment table, grabbed the forms, trying to steady her shaky grip. She didn't like dogs. Or boxers. Yet she'd found herself comforted by the former and attracted to the latter. Had she walked into some kind of *Twilight Zone*?

She forced her erratic focus on the looping words written on the pages. Brick was twenty-seven, the same age as her. He had beautiful writing, elegant and uniform. The type of cursive that would fill a nineteenth-century diary. She pictured a fountain pen in his huge hand dancing over the page in a flourish as he nibbled his bottom lip in concentration, and her traitorous body reacted again.

This was more than panic-induced attraction. The dating app must be to blame. Signing up had been a reminder of how long it had been since she'd felt the weight of a man on top of her. So long, even a boxing client was making her flush.

She blinked hard and bit her cheek. Started reading the form again, did a doubletake at the name he'd written. "Eric Kramarovsky?"

"You can read."

She looked up sharply. The man was smirking, challenge in the quirk of his lips.

"I practice every night," she answered drily. "I just thought your name was—"

"Brick?" The lift of his blond eyebrow said all he hadn't: what kind of idiot would name their kid Brick?

If one of them was dense, she was certainly taking lead. "Guess I didn't think about it."

He shrugged. "Guess not."

"Brick is part of your boxing persona then?"

"It is." Flat reply, not giving her an inch.

She deserved his irritation. "I feel like I've misjudged a lot about you, Eric."

He stared at her a beat, then said, "Happens."

He dropped his gaze as the word died on his lips, the challenge in his quips evaporating with the sad sound. He looked so defeated suddenly, this massive man beaten down by his alter ego, and Preston's words came floating back: *If anything, he gets pissed that they think he's dumb.* She could see it—the defensiveness, his sudden dejection—how much he hated the misconceptions. Thoughts of his thick thighs and the treatment table fled, replaced with the urge to say *hey, it's okay* and *I know you're crazy smart*. In an instant she *cared*.

The worst possible emotion.

At her former physio gigs, caring had led to worry. Worry had led to anxiety. Just ten minutes ago, she'd been panting by the door, fighting off a panic attack. She couldn't think about Brick's—*Eric's*—thighs or intellect or the sad slump of his shoulders. She was here to focus on her job and her father.

Another quick scan of his forms later, she said, "How's your hand, the one that was broken?"

"Strong. Gets stiff at times, but it's not an issue."

"And your left Achilles—how long has it been bothering you?" That was better. She sounded strong, sure. Like a physiotherapist.

He watched her before replying. "On and off for the past year."

"Why don't you lie down while we talk? Take off your socks and shoes. I'll poke around a bit, if that's okay?"

He grunted, still moody, but followed her instructions.

Once he was on the treatment table, she lifted his leg and palpated around his Achilles and ankle. A couple of nodules bumped along the tendon. "What have you done to strengthen it?"

Another pause, this one shorter. "I stopped skipping for a while, wore a heel lift in my shoe to take off pressure. Did typical strength building. My physio did ultrasound and electrotherapy on it."

"All good treatments." She stretched his lateral ankle. "Does this hurt?"

He stared at the ceiling, his face unreadable. "No."

She changed her angle slightly. "What about this?"

He grunted. "It's a bit tender."

They continued like that, with her stretching his Achilles and testing pressure points on his calf. He offered the odd grunt, but as they progressed his replies came more easily, each answer a bit more specific. Whit slept nearby, unperturbed by his new surroundings or his owner's physio assessment. A few times, Isla glanced at Eric, only to find him staring at her. He'd blush and glance away, like he'd been caught shoplifting tampons, and *her* face would heat.

He was likely trying to figure her out, a woman who'd been hot and cold with him. Whatever the source of those glances, she didn't dwell on them. This was her job. The familiar work settled her overactive mind. Until her phone chimed.

Whit's head lifted up. Eric frowned in the direction of the sound but didn't speak. She never normally had her phone nearby when working. Distractions were unprofessional. But she took this job to help her father, made him promise to call or text if he needed her. Since she'd never heard that particular sound, it couldn't be her father. Her only guess was she had a match on the dating app. She hadn't expected a match this soon or considered how disruptive the buzzing chime would be. The early riser reaching out to her better be this morning's only Casanova.

The second she got back to work another chime sounded.

"Sorry," she said, embarrassment seizing her as she lowered Eric's leg. "I should deal with that."

He didn't smile obligingly. Just gave another grunt.

Wonderful. Another misstep with her client.

She'd left her purse on the rolling table by the door. Flustered, she hurried toward it, feeling Eric's judgmental gaze on her back. One look at her phone confirmed her suspicions.

The goddamn dating app.

Ignoring the man's profile, she swiped the screen, trying to silence the app's notifications.

"Is our physical therapy session disrupting your personal time?"

She froze at Eric's curt tone. Fiddling with her phone was so not cool. Her clients deserved her undivided attention. Because she was a professional.

She used to be, at least.

Messing with her phone was about as unprofessional as a school teacher sipping from a flask. She debated muting her volume for the morning, but if her dad needed her, she wouldn't hear his call. She'd have to leave it until later, hope no other men reached out. Annoyed with herself for setting up the app right before her session, she shoved her phone into her purse.

6

Eric watched Isla as she made her way back to him. Her cheeks and neck were flushed. Not so different than when he'd found her flat against the door, her hand pressed to her stomach, freaking out over something. This flush looked more embarrassed.

"I don't like interruptions," he said. He didn't. It was unprofessional and rude, and cell phones were the worst culprits.

She put her hands on his ankle, cheeks still rosy, and resumed her prodding. "Agreed. It won't happen again."

He grunted. A sound he'd been making too often around her. She was stronger than she looked, her thumbs rubbing at his ankle joints with precision. She was also beautiful. Preston had been right about that. She inherited her father's dark eyes and wide mouth. Definitely not his busted-up nose. She had a softness to her face, rounded cheeks and a natural elegance you'd see in actresses of the forties and fifties. The rest of her was strong, yet feminine, lean muscles emphasized in a pink tank top and yoga pants. The birthmark on her long neck was sexy as hell. Yeah, he found her attractive, *on the outside*. Yesterday, with her snarky sarcasm, nothing about her had been appealing.

"I'm going to do some active release on your calf," she said.

He relaxed into the table's leather surface as her hands went to work, closed his eyes, using the quiet time the way he would if Gilpin were working on him. He visualized a boxing ring, punching patterns. The footwork he'd been practicing. He pictured himself standing over Joe Bradley, his opponent on the mat and—

Her phone chimed again.

Isla's hands stilled. Just a moment, then she continued putting pressure on his calf while flexing his foot. He kept his eyes closed, but her tension was palpable. *His* concentration was toast. Working one-on-one with a therapist was personal. Moods transferred easily through touch. Hers read agitated. His mood probably read annoyed. He tried to relax, ignore her intensity and her phone's intrusion. It chimed again. Whit barked.

"Do you need to get that?" His eyes were open now, narrowed at Isla's still-red cheeks.

Her jaw twitched. "No."

"Then turn off your phone."

"I need my phone on."

"Then why aren't you answering it?" If this was how she worked, he'd have to tell Preston he was out. He needed a capable physiotherapist. Not a person who couldn't put her life on hold for sixty minutes.

"It's not..." She looked up at the ceiling and mouthed something he couldn't hear. "That notification isn't why I have my phone on."

It chimed *again*. She cursed.

He pushed up onto his elbows, ready to get off the table and end this useless session. "I knew this was a bad idea."

"What?" She sounded panicked.

He swung his legs around and stood. "Everything about this is a bad idea: you stepping in out of the blue, my routine changing, your distraction."

Whit came to his side, probably sensing his irritation. Eric moved to leave, but Isla touched his arm. "I'm so sorry. Please don't go."

He should go. Take Whit on a walk and get some air. Nothing about working with Isla was good for this fight. Instead he faced her. "I need a serious physiotherapist."

"I promise you, I am serious. The phone notifications were an accident." He wasn't sure how his face looked, but she frowned and removed her hand from his arm. "I can't believe I'm telling you this, but"—she sighed—"I signed up for a dating site right before our session, and the stupid app chimes when a guy reaches out. I tried to turn it off, but it was taking too long, and you were frustrated, which I totally understand. I'd be annoyed, too. So I left it, assuming I wouldn't have eleventy million matches reaching out this early, and now I'm embarrassed and sorry and would love the ground to swallow me whole." She slumped, covering her face with one hand.

He surprised himself by chuckling. He could add cute to her list of attributes: adept hands, beautiful face, adorable when embarrassed. Rude and judgmental on a whim. But she'd apologized earlier, and her actual physio work had been on point. If nothing else, he owed Graham enough to give her another chance. "Let me see your phone."

She dropped her hand from her face. "What? No."

"Do you want to silence the mating calls?"

She smiled. "Clever. I like that."

One minute she was suggesting he was stupid, the next clever. "I'm good with apps and phones. Let me see it."

"You're not good with phones."

"Are you calling me dumb again?"

"No, Rick Rosner. You're far from dumb, but I saw you on the plane. You were struggling with something on your cell."

Right. The plane. Where she'd ridiculed his intelligence. If that Rick Rosner comment was another jab, that would be her last chance. "I was installing a new firewall on my phone, and it was complicated. This is easy. And who's Rick Rosner?"

"I thought you were smart."

"I thought you wanted to keep this job."

She smirked. "He's a writer and former stripper."

Fresh irritation had him standing taller. "And you called me Rick Rosner because?"

"He has a crazy high IQ. Like the second highest in the world. I read an article about him once, and your name rhymes with his, so..."

She spouted off this trivia casually, like it wasn't a startling compliment, minus the stripping part. *Clever. High IQ.* The opposite of how most people saw him.

He used to think of himself as a showman, donning a persona for the press. Like a Shakespearean performer duping the audience. His fists did the talking in the ring. His family knew the heart of him. No one else had mattered. These days, the dumb jock image made him feel foolish.

He watched Isla's face, searched for ridicule behind the comment. All he saw was good-natured teasing in the quirk of her lips, and he relaxed. Whit waddled away and lay down. Always attuned to the energy in a room.

Eric held out his hand toward Isla. "How about I silence your app?"

"Only if you don't read my profile."

"I don't want to read your profile." He hadn't contemplated it, at least. Not until she'd told him not to. She probably liked Wall Street types who owned fancy yachts and luxury cars. The lavish lifestyle Swinging Graham Slade had provided for her growing up. It would jive with her whiplashy personality. Or maybe she was a closet *Star Trek* fan and loved cosplay and had a massive comic book collection. Wouldn't that be something?

She hesitated, then fetched her phone and gave it to him.

While she went to find the ultrasound machine, he tapped through her settings. Silencing the app was as easy as predicted. He was done in seconds and flipped back to the home page. She had longer hair in her profile photo and looked incredibly happy. Her smile was disarmingly attractive, genuine and carefree. The opposite of her entrance earlier, when she'd seemed upset while leaning against the door. He hadn't asked if someone had made her uncomfortable. He'd still been annoyed with her sarcastic jabs on the plane. His irritation had begun to fade, and he felt rude for not asking more.

Probably better he hadn't meddled. He certainly shouldn't read her profile now, as she'd asked, but it was right there, down the screen. And curiosity was a tempting devil. He scrolled lower, aware he was invading her privacy, but he had to work closely with this woman. Finding out some background might help him relax around her. Plus it was public information.

She wheeled the ultrasound machine next to the treatment table, plugged it into the wall. "You almost done?"

"I've saved you from your throngs of male suitors." But not from his curiosity. He looked at the phone as he spoke, reading her profile before he could stop himself.

I love poetry. I love how words can build worlds and mean different things to different people. I prefer reading over watching

Netflix. I consider myself a strong, independent woman, but I also appreciate a man with manners, who wants to hold a door open to be polite. Chivalry is not dead. Family, humor, and loyalty are my pillars of strength. I hate boxing.

"I'm ready when you are," she said.

He startled and cleared his throat. "Yeah, sure. Here you go."

He handed back her phone and their fingers brushed. It was a tiny touch, but all he could think was *poetry* and *reading* and *words can build worlds*. If he'd read that profile, had seen that photo with the carefree smile and crinkled eyes, he'd have asked that woman out in a heartbeat.

Except for her last line.

This new information had his mind spinning like when he studied languages, one question kicking into another. He wanted to ask if growing up with her father had been tough, if it had scarred her in some way. He was curious what poetry she loved and why a smart, beautiful woman needed a dating app. Maybe it was her hot-and-cold personality. Unless there had been a reason she'd been rude on the plane. Maybe she'd had a particularly bad day yesterday, something to do with how unsettled she'd been when practically hyperventilating against the door this morning.

One of his favorite Walt Whitman quotes urged people to be curious, not judgmental. But judgment often came easier than curiosity. Maybe Eric had judged Isla as quickly as she'd judged him.

She returned from putting her phone away and gestured to the treatment table. "Let's get back to it, shall we?"

"*Sii curioso, non critic,*" he said, repeating the sentiment of Whitman's quote in Italian. The romantic language was the first to come to mind. He liked how the sounds curled around his tongue, softened on the roof of his mouth, as though the harder consonants had been dipped in honey.

"What does that mean?" she asked, her lips slightly parted. Her dark eyes swept across his face.

"It means I'd like to offer a fresh start. I think we got off on the wrong foot."

She pressed her palm to her chest. "I'd really like that, Eric. I've been awful to you. It's not who I am."

He had no clue who she was.

Once he got back on the treatment table, she resumed her work, used the ultrasound on his ankle, her phone thankfully silent. Their conversation gradually resumed, light discussions about his diet and training and workout schedule.

"4,000 calories a day is insane." She whistled while moving the ultrasound probe around his Achilles. "I'd have to be carted around in a wheelbarrow."

"I'm a lot bigger than you."

Her gaze moved up his body, lingering on his torso. "I assume forty to fifty percent is protein."

His abs tightened under her steady perusal, like he was his sixteen-year-old self, flexing to show off, amazed a girl was even glancing at him. A ridiculous reaction. "I eat lots of salmon and chicken," he said, forcing himself to relax.

Her focus darted to his ankle. "I hate salmon."

"What did salmon ever do to you?"

"It makes my teeth feel weird." She rolled her tongue over her teeth, grimacing, like she could feel the offensive texture.

There she went again, being cute. "Maybe your teeth are the problem."

"Or I need to eat it more. I used to hate olives, then I forced myself to eat them every chance I got. Now I love them. Just the green ones, though. And they're better with the pits in them. Firmer texture."

He relaxed further as she worked, no longer flexing like an idiot, but he wanted to keep her talking. Something about the change in her voice was soothing. Like he could hear the smile in her tone. "You're a picky eater."

"I prefer the term *particular*." She gave him a saucy look. "My toast has to be super burnt because butter tastes better on it that way. Marshmallows too—charred to a crisp. And if you put a raw onion anywhere near me, I'll melt like the Wicked Witch of the West."

She did a funny little shiver. Theatrical and silly. Amusing as hell. "I'll make a mental note not to eat raw onions before coming here."

"My sensitive sense of smell would be in your debt. What about you?" She slid him a sidelong glance. "Fussy or experimental?"

"I'll pretty much eat anything."

"Have you had live larvae?"

He curled his lip. "Why would anyone eat live larvae?"

"Oh, so you're a picky eater, too." She winked at him.

He laughed, surprising himself. He hadn't expected to like talking with Isla this much, but he was grinning outright, enjoying her company, when he'd spent most of the flight irritated with her.

She put the ultrasound machine away and wiped his ankle, then started doing some deep tissue work on his calf. She worked him patiently and thoroughly, as good as Gilpin, if not better, but when her fingers smoothed over his skin, the friction sent tingles up his thighs. When the tingling traveled to his groin, he clenched his stomach.

Eric's wellness team at home always had their hands on him: massage therapist, physiotherapist, acupuncturist, chiropractor. It wasn't like he hadn't worked with women before. After reading Isla's dating profile—*words can build worlds*—and chatting easily with her, her attention suddenly felt…different.

First the idiotic flexing, now this.

Talk of dating apps must have infected his mind, reminding him how isolated he was socially, romantically. Useless thoughts that didn't serve him while training.

Preston breezed into the gym as they finished, wearing slacks and shiny shoes, always stylish. "How'd it go?"

Isla glanced at Eric and bit her bottom lip, a question in her eyes, as though asking if things had actually gone well. He gave her small nod.

She beamed at Preston. "We're off to a solid start. We'll split our time between his Achilles and any other issues that come up. Your boy's in great shape." She bustled through the space, gathering her things, not giving Eric a second look. "See you this afternoon," she said, then slipped out the door.

Whit trotted over to the closing door, like he wanted to follow her. Eric watched the door, suddenly restless and antsy.

Preston clapped. "See? Told you you'd like her."

Eric blinked, unsure why he felt fidgety. Like he didn't know what to do with his hands. He crossed his arms. "She's smart and knows her stuff."

"Yeah, we talked a bit on the plane." Preston glanced at the door she'd walked through. "She was honest and interesting. Also turned me down flat, which of course makes me like her even more."

Eric tightened his crossed arms. "You asked her out?"

"I told you before we boarded—Graham kind of suggested I date her. He doesn't like her doing the online dating thing. Thinks we'd be a good fit."

Nothing about Preston and Isla was a good fit. He binged Netflix regularly; she preferred reading. He thought studying and learning was a waste of time; she loved poetry. But Preston was loyal and loved his family. Chivalry might be pushing it, but the man could turn on the charm. "She hates boxing," he blurted.

Preston glanced again at the closed door, head tilted. "Maybe that's why she won't go out with me." His attention shifted to Eric. "Do you have more intel? Anything that might help me?"

"It's a bad idea for you to date Slade's daughter." He winced at his harsh tone, but he needed stability on his team. Focus and support. "If it ends badly, Slade might be pissed. Tension between you two could rub off on me. Make training harder."

"You come before everything," Preston said, adjusting his cufflink. "And I admire Graham. I wouldn't dick over his daughter. If you won't help me, I'll woo her on my own."

Isla's profile had said she appreciated chivalry. Wooing certainly fell under that category, and Eric agreed with her father. Dating online could be dodgy. Plus, Preston and Isla were adults. They knew how important Eric's training was. They wouldn't do anything to jeopardize his fight. This might actually be nice, helping two good people get together. Eric pictured Isla and Preston out together, laughing, enjoying each other's company, but the effort of it—the bitter taste in his mouth and his reaction during this whole conversation—had his fingers digging into his biceps.

This wasn't good. Not even a little. The last thing he needed was to be attracted to his physiotherapist, but the idea of Preston and her on a date had him clamping his jaw. A flicker of jealousy he needed to squash. Eric wasn't in a position to ask her or *any* woman out. For the short term, his life was all boxing all the time, and she was his employee. For the long term, she hated boxing, which meant she hated boxers. And him.

He swallowed roughly, ready to nip this awkward situation in the bud. "I learned a few things that might help."

"Yeah?" Preston edged closer, like an eager kid, excited about his first crush.

"She loves reading, poetry in particular. Not so much a Netflix woman."

Preston frowned. "I don't know shit about poetry."

"Do some reading. It'll give that atrophied brain of yours some exercise." Eric could use more exercise now. A grueling run. An hour with a speed bag.

"Come on, man. I need more than that. You're the fucking genius here. Give me a line to use. A poetry passage that'll sweep her off her feet." He bounced on his toes, threw a couple of jabs at the air. "I'm killer on dates and can do the rest."

Preston looked ridiculous air boxing in his slacks, and Eric chuckled. Yeah, giving his manager some pointers was a good thing for them all. Preston and Isla might really hit it off. Eric's sudden interest in her would fade. He thought back to Isla's tough demeanor when they'd first met, how fragile she'd seemed when she'd been upset this morning, her cute humor as they'd relaxed around each other. The surprising depth in her profile. The quote he had in mind was one he'd found on the internet, a passage he'd read by some random guy name Eric Enyert.

The romantic note spoke more of his own sudden fascination with Isla—a fascination that *would* pass—but it would work for Preston, too. "Yeah, okay. I have a quote for you."

7

AT NIGHT, Las Vegas was all flashing lights and drunken tourists outside. It was also flashing lights and drunken tourists inside the casinos. Neither scene appealed to Isla, and thankfully her father wasn't a gambler, his spendthrift nature aside. She, however, wasn't sure where he was. He was the reason she was in Sin City, away from her business, and they hadn't spoken all day. His curt replies to her five texts didn't count.

She knocked on his door, ran through a list of choice words she'd launch if he wasn't inside relaxing. *Careless. Reckless. Heedless.* Along with a bunch of other *less*-es. She had a spare keycard for his room. He'd said it was only for emergencies, in case she needed anything and he was asleep and couldn't answer. He'd warned her not to use it to check on him.

She reached to knock again, ready to pull out the forbidden keycard, but the door opened.

Her father was wearing the hotel's plush robe. He looked annoyed, but then again, that was his resting face. "What's up?"

"I was in the neighborhood. Thought I'd stop by."

He watched her, his lips pressed into a stern line. Graham Slade had two scars around his left eye; his right eyelid hung lower than his left ever since that Hector Narvarez fight. Droopy eye or not, his stares were skewering—an interrogation technique he'd used often when she was growing up.

As a kid, if she'd lied—*of course I did my homework...no, I didn't break your massage chair*—he wouldn't yell or threaten like her mother. He'd just stare. And wait. Like now.

"What?" she asked, on the defensive. "I live down the hall. It's the same neighborhood."

He stood his ground, waiting for her to crack and admit why she was really there. To ask how he was feeling, obviously. Make sure he hadn't tired himself out and that he was taking his medication and getting enough fluids and vitamins.

All forbidden topics, thanks to Stubborn-Ass Slade.

He blinked once. Then resumed his role of Stare Champ.

She opened and closed her mouth, squeezed her hands into fists while matching his look eyeball for eyeball. But giving good stare was hard, and not talking about his illness was excruciating. Why did he have to be so infuriating?

She closed her eyes, defeated, and remembered a simple yet powerful Ramona Estle quote:

> "where we have wounds
> we heal"

Swinging Graham Slade had been dealing with his Parkinson's on his own for two years. Isla hadn't noticed any obvious symptoms. For now, she'd follow his lead, quit checking on him. When they got home, all bets were off. She'd force him to finally relax.

She shook out her cramping hands and kissed his cheek. "Just wanted to wish you a good night. Sleep well."

He huffed but didn't call her on the lie. "Heard you did well with Brick today."

"You mean Eric?"

"No, I mean *Brick*. He's got an image to uphold, Isla. In public, you call him Brick."

Don't ask me how I'm feeling. Don't call Eric by his actual name. This whole dictatorial situation was testing her last nerve. She saluted him and walked to the elevator, desperate for a drink and change of scenery. A moment without worrying over her impossible father.

The hotel had at least three bars in it, not to mention a number of restaurants and shops to tantalize the senses. Heaps of food and grandeur and *buy, buy, buy* in this town. She found her way to the most low-key establishment, a dimly lit speakeasy-style bar with velvet-padded booths and a wall filled with enough booze to drown an octopus.

She sat on a stool and smiled at the bartender. "What's your best cocktail?"

"The Gangster's Mistress," he said. "Tequila, triple sec, lime, cucumber puree, agave nectar, and mint." He wore a bowler hat and bowtie. His dark skin and eyeliner made his brown eyes shine. "Goes down nice and easy."

Nice and easy sounded like heaven. "I'll take one of those."

"Your wish is my command, ma'am."

"I wish you wouldn't call me ma'am."

"Noted and abided, miss. You can call me Jason."

Miss wasn't much better, but Jason played the part of old-fashioned server well, and she wouldn't mind gazing into those deep-brown eyes all night. Or she could extricate her phone and scroll through her thankfully silent dating app. Between this afternoon's second physiotherapy session with Eric, her hours on her phone and the internet trying to figure out how to navigate her new appointment-booking software, she hadn't given the app a second thought.

The bar's atmosphere was the perfect place to sneak a peek. The room was half-full with low-talking patrons. Freshly roasted, spiced nuts were delivered to the couple at her left. She inhaled the tempting aroma as Jason slid her drink in front of her. She took a sip and added talented to his list of lovely attributes. The man made a mean cocktail.

Another sip sliding down her throat, she pulled out her phone and tapped on the app.

First up was Brett. Brett's photo showed him holding a huge fish. The caption read: *Size matters.* She clicked the X icon to delete the match. *Brain size matters more, Brett.*

Vincent was next. He was handsome and athletic. His picture had been taken while on a hike, amid towering trees. Promising. When she read his profile's last line—*Modern technology will be the downfall of the world*—her lips puckered. A tad dramatic for a dating profile *on the internet.*

X marks the spot, Vincent.

The next two had selfies that screamed Cocky Womanizer. They got axed so fast she nearly knocked over her Gangster's Mistress. Not a fabulous start, but there was one more, and all it took was one intriguing profile, one fun date, one first kiss to find her match.

She clicked on the last notification and sat taller. Lance looked like the intellectual type she usually dated: trim beard, glasses, a kind smile. His name made her think of a pampered frat boy, but his profile didn't set off any sociopath alarms. He was an algebra professor and even made a cute math joke: *I'm looking for a relationship like an exponential curve: unbounded.*

Her thumb hovered over the screen, ready to swipe right and open a chat, but no flutter of excitement rose—the hint of butterflies that accompanied the stirrings of attraction. All she felt was hungry for the yummy smelling roasted nuts.

Earlier, when treating Eric, those butterflies had sparked to life. During their afternoon session, while she'd worked on his shoulder mobilization and lower back, he would occasionally say something in Russian. A random word when he was in pain. The guttural sounds had been oddly sexy, even though nothing about their interaction had been intimate. She'd used traction on his back, active release on his shoulder. All the while she'd avoided asking about his studies, his language skills, anything outside of their professional relationship. Questions that still nagged at her.

What would his dating profile say? *Handsome boxer who loves languages and pretends to act like a dimwit. Enjoys punching faces and kidneys on weekends.*

She glanced again at Lance's photo, tried to muster enough interest to swipe right. She motioned for Jason to fill her drink instead.

"Hello, beautiful." Preston slipped onto the stool beside her.

This man and his flirtations. "Somehow I'm not surprised to see you."

"It must be fate."

"Or we happen to be staying at the same hotel and both wanted a drink in the quietest bar."

"See? We already have so much in common." He slid his credit card over to Jason, who was doing a fine job of shaking up another Gangster's Mistress. "Her drink's on me. I'll have a martini, extra dry. And some of those amazing smelling nuts."

Those nuts really were making her mouth water. "If I ask to share your nuts, will you misguidedly assume I'm flirting with you and ask me out again?"

"That's a given." He swiveled on his stool, angled his body closer. "And you don't have to ask to have at my nuts."

She half-snorted a laugh. "You don't do subtle."

"Subtle is for the weak. And you were on a dating app when I got here. Guess things didn't work out with that other guy."

So much for that lie keeping his flirting at bay. "Things fizzled."

Instead of pushing the point, he pulled out his phone, checked the screen, and set it down. "Brick seems happy working with you."

"Yeah?" There were those butterflies again. At the wrong time. For the wrong man.

"He's bluntly honest when he's not happy. I actually don't think I've ever caught him in a lie. If he says he likes working with you, it's true."

"That's nice to hear." A relief she'd redeemed herself after their first meeting and the morning's blunders.

"Feel free to push him. He'll work his ass off for you."

"Like most boxers, he needs plenty of treatment." She pictured a jab connecting with Eric's face, his head jerking back. The damage to his neck and face and brain. She winced.

Preston scrubbed his jaw, studying her. "You don't like boxing."

Understatement. "It's a rough sport."

"It is, but it also gives kids confidence. Promotes a better sense of self, helps make them aware of their strengths, their weaknesses. Gives people an outlet when their other options might be less constructive. Plus, it's a great workout."

Easy to say when he earned a mint off his clients. "For the average Joe, sure. For professionals it's all about ego and money."

He shrugged a shoulder. "There's nothing wrong with using your skills to earn money. Your father certainly benefited from his fists."

Any butterflies lingering from discussing Eric died a fiery death. "He also benefitted from lots of hospital visits."

"Most things in life come with risks."

"Ninety percent of boxers sustain a brain injury."

She bit her cheek and shut the hell up. Her father would lose his mind if he'd overheard that harsh remark. It teetered too close to his illness. Not close enough for Preston to guess why she was steadying her breaths and calming her urge to keep arguing. But still.

Jason, thankfully, delivered their drinks and the nuts, but the spice-laden aroma had lost its appeal. She focused on her drink. Preston snacked readily, sipping his martini as the negative energy between them lingered.

"I'm not a boxer," he said finally.

He sure had the tenacity of one. "Because you don't want to damage your pretty face?"

He swiveled toward her, dimple flashing. "So you think I'm pretty?"

She laughed. "You know you're pretty."

"Go out with me, Isla."

"We're out right now."

He picked up his phone, scrolled through it for a second, then placed it down. "We are, but it's not the same. I promise we'll have fun."

Dating Preston wasn't the same as dating a boxer. His brain cells wouldn't be rearranged, while blood-hungry fans cheered or booed. Still, he was entrenched in that world, would always talk about Eric and his other clients and engage in heated discussion on the topic. She also couldn't imagine him lounging around on a Sunday, a book in his hand as they traded thoughts on their readings.

Tired of turning him down, she stayed quiet.

Preston ran his finger over the base of his martini glass,

eyes downcast. "'I know the shape of your hands,'" he said, still not looking at her. "'I want to know the shape of your heart. How it beats that intoxicating tune, both sad and beautiful.'"

She stared at him as his words sunk in. *No*, not words. A poem, the meaning implying he was looking deeper, wanting to see more in her than she'd shared. A few charred butterflies rebirthed, ash falling from their fluttering wings. "Who wrote that?"

His cheeks looked pinkish in the low light. Like he was embarrassed or shy. Two descriptions that didn't fit with the Preston she'd met. "No one famous. Eric..."

"*Eric* wrote that?" Forget a few butterflies. This was a swarm.

"Brick? No, not *Eric* Eric. His name's Eric *Enyert*. Some random guy." He dipped his head slightly, as though nervous. "I read it online and thought of you."

She wasn't sure why he wasn't meeting her eyes. Up until now, his confidence had been an entity of its own. Maybe, under his cocky exterior, Preston was a sensitive guy who liked to read poetry and imagined himself a romantic. "What stood out about that piece in particular?"

He glanced at his phone again. Was he waiting for a call?

He swallowed and faced her. "You're a complex woman who keeps a lot of herself hidden. I'd like to get to know you, understand what makes you tick." A gleam returned to his eyes. "And you're beautiful. I'd be lucky to look at you from across a table all night."

Cocky Preston was back, and she felt off balance.

She'd misjudged Eric horribly before they'd met. Could be she'd done the same with Preston, everything with her father throwing her judgment askew. She certainly wouldn't have expected Preston to recite poetry in an effort to win her over. Saying yes to one date wouldn't be the worst thing. One night to see if they actually had anything in common, as long as she set a ground rule. "If we—"

"Sorry, hold that thought." He grabbed his phone again and pulled up the sports highlights. "There's an interview on—Brick on ESPN. I need to make sure they didn't mess up the editing."

She fought a laugh. She was about to agree to a date, with one rule: they wouldn't discuss boxing. Here he was, interrupting her to watch his star athlete shit-talk his opponent.

Note to self: trust your instincts.

She gathered her purse to leave, but Eric's huge frame filled Preston's phone, and curiosity had her pausing. Eric had been focused and thoughtful in their sessions, fun to talk to, his face pensive more often than not. Brick Kramarov was a scowling monster.

She inched closer to Preston, fascinated.

The camera panned back slightly, revealing the interviewer. The woman was pretty, with long dark hair and bright red lips. She looked up at Eric's towering figure, microphone in hand. "How are you feeling about next month's fight, Brick?"

He grunted. "Joe Bradley's toast and he don't even know it. Gonna cream that guy."

"This fight's been a late addition for you, but Joe's been training for months. Are you doing anything different to prepare?"

"Prepare?" He sneered at the camera. "I was born ready. Gonna knock that amateur out."

The interviewer gave him a condescending smile. "Joe won the last defense of his title in a third-round knockout. I wouldn't call him an amateur."

"He ain't no challenge for me." Eric dipped his head lower, getting right in the camera's view. "Enjoy your belt, Joe. Give it a smooch goodbye before our match. That'll be the last time you see it." He snarled at the TV audience and finished with a vicious, "Brick Smash!"

Preston smacked the bar top and turned off his phone. "A thing of beauty."

"What about that was beautiful?" A man didn't need to dumb himself down for fans, just like a woman didn't need to hide her smarts to be liked.

"That Brick Smash stuff is gold. Crowd loves it."

She opened her mouth to tell him this ruse was silly and demeaning and, as far as she'd surmised, emotionally scarring for Eric, but that would entail standing up for her client. A boxer. One she found attractive. Exactly what she shouldn't do if she wanted to keep her emotional distance from Eric. "Thanks for the drink. See you around."

She was one step away when Preston said, "What about our date?"

"Strike two," she said, without turning around.

She could have sworn he laughed, but she didn't look back to check. Preston wasn't her type. That poem had been a one-off. But she *did* need to find a date. A man through her app. Someone who'd help her quit thinking about Eric's intellect and his rough Russian words and his slumped shoulders when she'd admitted she'd misjudged him, thinking he was as Neanderthal as his image. Lance might be getting a right swipe after all.

LANCE HAD GOTTEN A SWIPE. But it had been to the *left*. A quick internet search had showed several horrifying Facebook posts with him on a hunting trip, standing over a dead elephant. That was a hard *no*. Something else that was hard was Eric's ridiculously toned body as he did his weighted heel raises the next morning.

"Slower on the way down," she told him. "Make your muscles do the work. Don't rely on momentum."

He nodded, sweat dripping down his neck during his last few reps. He finished with a satisfied grunt. Tank top sweat-slicked to his body, he grabbed his water bottle, sucked back a huge amount of water, then wiped his neck and face with his towel. "My sister always tells me I do my exercises too fast."

"Is she a physiotherapist, too?"

"She's a know-it-all."

Isla laughed, picturing Eric—the man who was all Brick Smash in his interviews—being bossed around by his sister. "Are you two close?"

"Yeah." He took another swig of water. "When we were younger she drove me nuts, but we laughed a lot. As we've gotten older, she's become more subdued and crazy busy with her kids. Getting pregnant at nineteen, then going through a rough divorce has aged her in ways that upset me. So I do what I can to help her, but it never feels like enough. I wish I could've brought her to Vegas, given her a break."

Isla had been battling panic attacks at nineteen, barely able to take care of herself. She hadn't met his sister yet, but she was already awed by her strength. "She's not missing much with Vegas. It's pretty much like being stuck in a Spice Girls video."

The edge of Eric's lips curled up. "More like Lady Gaga crossed with Guns N' Roses. Flashy and loud."

"You know, I kept thinking you must be a Gaga fan."

He let out a low laugh. "I get that a lot, Sporty Spice."

"I'm the missing sixth Spice Girl: Neurotic Spice." With a dash of Workaholic Spice. "And seriously, the crowds here are brutal."

He took another sip of water, wiped his mouth. "I can't stand the music blaring from the cars."

"Everything's so noisy." They should get to work, head to the treatment table, but Eric leaned against the cable machine, and Isla liked looking at his crooked smile, the softening of his gray eyes as he regarded her. He was nothing like the brute in last night's interview. This morning, all she saw was a kind and curious man. A *really hot* kind and curious man.

"Tell me something about Vegas you love," he said.

"The food." She leaned her knee into the workout bench beside her. "I love the variety."

He twisted the towel in his hands, watching her. "But you prefer the smaller places."

A flutter moved through her stomach. He was certainly perceptive. "I do. What about you? One thing you love."

"The shows. Preston took me to Cirque du Soleil our first night. It blew my mind."

"You loved the athleticism?"

He rubbed at his chest. "Of course. Their skills are unbelievably impressive. But it's the magic of it. The spectacle."

"Like you've been transported to another world."

He cocked his head, another slow smile forming. "Yeah, exactly. Did your dad take you to those shows as a kid?"

"He did, and I loved them." Swinging Graham Slade had loved spending his money on anything and everything, but the memory made her think of her dad back then, big and strong and healthy, attacking each day, not caring if he spent every dime, because he lived in the moment. Even now with his diagnosis, he wasn't worrying about the future. He was focused on the present, working, doing what he wanted to do *now*.

"Did I bring up a bad memory?"

Aware of her frown, Isla focused on Eric, the compassion on his face. He may not know what she was going through, but his tenderness was a balm. "Not bad, exactly. My father's my favorite person in the world, but we've had our ups and downs, always related to his career. Going to shows and extravagant things like that brings back some of those tougher moments." Her toughest moment was in the present, but it was all linked.

"Family's like that," he said gently. "They're the most important people in my life, but they also contribute a lot of stress. Unconditional love is amazing and complicated."

They stared at each other, mutual understanding drifting between them. He opened his mouth slightly, as though about to speak again. He didn't, though. Just bit down on his bottom lip and smiled that slow smile of his, while Isla's heart raced faster than it should.

8

ERIC WALKED THROUGH THE PROMENADE, eyeing the busy shops, searching for inspiration, coming up short. He didn't have much spending cash, but he wanted to bring his niece and nephew something cute from Vegas: a new stuffed animal for Eliza's tea parties, a cool eraser for Asher's colorful eraser collection. Rock music flowed from one restaurant. Mexican guitar strummed from the bustling balcony above—loud people eating tacos, drinking margaritas. A guy dressed as a gorilla hawked theater tickets up ahead.

Then something wet landed on his head and dropped to the ground—a fucking lime wedge.

"What do you call a lime that falls on your head?"

He whipped around, unsure if he'd imagined Isla's voice. But no. There she was. Sitting on the edge of the promenade's fountain, sunglasses on, bottle of water in her hand, smirking at him.

He wiped his head and waited for a family of five to pass, then he moved toward her. "I call it disgusting."

"I call it a fruit punch."

He snorted, then schooled his face. "If that was funny, I'd laugh."

"If you had a sense of humor, you'd laugh."

"See that gorilla with the blue sunglasses?" The fact that he could utter that sentence without a hint of irony said so much about this town.

She followed his gaze. "Yeah."

"Why doesn't he use Twitter?"

Head tilted, she tucked her wavy hair behind her ear. "Because he's too sick with jungle fever?"

"He hates being followed," he said, straight-faced.

Isla pulled her sunglasses down her nose. "First a Lady Gaga lover, now a crappy joke teller. You continue to surprise me."

Bantering with Isla and enjoying her company still surprised him. "My joke was better than your joke."

"Is this where I'm supposed to tell you my dad can beat up your dad?"

"Your dad would kick my dad's ass, and I'd happily watch." Eric held no affection for the man who'd left him and his mother, no support offered, no birthday cards sent or phone calls made. Assholes like that deserved an upper cut from Swinging Graham Slade, and Eric didn't want to think about that waste of a human any longer than necessary. He nodded to the empty space beside Isla. "That seat taken?"

"It's only free if you grace me with another of your awful jokes."

An easy challenge. Asher was a fan of stupid jokes, and Eric loved cracking the little guy up. When Asher lost it, he belly laughed so hard, he cried. And sometimes farted. "What's often on the ground that's brown and sticky?"

"I asked for a cute joke, not toilet humor. Consider this seat occupied." Sunglasses pushed back into place, she planted her hand in the vacant spot, stretched out her legs, and crossed her ankles. Sassy and cute.

He paused, letting her wait for it, then gave the punchline: *what's often on the ground that's brown and sticky.* "A stick."

Her face puckered, then she laughed. "Wow. You really do excel at dumb jokes."

Where he might have tensed at any association with the word dumb, he was past that point with Isla, knew she was only teasing. Amused, he stepped over her outstretched legs, nudged her arm away, and sat beside her, coming flush with her side. It was either that or cozy-up to the man at his left wearing a mesh crop top. "At least one of us has a sense of humor."

She lifted her face to the sun. "Don't go getting cocky on me."

"Oh, this isn't cocky. My mastery of dumb jokes is fact."

"Two jokes is barely a scientific study."

They weren't, but he latched onto her mention of science. "Why can't you trust atoms?"

"I don't know, but I bet you're gonna tell me."

"Because they make up everything."

She made a cute snorting sound. "Is there a heavyweight belt in stupid jokes? You could totally win."

"Mom always said I was a natural." The mesh-wearing guy at his left pushed closer, giving someone on his other side room. Without anywhere to go, Eric slid his arm around Isla's back, planted his palm on the stone at her right, shifting even closer to her. "Sorry," he murmured. But he wasn't. He liked being this close to her, feeling her body shake with laughter.

She tensed a beat, then softened, leaning more fully into him. "Your niece and nephew must love you."

"Not as much as I love them, which is why I'm out here in the madness getting assaulted by limes. Finding cute gifts isn't easy."

"If all else fails, I got a flyer for an adult-only store. They sell fuzzy pink penises. You could pass them off as stuffed toys."

"And invite child services to my house when the twins bring them to school for show-and-tell? I'll pass." But his thighs flexed. The word *penis* coming from Isla's lips did things to him. Knotted up his stomach, made him wrap his arm more firmly around her back.

She tilted her head back, sunshine spilling over her sunglasses and smooth skin. "I could help you find something kid-friendly, if you want. Under one condition."

He wouldn't mind the help, but that would mean standing up, losing the heat of her pressed into his side. He didn't remember the last time he was out like this, with a woman or a friend, just hanging out for the sake of hanging out. "If your condition's another joke request, the answer's no. My limit's three an hour."

"Don't limit yourself, Kramarovsky, or you'll never win that Stupid Joke heavyweight title you've been training for."

"Is that why you're sassing me? Is there a Sass heavyweight title, too?"

She glanced at him over her shoulder, chin tipped up. "You haven't seen my sass."

He'd sure as hell like to see her *sass*, couldn't deny how much he enjoyed feeling it bumped up against his on the hot stone ledge. He also liked hearing her laugh. "Where do animals go when their tails fall off?"

She scrunched her face like that gross lime wedge had fallen on *her* head. "First toilet humor, now gruesome horror stories."

"Is that the sass of which you speak?"

"We've barely gotten started on my sass."

It felt like they'd gotten started on something, though. Fun banter. Sunshine on his face. Fountain water splashing behind them. Isla loose and happy, practically in his arms. Nothing about this happenstance chat was romantic. They were colleagues and friends, who'd randomly bumped into each other, but being this close to her, his body reacting when she moved, his smile so constant his cheeks hurt—this was how relationships began, and he wasn't sure how to feel about that. Preston was into Isla. Eric had helped hook them up with poetry. He had no clue if Preston had used the romantic passage, or if his manager had asked Isla on a date. Not that any of it mattered when Isla hated boxers.

Jokes, though. They were simple. He could do jokes: *where do animals go when their tails fall off.* "They go to the retail store."

"Oh my God." She downright cackled this time. The kind of laughter that had her doubling over, pushing into him as her shoulders shook. She braced her hand on his thigh. At the touch, heat fisted his groin; his heart pounded against his ribs.

She wiped at her eyes. "I need one of those jokes every physio session. They're so awful, they're good. But hearing your stupid jokes wasn't my stipulation. I'll help you gift shop for your niece and nephew if we get ice cream on the way."

"I can't eat ice cream." He didn't want to move either. Not even a little.

"Are you lactose intolerant?"

"Strict diet."

"When's the last time you had ice cream?"

He had to think about that, and the fact that he had to think about that was sad. He missed ice cream and Kit Kat bars and eating Doritos. Junk food. Unhealthy food. Fun food. "I had a bite of ice cream cake at the twins' last birthday party. Seven months ago."

Her mouth dropped open. "One bite...seven months ago. As in one, tiny forkful?"

"Yeah?"

"That's so sad I might cry." Abruptly, she hopped up and held out her palm toward him. "You can have a lick, though. Right?"

Jesus. Was she trying to murder him? *Penis. Lick. Thigh grabs.*

He cleared his throat. Her outstretched hand was meant to help him stand up. Unnecessary and impractical. With his bulk, if he tugged on her, she'd topple onto his lap. Not an unpleasant option, but...yeah. *Preston. She hates boxers.* He fitted his palm against hers, tensed his legs and stood, towering over her. He didn't let go right away. She didn't move either and he could feel her pulse point, the fast jump at her wrist. Her chest seemed to swell faster, too. Her eyes were hidden by her sunglasses, but her nostrils flared slightly as her fingertips dragged over the heel of his hand.

There went his body again, tensing at the simple contact.

Then she jerked her arm back, smoothed her hair behind her ears, clearly not as affected by the touch as him. "Let the ice cream mission commence. You get one lick, and I get the rest. Which is a pretty fair deal, I think."

One lick didn't sound like enough, but he followed her.

ISLA HAD no clue how she'd wound up walking through an outdoor mall with the heavyweight contender beside her. Spending social time with Eric wasn't a brilliant idea. Laughing with him didn't fit into her keep-their-relationship-professional plan. But fifteen minutes ago, she'd been sitting on that fountain ledge, surrounded by people and music and happiness, and she'd been on the verge of tears. Alone. She'd felt incredibly alone, unable to check on her stubborn-ass father or talk to anyone about his illness. Now she was smiling.

A man in a neon yellow tank top blocked their path, beaming up at Eric. "You're Brick Smash."

The creases around Eric's mouth flattened. "Yeah."

"Dude. This is so cool. Can I get a video?" He nudged his buddy to take his phone and maneuvered next to Eric, pretending to punch him in the face. "Do that Brick Smash line."

Eric scowled, but he obliged. The dude looked like he won the lottery.

A second later the fans were gone, high-fiving each other, and Eric's shoulders were hiked toward his ears. Isla's stomach dipped in the opposite direction. She didn't like seeing the frown lines by his mouth, especially after he'd lifted her mood with his silly jokes.

Instead of heading for the ice cream shop, she grabbed his hand and bee-lined toward a store on their left. She didn't think about how tiny her hand felt in his, or how much she liked the roughness of his callouses scraping against her skin, or how the heat between their palms tingled up her arm. She definitely didn't think about how good it had felt to have his arm around her back on that fountain ledge.

Once they made it across the promenade without getting body-checked, she dropped his feels-way-too-amazing-in-mine hand and gestured to the shop. "We've arrived."

Eric glanced at the hat store's display. "They don't sell ice cream here."

"Excellent deduction, Sherlock. But they do sell disguises, and you're in need of one."

His blond eyebrows quirked up. "You think you can hide me in plain sight?"

There was nothing subtle about this mountain of a man, but she was on a mission. "Do you trust me?"

His eyes did that thing where they focused on her so

intensely the throngs of people and noises disappeared. There was nothing but her and Eric and the loud beat of her heart. "Yeah," he said quietly. "I trust you."

Okay, then.

Feeling a tremendous need to keep busy, she marched into the store with Eric on her heels. A few shoppers were inside. She skirted a man with a tattooed head and grabbed an old-fashioned flat cap from the shelf. Eric sidled up next to her, looking uncomfortable, his huge body liable to knock over one of the displays.

She pushed up onto her tiptoes, tried to get the plaid hat on his head, but he was too damn big. "Mind helping me out here?"

His cheek twitched. "Help you make me look like an idiot? I'd rather not."

"What happened to you trusting me?"

"That was before you picked a hipster hat that belongs on a bearded guy who wears suspenders and bowties."

She pictured him in suspenders and a bowtie and surprised herself by flushing at the appealing image. There would be no flushing while shopping. Mission Disguise Eric was underway. She planted one hand on her hip, held the hat up with the other. "Would anyone expect Brick Smash to wear this too-cool-for-school hipster hat?"

His attention flitted around the store, like he was a cop on a stakeout. "No."

"Then bend your big body down and let me put it on you."

He gave her a bland look, but there was no missing the slight upturn of his lips. He bent low enough for her to place the hat on his head. She didn't mean for her fingers to trail through his buzzed hair—spiky and soft—or graze the shell of his ears. His breath hissed. More tingling sparked through her body.

She bit her cheek and forced a swallow.

Hat on and tingles squashed, she stepped back and examined her work. "If we add shades and a wig, *and* those suspenders and bowtie you mentioned, you'd be incognito."

"You're not putting me in suspenders."

"You're no fun."

He adjusted his hat, the movement so awkward it was adorable. "You're worse than my niece, whose favorite thing after stuffed-animal tea parties is playing dress up. She's seven, by the way."

"She sounds extremely mature. Please tell me she put you in a dress."

His cheeks reddened. "There may have been a feathered boa and nail polish."

God, that was just too much. Too cute and sweet, and the shop's temperature suddenly felt Hades hot. She swiveled and marched to the cashier. Paid for the hat, then dragged Eric out to find sunglasses. She unfortunately lost the fight for suspenders.

Partial costume in place, they finally hit the ice cream shop. Tourists milled around them, no one giving the large man with the flat cap and cool shades a second glance.

She held up her strawberry cone for him. "One lick, as promised."

She couldn't see his eyes behind his sunglasses, but his tongue poked out, swiping the corner of his upper lip as he studied her ice cream cone. "One lick," he agreed.

He gripped her hand, moved it closer while he dipped his head and proceeded to give a Not Safe For Work lick, slow and erotic, lapping up the strawberry sweetness so languidly her insides turned liquid. Also? He moaned.

Eric released her, licked his lips again. "That was amazing."

If amazing was turning ice cream licking into food porn,

then—yeah, sure, that. "You can order a cone if you want." But if he licked a whole one, she feared what her body might do.

"Naw, I'm good."

At least one of them was. She might never date a boxer, but attraction apparently wasn't an impulse under her control. She focused on eating her ice cream. Eric's focus seemed to stay on her, lingering longer than felt comfortable, no conversation offered to bridge the silence. With his sunglasses on, she couldn't see his eyes, decipher why he was suddenly so quiet, so intent on her. Then he turned toward the walkway.

A moment later, he said, "I bet that couple just met last night. Crazy Vegas outing."

She followed his line of sight. A young couple in trendy clothes was in that clingy stage of happiness where touching was their oxygen. Jealousy tightened Isla's ribs. Yeah, she really missed dating. Flirting. Having a special someone in her life. Without meaning to, her attention slid to Eric. A fascinating someone who was easy on the eyes and had been fun and sweet today. A man who fell under a strict category: Off Limits.

She forced down a mouthful of strawberry goodness. "They'll for sure get married by Elvis tonight."

He watched the couple, who stopped to kiss. The man then whispered something to the woman, who blushed and giggled. Eric's lips quirked up. "Annulment by month's end?"

"Heartless much? They'll be telling their grandkids about their wild Vegas wedding."

"Yeah, you're probably right." Where Eric had looked amused before, a different look crossed his face now: envy, longing. "They found their soulmates in Vegas," he said softly.

The couple had sure found something, all right.

She and Eric people-watched a bit longer, making up stories, teasing each other, while she enjoyed her strawberry bliss, thoughts of food porn and off-limit crushes fading as their conversation moved to Eric's family and Isla's new business venture. They tossed pennies into the fountain and found a cute stuffed pony for Eliza, a firetruck shaped eraser for Asher. All that time, she didn't stress about her father—wonder how he was doing, worry if he was tired or nauseous. For the first time since arriving in Vegas, she didn't feel like she was alone in a crowded town bustling with people.

9

ERIC DODGED pedestrians along the Vegas strip, which had become a habit in this town. Whit was by his feet, Preston beside them, on his phone as usual. The sun was scorching hot. Eric was sweating buckets, new sunglasses on to avoid eye contact with the throngs of tourists. Some pedestrians pointed at him and whispered. Others paid him no mind. With the glitzy hotels, buskers, fountains, and music blaring from passing cars, a six-foot-six, 249-pound boxer could often go unnoticed. Still, he should have worn the hipster hat Isla had bought for him.

Eric's phone vibrated in his pocket while Whit stopped to sniff a garbage can. Eric pulled out his cell and frowned at his sister's name. "Hey, Rosa."

"Did Mom call you?"

He didn't like the sound of that question. "Why would she be calling me?" Hip-hop blasted from a Porsche at the stop light. He plugged his free ear, hunching away from the street. "What's going on?"

"I would've called earlier, but I've been up to my eyeballs in errands and chauffeuring and cooking."

"Since when is Mom not shoving you out of the kitchen to cook for everyone?"

"Since she tripped on one of Asher's toys and broke her wrist."

Eric winced, picturing his mother hitting the floor, howling in pain. "Why didn't Mom call me?"

"She knows you need to stay focused. I shouldn't have called either. She's doing fine, and I'll figure out the rest. I just thought you'd want—"

"Rosa, don't you dare hang up." They were always considerate of his training schedules. Too considerate, going out of their way not to bother him. Overprotective caution that stemmed from love. Rosa and his mother always boasted to their friends about his big wins. The kids loved shadow boxing with him when he was home. Their pride in him was another push that kept him training; the prize money kept him fighting. But he suddenly resented being away. Not being home when his mother broke her wrist felt like failure. "How's she feeling?" he asked.

"She's frustrated, but the worst of it's over. Except for our electric bill, which is due. She obviously can't work, and I emptied our savings paying for the hospital visit."

Whit went to smell a cigarette butt on the sidewalk. Eric tugged his leash. "Leave it, buddy." They were in front of the Bellagio. All was calm in the massive fountain, no water shooting in time to lights and music at this hour. Eric felt the opposite of calm.

He hated how tight of a string they lived on. Training cost money. Preston cost money. His wellness team cost bundles, all to keep him healthy enough to box one more match, clinch one more win, make enough money to last until dental work and medical bills bled them dry again.

He could ask Rosa to find something full-time but being home for the kids after school was too important. She'd end up spending her few free hours fighting with the kids to clean up and do their chores and schoolwork. Exactly like it had been for their mother. He didn't want that exhausting life for her.

"I'll get the money to you this afternoon. And I'm sorry. I hate that you have to deal with everything on your own."

"We'll be fine. Just focus on your boxing."

She hung up before he could apologize again or ask to speak to their mother. He'd call his mom later, after he figured out the money issue.

Cellphone stashed away, he faced the bustling, noisy street. A person dressed like Spider-Man pointed at Eric's dog and shook his finger. Yeah. Eric knew he was breaking Vegas law: no dogs allowed on the strip between noon and five a.m. Eric stood taller, daring the guy to make a scene. Spider-Man mimed some nonsense and hurried off, melting into the sea of pedestrians. At least Eric's tough-guy image paid off at times.

"You could totally take Spider-Man," Preston said, pocketing his phone. They waited for Whit to quit his investigations, then moved with the throngs.

"Spider-Man can climb on walls and shoot webs. All I can do is throw a punch."

"A damn good punch."

A group of men walked toward them, red-faced, weaving slightly. They all held large plastic cups. One spotted Eric and awkwardly shadow boxed. "Brick Smash! Man, do you see who that is?"

His buddy burped. "Dude's gonna have his ass handed to him in that fight."

They passed, laughing.

Preston sneered. "Vegas brings out the schmucks, *but* it also brings out the dough. That was BDA on the phone. They're caving on negotiations for your endorsement deal. Once you win this fight, you'll be buying your own private jet."

He sure as hell hoped so. Not the jet part. The having loads of money part. He wanted to prove to his family that some men stuck around and provided for the people they loved. Show Eliza and Asher what it meant to have a responsible father figure, even if he was only their uncle.

Unfortunately, waiting for that win was getting harder by the day. "I hate to ask you this, but I need some cash until then."

Preston didn't stop abruptly or cut him a questioning look. "Sure," he said, nonplussed. "Tell me what you need."

No judgment. No guilt. The time Eliza's asthma had landed her in the hospital with acute bronchitis, Preston had helped pay the bills, zero hesitation. Eric had been flattened during that time, devastated seeing his niece in a hospital bed, unable to help. There hadn't even been a huge match on the horizon to pay Preston back quickly. His manager hadn't once held it over him.

"I owe you, man," Eric said.

"You do, and I'd like to collect."

They turned off the main drag, headed toward their hotel. "Unless you want to be paid in slobbery kisses from Whit, you'll have to wait."

"This is more of a quid pro quo situation. I do you a solid, you do me one."

"Way to make it sound shady."

They dodged a group of giggling girls, never breaking stride. Navigating Vegas sidewalks was a sport of its own.

"It's not shady," Preston said. "I need more help with Isla. She's a tough nut to crack."

Preston might not have hesitated with his financial help, but Eric sure as hell hesitated now. With how much time he'd spent with Isla—six days, two sessions a day, plus that fun afternoon shopping together—he'd felt off about helping Preston with that poem. The more time he spent with Isla, the more he liked her. Thought about her when they weren't together. Imagined asking her out, going on a proper date to talk more, learn more about her, tell her more stupid jokes so he could watch a smile break over her beautiful face.

The flare of interest in her he'd hoped would pass was only growing, but she likely never thought about him outside of their sessions. Would never consider dating a boxer. Helping Preston by telling him what to say would only add to his frustrations.

"It is completely shady," he told his manager.

Preston stopped outside of their hotel. "How's it different than me looking up poems online? You're a better resource. You see her every day."

"It's just different."

"What happened to you owing me?"

A woman with a massive hat and shoulder bag sashayed toward the revolving door, practically knocking into Eric. Pulling Whit closer, he stepped aside, feeling anxious. Irritable. He was worried about his mother. Hated borrowing money from Preston. It was more than that, though. Eric liked Isla. He was developing feelings for her, looked forward to their physio sessions. He wasn't sure how to separate those emotions when coaching Preston on how to woo her, or if Preston was pursuing her for the right reasons.

"What do you like about her?" he asked.

Preston crossed his arms, smirking. "You have seen her, right?"

Most nights, instead of working on his visualization, he

closed eyes and most certainly saw Isla: intelligent eyes, full lips, that birthmark on her neck. He wanted to knock Preston's smirk off his face. "I'm not talking looks. Why are you suddenly so interested in her?"

He dragged a hand through his hair. "The women I've dated have always wanted something from me: gifts, vacations. My money, basically. Isla's different and down to earth. Smart and gorgeous, but she's also a ball buster, which is refreshing."

"You enjoy the challenge."

"It's not like that."

Eric wasn't sure. "So you want more than a hookup with her? You're actually after something serious?"

A couple near them stopped to take a selfie, big smiles, hearts in their eyes. They laughed and kissed afterward. The closeness reminded Eric of the in-love couple he and Isla had joked about.

Preston sighed. "You know how my parents are? Always teasing each other, touching when they think no one's looking?"

Their affection was impossible to miss. Preston had invited Eric to several family dinners—Thanksgiving, birthdays. Rebecca Church always fussed over Eric, made sure he had enough to eat, while Preston's two older brothers talked sports and his father badgered them to take a family fishing or camping trip. "Like the old days," he'd say.

Jokes about burned food and landing a fish hook into Preston's thigh would follow.

They were a boisterous, male-dominated family, but the second they left the dinner table, Preston's father would take a plate from Rebecca's hand and kiss her cheek while clearing the table together. He'd sit right beside her on the couch, arm draped over her shoulder, fingers in her hair, when there were three roomier seats to be had.

The only romantic relationships Eric had witnessed growing up had both ended with tears: the father who'd left them in Russia, Rosa and her husband splitting apart. The love and affection in Preston's house had been a revelation. "Your parents are lucky," he said.

"They are, and I've been thinking about them more lately. How I've had so much success in business, but I don't have someone to share it with. I'm kind of envious."

The word *success* hit Eric in the gut, so forcefully he felt slightly ill. He'd spent his life striving for success, earning money to support his family. He'd done an okay job of it at times. If he really thought about it, though, he didn't feel particularly successful. He studied secretively, never pushing his mind as hard as he pushed his body. He wasn't working the job he wanted, he was doing his duty, and he was so far from having a relationship like Preston's parents he may as well claim celibacy.

What would it be like to just walk away? Quit boxing, study full-time. Get a job translating for people who needed his help. Affect lives, beyond offering brute entertainment. He'd even be able to ask Isla on a proper date instead of helping Preston charm her.

He rubbed the back of his neck, unsure where the hell those reckless thoughts had come from. Some people had the luxury of living selfishly. He wasn't one of them. "Thanks for the loan. And yeah, I'll help you with Isla. I have a session with her in a bit. I'll send you a couple poems this afternoon."

Ashamed at having to ask for the handout, he dropped his head and followed Preston to his room to get the check. He really did owe the guy. Big time. He still planned to make sure Isla was on the same page, that she seemed interested in Preston. Check that she wasn't already dating someone else she liked through that stupid app. Or maybe those precautions were excuses because he didn't have the stomach to play cupid with her and his manager.

ISLA SPREAD GEL on Eric's Achilles and switched the ultrasound machine on. She liked finishing their sessions with ultrasound. Mobilization and strength building to begin, localized treatment promoting local healing and blood flow to end.

Eric lay on his stomach, eyes closed. He inhaled deeply and exhaled a long breath as he relaxed. She'd treated him for six days now. At the end of every session, he'd grunt out the same slow breath. Like he was on his first vacation in ten years. Whit, always nearby, sighed in tandem.

"You did great today," she told Eric. "But your calves are crazy tight."

"The running and skipping are murder on me. Seems worse lately."

"Because your training's too intense. All you do is workout, eat an insane amount of calories, and walk your dog, which is also exercise, by the way."

The dog in question gave a snort.

He laughed. "I sleep, too."

Maybe, but there were dark circles under his eyes. His rotator cuff was paining him more than usual. She wanted to prod, ask if he planned to beat his body down until he was as sick as her father, but those were landmine topics.

"Do you exercise this much in your home gym?" she asked.

"Home gym?" He made a scoffing sound. "My house is barely big enough for Eliza and Asher's toys."

Isla blinked at Eric's back. She knew he lived with his family, had assumed they lived in an extravagant mansion, not a house too small for a home gym.

She didn't prod and ask if he hadn't made as much money as she'd assumed. Not exactly polite conversation. She focused on her work instead, moved the ultrasound's probe around his ankle in slow circles. Unfortunately, her gaze also moved, roaming over the expanse of his muscled back and shoulders, emphasized in his sparse workout clothes. The man was criminally attractive.

He angled his head to catch her eye. "How's the dating app going?"

Her movements jerked slightly. Had he sensed her heated perusal? Unlikely. That hadn't been the first time she'd taken an eyeful of his body, but she was always quick to school her features, lead them to neutral conversation.

"It's going slow," she said. A noncommittal reply.

More like it wasn't going at all. She'd been busier than expected while away, communicating with the contractor who was finishing her office space, putting out fires when they'd painted the bathroom the wrong color, taking an accounting course to brush up on her bookkeeping. Dating had once again taken a back seat.

Eric shifted his hips. A small move, but heat moved through her. She suddenly envied that treatment table, wished she was the one under him feeling the hard press of his body.

Jesus. She really needed to deal with her extended dry spell.

He stilled, but his dating inquisition persisted. "With all that chiming, I figured you'd have met someone by now. I mean, unless..." The tips of his ears pinked. "Forget it."

She gripped the probe harder. "Unless what?"

Was he insinuating she was too picky? *Picky with food. Picky with men.* A high-maintenance woman who was too difficult to date?

He turned his head face down on the pillow. "Nothing," he mumbled.

"If it was nothing, you'd tell me what you meant."

He didn't reply.

She moved the ultrasound in faster circles. "You're seriously going to say something like that and leave me hanging?"

Whit whined from the floor.

"See?" Isla said. "Even your best friend thinks you're being rude."

Eric laughed, a muffled sound that shook his body. He lifted onto his elbows and rotated enough to look at her. "*Unless* you're only after a hookup. I assumed you wanted a relationship, but then realized in this day and age most people use those sites for other things."

"Oh."

She did want to fool around with a guy. Feel desirable and let loose. She also wanted to date with an eye on the future and didn't like the idea of Eric thinking she was careless with her body. They should switch topics, talk about why he'd named his dog Whit or discuss the rain expected tomorrow. "It's not for a hookup," she said.

He stared at her, rolled his tongue over his teeth. "Do none of them like poetry?" he asked, then winced. "Sorry, forget I asked that."

Well, now, that was impossible. Prodding about poetry hadn't been a random question, and they hadn't discussed books or reading or anything of the sort the past week. Delving into Eric's intellect would have only exacerbated her attraction to him.

That left one explanation. "Did you read my dating profile?"

He shrugged weakly. "It was right there that day."

"Yeah, *Snoop Dog*, it was. That didn't mean you had to creep my profile."

"You hate boxing."

She kept working the ultrasound probe, quiet, hoping he'd drop the subject.

He laid back down, his head twisted to the side, his gaze on the gym equipment at their left. "If you hate boxing, why are you here?"

She wasn't sure which topic was more difficult, his sudden intimate knowledge of her likes and dislikes, or the real reason why she'd taken this job. "My father and I haven't spent much time together lately." The truth. "When he mentioned this last-minute fight, I asked if I could come." Not the truth. She didn't have any other choice.

"But you hate boxing," he said again.

"Huh." She glanced around, wide-eyed. "Is there an echo in the room?"

He laughed, a deep rumbling sound that filled the room. "Who's your favorite poet?"

She should never have let him silence that app. "Aren't we due for another stupid joke?"

"I'll only give you a stupid joke if you answer my question afterward."

"Holy demanding Batman."

"My jokes aren't free."

"You're right. I pay for them in my embarrassment for you." But talking poetry shouldn't be a big deal. She'd occasionally tried to convince Heather to read passages, so they could share their thoughts. Heather would get distracted by a random food craving for pickled beets or prosciutto or fiddleheads, and they'd end up on a food mission. Heather was a food stylist who spent her days making dishes look mouthwatering for photographs and commercials, a job that bled into her daily life. Poetry was a hard sell.

Talking poetry with Eric would be a treat. It was also safer than talking about her dislike of boxing. "Fine. Joke first, then I'll divulge my poetry secrets."

He smiled, clearly pleased with himself. "How do you catch a squirrel?"

"By baiting it with a crappy joke teller?"

"You climb a tree and act like a nut."

Oh, man. Those really were too lame. And cute. She tried to muffle her snort, but it snuck out. "You continue to amaze, Kramarovsky."

"Favorite poet," was all he said.

"Ramona Estle," she finally admitted. "When I stumbled on her, I felt like I discovered gold."

"She writes Instagram poetry, doesn't she?"

Isla stilled. "You know Ramona Estle?"

"Not intimately, but her work's really accessible. Not as hard to untangle as some poets. Everything she writes feels tangible."

Eric was still focused on the gym equipment, but she felt exposed. Seen. "That's exactly it. But I'm honestly shocked. I've never met anyone who knows her."

"Shocked because I'm Brick Smash?" Accusation crept into his tone.

One hint she still thought he was stupid and he was back on the defensive. His PR team had really done a number on him.

She pressed the flat of her hand against his calf. The muscle was bunched. "Not at all. Estle just isn't as popular as Poe or Angelou or Whit..." She stared at his back, her mouth dropping open slightly. "Your dog—you named him for Walt Whitman, didn't you?"

He nodded. "Still no cat named Smart, though."

"Wow, I am such an asshole." His dog's name hadn't been misspelled as Whit, short for witty, as she'd first assumed. He'd named his pup after a famous poet. She couldn't have misjudged a person more harshly if she'd tried.

"Assholes don't love Ramona Estle," he said, his lips curving up slightly.

She released his calf, still horrified with herself. She tried to focus on the probe in her hand, applying his therapy. "Not an asshole then. But I'm an awful, judgmental woman."

"Why Ramona Estle?" he asked, not disagreeing with her self-assessment.

She shook her head, tried to quit mentally flogging herself long enough to form a reply. She'd never forget the first Estle passage she'd read, the one that had struck an immediate chord:

"the longer
i stayed
the uglier
i became
leaving wasn't a choice
it was for you"

That poem had sucked the breath from Isla's lungs. She'd thought of her mother instantly, wondering if there'd been more to her abandonment than her husband's boxing, her resentfulness toward her daughter. Maybe she'd been depressed or simply hadn't been capable of love. After reading that passage, Isla had felt the first stirrings of forgiveness in her adult life.

"Something about her words speaks to me," she told Eric. "Like everything I read feels relevant."

He folded his hands under his head, looking deep in thought. A night-and-day contrast to his scowl when playing his role of Brick Kramarov. "Poetry is magic like that. Like your profile said, words can build worlds, and we're the architect of those worlds. We read and interpret writing to suit our needs in that moment. We let those poems build us up or tear us down. We have the power in the end, not the author."

"Yeah," she said, her voice turning breathy. "Exactly."

Eric shifted on the table, his hips moving slightly. The move shouldn't have been erotic. Lying that long on your stomach was uncomfortable. But a yearning took root—the urge to spread her palm along his upper back, trail it up and drag her nails across his scalp, trace the shell of his ear. Lie on top of his back and mold herself to him, soft breasts to hard muscle, her pelvis rounded over his ass.

"I'm surprised you're single," he said.

The compliment sent a rush of heat up her neck. "I'm busy, and it hasn't been a priority."

He didn't reply right away, but she sensed his mind spinning. Was he thinking about her? Considering asking her out? She trembled at the possibility. Trembling that should not happen. *I hate boxing.* The last line in her profile was there for a reason.

"What about that dating site?" he asked. "Have any of the guys interested you?"

More men had been matches. A couple had been cute and not overtly weird. Something had still held her back. "I think I'm a bit nervous about meeting a stranger. I know it can be fine, not all guys are catfishing or trying to take advantage. It's still daunting, or I'm just…" Spending too much time with a man more interesting than the profiles she'd read.

She remembered the soft-spiky feel of Eric's buzzed hair when putting on his incognito hat, the warmth that had zapped up her arm.

She glanced down sharply.

"Isla?"

Her face felt flushed, her body alive. She should never have allowed them to get this personal. If this were her own practice, she'd ditch Eric as a client. Move on and not let whatever this was develop further. This wasn't her practice, though. She was here for her father, not herself. Her father who'd been blatantly avoiding her and keeping her at a distance. He was being his usual stoic, stubborn self. But there were five more weeks of training ahead, tiring days, and she wouldn't risk leaving him alone.

"I heard it's supposed to rain tomorrow," she said. A pathetic attempt to change topics.

"Or you're just *what*?" Eric pushed.

"Not sure what you mean." The ultrasound beeped. Their session was over. She busied herself wiping his ankle, wrapping the cord meticulously around the cart.

Eric rotated so he was sitting on the table, powerful legs dangling off. "You were about to say something before, about why you haven't contacted any matches."

She wasn't sure why he was pushing. He'd never flirted with her or hinted that he was interested. More reasons why she should cut her losses and cut this conversation short. Whatever interest she felt in Eric, it was purely physical, not emotional, and he didn't feel the same.

He stood from the table, moved closer to her. "What's holding you back, Isla?"

His question was so quiet, so earnest, her heart gave a soft whump.

She wanted to look up into his hypnotizing eyes, see her desire reflected back at her. No, *dammit*. She didn't want to be on the receiving end of his sexy looks. As attracted as she was to him, tempting herself with something she could never have was idiotic. Eric was in training mode. For now, he was just an athlete honing his body. She hadn't had any more panic attacks since that first one, but in five weeks he'd be in the ring, punches connecting with his head and body, and everything would change. She couldn't go through that again, even for a fling with a beautiful man. But his quiet question, the expansion of his chest as he breathed slowly, waiting on her.

"There's someone who interests me more," she said, her hands shaking slightly. She forced herself to meet his eyes. "But we're not a good fit."

She wouldn't admit it was him, there was no point. The partial admission on its own had her heart racing.

He didn't back away or even blink. "Why isn't he a good fit?"

Better question: why was she playing this game? Lighting a match next to spilled gasoline was less dangerous for her than exploring attraction to a boxer. Still, traitorous words rose, a bit of truth she couldn't contain. "There are things from my past that affected me deeply. Things I don't want to revisit. This man would bring it all back."

Heat flared in his eyes and she stepped back, worried she'd said too much. Damage control was needed. "Plus," she said quickly, "you and my father know him. The last thing I want is to date Preston and make things awkward with everyone."

She didn't want to date Preston. She didn't want to date Eric either. This was desire, pure and simple. But the heat in his eyes chilled, and her gut hollowed.

"Right." He turned his back on her and grabbed his shoes and socks. "You should go out with him, if it's what you want. It won't be awkward. I'll see you tomorrow."

He clicked his tongue for *Walt Whitman* to follow his master out the door. She watched Eric leave, feeling anxious and more confused than ever.

10

"THAT WAS NICE, Princess. It's a treat spending time with you." Isla's father stood from paying their bill and helped pull out her chair.

"I'm full to busting," she moaned. Dinner with him had been more than a treat. She'd been thrilled when he'd suggested they go out, relieved he wasn't pushing her away completely. More importantly, she hadn't been sure she could sit across from him without worrying over every move he made. But they'd talked easily, perusing the menu, discussing her accounting course, joking about Brick's slobbery dog.

The relief at their normalcy had been exactly what she'd needed. They were still *them*. His illness wouldn't define their relationship or weaken their bond.

"broken hearts
are messy
splintered things
that break time
and again

but keep ticking"

The Ramona Estle quote could apply to many situations: heartbreak, the strength to keep fighting, resilience of spirit, hope for new love. Readers did have so much power, as Eric had said. The choice to redefine a passage, depending on the day or mood or person reading between the lines. Tonight, as Isla walked into the hotel elevator with her father, belly full of delicious food, smile lingering, she spun the poem in her mind, deciding it meant pain was a gift. If you had to endure discomfort, it meant you were still living and loving against the odds.

In the elevator, she nudged her father's foot with hers. "Remember when you took me to that fight in Atlantic City and you had to pee really badly, and I hit every button in the elevator?"

He laughed. "Told you, you're a hurricane."

"The look on your face was priceless."

He hit the button for their floor, amusement fading as he stepped back. "We had good days, didn't we? Even with your mom and everything. You still had a good childhood?"

She wasn't sure where this melancholy was coming from. His illness giving him perspective? She wrapped her arms around his barrel chest and squeezed. "Mostly good. I mean, I got to drink champagne at twelve and splatter painted a hotel room wall while you trained."

"You didn't ask to paint the hotel wall."

"You didn't tell me I couldn't."

"Hurricane," he mumbled, holding her close.

The elevator opened and they got off. She'd been tired earlier, drained from this afternoon's session with Eric and lying to him about Preston, looking forward to sleep. Now she felt energized, might finally tackle the biggest thing she'd put off with her business: building a website. She opened her purse, searched for her keycard, which always seemed impossible to find.

A loud *thump* had her spinning around.

"Dad?" His shoulder was pinned to the wall, a dazed look on his face. She rushed over, gripped his arms. "What is it? What's wrong?"

He righted himself but swayed slightly and braced his hand on the wall. "Just tripped. No big deal."

She scanned the floor. The only thing to trip over was his own feet. "Has your balance been off?" Balance was a Parkinson's symptom. A scary one when motor skills were affected, shorter shuffling steps and freezing muscles making falls likely. She hadn't noticed any of those changes.

"My balance is fine. Just a bit dizzy. Must have been the wine." He stood taller, took three steps, paused, and swayed.

Her stomach lurched.

She moved to his side and looped her arm around his waist. Not an ideal support. If he fell, his bulk would drag her down for the tumble. She gripped him tighter, but he shrugged out of her hold.

"I'm fine, Isla. Like I said, it was the *wine*. I'll see you tomorrow." He marched to his door, flattened his huge palm on the wall, pulled out his keycard, and swiped it without another word, shutting her out when his door clicked shut.

She stared at his closed door, her eyes stinging as helplessness and anger fought for dominance. She wanted to knock on his door, help him lie down, hum him a song while he fell asleep. He'd done the same for her growing up when she'd had a nightmare. But he'd closed his door in her face.

"broken hearts
are messy

splintered things
that break time
and again
but keep ticking"

Estle's poem morphed in her mind, tangling with her ugly thoughts into a new meaning: to live and to love was to suffer.

She glanced down the hall toward her door. The excitement of working on her website drained out of her. The idea of being in there alone tightened her throat. There wasn't even anyone to call. Heather was on a date. Isla's other acquaintances weren't the type she'd call on a whim, certainly not to discuss anything this personal.

The elevator opened, drawing her attention. Eric walked off with earbuds in his ears and Whit on a leash. She hadn't seen him since she'd lied about liking Preston and he'd stalked out of the training gym earlier. He was the last person she wanted to see now.

When he noticed her, he jerked to a stop. "Isla."

She tried to force a friendly smile. Her face felt too stiff to function, and those too-intense eyes of his roamed over her. She wasn't sure how she looked, but he frowned. Apparently, she wasn't hiding her stress well.

He didn't move toward her. Whit did, though. He tugged on his leash and Eric let it drop. Whit trotted over and leaned his thick body into her shin. The pup made his usual snorty sounds. Ridiculous, ugly sounds. But that pressure, the solid heat of him grounding her...she almost released a sob. She squatted quickly, hid her face from Eric and pressed her hands into Whit's wrinkly coat. Eyes closed, she exhaled. Whit pushed closer. She massaged the dog, tension easing with each press of her fingers.

"He's a great therapy dog. Senses when people need some love."

She didn't open her eyes, but Eric's deep voice was whisper-close, so near his warm breath kissed her hair. She chanced a glance at him. He was squatting, too, his knees almost touching hers. With his legs folded like that, his muscled thighs looked even bigger, his corded forearms balanced on them. His earbuds dangled around his neck.

"You okay?" he asked softly.

No. The answer was a big, neon *no*. But she wasn't allowed to talk about her father's illness and how she suddenly felt like she was drowning in all this silence. "Tough night," she said.

He put his hand on Whit, too. His palm was massive, splayed right next to hers. The dog wheezed out a happy chuff. Eric spread his fingers wider, giving Whit an affectionate rub, his pinky finger grazing her hand. She froze at the contact, but he didn't.

He lifted his pinky and placed it over her thumb. "If you need to talk, I'm here."

Cry. She needed to cry. Another thing she couldn't do in public, certainly not in front of Eric. And facing him like this, their bodies crouched and heads bent close, a slew of other unclear feelings crested over her.

She yanked her hand back and stood, turned to head to her room, but the prospect of closing the door, being in there with nothing but her thoughts...she just couldn't.

"I have to ice my shoulder," Eric said from behind her. "Any chance you mind helping? Wrapping it up is tough one-handed."

She swiveled back and narrowed her eyes. He was either a mind reader and was taking pity, or he actually needed help. She'd worked his shoulder. Had seen firsthand how it could flare up. He probably could use her help, but being in Eric's room alone with him might make those unsettled feelings flare brighter.

Still, she said, "Sure. Let's get you iced."

ERIC OPENED the door to his room, doing his best not to crowd Isla or ask again if she was okay. She wasn't. That much was clear. She hadn't been as distressed as their first physio day, but there was no missing the glassiness in her brown eyes.

He unhooked Whit's leash, dropped it on the coffee table, and scanned his suite. The door to his adjoining room was open. His bed was neatly made, thanks to housekeeping, but textbooks were on his sofa, a number strewn on the floor. The hotel staff had strict orders not to touch his books. If he'd known he was having company, he wouldn't have left such a mess.

Whit flopped on his dog bed, tongue flapping as he breathed heavily. Eric started gathering books.

Isla lifted one from the floor. "You know Latin?"

"I'm far from fluent." He struggled with it most days, hadn't had the time or mental energy to focus lately.

She flipped through the textbook, stopping periodically to scan a page. "But...why Latin? It's not exactly something that comes in handy when on the road."

He piled his books on the floor and sat on the couch, unsure how much to say. After this afternoon's gut punch when Isla had admitted her feelings for Preston, he'd decided to keep things strictly friendly with her. Talking poetry together had enflamed his interest. He'd ached to take her out, get to know her better, kiss her until neither of them could recite their names, let alone a verse from Ramona Estle. He'd thought he'd sensed her interest, too. A two-sided connection he wouldn't have ignored.

Then she'd said she liked Preston.

It was fine. More than fine. Dating was a distraction, and his focus hadn't been optimal. Thinking about Preston's parents today—the envy of that normal life, wondering how it would feel to love someone freely, work a normal nine-to-five, study and use his brains, not his fists—all of it had been infecting him. The tease of things he couldn't have.

Now Isla was in his room, wearing dark jeans and a shimmery yellow top, like she'd been on a date. That possibility was enough to cool his desire for her, but she was asking him about Latin, as though it was nothing. She wouldn't understand that he'd never dated anyone who'd cared for his studies. The women in his life had teased him with a sharp edge: *A guy with your face doesn't need to speak one language, let alone two.* Most people thought his studies were a joke. Even Preston and Eric's family called his coursework a "silly hobby."

Not Isla, who was flipping pages, seemingly fascinated.

She glanced up. "Seriously, I have to know. Why Latin?"

He picked at his cracked cuticles, a bead of excitement rolling under his skin. The chance to talk about this part of his life with someone who cared was too enticing. "Latin is part of everything. Hardly anyone speaks it anymore, but it's not dead. It's the language of law and government and theology. Subpoena, habeas corpus, pro bono, non sequitur—those are Latin terms we still use. Beyond that, so many words are rooted in the language. It helps develop and train the mind. Gives us a foundation to learn the other romance languages. Learning it is a gift." He blew out a rough breath and hedged a glance at Isla.

She stared at him, blinking. "You're a surprising man, Eric Kramarovsky."

"Surprising good?"

Her teeth grazed her bottom lip, sinking down, then slipping off. "Depends, can you tell stupid jokes in Latin?"

"Not even close."

"Then I'm undecided."

His hotel suite—covered by Preston with cash Eric would have to reimburse after the fight—was massive compared to his small room at home. It wasn't a lavish penthouse, but it was stylish with its old-money vibe, ornate curtains, framed Renaissance art. The most beautiful thing in the space was the woman eyeing him curiously.

"Which is your favorite language?" she asked.

Her question was eager, as though she hadn't been on the verge of tears in the hall. He'd thought asking her to ice his shoulder would be the thing to calm her. Rote activity was a great distraction. She hadn't brought up the subject since coming in, and he didn't bother. Whatever was relaxing her, he liked being part of the reason. "Japanese, for sure."

"It must be crazy hard."

"It takes discipline, not so different than boxing. But Japanese kanji is more like a puzzle. It's a language written in pictures, with culture and history infused into the symbols, but there are no familiar references for English speakers to draw from. The challenge is exciting."

She knelt by his books, checked out the other spines. "You spoke Japanese on the plane, didn't you?"

He thought back to their first unpleasant meeting, coming up blank. "Not that I remember."

"After I thoughtlessly insulted your intelligence because I'm a judgmental asshole." She gave him a sheepish grin. "I left you the forms to fill out and you said something under your breath as I was leaving."

"Right, yeah." He chuckled as it came back to him—his

utter irritation, her quick escape to the front of the plane. "I said: *Hana yori dango*."

"What does that mean?"

No way was he going there. "I'd rather not say."

She looked pointedly at Whit. "Your dad's being rude again."

He laughed harder, tried to think of a way around the truth. He settled on a direct translation. "It's a proverb of sorts. Means dumplings over flowers."

She scrunched up her face, completely adorable. "I don't get it."

"Look it up."

"Why are you being so difficult?"

"Why are you being so pushy? A guy shouldn't have to explain his insult. I said it in Japanese for a reason."

"Fine. I get it." She closed his book and glanced around, her mood dimming again. "Where's your ice?"

Her walls were coming back up and he paused. A moment ago she'd been open and curious, talking with ease, but telling her the truth was tricky. He was bound to offend her.

When she looked ready to stand up, he sighed. "Dumplings over flowers, from what I gather, means to prefer something real and useful over empty outward beauty."

She shifted to sitting and scratched her nose. "What does that have to do with me being rude?"

"You're beautiful, Isla." As stunning as a rare flower. "But your inside was ugly that day. The opposite of that saying, and I didn't like you much."

"Wow." She focused on the floor, swallowed a couple of times.

Had he gone too far? Or did she sense the dual meaning behind those words: *you were ugly that day, but I can't look at your beauty now, inside and out, without wanting more.* "You asked for honesty," he said.

She rubbed her hands down her jeans and glanced at him shyly. "And now? Do you still feel the same?"

"*Shiranu ga hotoke,*" he said. No hesitation.

She nibbled her lip again. "What does that mean?"

Not knowing is Buddha. Another form of *ignorance is bliss*.

He wished he were ignorant to Isla's true nature. That he wasn't impressed with her physiotherapy work, fascinated by her love of poetry, intrigued by the sadness she'd been fighting. He wished he didn't want to drop to his knees, crawl over to her until she was flat on her back, her legs hooked around his waist as he settled his weight on her. God, the things he'd do to her.

Ignorance could be bliss. And he was no longer ignorant of Isla.

"It's your turn," he said, done torturing himself. That was one explanation she wouldn't get. She wanted Preston, not him. "Give me another Ramona Estle poem."

She looked about to argue, but she lay on her back, attention on the embossed ceiling tiles. He glanced at Whit, who usually took advantage of people lying on their backs—a direct invitation for a face licking. Whit didn't disappoint. He was up and slobbering all over her before she could protest.

Isla cackled, grinning and pushing at his big head. "That is so gross."

Maybe. But Eric's chest warmed at the sight. "Poem," he said roughly and whistled for Whit to return to his bed.

When Isla's laughter ebbed, she said, "'Turn the last page. Keep reading. Keep turning. It never ended.'"

He'd read that quote before, had spent time dissecting it. He liked it even more spoken in Isla's soft voice. "Never give up," he said. His favorite interpretation.

She shook her head. "The end is just the beginning."

"Nothing truly dies," he said. Another possibility. So many.

Her interpretation: "Challenge yourself to do more."

His: "Let your imagination guide you."

"I don't," she said, sighing. "I'm a planner, always ten months ahead, checking off my to-do lists."

"You're a control freak."

"Guilty as charged." She reached up as though to touch her hair but switched tactics and fiddled with the hem of her yellow top. "I felt like I had zero control growing up. My mother came and went until I left for college and she just *went*. My dad's fights were terrifying for me. I was always waiting for one bad hit to hurt him irreversibly. As an adult, I thought I had control. But…" She flattened her lips. "Control is an illusion."

I hate boxing. The last line of her dating profile made more sense now, how hard the lifestyle could be on a child. How damaging it had been for her. "Sometimes control is a hindrance. Chasing it keeps you from experiencing life fully."

She cut an accusing look his way. "Have you ever considered giving your body a break? Not working so hard that you need physio twice a day?"

Her sharp turn in conversation was aggressive, and his gut hardened.

On top of the odd feelings about his stagnant life and lack of success weighing him down today, this morning's call from his sister and learning about his mother's injury had been rough. Not as bad as the call he'd placed to his mother afterward. She'd been dismissive of his worry and positive in general, but he'd heard the tiredness in her voice. Her frustration at being hurt. He should be home, helping Rosa with her kids, making sure his mother was healing well. He wasn't boxing for fun, damaging his body for the thrill of it, pushing his studies to the background for shits and giggles.

"I don't have a choice," he told Isla, more forceful than intended. "Not with this fight coming up."

"What about after?" She moved to sitting, gestured angrily at nothing. "Why don't you go lie on a beach somewhere? Take a break and not make your family worry so much."

"My family understands my job. They're proud of what I do. The kids love having a boxer uncle to brag about."

"Or they're too scared to tell you how they really feel." Her eyes were glassy again and kind of ferocious.

He wasn't sure they were still talking about his family, and he was done justifying his situation. She wasn't a lover or a girlfriend. He didn't need to explain his reasons to her. And Isla's experience of the sport didn't compare to his family's. She'd been a kid watching her father. Rosa wasn't young and vulnerable, and the twins thought Eric's fighting was cool. Isla was projecting her childhood trauma onto him.

Still, he wasn't okay with her leaving distraught, not with how he'd found her. "What happened before I stepped off that elevator? Why were you upset?"

She glared at him, the pinched expression so reminiscent of her father he almost laughed. "I think we're done here. You can ice your shoulder on your own."

She started getting to her feet, but he was bigger and faster and blocked her path to the door. "If someone hurt you, I'll be dealing with it."

Her frown softened slightly. "No one hurt me, but thank you for your chivalry. Consider it noted."

Chivalry had been in her dating profile. An attribute she liked. He'd happily uphold the sentiment, but she was still upset. "Let me help you."

"You can't help with this," she said bluntly. Angry. Eyes shimmering with more tears.

She wasn't ready to confide in him. That didn't mean he couldn't help.

When he'd been on the road and Eliza had been rushed to the hospital with asthma, there had been no one to turn to. No one to offer an ear or words of wisdom or a simple hug. He'd flown home the next day, paced angrily outside her hospital room while staff had cast worried glances his way. Preston had showed up and helped pay the bills. His mother and sister had sat vigil, supporting each other. The whole while, no one had offered him the one thing he'd needed in that moment. They always assumed he was strong on his own.

He approached Isla and brushed a few hairs from her face. "Sometimes physical contact is the best medicine."

She tensed, her chest barely inflating. "Whatever you're thinking, please just...don't."

"I'm hugging you, Isla. Nothing more. Just one friend giving another comfort. Can you handle that?"

He wasn't sure he could. It didn't change his resolve.

She crossed her arms. "Why?"

"Maybe I'm the one needing comfort. I think you're a flower *and* a dumpling, the best attributes of both, and I want to apologize for saying otherwise."

"Fine," she said slowly, going along with his pretense. "If it'll make you feel better." But she stood stiffly, her eyes wide and wary.

Sensing what she needed, he did the hard work for her, reached out and folded her in his arms. She stayed rigid, her hands barely touching his sides. Her heart pounded hard against his chest.

"'Let it go, let it fly. Set it free before you forget how.'" He whispered the Ramona Estle quote, tucking her closer.

Finally relaxing, her hands slid around him, her fingers pressing into the muscles of his back. He tightened his hold on her, breathed in her soft smells of perfume and eucalyptus, holding her steady and strong. He would be the ground beneath her feet if that was what she needed. Her strength on a tough night. He would be her *friend*.

She shuddered and burrowed deeper, pressed the side of her face to his chest and nestled against him. The feel of her like this, tucked into him, was a tonic and a dangerous drug. She felt too right and too perfect, this woman who wasn't his. Still, he rubbed her back, used his other hand to cup her head. Her heat seeped into him, hot prickles spreading across his skin. When his fingers tangled in her hair, she released a sob, and his ribs tightened.

Whatever was going on with her, he'd bet she'd been dealing with it on her own, not leaning on anyone. Being the brave, stubborn woman she was, not unlike her father: Strong-minded Isla Slade. He kissed the top of her head, put as much warmth into the hug as possible. Her heat seeped deeper into him, gave him a sense of peace so intense he felt like crying, too.

Her support. Her friend. If he couldn't have more, he'd take this.

11

ISLA SAT in the hotel's sports-themed diner, laptop open, her attention beyond frazzled. Between the crying kid beside her, the multiple TVs playing, and the low hum of fifties tunes in the background, the place was far from quiet, but she normally excelled at tuning out white noise.

Today proved challenging.

She should be working on her accounting course or putting her website together, but her father's texts this morning had been abrupt and dismissive. His usual *I feel fine, quit worrying* had made her feel anything but fine. She was tempted to use the emergency keycard he'd given her, go check on him and be sure, but he'd be livid, and she didn't want to add to his stress. So she was researching Parkinson's symptoms for the millionth time, trying to predict his next episode. It was either that or relive last night's hug-athon with the hottest man she'd ever known.

"This seat taken?" Preston was dressed for a board meeting, as usual. Slick from his gelled hair down to his shiny shoes. The opposite of her yoga pants and worn *Ghostbusters* T-shirt.

"It's all yours," she said as she closed her laptop, hiding her searches. *Nothing to see here. No father pretending he's not sick so he can stay on the payroll.*

She plastered on a smile and waited for Preston to get settled. She hadn't seen him for a few days. Hopefully he'd given up pursuing her.

He sat and motioned for their server. With his coffee ordered, he settled his elbows on the table. "Did you miss me?"

So much for him giving up. "Were you gone?"

"Of course you missed me. I flew to Florida for a few days, damage control with another client." He smoldered at her. "The view wasn't as nice."

The baby beside them tested his vocal chords. Isla winced and leaned closer to Preston. "Why do you keep flirting with me?"

"Because I like you and want to take you out." He tapped his fingers on the table, lips quirked up. "You, Miss Isla Slade, haven't given me enough of a shot. One date's all I want. If you're still not interested, I won't pester you. We'll be friends, nothing more."

Just friends. The same label Eric had offered her last night. The only problem was she wanted to add *with benefits* to Eric's label.

Their hug had set off something primal in her. Afterward, back in her bed, an ache had throbbed through her so intensely she couldn't sleep. She'd wanted more of his arms, his body, his physical strength. She'd even debated knocking on his door in the middle of the night to seduce him. Her rationale: her feelings were lust and nothing more. Professionally, he wasn't a long-term client and no one had to know they'd fooled around. Personally, she hadn't had any new panic attacks. She could have sex with a boxer and emerge unscathed. Especially if there was no actual dating or emotional attachment when he hit the ring.

That idiocy had lasted all of one minute before she'd remembered how much she'd loved talking poetry with him, listening to him discuss why he loved Latin.

There was no point lying to herself. The worst thing of things had happened. Her developing feelings for Eric had crossed that scary line, beyond lust into I Really Like This Guy territory—just down the block from I'm Totally Screwed, around the corner from My Life Sucks.

Their waitress came with Preston's coffee and Isla's poached eggs on avocado toast. Preston got busy with something on his phone. Isla ate her food and glanced occasionally at the TV closest to her, her heart knocking anxiously at her ribcage. Race cars zipped around a track. That baby was back to crying. A pair of boxing gloves hung on the far wall, among a slew of other sports memorabilia. She knew those gloves. Her dad had signed them after his awful Hector Narvarez fight, sold them for cash when things had gotten tight.

She put down her cutlery and pushed her plate away.

Preston placed his phone on the table and waved at someone over Isla's shoulder. She turned, only to spot the last person she wanted to see.

Eric stood in all his six-foot-magnificent glory, wearing cargo shorts and a T-shirt that didn't leave much to the imagination. The man was an action figure come to life, every muscle on his body defined, his bone structure devastatingly handsome.

Eric looked at her and Preston, then at his feet, then at the exit, like he didn't want to come over. She didn't want him any closer either. Not with last night fresh in her mind.

Preston hollered, "Brick! Get over here."

She slumped on her seat.

People around them pointed and whispered as Eric walked over. He stopped at their table and rubbed the back of his neck. "Don't want to intrude if you're..."

His eyes darted between them, and Isla wanted to shout NO. Confess that she'd lied and there would never be anything going on between her and Preston Church. She wanted to climb *Eric* like a tree, not his manager. Yank off his clothes and ride him until he growled her name in ten languages. She shoved a bite of toast in her mouth and chewed.

"You're not intruding," Preston said. "I'm just waiting on Isla to agree to go on a date with me."

She choked on her toast and struggled to swallow. "You're unbelievable."

"That's what the ladies tell me. Right, Brick?" He pulled out a chair from the table and motioned for Eric to sit.

The big man obliged. His knee touched hers under the diner-style table. He didn't glance at her, but she clenched her thighs.

"Preston's as loyal as they come," Eric said. "You two should go out."

There was no hesitation in his voice. No questioning look shot to Isla, and she felt...hurt. *Resentful*, almost. Both of which were relationship feelings, more proof the worst thing of things had happened: she liked Eric on a deeper, intimate level. She could feel it—how badly she wanted him to want her. For him to care. These traitorous feelings were no doubt his big brain's fault. The man's overdeveloped organ had tipped the scales, his language knowledge and poetry talk casting her under his smarty-pants spell. A freaking boxer.

Her only option was to train her mind to plant him firmly in a professional zone. There would be no more friendly hanging out. No fantastic hugs. She wouldn't ask about his language studies or discuss poetry with him again. He likely wouldn't notice or care. He'd been the one to suggest the friend boundary last night. He was pushing her to date Preston now.

Which was good. Smart even. If her *friend* Eric thought Preston was worth dating, maybe that poem in the bar hadn't been a one off. Maybe Preston's time with Eric had brought out Preston's intellectual leanings.

The two men were watching the car racing on TV.

She chugged some water and wiped her mouth. "I'll go out with you," she told Preston.

They both swiveled toward her. Preston positively beamed. Eric looked...uninterested, like he was bored. Sinking disappointment took her belly for another drop.

"Yep." She nodded so quickly her neck hurt. "Tonight works. Or tomorrow."

"Tonight, it is." Preston leaned back in his chair, looking pleased with himself. "I'll pick you up at your door at eight."

The baby screamed. Isla shuffled through her purse, desperate to find her wallet and pay for this meal. Get away and regroup before her physio session. Eric was talking to the table beside them, low tones she couldn't decipher. By the time she found her cash, he had that baby in his arms, nestled against his man-chest, as he cooed in a foreign language.

Her ovaries exploded. Along with her heart.

His guttural words sounded Russian, low and gravelly. The kid quit crying, of course. She knew the power of his hugs. *Lord help me.* People in the restaurant held up their phones, snapping shots of the adorable scene. Isla didn't need a photo to burn that heart-melting image into her mind.

She slapped her money on the table and gathered her things in a rush, making vague utterances about why she had to bolt. This date with Preston would be wonderful. Really great. Absolutely fan-fucking-tastic. She'd be open-minded and give him a real chance to win her over. She'd kick these unwanted feelings for Eric cold turkey like the bad habit they were.

ERIC WATCHED ISLA RUSH OUT, unsure what had set her off this time. He focused on the baby in his arms, rocked him until he settled. He'd loved holding Asher and Eliza after they'd been born. So tiny and fragile, innocent and trusting. He smiled at the kid's parents and passed the little peanut back. "He's beautiful," he told them.

"We're huge fans," the father said. "Mind signing this?"

The man held out a napkin and pen. Eric obliged and passed it all back, a final smile aimed at their now-sleeping son. "Have a great day."

He sat back down with Preston, who was scowling at him. "You can't do stuff like that."

Eric sipped his water and crunched an ice cube. "Like what?"

"Holding a baby—'*he's beautiful, have a great day.*' In public you've got to maintain your persona."

Eric's neck bristled. "There's nothing wrong with being kind to a family and their child."

"There is when half the restaurant snapped photos of it." Preston pushed his empty coffee cup aside. "We've spent thousands on PR for a reason. Part of why you were booked for this fight was because of your image."

And the fact that Eric was willing to sign their shitty contract.

If Eric beat Joe Bradley, not only would BDA be begging him for that endorsement deal, he'd walk away with thirty million large. Enough money to keep his family happy and healthy for the rest of his life. If he lost, his earnings would barely cover his travel costs, the hotel and private training room and salaries for his manager and agent and trainers and the rest of his team. The other boxers who'd been asked to step in for the fight had refused the pathetic terms. Eric didn't have that luxury, and he understood his position. Advertisers had pulled out when the original fighter had broken his wrist. Eric wasn't the draw for this match, the big name bringing in viewers. He had no leverage.

What he had was a ridiculous image that felt increasingly offensive by the day. "It's demeaning and a lie," he said anyway.

"It's the business. Like wrestling. You're a showman, and you've almost got that belt in your hands. Why the hell are you pushing back now?"

He'd been off since landing in Vegas, and last night hadn't helped. With Isla, he'd remembered how good it felt to be *real* and talk about his passions. Hold a woman who understood him, even platonically. He thought he'd be okay with only being Isla's friend. This morning, sitting beside her, watching her accept a date with Preston, had been a reminder of how phony his life had become. He didn't want to just be friends with her. He was lying to the world about who he was and to himself about his feelings.

Envy sunk its claws in deeper. "I'm just tired," he said.

"Look." Preston leaned closer. "Behind closed doors, you're still the brainy guy who sticks his nose in textbooks for some unfathomable reason. You're the nicest, smartest client I have. Out here"—he glanced around the restaurant—"you belong to them."

There was only one person he wanted to belong to, and she wasn't interested in him. "I'm skipping my physio this morning. I need to go for a run, clear my head. Maybe a swim, too. I'll be your darling brute by this afternoon."

"That's my guy." He picked up his phone and sent a

message to someone. "You'll also have to reschedule the afternoon physio session. The crew filming your training changed today's schedule."

The change would mean not seeing Isla again until tomorrow, which was probably for the best. Still, the last thing he felt like doing was strutting around, growling *Brick Smash*. "How long is the filming?"

"An hour, tops. Your usual training stuff and an interview. But back to the Isla situation, I need your help again."

Scratch that. *This* was the last thing he felt like doing. "She said yes to a date with you. Just be yourself."

"You saw how reluctant she was, and I say stupid shit around her sometimes. Like, I actually get nervous. The poem last time piqued her interest. I just need a little help at the start, to soften her up so she gives me a chance."

Choosing poems inspired by Isla was no chore. There were endless passages that spoke to her complexity and wit, her beauty and strength and the sadness that lived deep in her soul. He wished he knew what had been upsetting her last night. He sure as hell wished Preston would quit asking him for help. Eric wouldn't be able to keep his feelings out of it. "I can't do it."

"Come on, man. Just find me a couple poems."

"Why can't you find them yourself?"

Preston raked a hand through his styled hair. "I got to where I am in business by working with my strengths and delegating to shore up my weaknesses. Poetry's a weakness. How often do I ask you for a favor?"

His manager didn't mention lending Eric money, holding it out there as bait, but it seemed implied. *You ask me for money, and I oblige. I ask you for help with a woman, and you say no?*

What could Eric say to that? Preston had come through for him time and again, never asking questions, always willing to help. All the guy needed was for Eric to choose a couple poems, sentiments that would capture Isla's attention and give Preston an edge. The rest would be up to him. "Fine, I'll help you. But this is the last time."

After his breakfast of six poached eggs, yogurt, fruit, and toast, he changed into his running gear and went on an exhausting run, each hard pound of his feet vibrating up his legs. He hit the swimming pool next, feeling spent but invigorated afterward, his mind clearer. Sifting through poetry for Preston undid all that hard work. Eric found the perfect passages, words that embodied the woman he'd come to know, but his feelings for Isla swelled to the surface so keenly his heart ached.

He sent Preston two poems and suggested he bring her flowers. A mix of light blue hues. According to one website they represented peace, openness, and serenity. It was what he'd have given her, if he'd had the chance, and he liked the idea of her seeing them every day. He even told Preston not to take her to some flashy restaurant. Preston didn't agree, and Eric had to explain that a woman who loved poetry and nuance would prefer quiet elegance, which of course made Eric picture himself on the date, holding Isla's hand, being lucky enough to make her laugh.

Frustrated, he gathered his gym bag, ready for another grueling workout. Training specifics weren't on his mind. He just had an overwhelming need to punch something.

Eric met Graham in the locker room attached to the hotel's training facility, dumped his bag on the floor, and hopped onto the table.

"You're early," Graham said as he got to work wrapping Eric's hands.

"Needed out of my room." Out of his head.

Graham wove the elastic cotton over Eric's knuckles, then around his thumb and between each finger. The methodical process calmed Eric's unwelcome thoughts. He visualized hitting the double-end bag with consistent combinations, quick punches: 1-2-1-3-1-2. He repeated the combination in his mind, then pictured a 3-1-2 pattern of hooks and jabs, with pivots between, hitting the bag at different angles.

"That should do you." Graham secured the Velcro at the end of the wrap. "Good?"

Eric made fists, checked that the wraps felt solid, but not so tight they'd cut off circulation.

The day he'd fractured the metacarpal bones in his hand, his wraps had been part of the problem. Eliza had had an asthma attack that afternoon. Worried about her, he'd been late to his fight, and his coach had been in a car accident. Nothing brutal, but Eric had done his own wraps, rushing to get into the ring. The injury had happened in the third round. Eric had been distracted, the day's string of frustrations eating at him. He'd put his entire body into that calamitous punch but must not have fisted his hand tight enough, and the wrap hadn't been snug enough to protect his bones. The memory of that sickening crunch still made bile rise in his throat.

Months afterward, the thought of his fist connecting with a body had still curdled Eric's stomach. When he'd hired Graham, he hadn't spoken those fears aloud, but his coach would spend extra time wrapping his hands, talking about the strength and purpose of the ritual: to protect the hands' twenty-seven small bones, maintain proper distance between knuckles. A barrier. A way to absorb impact and keep him safe. Like Graham had known how nervous Eric had been to put his full strength into a jab.

"Feels solid," Eric said, shaking off the memories. He was smarter now, had learned tricks to keep his head focused. He'd never slack on wraps again. "Are the TV crews here yet?"

Graham gathered a couple towels and slung them over his shoulder. "They are, but there's been a change."

The irritation in Graham's tone had Eric sitting taller. "What kind of change?"

Graham's jaw flexed. "Preston brought in a tire, an axe, and massive stone slabs for the show. You'll do a circuit, flipping the tire, cutting wood with the axe, and moving the stone slabs into a stack, with speedball and double-end bag work between."

"Stone slabs and an axe?" Did he want Eric to gnaw on a massive turkey leg as well? "That's ridiculous and wasn't what we discussed." Preston must have officially lost his mind.

Graham ran his hand over his buzzed head, a slight snarl on his weathered face. Not unusual. The snarl was a permanent fixture. "He said something about a baby and you screwing up your image. Wants your training to look rough and old-school. Get into Joe Bradley's head. I believe his exact words were: make it look like that *Rocky Four* training montage."

"You have got to be kidding me." Eric hopped off the table and grabbed his phone from his gym bag. He shot off an angry text to Preston and glared at his cell until it chirped with a reply.

Preston: **The baby incident is all over social media. This meme is my favorite.**

A side-by-side image came through, with Eric on the left holding the baby, a content smile on his face. The image on the right was of a vicious-looking Joe Bradley, his fist connecting with a man's face. The caption read: *Who would you bet on?*

Eric fisted his hand and breathed deep to keep from crushing his phone. Holding a baby wasn't a crime. What fighters did in their down time shouldn't impact a fight. They were tested in the ring, not on social media.

Preston didn't send anything else. He'd made his point. This absurd televised training was his team doing damage control. "Social media is evil," Eric mumbled.

A new text came in while he gritted his teeth.

Rosa: **Call Mom and tell her to stop trying to cook with her broken wrist. She won't listen to me.**

Their mother didn't listen to anyone, and frustration knotted tighter in his temples.

Graham patted Eric's shoulder. "The circus sucks, kid. I know. But you gotta play the game. Growl for the cameras. Be the big, strong brute your fans want. Then we buckle down and keep your head focused. You're fighting for yourself, not them."

Eric wasn't fighting for himself. He was fighting for his family, and he needed to remember that. More televised humiliation was nothing compared to the tough hours his mother put in on the factory line, when her wrist *wasn't* broken. Rosa's daily burdens put his stress to shame. "We're training after, though?" he asked Graham. "Without the media?"

A loud bang came through the door to the training room. A stone slab landing? Graham sucked his teeth. "I'm bringing Sanchez in for sparring. He's fast on his feet, like Joe. We'll work on matching his speed and mobility. Try to stay ahead of him, and don't let him work you into the corner."

Eric nodded. Time with Sanchez would help sweat off any lingering irritation from chopping wood.

Graham collected Eric's boxing gloves, moved some stacked towels to the left, then back to the right. "How's the Achilles?" he asked, something different in his voice. Hesitation? "Did today's treatment go okay?"

This locker room, like the private gym where Eric worked out, had been built to attract athletes and the publicity that followed them. The attached training area, complete with boxing ring and necessary equipment, had been tossed together for this fight. The equipment was modern, the space comfortable enough for their needs, but the gray walls in the locker room were bare, the general vibe antiseptic. Graham was studying the stark room like it was a rare archeological site.

"I didn't work with Isla today," Eric said. "Went for a run and swim instead." Followed by a lunch of three chicken patties and a load of roasted vegetables. Enough to fuel him for the afternoon. One mention of Isla, and his gut gnawed at him like he hadn't eaten at all.

Graham quit pretending to stay busy. He crossed his arms and narrowed his eyes at Eric. "You haven't seen her today?"

"Well, yeah. I saw her this morning. At breakfast."

"And she canceled the physio? Is she not feeling well?"

She'd seemed fine health-wise, both last night and this morning. He wasn't sure why Graham was grilling him when the man could just call his daughter, but he remembered how sad and lost she'd looked standing in the hallway, not far from her father's door. He'd assumed a date had upset her. She'd been dressed as though she'd gone out. Maybe the source of her turmoil was standing in front of Eric.

"*I* actually canceled the sessions. Needed a different outlet this morning." A breather from a woman who wasn't interested in him. Still, his curiosity persisted. "She has been off, though. Did you see her last night?"

Instead of getting defensive, Graham scratched his nose and resumed busying himself. "We had dinner. Great meal at the Japanese place in the hotel, but she seemed tired afterward. Just wanted to make sure she was okay."

DeAndre poked his head in the door, glancing between Eric and Graham. "You fuckers ready yet?" Eric's assistant coach had a chipped front tooth, crooked nose, and seriously foul mouth, but the man was killer with pad work and strategy.

"Be right there," Eric said, wanting to finish this

conversation with Graham. Figure out why the man was clearly lying about Isla. Something had gone down between them last night. Whatever the conflict, it was bad enough that Isla had all but sobbed in Eric's arms. Before he could push for answers, Graham spun around and walked out the door. Probably for the best.

Their family drama wasn't Eric's business. He needed to focus on what mattered: getting through this farce of a spectacle so he could get down to the real business of training. Winning that thirty-million-dollar pot. Stop letting his mind wander to useless things like wishing he was at home cooking for his mother. He'd work his body hard enough that he'd crash the second he got to his room, not leaving himself time to think about his family, or about Preston going out with Isla tonight. Preston holding her hand. Preston using Eric's words to pursue her.

Maybe chopping wood wouldn't be so bad.

12

ISLA HUNCHED over the bathroom sink, swiping on the last of her mascara as the name Brick Kramarov came from her TV. Like some pathetically trained Pavlovian dog, she hurried into her room and perched on the edge of her bed.

A bizarre image filled the screen: Eric chopping wood, with a feral look in his stormy eyes. The segment showed him hauling stone slabs, his biceps and forearms bulging with exertion. He flipped a tire, attacked a speedball so viciously she had no clue how it didn't burst. The screen switched to a still image afterward—Eric holding that baby in the restaurant, gently and carefully, as the telecaster questioned if the boxer had what it took to clinch the title.

Next they had him baring his teeth at the camera. "Joe Bradley's gonna learn how it feels to be hit by a Brick."

Isla frowned at the screen. She'd seen several of his interviews this week. Not by accident. Prior to the hug-athon and her vow to quit thinking about Eric, she'd looked them up, fascinated by his performances as Brick. In the clips she'd seen, he'd been intense and intimidating, loud and boastful, but he'd never looked this furious.

The act was likely a way to restore his Neanderthal image after those baby shots. Still, she worried how far Preston was pushing him. If a man that big and strong snapped, the fallout wouldn't be pretty. But it wasn't her business.

A knock sounded from her door, a reminder of why she was wearing her favorite teal dress, low cut enough to make her minimal cleavage appear larger. She'd pulled out all the stops tonight—smoky eyeshadow, eucalyptus cream on her skin, her hair styled in loose waves—trying to look her best. She was committed to this date, kind of desperate to focus on someone who didn't get punched in the head for a living.

She answered her door, and said, "Please don't talk about boxing tonight."

Best to get them off on the right foot.

"Hello to you, too." Preston took her in from head to toe. "You look breathtaking."

He looked handsome, too, wearing a button-down in shades of thinly-striped purple. He ducked his head slightly and held out a small bouquet of blue flowers. The arrangement was beautiful. Not big and bright and ostentatious as she'd have expected from Preston. These flowers were feminine and understated, and any reservations about this date fled.

She stuck her nose in the bouquet and inhaled. "Thank you. They're gorgeous."

"Not as gorgeous as you. And agreed on the boxing. Tonight is about us, not about business."

More at ease and excited for their date, she grabbed her purse and joined him in the hallway. He stayed close as they walked toward the elevator and for the ride down. When they exited, he pressed his hand to her lower back, a move she generally loved—the simple confidence of it, a man knowing what he wanted and taking charge, without doing so aggressively. Her body didn't get warm and tingly. No fluttering butterflies birthed, but his proximity was nice.

"Where are we going?" she asked as they skirted tourists in the busy lobby.

"It's a surprise."

She smiled at him, touched he'd put the time into planning something special. He even had a private limo waiting to whisk them to their surprise location. When the limo pulled up to a quiet French restaurant off the strip, she couldn't hide her impressed, "Wow."

The driver opened Preston's door, but Preston waved him off and turned to help her from the car. "Wow, as in you approve?"

She took in the understated vine-covered exterior, the soft lights and green awning beckoning patrons inside. "I definitely approve."

Inside, the distressed brick and concrete walls gave the space an intimate cavern vibe, the white tablecloths and antique chairs adding elegance. Between Preston's private jet and slick wardrobe, it was clear Preston liked the fancier things in life. She'd have expected him to take her to one of Vegas's fancy hot spots, something loud and garish and exactly what she disliked. But no one here was dressed to excess, hoping to be seen. First the flowers, now this charming restaurant. Preston was proving more appealing by the minute.

Once they got settled at their table, he perused the wine list. "Is red okay with you?"

"Red is lovely." Most other tables were filled with couples. Some talked while bent close, holding hands. The din of tinkling cutlery and light laughter rose around them. She felt a rush of pleasure at being out on a romantic date with a handsome man. It really had been too long.

The waiter brought them water and told them the specials.

Preston angled the wine menu toward her and pointed at a bottle in the red column. "We'll have the 2005 Basco Simone." His finger followed the description, stopping at the astronomical price.

Her jaw dropped.

The second the waiter floated away, likely high on his night's impending tip, she said, "That bottle of wine was 445 dollars."

"I told you when we met on the plane, if you went out with me, I'd show you my version of a good time."

Exactly why the restaurant choice had surprised her. "Honestly, I won't be able to taste the difference between a sip of that and a sip of a twenty-dollar bottle from the corner store. I'm sure it's good, but no wine tastes 445 dollars good."

"It was the best on the list, and you deserve the best. Is there any harm in spoiling my date?"

Technically, there wasn't. But the move made her uncomfortable. Like there was more pressure on this evening.

He clasped his hands on the table. "You really do look ravishing tonight. That color is stunning on you."

Her face flushed, despite her misgivings. "You don't look so bad yourself. But you're always dressed this nice."

He twisted his diamond-studded cufflink. "My closet at home is bigger than my kitchen."

Definitely not a surprise. "At least you own who you are."

The excess reminded Isla of her father's extravagant spending in his heyday: another useless fancy car, gold necklaces and ruby-studded rings no one needed. It had irked her then, and Preston showing off his wealth kind of brought it all back. She understood the wanting of things. The excess was what confounded her, as though material goods defined who you were. She should have added no money talk to her list of conversation landmines.

The waiter arrived with their overpriced wine, uncorked it, and poured a measure into Preston's glass. Preston sipped it and talked with the server about the age and finesse of the vintage. His knowledge was impressive. Maybe purchasing that bottle hadn't been all posturing for her benefit. Maybe he was passionate about viticulture and thought he'd treat himself to something special.

She took a small sip—it was better than her twenty-dollar bottles, but *not by much.* She glanced around the dimly lit room, grasping at conversational straws. "So..." she said. Not her best opener. "How'd you find this place?"

Preston swirled the wine in his glass. "A friend suggested it."

"Well, if the food is as lovely as the ambiance, you'll have to thank your friend."

He smiled tightly. "I will."

Silence descended. Preston pulled out his phone, checked it, and put it on the table. Isla struggled not to comment. People who couldn't put digital interactions on hold while socializing with real, live humans confounded her. She needed her phone with her as well, in case her father called. But the device was in her purse, not a blight on their pretty tablecloth.

She focused on the menu, decided on the frisée salad and steak frites. Feeling first-date awkward and conversationally inept, she reread the menu two more times.

Preston cleared his throat. "'Dreams are water, vast and powerful. Clear enough to show you the way, strong enough to hold you down. She drowns me every night, yet I wake.'"

She looked up sharply. Another poem. This one startlingly personal. "Who wrote that?"

More like, *who are you?* One minute he was buying astronomically expensive wine and checking his phone, next he was spouting incredibly deep poetry. Those dormant butterflies flapped to life in her stomach.

"Ekram Rahal," he said. "The date inspired me to do some reading." He held out his hand on the table, an invitation for her to place her hand in his grasp. She hesitated, didn't feel the pull of intimacy between them, despite his beautiful words. But she'd promised herself to give him a chance. She slipped her hand into his.

He ran his fingers over her knuckles. "Have you always loved poetry?"

"Have you?" Preston finding her weak spot was an odd coincidence. Maybe too odd. Most men in the sports world weren't poetry buffs. Except Eric, who'd been a sneak and had read her dating profile. Which could mean... "Did Eric tell you I love poetry?"

Preston stared at their hands briefly. "Will you be mad if I say yes?"

She wasn't mad, exactly. More like wary. And slightly annoyed. "So you guys have talked about me?"

"I just asked about you is all. You two spend a lot of time together, and I was curious. But poetry isn't new to me. Working with Brick has opened my eyes to a lot of things."

She didn't doubt that. Eric was an intellectual. Being around him could easily inspire someone to read and learn more. Her discussions with him last night had certainly been engaging. The hug had been something else entirely. As were these dastardly *feelings* that kept creeping up. Which was why she was on this date, with a kind man who didn't box for a living. A man who'd gone out of his way to plan a lovely night.

"I guess I can't fault you for that. If my friend Heather knew a guy I wanted to date, I'd ask for intel." Still, she pulled her hand from his, fiddled with the edge of the napkin on her lap. "Who's your favorite poet?"

He sipped his drink, checked his phone again. "Can't say

anyone in particular. I just get lost on the internet sometimes, reading and thinking."

She could relate. She often lost hours perusing passages, only to look up and realize she hadn't eaten dinner. "Why did that poem make you think of me?"

It had been beautiful, but too intimate almost. Words she'd have expected from a lover consumed with their early days.

Instead of replying, he pulled his menu open and perused its contents.

She squinted at him. "Sorry, did you not hear my question?"

"Oh, no. I heard it. I just believe in leaving a little mystery." He glanced up, winked at her. "It's up to you to interpret the poem as you like."

Okay. Sure. But the evasive reply was odd.

French music drifted through the room. She rolled out her shoulders, choosing to focus on the romantic vibe and delicious smells of hot bread and savory meats, not Preston's strange comment.

The waiter returned with a notepad and smiled at Isla. "Have you decided what you'd like this evening?"

"I'll have the frisée salad and steak frites. Steak well done, please."

"Excellent. And for you, sir?"

"I'll have the tartare," Preston said, scanning the menu. "But hold the pickled onion. If you can sub in the potato crisps for the bread, that would be great. For my main, I'll do the lamb shank, but no cauliflower. I'd rather the beans from the chicken, if the chef doesn't mind."

"Of course." The waiter left with their menus.

Isla did a crappy job of keeping a straight face. "Do you always rewrite the menu when you order?"

Preston smirked. "I'm particular with my food. What about you? Do you often eat shoe leather?"

She snickered. "Touché, sir. And yes, I'm a fan of *well-done* steak. I don't need to see my food bleed."

"Note to self: don't take Isla to a slaughterhouse on our next date." He grinned, his eyes playful, as though he enjoyed their sparring.

She liked their banter, too. Things were starting to feel less stilted between them, but the mention of a second date had her realizing fun didn't equate to chemistry. So far, aside from the romantic flowers and that moment when he'd recited the poem, things between them had felt more friendly than intimate. She shifted on her seat and sipped a bigger mouthful of wine. She'd been timid before, uncomfortable with the price tag on each swallow, but wine might loosen her up for the rest of the night. Preston seemed slightly awkward, too, tracing the stem of his wineglass, then the rim, then the base.

When he moved to touch his phone *again*, Isla leaned back in her chair. "Am I that boring?"

He froze with his hand on his device. "What?"

"I know I'm not Taylor Swift and can't entertain you with my dating history via song, but the phone-on-the-table thing is a tad obtrusive."

"Oh, yeah. Sorry. I just..." He let out a weird high-pitched laugh and removed the phone from the table. He put it in his jacket pocket, his hand lingering there like taking it out of eyesight pained him. "Just work stuff, and you're right. It's not gentlemanly behavior. No phones on tables and no boxing talk."

"When you say it like that, I feel like I'm some awful datezilla." No wonder he'd been more interested in his phone.

He settled his forearms on the table and leaned in. "You say what's on your mind, not what you think I want to hear. Honestly, that's part of the reason I asked you out. Most women I've dated are the opposite."

"So you like when I tell you your pick-up lines are awful?"

He grabbed his chest, feigning pains. "Low blow, Slade. But yeah. Hanging out with you keeps me on my toes." He unleashed his smolder, and a lock of hair flopped on his forehead like he was a Disney prince. "Plus, I get to look at your beautiful face all night."

The flirty compliment didn't send a rush of heat through her. Certainly not like when she'd talked with Eric last night. The boxer's rumbly voice uttering Japanese was the definition of sexy. Sexiness she should not be fixating on. This date was supposed to help her drown thoughts of Eric, but she found herself picturing Eric's huge body relaxed on his couch while they'd shared poetry interpretations, Eric holding that baby, Eric in the gym, Eric's biceps and deltoids and triceps glistening with sweat.

She took a cleansing breath and focused on her date. "You must travel a lot for work. Any favorite places?"

Preston talked about a trip to Portugal for a soccer client, drinking local wine and lounging on white-sand beaches, visiting Vancouver and Texas, and one hail-Mary trip to Belize, where he'd had to coax a client away from the beach and booze, back stateside, to uphold an endorsement contract. He boasted plenty, but he also asked questions about her work, what she was struggling with in the set-up, which aspects had been the most fun. She answered between bites of her delicious *well-done, shoe-leather* steak. Made a show of enjoying her food. He belly laughed at her antics.

Preston also pushed back while they talked, suggesting she not rely on her father for connections, after she'd told him about the Álvaro setup and landing her first client. She volleyed back about his need to buy the most expensive wine and show off his wealth, no longer shying away from the obvious.

Instead of getting defensive, he laughed harder and said, "Next time I'll ask for a box of wine."

At the end of the night, when he walked her to her hotel door, she felt happy and light. An easy smile lingered on her face. But every time she tried picturing herself kissing him goodnight, a fizzy rush didn't spin her stomach. Excitement didn't have her wanting to hold his hand or touch some part of his body just to have a connection.

They stopped at her door. His eyes dropped to her lips. He angled toward her.

Before he got any closer, she planted a soft kiss on his cheek. "Thanks for the evening."

"Can we do this again?" He leaned his shoulder into the wall, his hands stashed in his pants pockets. "I had a nice time."

She'd had a nice time, too. Although aspects had been awkward at the start, the night certainly hadn't been boring, and the flowers and restaurant choice and poem had been lovely. She hadn't even thought about Eric for parts of the evening. She and Preston might not be destined for coupledom, but another date wouldn't hurt. One more night to test if attraction might bloom.

"Okay," she said. "Let's go for drinks in a few days. I'll probably do room service this week—work on my accounting course while eating. And it's my treat next time."

Preston pushed off the wall and walked backward toward the elevators, doing some kind of old-timey two-step as he went. "Drinks work for me, Miss Isla Slade. But it'll be *my* treat. I'll come with new poems, and I won't bring my phone or talk about boxing."

She laughed at his goofy retreat, charmed by him despite the lack of chemistry on her end. Then her eyes snagged on Eric's closed door. Immediately her mind filled with images of *him* kissing her goodnight, his massive bulk pressing her against the wall, his hands sliding down her ribs, over her hips, his lips on her neck...

Abort. Desist. *Someone save me from myself.*

She rushed into her room and slammed the door, breathing too damn hard.

God, it wasn't fair. The old Isla Slade would never in a million years fall for a boxer. She wouldn't tempt the anxiety and heartache of that connection.

She wouldn't melt at the mere thought of a heavyweight contender.

Agreeing to another date with Preston was smart, even if their chemistry remained dormant. The distraction had worked relatively well tonight, and they'd have fun regardless of the outcome. Tomorrow she could focus on the playful arguments she and Preston would have, while she worked one-on-one with the Baby Whisperer. She'd keep her desires in check and any fantasies on lockdown. She totally had this.

13

Isla didn't have this. Not one bit. She'd been working on Eric for forty minutes, and she'd barely looked him in the eye. Aside from asking if an exercise hurt or telling him to adjust positions, she hadn't engaged him in any conversation. This had been the plan. She was in protection mode, doing her best to keep a blockade between him and her heart, but with every passing minute, her discomfort grew. "Give me six more reps and slow the movement down."

Eric was working his last set of reverse flies, pushing his range of motion with lighter weights. Instead of acknowledging her instruction or slowing down, he cranked his arms faster and blew past the number he was supposed to do.

"*Eric.*"

He stopped suddenly, his expression severe. "Yeah?"

"We're done. Those were the last reps."

He frowned and dropped the weights.

She barely refrained from giving herself a slap.

As a physiotherapist, client rapport was paramount. Relaxed clients focused better, engaged their muscles more effectively. Tension radiated from Eric so thickly his therapy was suffering. She may be in self-protection mode, but she wasn't doing her job effectively. It wasn't fair to Eric, who had no clue why she was freezing him out. He wasn't the one interested in someone off limits. He wasn't interested in her at all. She'd have to be a grown up about her feelings. Engage Eric for his sake. Ignore the rapid beating of her heart when he was near.

Whit dozed on the floor. Eric moved wordlessly to the treatment table and lay on his back.

Rolling out her shoulders, Isla grabbed some coconut oil and started performing soft tissue release on his calf and Achilles. When his body began to relax, she said, "How long have you been a lumberjack?"

His eyes cut to her. "A what?"

"I saw your televised training."

"Right. That." He turned his attention away, back to tensing.

This massive man's sensitivity never ceased to surprise her. He didn't bother hiding his emotions, and she couldn't pretend she didn't care. Couldn't look at the sad set of his mouth and not offer comfort. "The people who know you know it's all a show."

His calf muscle bunched under her touch. "It doesn't matter."

"You're upset, so I'd say it matters."

"What matters is winning this match." His jaw knotted. "If I need to act like a high-school dropout who can't form a proper sentence to get in my opponent's head and fill seats, then so be it. It's not a lie."

"Which part isn't a lie?" As far as she could tell, Eric was nothing like his Brick alter ego.

"The high-school dropout part," he said.

Eric was smart and studious. More dedicated to learning

than most college graduates she knew. Unable to compute his comment, she put his leg down and got more coconut oil. She started working on his vastus medialis and his rectus femoris. The anatomy words describing his quad muscles were probably rooted in Latin. If she asked him, he'd know the specifics. This supposed high-school dropout would give her a lesson on linguistics. "How does a high-school dropout end up studying dead languages?"

She shifted his leg as she worked on his other quad muscles. Eric grunted and hissed through his teeth. They didn't normally work these larger muscles, but he'd been favoring his left leg, his balance wavering when doing his single-leg weighted heel raises. She was about to ask him to shift to the side of the table, so she could stretch his hip flexor off the side of the bed.

He placed his hand on hers. "Please focus on the Achilles and calf."

"Is this hurting?"

"Not in the way you mean." He glanced down at his waist. No, not at his waist. *Below* his waist. *Oh my God.*

The slight bulge was unmistakable, and her whole body flushed hot. "I am so sorry. I didn't think…or mean to—"

"Isla?"

Mortified, she slowly met his eyes. "Yeah?"

"I'm in this state most of the time around you. I know you're not interested, and I'm pretty good at ignoring how I feel, but if your hand goes any higher, I'm going to embarrass myself worse than I already have."

I know you're not interested.

Ignore how I feel.

Those were not the vibes he'd given off when telling her they were just friends. There'd been no emotional reaction from him the day after the Hug. She should pretend he didn't say what he'd just said. But he'd said it, and her stupid hurricane nature couldn't ignore it. "You told me to go out with Preston."

He licked his lips, watching her. "Yeah, I did."

Her hand was still on his quad, his on top of hers. Neither of them moved, but his male firmness under her touch had her practically panting. He was a mountain of muscle covered in smooth skin. He had cut cheekbones. A strong nose. Shoulders so thick and wide she itched to run her hands over them. She moved her thumb a smidge, enthralled, curious to see if she affected him as much as he suggested. He hissed another breath, and the bulge in his shorts twitched. His hand pressed harder on hers.

"So," she said carefully, "when you say you're good at ignoring your feelings, what exactly does that mean?"

He worked his jaw, staring at her, unblinking. "It means I'm very interested in you, Isla."

Butterflies. Lots of them. And a horrifying amount of sweat gathered under her T-shirt. "But you told me to go out with Preston," she repeated.

"Because you told me you liked Preston."

"Because it's a hell of a lot easier to like Preston." Not Eric. A boxer. A man who could end up sick like her father. *God, why is it so hot in here?*

"Easier," Eric murmured. His wide chest expanded as his gray gaze roamed her face. "And how do you feel about me?"

What *didn't* she feel? They had fun together. His mind interested and challenged her. He'd offered her comfort on a night when she'd been spiraling, no hesitation on his end, ignoring his supposed one-sided feelings, all to make sure she was okay. Eric was sensitive and smart and strong and cared deeply for his family. He was a dumpling and a flower, and a *boxer*, and she was insanely attracted him.

An Estle poem bloomed in her mind, one that spoke of the intensity of wanting. Desires impossible to control:

"petals spread
at the sight of you
desperate
for your attention"

Feeling that poem in every goose bump descending her neck, she said, "You scare the shit out of me."

He held her hand in place as his Adam's apple dragged down his throat. His nostrils flared, then he released her hand and lay back down, clasping his fingers casually over his stomach. "When I was seventeen, my mother lost her job and I had to make a choice about finishing high school or taking boxing more seriously to help support the family. I chose boxing."

Isla blinked, unsure how they'd gone from confessing their feelings to Eric's early boxing days. Then she remembered her question: *How does a high-school dropout end up studying dead languages?* She wasn't sure if this was a tactic. If he'd sensed her urge to flee and hide from her admission. She wasn't sure of much, except that Eric had her captivated.

She resumed working on his Achilles and calf, *not* his upper leg. "Did you finish your diploma later?"

"Night school when I was twenty-two."

Whit snorted in his sleep. Isla laughed at the sound, then glanced at Eric, who smiled back at her. Dimples. Quiet affection. The fluttering in her stomach erupted into a tempest.

"And language?" she asked, keeping the conversation neutral. "What sparked that interest?" She still couldn't believe she'd admitted a fraction of her complicated feelings for him, but his blunt *I'm very interested in you* had usurped her sense.

"A woman's sick husband," he said.

"Care to elaborate?" She glanced at him out of the corner of her eye. Her movements on his Achilles had become more of a soothing rub than therapeutic pressure. The change was unprofessional, but she wasn't sure how to stop. She felt out of control and out of her depth.

Eric still lay with his hands clasped over his abdomen, as though unaffected by their proximity and personal conversation, but he hummed a soft purr, like a satisfied cat. "My father left us when I was six and Rosa was four. We were still living in Russia, but my mother had it in her head that she could give us a better life in the States. She had a friend here, a woman who married an American. They helped us come over, but the transition was harder than my mother expected."

"Because of the language?"

"In part. Her English was bad, and the only job she could get was at a vinegar manufacturing and bottling plant—another connection with a fellow Russian immigrant. She's at another factory now, but she worked long hours then, would come home smelling sour, like she'd bathed in vinegar. I hated that smell. Hated that she was exhausted all the time. And school was hard for me. I got bullied for how I spoke and the foods my mother would pack for me: cabbage rolls and potato knishes."

"Knishes?" She'd seen those on a menu before, at delicatessens on trips to New York with her dad. "Are you Jewish?"

He shifted on the table. "I am, but Preston thought it was best to keep my religion out of the press. Thinks it's better to present a more neutral front, attract as much attention from the largest number of fans."

More sides to Eric she was discovering, endless complexity that upped his appeal. But the choice to suppress such a fundamental part of him didn't sit right. "Why would you agree to hide who you are?"

He focused on his hands, picked at his cuticles. "My Brick Smash routine isn't any different. None if it's who I really am. And I'm not religious. I feel a strong connection to the cultural aspect of Judaism, to the history my people have suffered, but it's not part of my daily life."

"Is your mother religious?"

Frown lines sunk between his brows. "She lights candles on Friday nights and makes sure we all celebrate the High Holidays and Passover, and that I had a bar mitzvah when I turned thirteen, but religion was part of the reason her immigration was so tough. Not speaking English well made attending synagogue tough. She felt very alone and lost, I think."

Isla couldn't imagine raising two kids alone in a new country, with a new language, few friends, a new culture, and no family to ground you. "Your mother must be incredibly strong."

"She's the most amazing person I know." He said the words while staring at Isla, a different expression on his face than she was used to. Warmer. Searching. "Do you mind working on my rotator cuff a bit? It feels tight after those exercises and could use some active release."

She liked being given a task, something to focus on besides the palpitations threatening her equilibrium. He adjusted on the treatment table as she moved, so he was sitting upright. The change brought them closer, near enough she could see the small scar under his right eye. His lips looked softer from this proximity, the stubble on his cheeks deliciously rough.

"Language," she said, her voice suddenly husky. "You still haven't explained how you got into language."

She pressed her thumb into his infraspinatus, got him to

actively move his arm, creating tension in the tight muscle. An attempt to break down a fraction of the scar tissue that had built up over the years.

Eric adjusted his position, a small shift, enough that his warm breath grazed her neck. "When I was nine, my mother had a friend at work whose husband got sick. The woman came to America a year after us, and her English was still horrible. My mother's wasn't much better, but I worked my butt off to lose my accent and perfect my English."

"Always a natural at languages."

He huffed out a flat laugh. "Bullying can be a powerful motivator, and I wasn't big enough to intimidate those cowards into silence back then. But yeah, I had an aptitude." He inched closer to her. She wasn't sure if it was for a better stretch or to shrink the distance between them. She wasn't sure which option she preferred.

"My mother's friend was in a panic," he said, his tone low and intimate. "She couldn't understand the doctors and didn't know what to do. So my mother brought me to the hospital to translate for her. I helped her and the doctor make decisions together, then helped her buy medicine at the pharmacy."

Isla pictured Eric as a young boy, blond hair longer, gray eyes inquisitive and determined as he made a staggering difference in those people's lives. "That's some pretty astounding work for a kid."

He gave a slight, unaffected shrug. "It made me realize how important language is. It can be a barrier and provoke bigotry toward immigrants. It's also a powerful key that connects people. I was proud of what I did, amazed something so simple could have so much impact, and I was hooked. I studied Hebrew and French to start. When other kids my age were reading comics and messing around on skateboards, I used my free time to pore over books. Later, after I got my high school diploma, studying linguistics was a natural move."

More pieces of his puzzle clicked together. But not the biggest one. The central piece that made her growing feelings for him terrifying. "That's a powerful story. And inspiring. But how did a book-obsessed language nerd become a boxer?"

He was still so close, his warm breath ruffling the loose hairs of her short ponytail. "You're asking a lot of questions, Isla."

She was. She wanted to understand all of him. Couldn't fight the urge. But these questions weren't just curiosity. She was collecting evidence, proof that following her reckless heart and giving into this incredible pull to be with Eric wouldn't ruin her. Every fascinating detail about his life was a checkmark in the YES column. *I can date him. I can survive him. He will make me happy.* Learning about his boxing life could fill the NO side with one measly point and tip the scale.

"I'll stop the inquisition if you want," she said.

He stilled her hands and swung his legs around. With him sitting on the edge of the table they were at eye level. He spread his thighs wider, invited her to move between them. She did —*of course* her traitorous body did.

He gathered her hands in his. "I know talking about boxing is hard for you."

"All of this is hard for me." The statement came out angrier than intended.

Eric tipped his head forward in quiet understanding. "My bullying was bad enough that I came home a couple times with black eyes. The woman whose husband I helped owned a boxing gym. When my mother told them how rough school was for me, he suggested I start to train. No cost to my mother. They were beyond thankful for my help, but I had to clean the gym and do the laundry. I worked for my training."

"And the rest is history," she said bitterly. The quiet kid who'd loved language had tossed it all away for a chance at the brass ring.

"I'm a boxer, Isla. It's my job and what I need to do to support my family. I have a shitty contract on this fight. If I lose, I'll barely make enough to cover my expenses. I fight to win and give my family the life they deserve." He pressed his thighs to the outsides of her hips, steadying her, still holding her hands tight.

Eric was a smart man. The sort who boxed and lived his life with an eye on the endgame, a chess player planning several moves ahead. He'd probably orchestrated their current intimate position from the get-go—moving to sit, then moving closer to her, so when they talked boxing, she couldn't freak out and run.

She wanted to run, though. Flee the cramping in her chest, the clamminess overtaking her palms. "I know why you box, but you don't understand how hard this is for me." How hard she'd fought to get her life back after watching her father get hurt time and again. How she'd have to watch that great man deteriorate because of their barbaric sport.

Eric's forehead puckered. "It's hard for me, too. The last thing I need or want is to fall for someone while training. That kind of distraction can kill my focus, but I've been dealing with a worse distraction lately."

Fall for someone. Fall for *her*.

His calloused fingers scraped her hands. He smelled like the definition of a man—musky and rustic, like he'd been in the forest chopping wood, his ridiculous television performance come to life. If she leaned in an inch, her lips would touch his. She wanted that taste more than she wanted a coffee date with Ramona Estle. She'd also never been this nervous to kiss a man.

"What's been distracting you?" she whispered, terrified of how much she wanted him.

He lifted her hands and brushed his nose along the pulse point at her wrist. He inhaled deeply, then released a sexy grunt. "Trying not to think about you has been consuming my thoughts. Knowing you went out with Preston put me in a particularly foul mood, and I was the one who pushed for that." He paused, ran his tongue over his teeth. "Are you interested in him?"

In her mind, the answer was a quick no. Preston had been fun and offered a distraction from what she really wanted: the man watching her with piercing gray eyes. But the question was a double-edged sword. She'd already admitted her feelings for Eric. If she said she wasn't interested in Preston, there was no going back. The door to her heart would be kicked so wide open she might never get it shut.

She settled for a neutral, "I don't know."

I don't know if I can survive you.

Eric's answering frown was so genuine and endearing she almost took back the lie.

"So you had fun on your date," he said, flat.

They shouldn't be talking about her date with another guy. Everything about this scenario was beyond messed up. Preston was his manager and friend, and she'd only dig herself deeper with more lies. She settled on a bit of truth. "Preston admitted you two talked about me, that you told him I love poetry. Which is fine," she added, when he looked about to apologize. "He came armed with beautiful, prepared words and brought me lovely flowers and took me to a surprisingly quaint restaurant. I'm not sure if the chemistry's there, but all of that was unexpected and nice. I agreed to go out again for drinks."

Instead of getting frustrated or upset, Eric grinned, a slow smile spreading as he laughed softly.

She didn't recall telling a joke. "What's so funny?"

He dropped her hands and rubbed at his eyes. "Isla, the reason you liked that side of Preston—the flowers and poem and restaurant—is because—"

Isla's phone rang. The specific ringtone she'd set up for her father.

14

ISLA HURRIED to her purse and fumbled around until her phone was pressed to her ear. "Hello?"

"Are you with Brick?"

Pulse racing, she glanced at the man in question. He was focused on her, as was Whit, both boys watching her with concern. Already, she missed being close to Eric, listening to his deep voice as he talked about his childhood. As challenging as her feelings for him were, facing the reality of her father's worried tone was miles worse.

She turned her back to Eric and dropped her voice. "I am."

"Don't tell him it's me. I'll call him in a bit. I'm feeling off today, more tired than usual and nauseous. We're supposed to train in an hour. I'm sending DeAndre instead. I'll tell Brick I promised to take you out."

"You're feeling sick?" Her voice wobbled. She pictured him in the hallway after their dinner, his loss of balance. "What can I do?"

"Keep it together, Princess. This is why you're here. Preston and Brick know I planned to spend time with you. I just need you to go along with it."

"Okay, fine, but I'm coming up."

"No, you're not. The door will be locked. I'll be resting. We'll talk later."

He hung up, but she didn't lower the phone. She gripped the device harder as she recalled his stubborn words that had convinced her to come on this trip: *If I rest, I die.*

Images of standing over his grave caught her breath. Earth filling that gaping hole, his mansion empty, her heart broken in half.

Which punch had done the most damage during his career? Which harrowing crash to the canvas had cast this die? Brutal memories followed her morbid thoughts: punches to his head, his big body staggering, blood dripping from his nose, blood under his eyes, his ribs taking a beating, fists connecting with his skull, his kidneys, his head snapping back again, and again, and again until she couldn't fill her lungs with enough air. Her chest ached. She heard a ragged sound, only to realize it was her, trying to breathe through the sharp pain.

"Isla." Eric. She'd forgotten about Eric. Now it was *his* head being hit, snapping back. The blood. His brilliant brain being jostled with every brutalizing punch.

The room took a dizzy spin. Her balance wavered.

"I've got you, *milaya*. Just breathe. I need you to breathe for me."

Big arms came around her, but it was too much. Suffocating. She pushed at him, clawed at her T-shirt's neckline. The room spun faster, walls closing in. She dropped to her knees and pressed her palms into the cool floor.

Ground. Firm. *Real.*

She squeezed her eyes shut, tried to count slowly from one, but she only made it to four. Her heart was pounding too loud and something wet nudged her cheek. Loud snorty sounds crowded her, followed by a slimy lick to her ear. Whit. That damn dog was coating her in his slobbery germs, but she didn't shove him away. She sunk to sitting, pressed her face into his wrinkly neck. He pushed back and made the most ridiculous sounds until the pressure on her chest eased. She counted her breaths again, made it to ten this time, focused on the air filling her belly like a balloon. Her usual technique.

Inflate, deflate.

I am here. I am fine. Nothing bad is happening.

I have my face stuffed in a stinky, slobbery dog.

She eased her grip on Whit and chanced a glance up. Eric was crouched in front of her, the worry on his face heartbreaking. Everything about this man was heartbreaking.

She forced a swallow, wanted to say something, explain what just happened, but she couldn't talk about that call, and she'd never told anyone about her attacks. Even now, sitting with Eric's compassion aimed at her, she felt silly. Foolish. She was freaking out over intangible fears.

He reached forward and brushed a tear from her cheek. She hadn't realized any had slipped out. "Should I call your dad?"

"What? No." She moved out of touching distance. "I'm fine. It's no big deal."

Turning away from his scrutiny, she tried to scramble to her feet, but her legs weren't cooperating. Her left knee buckled. She teetered. Instead of hitting the floor, she hit Eric. He caught her and folded her against his chest. "Your body's still recovering, Isla. Relax a second."

His arms had felt too oppressive before. Now? She wanted to sag into him, set up camp, curl up for the night. Or the year. Stake her territory and never leave. She wanted so much with Eric, and he was part of the reason she'd just had a meltdown.

Isla was shaking. Her skin was hot. Eric wanted to kiss the lingering tears off her face, hold her until she settled, or carry her upstairs, tuck her into his bed, dote on her, read her books until she fell asleep. Wake her up with his mouth on her, taste her, give her so much pleasure she never looked that scared again. "Was that a panic attack?"

When Eliza's early asthma attacks had struck, he'd thought they'd been panic attacks: shortness of breath, fear building alongside the symptoms. It had been asthma in the end, but he recognized some similarities in Isla's symptoms. He just wasn't sure what had caused them.

She nodded but wouldn't look at him.

He smoothed a hand down her back. "It's nothing to be embarrassed about."

"Because it's totally normal to freak out for no reason." She kept her head down, like she *was* embarrassed, her sullen vulnerability so unlike the strong woman he'd come to know.

He eased back farther, put two fingers under her chin, lifted her face up to his. "The body and mind are incredibly complex. We all have mental and physical issues we deal with, and what you experienced was real to you. There's no shame in being human."

Her lips wobbled. Another tear slipped out. "I've never told anyone," she whispered.

Jesus. She really was as stubborn as her father, intent on carrying the world on her shoulders. "Well, I'm here and I'm listening. So, please tell me what triggers your attacks."

She glanced at the phone she'd dropped on the floor. A tremor ran through her. Unwilling to let her sweep her episode under the proverbial rug, he lifted her into his arms and carried her to the treatment table. He laid her gently down, sat on the edge of the table next to her, keeping hold of her hands. "You're not leaving here until you talk, *milaya*." *Darling.*

He hadn't planned for the Russian endearment to slip out before. He'd been worried about Isla, and it was simply how he felt. Protective of her, connected to her. Saying it felt right.

She sniffled and played with his fingers, measuring her palm to his, so tiny in comparison. "They started when I was thirteen. Stuff was bad at home between my folks. My mother pretty much told me she never wanted me, and my dad had this insane match. With Hector Narvarez?"

"I remember it." The big men had traded bruising blows. A go-for-broke bloodbath that ended with Narvarez in a heap on the canvas and Swinging Graham Slade's fist punched up in victory. Eric had found the match thrilling. Slade's daughter wouldn't have felt the same. "Your dad won, but it must have been rough to watch."

She kept her attention on his hand. "He ended up in the hospital that night, and I thought I was dying watching the match. Those same symptoms—the fear, the chest pain, the difficulty breathing. Things were rough at home with my mother. She didn't leave us until I went to college, but she was barely around, and when she was around her unhappiness with me and my dad wasn't subtle. I'd watch all my dad's matches, terrified something would happen and I'd be left alone with her. The attacks happened more often after that, always when he had a fight."

She must have been so terrified, alone. He hated that for her. "You never got help?"

"I did briefly, but I didn't click with the therapist, and I never told anyone about it. The attacks make me feel weak, and I hate feeling weak. I did my own research, found techniques that helped me relax, and when my dad retired the attacks eventually stopped. Until I started working for physio clinics and they used my name to advertise and lure in boxers. If I got too close to them, I'd picture these nice men and women in the ring, and that same fear would rise. Not as intense, but I was terrified it would get worse, so I quit."

"And you started your own practice."

"With no boxers."

I hate boxing. Any random guy on that dating app would assume that line referred to the sport, the way people disliked golf or curling. Isla's distaste for boxing was wrapped in a painful childhood, watching her father get beaten up, fear of losing the one parent who loved her unconditionally.

"Did your father call now, is that what triggered you?" Graham had been with her the other night as well when Eric had found her shaken in the hallway.

Her eyes widened, another hint of fear dilating her pupils. "No. It wasn't him."

"Then who was on the phone?"

She sniffled, twitched her nose. "Just a spam call."

That didn't ring true. It didn't explain her panic attack either. "Then what set you off?"

She swallowed convulsively and closed her eyes. When she finally reopened them, his heart pressed against his ribs. Her dark eyes shimmered with so much pain he wanted to wrap her in his arms and never let go.

Just as quickly, she set her jaw. "I like you, Eric. A lot. I was in denial for a while, assumed it was just physical attraction, because you're..." She dragged her gaze over his body and sighed. "You're spectacular, but it was your mind that clinched it. You're smart and funny and interesting and compassionate, and you know Ramona Estle and have this power to excite and soothe me all at once."

Her breathing picked up pace, along with the rapid fall of her words. "I didn't want to fall for you. I tried to fight this thing between us. Then you held that baby and you told me stories about translating for immigrants, and those jokes are perfectly awful, and I really wish you weren't so amazing. Because honestly? You're a man I could fall in love with. I can't even believe I said that out loud. That's just how things are going for me today, and now I need to say the hardest part."

He should keep his distance, wait and hear her out. It was the gentlemanly thing to do. But she thought he was amazing. She was finally admitting how intensely she felt.

Fuck being a gentleman.

He leaned in, captured her lips in a kiss, scooped her close, finally taking what he wanted. She stiffened at first, only a moment. Then she relaxed, opening for him. Soft lips, tiny whimpers. He swiped his tongue against hers, a hot slide that sent a bolt of lust through him. He crushed her closer, kissed her harder. So deeply he was sure he'd lose a piece of himself with every needy sound she made. Christ, she undid him with nothing but a kiss, this woman who saw the real him and imagined a future full of love.

He was half a second from dropping to his knees, peeling off her yoga pants, tasting what he desperately wanted, but he slowed his kisses, finished with two soft ones as their noses brushed. "I'm sorry," he murmured.

He wasn't. He really fucking wasn't. But she'd just had a panic attack. She needed time to calm down, relax. And he wanted to be part of her recovery. Help her any way he could. Dote on her. Make her smile and laugh, banish all her worries.

She held him more tightly and started to shake. The bad kind of shaking. Upset. Panicked. When he pulled back, more tears were falling down her reddened cheeks.

"I can't do this," she said, her voice cracking. "I can't date you. I can't kiss you and feel all these things, when so much of you reminds me of the bad parts of my childhood. I thought I could. I tried to convince myself this was worth it, but..." Another tear slipped out. "You're what set off my panic attack, Eric. My developing feelings for you are why I lost it before. And I'm just...*fuck*."

She dashed at her face. Opened her mouth, closed it, then maneuvered off the table, grabbed her things, and left before he could catch his breath.

15

Eric hadn't felt this agitated and tense in a long while. He hadn't seen Isla since this morning's disaster. He'd trained with DeAndre, had eaten and walked Whit, the whole while feeling like a swarm of wasps were in his stomach. He kept replaying Isla's rough breaths, the tears on her face, her devastated: "You're what set off my panic attack."

He was actually relieved when Graham didn't show for their session. Eric doubted Isla had confided her issues to her father, but she'd been rational enough to realize she needed company. Family. Familiarity. Someone who wasn't Eric to offer her comfort.

Yeah, there were those buzzing wasps again.

He bent down and gave Whit a rub, pressed a kiss to the top of his head. "Love you, stinker."

Whit chuffed, nuzzled into Eric's neck. Eric didn't feel much like leaving the room—facing Isla for their afternoon treatment session, seeing everything he couldn't have. For half a minute, he debated canceling, but he needed to see her. Make sure she was okay. And his shoulder was acting up.

Steeling himself for the session ahead, Eric walked into the hall. And there she was. At her door. Eyes on something in her purse.

When she looked up and saw him, she froze.

He mirrored her statue pose. "Hey."

"Hi." Her eyes darted from him to the floor, back to him, then to something on the opposite wall.

He swallowed a frustrated sigh. So this was their new normal, reverting to awkward acquaintances who could barely look at each other. All the while, the only thought rushing through his knotted mind was: *Isla is my match.*

He'd felt this morning's kiss down to his soul. Consuming lust that went beyond physical attraction. In the weeks Eric had worked with Isla, he'd learned she reached to touch her hair when she was nervous and twitched her nose before she laughed or lied. He'd catalogued every fun food chat they'd had: she hated salmon and raw onion, loved green olives and the taste of burned toast, as long as it was dripping with butter. He *knew* she was a woman who enjoyed understated elegance, not the flash and money of Vegas. Delicate blue flowers. A charming French bistro. Poems that spoke to her depth. He knew exactly how he'd sweep Isla Slade off her feet, and how fucking *sweet* she tasted.

He'd also seen her panic attack, had felt gutted and helpless watching her, and *he'd* been the cause. There was no fixing their discord. The last thing he'd want was to be the source of anxiety in her life. His only option was to keep his distance, curb his emotions around her. Put her first and forget his needs.

When she finally walked toward him, he matched her stride to the elevator. "How are you feeling?"

She lifted her hand toward her hair—her nervous tic—then dropped her arm to her side. "Better, thanks."

"Glad you spent time with your dad."

"Yeah." She nodded stiffly. "It was nice. Sorry he missed your training."

"I'm just happy you had someone with you." Frustrated as hell that someone wasn't him, but he'd have to get used to that notion.

They waited at the elevator. Neither of them spoke. When the door opened, they moved at the same time and their sides brushed. Isla practically jumped out of her skin and stepped back. He stepped back too. Then they stepped forward at the same time, brushed again, the tiny contact like that one lick of Isla's strawberry ice cream, making him want to moan and go back for more. A stupid brush of their arms and he was on fire for her.

Frustrated, he took a bigger step forward and turned once inside. She followed, her face looking flushed. He tried not to glance at her lush lips. Tried not to remember the swipe of her tongue this morning, the feel of her fingers digging into his back. Tried and failed. His cock thickened, the thin fabric of his workout shorts doing him no favors. He clasped his hands over his crotch. He felt Isla's attention on him, but the second he glanced over, her focus was cemented to her feet.

The elevator stopped a few floors down. A family entered, filling the space between them. It felt like a football stadium worth of people could fit in that widening gulf.

Walking through the casino wasn't much better.

"It's always busy in here," Isla said.

Eric replied with a brilliant, "Yeah. Hot out today. Maybe people like the AC."

"Probably."

That level of awkward pretty much described the first half of their physio session. Eye contact was minimal. Conversation revolved around Isla giving him brief instructions and Eric asking the odd question but mainly grunting in acknowledgment, embodying his Neanderthal persona.

Partway through, they switched to resisted scapular slides, using lightly weighted cables and a triceps rope to increase his range of motion. Eric sat a distance from the cables, concentrated on his arms as he held the rope at chin level, slowly raised his arms above his head, then lowered them back down.

"Don't let the resistance pull your arms forward at the top," Isla told him. "Keep your hands in line with your ears."

He repeated the movement, noting her suggestions, sweat gathering along his neck. "Like this?"

"Exactly. Take it slow."

She crouched next to him, the closest they'd been all session, and his stomach swooped. Fucking swooped, like he was a love-struck teen. The sensation divided his focus, part of it staying on the rope in his hands, a fraction diverting to her proximity, another locked on his reacting body. She shifted positions slightly, seemed to hesitate, then she placed her hand on his back.

Forget divided. All his attention zeroed in on that one spot. *Isla. Hand. Hot.* So much heat concentrating where she touched. He leaned back a bit, couldn't control his body's urge to ask for more. More contact, more Isla.

Her fingers spread wider. "Don't overarch your back," she said, her voice lower, breathy. "Sit straighter."

He paused with the triceps rope at his chin, fixed his posture and turned his head, bringing them almost nose to nose. "Like this?"

Her gaze dropped to his lips. His thighs flexed.

"Yeah," she murmured. "Like that."

The moment lingered, sexual tension vibrating between them so thoroughly he was surprised the walls didn't shake.

And he was pissed. Angry at their circumstances. Upset for Isla and all she'd dealt with in her life. Mad that the easy friendship they'd developed had devolved in a matter of hours to broken sentences and awkward glances. None of it was okay.

Determined to salvage something from this mess, he worked through his next rep with slow precision, keeping his back straighter, his arms at the correct angle. At the end of the rep, he said, "What do you call spending the afternoon with a cranky rabbit?"

Isla made a startled sound, a muffled kind-of-laugh. From the corner of his eye, he caught the hint of a smile. "I don't know," she said.

"A bad hare day."

Her tentative smile grew. "Have I told you your humor hovers at a grade-one level?"

"Have I told you that you have no sense of humor?"

"I wouldn't know. I usually tune you out."

He chuckled at that, turned his head toward her, bringing their lips dangerously close again. Her hand was still on his back, maintaining his posture. Her thumb moved, a small stroke he felt everywhere. They breathed deeply at the same time, their chests expanding like their hearts were reaching toward each other.

Then they got back to work. Less awkward this time. They talked more easily. Joked occasionally. Everything out of Isla's mouth sounded like foreplay to him: *move slower, hold that position, yeah like that*. But he somehow found his focus, stayed attuned to his body's needs and pains, assessing when muscle fatigue meant a break was due. Neither of them crossed the invisible line they'd drawn. They were once again patient and physiotherapist, no different than during their early sessions. But everything was different.

16

ERIC SLAMMED his gloved fist into the punching bag, sweat dripping down his face as he danced around the swaying bag. Each hard jab shot tension up his arm, jolted his shoulder. He did pullups next. Bench pressed enough weight to have his pecs and triceps screaming. Sit-ups, one-handed pushups, box jumps, double-unders, and back to the bag. Wash, rinse, repeat.

His last punch rattled the punching bag's framework so thoroughly the whole thing nearly toppled. His breath raked through his lungs. Whit gave a disapproving chuff.

"Yeah, buddy. I know." Eric couldn't be in a worse frame of mind. Where he'd hoped his affections for Isla would mellow as their friendship rediscovered its footing, the opposite was happening. He was braindead from little sleep and heartsick for a woman he couldn't have. Add in his mother's injury, his sister's frustration, their money woes, and nothing in his life felt like it was in his control.

His phone rang from his gym bag. He peeled off his gloves and grabbed a towel, wiping his face as he checked the screen. The second he saw Rosa's name, his gut hardened.

It was just after 6 a.m. in Vegas. Chicago was two hours ahead. Rosa should be running around, wrangling the kids so they could get to school and she could get to work. Her morning shifts finished at one, leaving her time to shop, pick up the kids from school, spend time with them. Shaking up their schedule meant something was up.

He answered before it clicked over to voicemail. "Everything okay?"

"I'm sorry for calling again, but the heat's out."

"Shit." He scrubbed the towel harder over his face, wanted to shred it to pieces. He could hear the exhaustion in her voice. Could imagine how stressed she'd been with Mom's broken wrist on top of it all. "Have you called someone to fix it?"

"He just left. We need a new furnace. And I'm at my wits end, trying to hold everything together, not feeling like I'm doing a very good job of it."

She did the best she could as a single mother. Eric was the one who should've done better, earned more money over the years. How could he have left them so strapped for cash? Frustration thrummed through him, so hot and fast he kicked his gym bag, sending clothes and boxing wraps flying. He pressed his fist to his forehead, worked to calm his voice. "I wired you extra money for the medical bills. Is there any left?"

"Not enough to buy and install a new heater. And Asher needed new sneakers. He grew out of his." Her sigh was bone weary. "Honestly, I think it's time I figure out a full-time job."

"We're *not* talking about that again." He wouldn't stand by while she worked herself to the bone. She'd end up spending half that money on after-school daycare, being ten times more exhausted than she was now. If he couldn't provide for his family, what kind of man was he?

Last night, unable to sleep, he'd tortured himself by googling Ramona Estle and reading various quotes. A way to feel closer to Isla and get into her head, even though it was the last place he should be. One poem came back to him now, along with a heaping of shame.

"daughters soak up
hate
faster than
love"

Rosa was his sister, not his daughter, only two years younger than him, but Eric had assumed the role of man of the house, earning money, making sure she studied and finished high school. He'd reprimanded her when she'd made bad choices, like the time she got caught cheating on a math test, and the night a parent called because Rosa thought it was a genius idea to drink a bathtub worth of peach schnapps.

Without their father around, he'd grounded her as needed and showed up for science fair presentations. He'd sacrificed his schooling and wants and had taken care of his family, as it should be. He wanted her to experience unconditional love and support from a man in her life.

He wouldn't fail her now.

There was a leather sofa in the corner facing a TV, where he often watched videos of Joe Bradley with Graham and DeAndre, analyzing Joe's fighting style, strategizing techniques.

He dragged his ass over there and fell onto the cushioned seat. "I'm sorry for raising my voice. You're just such a great mom who always puts her kids first, and I want to keep it that way. Aside from more money, is there anything you need?"

"I need a week's worth of sleep," she said, sounding exhausted enough to need it. "And a magic kitchen that cleans itself, and I'd kill for one of those spa days, with the manicures and pedicures and fruity water. For now, I'd settle for a hug from you."

Something else he couldn't give her. "I'll be home as soon as the fight's over. I'll clean the kitchen and make you fruity water. And when I win this fight, I'll buy you a year's worth of spa days."

Silence lingered. Then she said softly, "I'm so glad you're doing what you love."

He almost let out a harsh laugh. He had loved the sport once—the challenge of it, the athletic outlet. In the early days, his mind was always on training and visualization. Then he'd finished high school remotely, had started studying in his free time. Gradually, over the years, something had shifted. He knew his boxing made his family proud. He got a thrill when they boasted about him, but lately any love for the sport felt tainted. Bitter greens he had to swallow.

"I'll wire more money today," he said. Money he'd have to borrow.

A distant "give it back" sounded through the line: Asher's pained whine.

"Goddamn it," Rosa grumbled. "Gotta go. Love you."

She hung up and Eric stared at nothing until his eyes blurred.

"Did a tornado blow through here?" Preston stood at the training room entrance, glancing at the contents of Eric's gym bag sprawled over the floor.

"It's been a rough morning." His sweat-slicked skin was stuck to the leather couch. Clamminess settled in the wake of his intense workout. He pushed off the couch, wiped the leather down with his towel, then joined Preston, who was already on his phone, meandering toward the punching bag.

Preston finished his business and jerked his chin at Eric. "I need a favor."

Eric tensed. *He'd* been about to ask Preston for another massive favor, more cash to get the heat on in his house. Chicago in November wasn't freezing, but nights dipped low. Low enough that he needed this work done. Asking for another handout was a blow to his pride. One he'd suck up for his family, but Preston's comment had him on edge. The last two favors his manager had asked for had centered on Isla.

He'd worked with Isla for two days since her panic attack. Four more painful sessions of them being polite, skirting any discussions of substance, when all Eric wanted to do was kiss her again, take her on the treatment table, against the wall, anywhere and everywhere, as long as it meant he could have her. Now Preston needed another favor.

Eric slung his towel over his shoulder and crossed his arms, squaring off to face his manager. "What do you need?"

"I'm taking Isla for drinks tonight, and I need more of your romance skills."

Jealousy careened into Eric. He bit down on his molars, surprised he didn't crack a tooth. The last time Isla had mentioned Preston, before her panic attack, she hadn't denied having feelings for him, but she'd admitted the chemistry was lacking. Still, she'd said they planned to have drinks. The subject hadn't been broached since, not that their conversations had been personal lately, and she didn't owe Eric anything. But he hadn't expected her to keep that date.

Maybe she was as frustrated as him by their forced separation and needed a night out with another man, someone to help her forget what she couldn't have. Maybe she really liked Preston.

That notion had him grinding his teeth harder. "Last time you said you needed a little help to soften her up, then you'd do the rest. This is the rest. She wouldn't have agreed to another date if she didn't like you as you are." Eric wanted to choke on his pep talk, hated the idea of them on another date. The idea of her on a date with any man but him had him itching to go ten rounds in the ring.

Preston waved his hand in vague dismissal. "She does like me. And I like her. I mean, nothing's happened between us physically. But we laugh a lot, and she doesn't take my shit, which is refreshing. I can actually picture her with my family, getting along with everyone. She agreed to another date, and I don't want to mess it up."

Hearing they hadn't been intimate loosened Eric's fists. Slightly. Jealousy still simmered behind his sternum, and that call with Rosa was a massive concern. Preston was the only person he could ask for money. Preston, who couldn't deal with his love life on his own. "I don't see the problem. Take her out again and leave me out of it."

"Yeah, well, there was a hitch last time." He faced the punching bag, all done up in his pressed shirt and tie, and gave a few pitiful jabs. "Those poems don't stick in my head. I have them on my phone as a cue, but she hates me leaving my phone out, which I get. So I put it away and tried to wing conversation. But I get nervous with her, especially when the night starts out. I just have a feeling this date is a make-it-or-break-it one with her. I need a wingman with me at the table."

"I'm not tagging along on your date with Isla." Death by elephant trampling was preferable.

"That's where being rich comes in handy." He spun to face Eric and opened his suit jacket. A small black cone was attached inside, with a wire hanging down. "I'll be wearing this microphone, so you can hear everything we say, and I have a matching earpiece. If our conversation goes off the rails, you tell me what to say—those fancy poems and romantic words. When I'm more myself, less nervous or whatever, I cut the cord."

Eric stalked over to his scattered clothes and started shoving them forcefully back into his bag. If boxing wasn't an issue for Isla, Eric would have told Preston about his feelings for her. Apologized for going after the same woman as his manager, but he'd have taken what he wanted. Eric wasn't a saint. And Isla was no ordinary woman. Eric had never lain awake wishing he could ask a woman's opinion on a poetry passage, while hungering to whisper those beautiful words along the outer swells of her breasts, down the curves of her belly, against the hot center of her. His unmitigated desire was a roaring, living thing.

If there were any chance she could handle a relationship with him, he'd have told Preston in a heartbeat, dealt with the fallout. Found a way to balance her and his training. But there was no chance for them. Explaining to Preston he'd already fallen for her would be useless. Helping him on another date? That would make him masochistic.

"You've officially lost your mind," he told his manager.

"Or sharpened it. I saw it in a movie once. They did the earpiece thing and it worked perfectly."

Except this wasn't a movie, and Eric was way too invested in the other half of that prospective date. But he paused. His focus had been abysmal lately. He had an edginess he couldn't contain. Isla wasn't the only source of his frazzled head space, but she was a big part of the problem. Maybe speaking through Preston could settle his mind.

After her panic attack, Isla hadn't given Eric the chance to tell her how he truly felt. He may have confessed he was interested in her, but she'd run out before he could praise her beauty, tell her how smart and wonderful she was, that he'd also imagined a future for them. He couldn't tell her now. Not in person. It wasn't fair to her. But he could bare his heart under the safety of a disguise. Use the confession to find some kind of closure, then shove his feelings down and walk away.

The prospect was absurd. Royally fucked up. So why wasn't he saying no?

"Our furnace broke at home," he found himself telling Preston. Not the topic at hand, but an important one. "Rosa just called."

He winced. "Shit, man. That sucks. You need another loan?"

Preston's instant kindness reaffirmed he was a solid guy. Never one to latch onto Eric's shame and make him feel like more of a mooch for needing cash. Preston may spend his money on ridiculous things, but he'd be good to Isla. He wouldn't cause her to have panic attacks.

"The cash is needed and appreciated. It'll come back to you with interest. And sure, I'll be your wingman with Isla. But if you can't fly solo after that, you two aren't right for each other."

Preston gave his shoulder a hard slap. "You're the best, man."

Or the worst. He no longer knew.

17

Eric sat in his hotel room, feeling like a disgruntled cop on a painful stakeout. Preston's plan had gone beyond a simple microphone. He'd shown up with a laptop, explaining that a fancy pin on his lapel would video his date, so Eric could better follow the conversational flow and read visual cues. Eric would rather read his own obituary.

"I'm an idiot," he told Whit.

He should have backed out when Preston arrived. Made an excuse. Apologized and washed his hands of this absurd situation. Preston may have gone above and beyond to help Eric's family, but this was *durast. Insensé. Insipiens. Unsinnig.* Whatever language popped into his head, the results were the same: this situation was *foolish*.

He picked up his phone, ready to text Preston, explain he had to bail. But the screen came to life, with Isla front and center. She wore a sexy purple dress that had thin straps over her shoulders and hugged her lithe form. Her makeup was subtle but pretty, highlighting her dark eyes. Her lips looked full and shiny, her shoulder-length hair loose with its usual wave. The dim lighting emphasized the old-Hollywood look he loved about her: the smooth roundness of her cheeks, the elegance of her long neck.

"Flowers would follow you," he said, gruff. Only to remember the listening device was on.

A second later, Preston's voice said, "Flowers would follow you."

Isla tipped her head slightly. "What?"

Eric said, "Shit."

Preston parroted the curse.

Isla scrunched her face in that cute way of hers, and Eric muffled another curse. This was more insane than he'd thought. Completely ridiculous, with Preston mimicking every sound Eric made. Was his manager really this nervous with Isla? Whatever the guy's deal, it wasn't Eric's problem. He couldn't go through with this charade. Even Whit snorted and gave Eric a dubious look.

Done with this nonsense, Eric leaned forward to switch off the program, but Isla reached to touch her hair, then lowered her hand below the table, probably placed it on her lap to twine her fingers. Her nervous tics. When she nibbled on her bottom lip, Eric's stomach tightened. He couldn't see much of the dark bar. Judging by the leather couch and crooner music, it was the hotel's throwback lounge, where people schmoozed and flirted under low-hanging lights. She was there, feeling awkward and nervous, and he had the power to put her at ease.

Hating himself, he muffled his rising sigh and said, "Flowers lift their heads to the sun, because it's the brightest light in the sky. Everyone you pass does the same."

At least she had that effect on Eric. A magnetic draw.

Preston repeated Eric's words.

Isla smiled. "The poet returns."

"You inspire poetry," Eric said, like they were on a date, just the two of them. A total sham, but Eric was suddenly hooked. He didn't care that Preston was repeating his words, or that Isla wasn't looking into his eyes. This was a stolen moment, a night to admit his feelings without hurting this beautiful woman.

"There's no phone on the table," she said, smirking.

"I don't need a phone when I can spend a night talking with you." Preston's words flowed after Eric's prompt.

She ducked her head, a sweet move he hadn't seen her do before. "If you don't start spending money recklessly, I might think someone's taken over your body."

Eric waited, wasn't sure if Preston would interject, speak on his own. The lingering pause felt like a poke for Eric to keep talking. "Money is necessary," Eric said. "It drives a lot of my choices in life, but at the end of the day, it's not what truly matters."

Isla's eyes widened. "I couldn't agree more. So what matters to you?"

"The people I care about." It was an easy answer. His family's health and happiness had driven every decision of his teen and adult life. If given the chance, he'd have added Isla to that selective group. Actually, she was already there. He was keeping away from her so she'd be healthy and happy.

"You're close with your family?" she asked.

"I am." Preston answered that time. He steered the conversation, asking Isla about her last couple of days, being his usual charming self. She smiled while she talked, happy with another man.

Eric's lip curled, his hands fisting of their own accord.

A waitress came by to take their drink order while Eric tried to relax. Preston ordered a Manhattan, asking for a top-shelf bourbon to be used. Isla ordered a strawberry daiquiri.

When the waitress left, Preston said, "You like to eat shoe leather *and* drink girly drinks."

Isla raised an eyebrow. "What do you mean by *girly* drink?"

"Fruity. All sugar. The type of drink that comes with an umbrella. It was an unexpected choice."

Eric winced at the jab.

Isla relaxed into her seat. "Funny, I *did* expect you to ask for a fancy bourbon. I assume you're compensating for something." Her gaze drifted downward, toward Preston's lap.

Eric chuckled.

"No compensation here," Preston said, more amused than defensive. "And you don't have to make excuses to check me out."

"I wasn't checking you out. I was judging if a glass of ice water on your groin would stop you from mansplaining what type of drink I *should* order."

Preston laughed, clearly not offended by Isla's quick wit. "If I just rolled over and agreed with you all night, you'd miss our fun banter."

Isla cocked her head and studied him. "You know, I probably would."

She no longer seemed nervous. The two of them shared another few jokes, at ease and having fun with each other, and Eric's gut hollowed. Maybe Preston was the man for her in the end, not Eric, everything having happened for a reason. Maybe this was all for the best. Either way, she clearly didn't need Eric's help any longer. Their drinks were served. They both made cracks about their choices again.

Eric should shut this circus down, go for a walk. Or a run. Or bang his head against the wall for an hour. But Preston didn't cut the connection, and for some unfathomable reason Eric couldn't tear himself away from the screen.

Isla's laughter died down as Preston sipped his Manhattan. Tonight may have begun awkwardly again, but their easy jokes had resumed. Teasing each other was fun. Still, the chemistry she'd hoped to kindle remained absent. Her mind kept drifting to Eric, wondering what he was doing, if he was studying or reading or scratching Whit's wrinkly neck.

She wondered what it would be like to sit across from *him* now, except in that fantasy they'd be beside each other, not across, her hand on his thick thigh, his fingers in her hair as they talked and flirted and pretended they were the only people in the room. If she were a normal girl who could handle a normal date with Eric, that was exactly where she'd prefer to be.

She swallowed a sigh. If she had the same intense attraction to Preston, everything would be easier. But she didn't. The more they joked, the more he felt like the sibling she never had.

"I want more poetry," she said. Not because she wanted to up their flirting. As much as she'd hoped this date would spark their romantic flames, that ship had sailed for her. She was too stuck on Eric for any man to interest her. But talking poetry was fun, and she was curious what he'd come up with.

They were sitting on low-slung couches, smooth velvet and comfy cushions. Everything about this lounge was elegant, including the impeccably dressed man across from her. Preston leaned back and rested his ankle on his knee, going for cool, when he was clearly delaying for time. She sipped her *girly* cocktail, pleased he was on the defensive.

Then he said, "Love is sunshine and rain, flowers and decay. It's happiness and pain, but it's worth every struggle."

She didn't know that quote, but it hit her in her heart. It was another reminder of Eric, who had the potential to be all those things wrapped in a muscled, handsome package. A man who kissed like sin and was permanently stuck on her mind.

She shoved her straw around her cocktail as she replayed her panic attack. Her dad's call. How closely linked Eric was to that world. "The prose is idealized and impractical," she told Preston.

He paused, scratched his neck. "True love is worth suffering some pain."

"It's false utopia. In the real world love is dangerous. It makes people do irrational things."

More neck scratching. Did the guy have some kind of funky rash?

"Love is hard," he said, "but anything hard is worthwhile. You don't strike me as the type to like things easy."

She didn't. At college Heather had refused to join any clubs, saying she hated wasting her time on lame things. Aka: she hated not being the best at a new task. After Isla's tough first year, she'd eventually branched out and joined rock climbing and calligraphy clubs. Activities that were hard and challenged her. She hadn't stuck with either hobby, but pushing herself to learn and test her boundaries had given her a punch of pride. Opening her new business was terrifying on many levels, but that fear and the challenge had also been a draw.

Love was a wild card, though. It left you open and vulnerable. She'd had enough open and vulnerable to last a lifetime.

"If you know me so well, Mr. Mansplainer, what type of person am I?" This would be good. More entertaining than discussing the complications of love.

Preston paused *again*. Re-crossed his legs *again*. Then he met her eyes. "I know you're as stubborn as your father and don't like leaning on others. I know you're smart and can do anything you put your mind to. I know your dark eyes remind me of the horizon as the moon rises on a cloudless night, and I know you twitch your nose before you laugh, Isla. I also know how you..." Preston trailed off, his gaze shifting away.

Isla froze, unprepared for the intimate turn in conversation, how *seen* she felt. By a man she hadn't spent that much time with. She tried to recall her conversations with Preston, what they'd discussed, how she'd acted. Nothing explained his intuitive words.

"You also know how I...*what*?" He hadn't finished his sentence, and she was on the literal edge of her seat, having scooted forward. Not because she was starry-eyed and fluttery. Their chemistry was still as dormant as a bear in winter, but his sudden knowledge of her drive to always go it alone had her itching to hear what else he had to say.

Instead of replying, he opened his suit jacket and touched the inside. He fiddled with the pin on his lapel, then tugged at his ear. "Sorry, what was that?"

"You didn't finish what you were saying."

"Yeah, I did."

"Uh, nope. No, you didn't." The guy was losing his marbles. "You said, and I quote: *I also know how you...*and then you stopped."

"Did I?" He rubbed his chin. "Guess I ran out of awesome things to say about you."

She sputtered out a laugh. Preston was certainly funny and a bit of an odd duck. Probably best if they steered clear of future poetry talk. Sparring with him was more fun. "I bet your head's too busy cataloguing the gold bars in your diamond vault to keep track of all your errant thoughts."

He grinned. "You mean the gold watches in my ruby jewelry box."

She stuck her straw in her mouth and sipped the rest of her fruity drink, making extra sucking sounds at the end. He made a face. She sucked harder. "Do you actually have a ruby jewelry box?"

"Of course I do. Should I order you another strawberry slushie with a shot of insulin on the side?"

"Only if you order yourself the most expensive bourbon on the menu."

"Is that a challenge?" The gleam in his eye was too much.

She laughed. "You know it is."

He snorted and waved the waitress over. She was blonde and petite, wearing a bustier and slacks. Compared to the other servers, she was shy and soft spoken, pretty in a girl-next-door kind of way. The second Preston ordered his Scotch, she blushed something fierce. "No problem. I'll get right on that." She ducked her head, looked back once as she walked away, smiling at him.

Isla leaned forward. "She likes you."

He darted a glance to the pretty waitress then back to Isla. "She barely spoke to me."

"She had that shy, overwhelmed vibe about her, like she was smitten. You should ask her out."

He gave Isla an appraising look and ran his hand through his hair. "Aren't *we* out on a date?"

That might have been the intention, along with distraction. But there was no point pretending this might go somewhere. "Tell me honestly—do you feel chemistry between us? Like rip-my-clothes-off chemistry?"

He eyed her body. "You're hot."

"Not what I asked."

He peeked up at her bashfully. "You feel like a fun sister?"

She touched her nose. "Bingo."

"I really wanted to like you, though. You're the type of woman I pictured taking home to meet my family. I don't get what's missing."

The intangible thing that made relationships terrifying. The thing you couldn't name or bottle or choose. "That's sweet. And I wanted to like you, too," she said softly.

More to the point, she didn't want to like his client.

Two hours later, they were tipsy and laughing as they got off the elevator on her floor. Preston had secured a date with the sweet blonde, and they'd had an entertaining night. One she hoped would be repeated while in Vegas. But it would be back to the dating app for her. To find the impossible someone who thought and looked like Eric and acted like Preston when Preston wasn't showing off his money. Which was only about ten percent of the time. So ninety percent Eric and ten percent Preston.

Yeah, no problemo. That wouldn't be impossible to find.

She stopped at her door and punched her brotherly date in the shoulder. "That was fun, and you didn't have to walk me to my door."

"It's the gentlemanly thing to do. And it was fun. Especially since I left the night with digits. But I feel like I've failed you."

"If you make another daiquiri crack, I'm hightailing it back downstairs to tell blondie you still wet the bed."

He rolled his eyes and swatted at the air. "Drink whatever gross drinks you want. I mean the digits. I failed you on our quid pro quo. It's not fair that I met someone tonight, and you didn't. We need to find you a date. Someone who knows poetry."

She didn't mean to look at Eric's door. It was just down the hall, and Preston saying *quid pro quo* made her think of Eric's Latin learnings and the heart-melting kiss they'd shared. She immediately focused on the carpet, found the swirling gray pattern captivating. "Nope. No need. I'm good. I've got my dating app."

"Isla."

"So, I'll see you soon. Tomorrow, maybe? Or whenever. This was super fun." Yep, that carpet was *fascinating*.

Preston grabbed her arm before she could get her keycard from her purse. "You like Eric."

"What? No." Her laugh sounded brittle. "Don't be ridiculous."

He closed his eyes and muttered, "Holy shit. I'm such an idiot."

"You won't hear me arguing, and I'm turning in."

He didn't release her arm. "I'm an idiot because I didn't see what was right in front of my face." Concern replaced the cocky glint in his eyes. "You like Eric."

She wanted to keep lying, pull out of Preston's grasp. Pretend he didn't know what he thought he knew. But he totally knew what he thought he knew and she was a crappy liar. "Fine, I like him. But I can't date him."

"Because you hate boxing."

"Bingo, again. You're quick tonight."

He rubbed his brow and shook his head. "Yeah, well, not quick enough." He focused on her again, those concerned eyes now calculating. "There were some things you liked about me, right? On our dates? The flowers and restaurant and the romantic poems?"

"News flash: I'm not into you, money bags." And this night was going from odd to odder.

"I don't want to kiss you either, feisty. Just answer the question."

"Fine. *Yes.* Those things were actually fantastic, but the chemistry was—"

"Lacking. Yeah, I know. Which is why we need to have a serious talk."

He really was like an annoying big brother. She liked it,

kind of, and laughed at his antics, unsure what the heck he was getting at.

NEEDING MORE ice for his shoulder, Eric pulled his hotel door open, only to be faced with the last thing he wanted to see: Preston and Isla ending their date. He'd shut that stupid video down after he almost slipped and said something he shouldn't. He certainly didn't want to spy on them now. They were talking close, with Preston's hand on her arm. They spoke too low for him to hear their words, but the touch looked so intimate his stomach bottomed out. Dropped to his goddamn feet.

He kept out of sight but couldn't tear his eyes away.

Isla looked up at Preston and laughed, sweet and happy, then she opened her door and tipped her head, inviting him into her room. Preston followed. The door clicked shut behind them.

Eric slammed the flat of his hand into the door jamb.

He was right earlier. Nothing in his life was in his goddamn control, except this one thing: keeping away from Isla so she stayed happy and safe. And he had to live with the fallout. Accept Preston and her as a couple. Deal with seeing them together, flirty and affectionate. This was more than a sacrifice, though. This was some sick form of torture.

He'd go for another exhausting run tonight, a hard swim maybe. Try to burn that image of Preston following Isla into her room out of his head. Tire himself out so ruthlessly, dreams wouldn't breach his sleep.

18

"I'M SORRY, you're gonna have to repeat that. From the beginning. PowerPoint slides would be helpful." Heather practically had her face pressed against her computer screen as they chatted online.

It took all of Isla's energy not to flop on her bed. "I can't say it again. I can't believe this is my life."

"But it's the most romantic thing I've ever heard."

"There's nothing romantic about a guy telling another guy what to do and say on a date, basically lying to my face." And proving how perfect he was for her. The facts were unacceptable. Preposterous. So freaking unfair.

"This is the definition of romance, especially to a girl who orgasms from poetry. Forget the fact that he's a genius linguist, which basically means he's a master *cunni-linguist*, which is something you need to think long and hard about. He was baring his soul to you through someone else!" Heather inched back from her screen and lay on her stomach. Her blonde hair was tied in a knot on her head. She held a bottle of nail polish.

Bubblegum pink. "I just don't fully understand why he didn't tell you how he felt."

"He knows I hate boxing, which means I hate boxers." And she'd told him he'd been the cause of her panic attack. A partial truth that day. Her father's call had been the cause, but Eric had been a factor, and she was nervous to confess the ordeal to Heather. Shame still stewed in her gut. Embarrassment over her mental health issues, and the fact that she'd never shared her difficulties with her best friend.

Heather started painting her nails. "You may hate boxers, but the guy's gone out of his way to try and make you happy, even though it must have been crazy painful for him. Those aren't the actions of a guy who'd sit on the sidelines because you have an issue with his job."

"He didn't think I liked him then."

Heather froze mid-swipe of her nail polish. "*Didn't* think? As in past tense?"

Isla played the same statue game, furious her mind had betrayed her. "I mean *doesn't*. He *doesn't* think I like him."

"Ha. No. Don't try that bullshit with me, girly. *Didn't* means there's been a change in his understanding of the situation. Spill the details or I'm flying out there and will interrogate you by playing "Barbie Girl" on loop until your ears bleed."

Isla snorted, remembering the two of them having a Worst Songs of the Nineties dance party in their shared apartment, doing shots and devouring pizza. When "Barbie Girl" had played, Isla had plugged her ears and shouted lines from poems to save herself from the godawful song.

Heather pointed her pink-tipped nail polish brush at the screen. "You're lying to my face right now. If he knows you like him, and he's clearly smitten with you, why the hell is he letting another guy take you out?"

Last night, after Preston had confessed to asking for Eric's help the past weeks—planning their first date, choosing Preston's poetry, speaking to Isla through Preston in the bar—her heart had felt ready to burst. She should have been angry. She had been angry, but not at the guys. She'd been furious at herself. At her mother, her father. Everyone who'd turned her into what she was today: damaged goods. A woman too scared to pursue the most amazing man she'd ever met.

Feeling cheated, she'd thanked Preston for his honesty, but he hadn't been easy to shake. "You'll talk to him?" he'd pushed. "Tell him how you feel?"

"Shouldn't his manager be warning me away from his boxing client before a big fight? Aren't you worried about his focus?"

"I *am* worried about his focus. He's been off lately, distracted when training, and I think you're the reason. On a business level, staying apart would actually be worse for him. On a personal level, I love the guy and want him to be happy. You need to put Eric out of his misery and go out with him already."

The only reply she'd been able to form had been a sad, "It's more complicated than that."

Infinitely more complicated, and now she was staring at her best friend's beautiful face, trying to figure out how to share a secret she'd hidden their entire friendship. "I have issues," she told Heather.

"Tell me something I don't know."

Isla smiled, loving Heather's no-nonsense personality. "Remember those days when I worked at physio clinics and you'd ask me to go out? But I'd tell you I was tired or had a headache."

"And I felt like a jilted lover. But I get it. Those places worked you too hard, which is why you're gonna be your own boss."

Discomfort swirled through Isla's stomach. "Those places didn't work me too hard."

Heather's eyes widened. "Oh my God. Were you dating someone in secret? If the answer's yes, I'm definitely coming with the Barbie song."

Isla slumped forward, laughing under her breath, thankful for Heather. A best friend who could make her laugh, even in the most stressful times. A friend who might be upset with her shortly. Sighing, Isla said, "There was no secret lover. I actually suffer from..." She inhaled deeply, remembering the soothing feel of Whit's wrinkly skin under her hands, his slobbery kisses. "I suffer from panic attacks."

"Isla." The nail polish disappeared as Heather's face loomed large on the screen once again. "Since when?"

"Since I was a teenager."

"A teenager? Why didn't you tell me?"

"I was embarrassed?"

Heather's perfectly plucked brows drew together. "I'd never have judged you," she said softly.

Of course she wouldn't have. Isla had never questioned Heather's acceptance. Shame was the culprit. The self-loathing that came with weakness and led to secrets. "It was my issue, not yours. You're only the second person I've ever told. Well, no. The third."

"The third?" Heather's eyes and nose filled the screen now. "Do I have to unfriend you on Instagram?"

Isla laughed, but it sounded watery. "I should have talked to you about it. I just thought I had a handle on things."

"Because you're the daughter of Stubborn-Ass Slade and the apple didn't fall far from that immovable tree."

Heather's insight was more accurate than Isla cared to admit. Isla's father had kept her in the dark the past two years, not sharing his illness, barely letting her help him now. Since his bout of fatigue and nausea, he'd kept more distance from her, answering with short texts. Refusing to spend time with her.

Was it shame keeping him isolated, the way Isla had refused to share her weakness? Fear of what others would think? Were they so similar neither of them knew how to ask for help?

If that was the case, she had to stop running from her problems. She didn't want to end up like him, fighting issues on her own. Shutting herself in her room. Hiding who she was, warts and all. She'd been doing exactly that for years, the reality of her self-destructive behavior startling. And maybe, just *maybe*, if she quit keeping everyone in the dark, her dad would learn a thing or two from her.

She told Heather everything. From her first attack watching her dad fight, to the therapy that hadn't helped, to her learned techniques, the physio jobs that had brought it all back, and then about her father's Parkinson's.

"I knew there was a bigger reason you went on that trip." Heather propped her chin on her hand. "I hate you for not telling me, but I love you a whole lot, and love always wins. I wish I were there right now."

"Wish you were here, too. Dad listens to you more than he does to me sometimes. And we could have sleepovers."

"A Bad Eighties Music Dance Party this time."

Isla could use a ridiculous dance party, but she was also drained. In a good and bad way. Finally opening up to Heather was a huge weight off. The shame she'd expected to feel hadn't risen; the nervous rush of her pulse had slowed. Sharing the secret with her best friend was a relief on some levels, but her mind was still a tangled mess.

"I've fallen for Eric. Like, really hard. I told him as much and he feels the same. But when my dad called and I had that attack, my worry transferred to Eric. I pictured him in the ring, getting hurt, and I had a full meltdown. He kissed me, like the best kiss of kisses, but I ran out and we haven't talked about anything personal since."

"Was the kiss *Princess Bride* good?"

"*Notebook* in the rain good."

"Jesus. He's for sure a professional cunni-linguist."

Isla slumped forward and rubbed her eyes. She could *not* focus on that visual: Eric's wide shoulders between her legs, his tongue on her, hot breath, throaty sounds, brushes of his stubble. Would he whisper to her in Russian while devouring her? Say words in Hebrew or French?

She whimpered. "I think I need a shot."

"You and me both."

Isla fanned her overheating face with her hand. "He's too good to be true. Everything but the boxing. He has the power to bring my worst days back, but he also makes me incredibly happy. I feel so good about myself around him. And horny as hell. What do I do?"

"This is a tough one, sweet potato."

"Since when do you call me sweet potato?"

"I have a craving for sweet potato fries." Heather and her cravings. "What about therapy again? You said you didn't stick with it because you didn't like the therapist. Maybe try someone new?"

Isla was exhausted just thinking about dredging this all up again. As it stood, her hotel room was spotless, all her clothes neatly folded and put away. She'd rearranged the small amount of furniture twice. Avoidance and procrastination for the win. "Dating a guy shouldn't require therapy."

"Depends if the guy's worth it." Heather leaned forward and kissed the screen. "Gotta head to work. We'll talk later. Just see how you feel around him today. Don't make any rash decisions.

And if you have any more episodes or just need to vent about your dad, please call me."

Thrilled at not having to lie, she said, "I will. Love you."

They signed off, and Isla flopped back on the bed. She had no clue how she'd work with Eric after Preston's revelation. Eric understood her to the core and ticked all her ideal-man boxes. He'd told her, through Preston, that flowers would follow her, because they lifted their heads to the sun—the brightest light in the sky.

That was how he saw her: bright, beautiful, stubborn, strong, smart.

And she had to work with him shortly.

She left her room early, wanting to arrive at the gym first. Time to get settled and centered before she had to face him. She didn't trust herself to act normal, and she wasn't sure if she was ready to confront him with all she'd learned. She also couldn't quit picturing him in Preston's place at the bar, across from her at a table, holding her hand, whispering romantic words.

She walked by her father's door and scowled at it. Another man she'd have to deal with one day soon. Force him to open up the way she had with Heather. Quit fighting the world on his own. That would be as much fun as wrestling a hippo.

She hit the elevator button, feeling jumpy and nervous. The doors slid open and she stepped inside, her heart already pumping too fast. She just had to get through the casino and into the quiet of the gym. Clear her head. Play some music on her phone. Crappy eighties would be fun, but as the doors slid shut, a hand wedged between them.

A large hand.

Eric's big body followed, Whit trailing behind him.

So much for finding her center.

He moved to the wall opposite her, barely sparing her a

glance. She couldn't peel her eyes off of him, those thick thighs and huge calves. Hard muscles she'd be digging her thumbs into shortly.

"You planning on pressing the button?" Eric's voice was a low rumble.

She startled and glanced at his face. The mouthwatering view exacerbated her nerves. She stabbed the button for the lobby, forced what probably looked like a maniacal grin. *Nothing to see here. Just a frazzled woman doing her best Joker impression.* "Good night?"

His jaw knotted. "Fantastic. You?"

"Excellent!" Now she sounded like the Joker after sucking back helium.

Silence descended. Whit nudged up against her leg. She crouched to pet her new friend, while Eric stood rigid, seeming aloof. Distant. Nothing like the man who'd said *I know your dark eyes remind me of the horizon as the moon rises on a cloudless night, and I know you twitch your nose before you laugh, Isla. I also know how you...*

He also knew how she *what*? That unfinished line had driven her nuts all night.

She wanted to ask what he'd planned to say, what else he'd observed about her, but asking would require admitting she knew he'd been speaking through Preston, that she'd loved what he'd said, understood why he'd spoken about overcoming pain to experience love.

She cleared her throat. Neither of them spoke.

"silence
silence
silence
do you hear
how loud that is?"

Ramona Estle had a poem for every awkward moment of life.

The elevator stopped on another floor. Two women filed in and stood between her and Eric. One of them fawned over Whit. The other, a stunning redhead, looked at Eric from his feet to his head, blatantly checking him out. "You certainly make elevator rides more interesting."

Isla bit down on her molars. What kind of shitty luck had her stuck in an elevator, having to witness a woman hitting on the man she'd fallen for?

Note to self: avoid betting in the casino today.

Eric smiled at the woman, almost flirty, like Isla wasn't even there. "If I make the elevator more interesting, you need to get out more."

What Isla needed was to get out of their moving coffin. She was so far from centered she was surprised she hadn't toppled over.

The redhead moved closer to him. "Getting out sounds great. You free for a drink tonight?"

The elevator stopped on the main floor, but Isla's stomach kept traveling *down*, *down*, *down*, churning, making her ill. Jealousy in all its nauseating glory. She wanted to step between that woman and Eric. Tell her she'd never understand a man of his depth, give him what he needed. Unshed tears burned the backs of her eyes.

Eric watched Isla, a strange look on his gorgeous face, those sharp cheekbones and full lips too enticing. Even the dark smudges under his eyes were devastatingly attractive.

She tore her gaze away and hurried out of the elevator, not listening to his reply to the redhead's pickup. He'd for sure meet that woman. Why wouldn't he? She was beautiful, and as far as he knew Isla was dating Preston. This physio session with him was going to be some kind of fun.

19

"I'M FLATTERED," Eric told the pretty redhead, "but I'm in Vegas to work." He was dreading his physio session with Isla, though. Didn't understand why she'd looked upset just now. A confusing turn of events. Not that it mattered. He was tired of being affected by her. Analyzing her every blink and twitch.

The redhead pouted. "If you change your mind, I'm in room 517."

He wouldn't change his mind, but he might have to do something more drastic about Isla.

He grunted at the redhead, didn't risk smiling and being caught on someone's sneaky phone. He walked through the garish casino, the dinging bells a lullaby compared to his clanging thoughts.

If he wanted to win this match, he had to gather himself, quit this silent moaning over a woman he couldn't have. Give everything to his training. Win this for his family. But his mind kept skittering to Preston slipping into Isla's suite last night, the hurt in her eyes just now, and *fuck*. Normally he'd be focused on his body, his physio and training ahead. For some goddamn reason he couldn't shut everything out.

Maybe he should fire Isla. Try to get Gilpin back.

She did excellent physio work. Better than Gilpin at times, but Eric's focus had been off since arriving in Vegas. Exactly when he'd met Isla. Her distracting presence didn't fully explain why he'd felt down this morning, wishing he were at home, having a tea party with Eliza, instead of training to get his ribs punched. He'd rather be further into his Latin studies than grunting for fans. He'd rather be kissing Isla than any of those things, and he needed to get his head on straight.

A few fans stopped him as he crossed the casino. Asked for autographs, pictures. He played up his barbarian image, gave them what they wanted. The act made him feel sick.

At the door to the gym, he crouched and gave Whit a pat. "At least I have you, bud."

Whit nuzzled into his side, easing some of his tension. The second he walked past the security guard into the gym and saw Isla, he was back to agitated.

She was wiping down the treatment table, rubbing vigorously, like she needed to clean a blood stain. "Hey." She didn't glance at him. Just kept wiping. "We'll start with your Achilles. Work on lateral movement and endurance."

She turned, still not looking at him, and her hip knocked into the ultrasound machine. The gel tube hit the floor. She swore and bent to pick it up, then smacked her head on the table edge as she stood. "*Shit.*" She pressed her hand to her head, squeezed her eyes shut, and swore a few more times.

"You okay?" *You're fired*, is what he should say. Remove her from his life. Get back to normal and geared up for this match. But he'd never seen Isla this frazzled. Distressed, yes. Upset, yes. Frazzled and clumsy? No.

She rubbed her head some more, then slumped against the treatment table. "I'm clearly not okay."

He stepped forward. Pure instinct. *Go to her.*

She raised her hand. "Please, stay there. When you're near me I get muddled, and I need to be *un*-muddled for what I'm about to say."

Whit whined. Eric wanted to whine. He didn't understand why she'd seemed upset on the elevator, why she was twitchy and clumsy now, stewing over something she had to tell him. The way her night had ended with Preston, he'd expected her to be giddy and glowing. "Isla, what's going on?"

"What *isn't* going on?" Her tired voice trailed off.

He felt that weariness in his bones, and he suddenly regretted prodding her. He wasn't in any frame of mind to hear about whatever drama was going on with Preston. Not when the only thing he wanted to do was corner Isla against the treatment table and kiss her breathless. He certainly didn't have the stomach to fire her. "Let's cancel the session. I'll see you this afternoon."

He turned to go, but she said, "Wait."

He faced her, couldn't fathom why she was shaking slightly, red blotches dotting her cheeks. Another panic attack?

She shook out her hands and stood taller. "I wasn't sure I was ready to say anything, but I've apparently embodied a hopeless teenager and would rather not wind up with a broken leg when I get extra awkward around you and trip over a speck of dust. So..." She seemed to slow her breathing, then met his eyes. "I know you've been coaching Preston on our dates."

He flinched and dropped his gaze. Instinct had him wanting to raise his arms, block his body from incoming punches. There was no defensive pose to protect him from his bad choices. "I'm sorry. It was wrong and I—"

"I'm not mad," she said softly. "I mean, the move was

ridiculous, and I gave Preston a piece of my mind, but I'm more touched than mad. What you said to me, even through him—no one's ever made me feel that special."

He finally looked up. Saw longing, not anger on her face. Or was that wishful thinking? His heart kicked against his sternum, a desperate, hopeful pound, until he remembered last night. "Preston went into your room."

She frowned. "What?"

"Last night, I saw you. He went into your room after your date."

She nibbled her lip and fidgeted with her fingers. "That wasn't a romantic move. He came in to tell me what you guys had done, because I stupidly confessed to still being into you. And I am. Like off-the-charts into you, and learning you planned our first date and said all those beautiful words through Preston exacerbated how I feel. I want you so badly I'm in physical pain, but I'm still worried about how being with you will affect me. Then there was that whole elevator thing—watching you flirt with that redhead. Knowing you're going out with her is the absolute worst and working with you, seeing you now, I don't know how to do this with how much I feel."

He hadn't moved. Had barely breathed. His heart was about to pound out of his chest. He ached to erase the distance between them, but she'd asked him not to come closer. "I'm not going out with the woman from the elevator."

"She was beautiful," Isla said hesitantly.

"She's not you."

Tears shimmered in her brown eyes. "How do I do this?"

The question seemed rhetorical, directed more to herself than to him, but he wouldn't let its intention slip away. Not when he was so close to what he wanted.

Along with the stirrings of hope, his frustrations from the past weeks returned—the constant training and fighting and acting like a Neanderthal—when what he truly wanted was to study, maybe turn language into a real job. Could he do that? Walk away from this grind and unlock the secrets of language for others? Not right away, but after winning this fight maybe. The payout was huge. Maybe then he could start putting himself first.

He focused on Isla, her moon-rise eyes and cherry-blossom lips, her breathtaking beauty not nearly as enticing as her inquisitive mind. He soaked in this special woman and said, "I'll quit boxing."

An insane promise.

A future he'd never let himself contemplate.

With those words came a rush of utter *relief*.

IF THERE WASN'T a table at Isla's back, she'd have stumbled. Fallen ungracefully on her ass.

"You'll what?" She must have misheard Eric. Kept replaying his shocking words: *I'll quit boxing.*

He ticked up his strong chin. "After I win this match, I'll quit. You won't have to worry about dealing with the training and the fights. I'll just be a man, putting the woman he cares about first."

All the years she'd begged her father to quit boxing, he'd never entertained the idea. His first retirement had only happened because his vision had gone blurry.

After a particularly vicious match, the doctor had prescribed him steroids and told him to avoid punches. She'd been sixteen and thrilled for the reprieve, having convinced herself he was done boxing for good. Stupid sixteen-year-old naiveté. She'd doted on him and made his favorite salami sandwiches and talked about the fun things they'd do now that he didn't box: long drives in his fancy cars, a trip to New Orleans to see a fun magic act—The Marvelous Marlow Boys. He'd nodded along with her grand ideas, never promising anything, never explaining the retirement was temporary.

In her heart of hearts she'd known his intent. The knowledge hadn't stopped her from crumbling when he'd stood in front of her, his thick thumb gliding over his fisted knuckles, his square jaw pulsing as he'd avoided her eyes and broke the news: he was returning to the ring.

Now Eric stood before her, this brilliant, compassionate, incredibly strong man, offering her the one thing her father never had. "You'll quit boxing for me?"

"No." He massaged the back of his neck. "Not for you. I'm tired of the show and hiding who I am. I'm tired of squeezing studying in, instead of giving it my focus. I want to make a career out of it, maybe. Broaden my studies. Teach people languages or be a Russian translator and help people the way I helped immigrants when I was young. Honestly, I've barely thought it through, and it may feel sudden, but it isn't. This lifestyle's been eating at me for a while, making the Brick Smash image harder to stomach. But with this win, everything will change. I'll have enough money to support my family without worrying one hospital visit will set us back. I'll be home enough to be there for them when they need me. And..." He stepped closer, one small move, bridging the gap between them. "I can be with you."

Yes, she wanted to shout. *Yes, let's do this. I want to try.* But the brain was a complicated organ, and she'd barely begun to deal with her issues. Plus, there was a massive hole in his thoughtful, ridiculously perfect, too-good-to-be-true plan. "What if you lose the match?"

"I won't."

"You could."

He broke eye contact and paced, then stopped and faced her. "I *will* win. I'm hungrier and need it more. If I lose, I'll figure something out. It's time I make changes in my life."

Just like that. The man she wanted would change his life. For himself mainly. For her a little, the romantic gesture not lost on her. Either way, he was proving he wasn't a stubborn fool like her father. Swinging Graham Slade hadn't retired until forty-three. Old for a boxer. Eric was twenty-seven. If he retired after this match, that would be sixteen fewer years of punches to his head. Less likelihood of him developing a disease like Parkinson's. Not that anyone could guarantee a long, healthy life. But his choice to leave boxing would help his odds.

"I'm still scared," she said.

Another step closer. "I know. But I'm not going anywhere. We'll take this slow."

She gripped the treatment table at her back. "Like, really slow." Injured-turtles-walking-up-a-sand-dune slow. "And we can't be public about it until I stop treating you. I can't be seen dating a patient."

He took another step, then another. "So slow, *milaya*. And I'm fine keeping this quiet as long as needed." He stopped right in front of her, a tower of a man, gazing down at her with so much desire her stomach clenched. He threaded his fingers through hers, lifted her hand, kissed her knuckles. Soft lips, a hint of rough stubble.

She practically melted. "I told Heather this morning about the panic attacks."

"Yeah?"

"I think I'll try therapy again, look for a therapist I connect better with, which means I really can't rush this."

He released her hand and ran the tips of his fingers through her hair. The slight drag of his nails on her scalp sent shivers down her spine. "Take whatever time you need," he said, low and rough. "I'm not going anywhere. I won't push you for more than you can give until you're ready, but I don't want you pushing me away either. I'm done hiding how I feel."

Could she really do this? Get a handle on her anxiety and date a boxer?

"I like that plan," she said, her voice stronger than she'd expected. This *was* happening. It *would* happen. She'd be as brave as Eric and make a massive change in her life. Keep opening up to others and face her biggest fears.

He licked his full lips, looked at hers. More tingles erupted across her skin. If she wanted, she could fist the front of his shirt, drag him closer, taste him again. But giving into her desire wouldn't serve her. Getting too close too fast could instigate a panic attack before she'd found ways to better control her anxiety. She touched him, though. Trailed a finger down the length of his biceps.

The big man shuddered and blew out a ragged breath. "You're going to make this waiting painful, aren't you?"

She felt like a water dam about to crack. "What were you going to say, through Preston on our date, before you shut him out?"

He frowned as though he didn't know what she was referring to, then he said, "I know your dark eyes remind me of the horizon as the moon rises on a cloudless night, and I know you twitch your nose before you laugh. I also know how you taste and I can't go to sleep without thinking about the shape of your lips or the way your tongue felt sliding against mine."

Good Lord. Bad Lord. *All the Lords.*

Her belly tightened, heat flooding south.

"So," she said quickly, slipping out from between him and the treatment table. Now was not the time to turn into a pile of turned-on goo. Eric's fight loomed larger than ever. She desperately wanted him to win, and she had a part to play in his fitness. “Let’s get to work. We’ll focus on plyometrics—jumping exercises to push your Achilles. We need you in fighting form.”

He watched her a moment, a slow smile spreading. “Just tell me what you want me to do.” His voice was all honey and gravel, the simple statement hiding a world of innuendo.

If they weren’t working, and she wasn’t scared of having an episode, she’d tell him exactly what she wanted: to feel his hands sliding over her damp skin, digging into her hips, guiding her while he thrust so hard and deep she shattered into a million pieces. “Box jumps,” she said, hoarse. “We’ll start with those.”

His chest expanded on a deep inhale. “I’m all in.”

They somehow got to work, fell into their easy rhythm. She shouldn’t be surprised. Eric was a professional athlete. If anything, he seemed more focused than usual, regardless of the sexual tension vibrating between them.

“Focus on your knees,” she said as he jumped. “They’re collapsing in as you take off. Drive them out shoulder-width apart.”

He nodded, pushed through his last five jumps, fixing his positioning as he went.

“Rock star,” she said on his final landing.

Breathing hard, he smiled and walked toward her, grabbed his towel from the bench at her right. Where they’d given each other a wide berth while he exercised recently, he stood mere inches away now. Heat poured off him, his short breaths puffing up his chest.

“What’s next, boss?” He held his ground, not moving closer, but making it clear he intended to test her boundaries, invade her space, her heart.

Out of nowhere, she blinked, saw a sudden image of him in

the ring, his rough breathing turning harsher. Joe Bradley's fist sinking into Eric's ribs.

Her pulse rocketed, then Eric's knuckles were gliding down her arm, a soft brush—achingly tender—and the image vanished. All she saw was this incredible man, staring down at her with unrestrained emotion. His desire was clear in the heavy fall of his eyelids, but there was more swirling in those gray depths. The word *cherish* came to mind. Amazing, how quickly he could ground her, the lightest touch banishing her worries and lighting up her skin.

"Diagonal single leg hops," she said, back to being fluttery and overwhelmed with how badly she wanted to kiss him. "A zig-zag pattern over the taped line on the floor."

He didn't move right away. Just stared at her, his lips parting slightly. She wasn't sure what vibes she was giving off, but her body felt like it was a pheromone factory, every breath projecting the extent of her desire.

"Leg hops, it is," he finally said. He tossed his towel on the bench, crowded her as he moved, his huge hand landing on her lower back. "After you."

God, his voice did *things* to her. Thirst things. Molten-lava things, with nothing but a couple low-spoken words. Her belly did a delicious spin, and she couldn't resist one small move toward him, an angled twist that brought her lips toward his neck. She pressed a kiss to his damp skin, stole the tiniest taste of salt and Eric and everything she wanted.

He grunted, the pressure of his hand increasing briefly, then he stepped away. "You're testing all my strength today."

"Should I stop?"

"You better not."

Right, then.

In unison, they spun and strutted toward the taped line on

the floor, a simultaneous decision to get to work. And they did. Eric pushed himself through his exercises, once again switching to athlete mode, his single-mindedness the reason he was a heavyweight contender. Occasionally, he'd brush against her—a subtle press of his hand on her hip, a drag of his fingers along her skin as he grabbed his water bottle or towel—and heat would flood her body. But they worked hard, the familiar routine reminding her how fantastic they were together: they could rein in their sexual tension, support each other professionally. Give each other the best of themselves so they both thrived.

They finished on the treatment table, as usual. Ultrasound for his rotator cuff this time. He was more relaxed, his legs sprawled slightly apart, contentment on his face. "I like this part," he said.

She loved this part, especially today. Being close to him, feeling secure in their mutual feelings, no secrets between them. Except there was one, she remembered in a rush: her father's illness, which would be harder to hide as she and Eric got closer. Eric still believed he'd been the only source of her last panic attack.

"Of course you like this part," she said, wishing she could confide in him. Sharing her dad's Parkinson's would have to wait until after his match. "This is probably the only time you sit still."

"That's not the reason. I get to watch you. Have your hands on me."

There were those butterflies again, dipping and diving and fuzzing up her brain. "As long as I don't massage your thighs." But she'd love a repeat of the last time, watching the large bulge in his shorts display proof of his desire.

He shrugged. "Won't mind now. As long as you don't mind my body's reaction."

She darted a look at his groin, and hunger tugged at her

fiercely. With her history of dating hipster types, she'd never had sex with someone this big and strong. Incredibly muscular, *everywhere*. What would it feel like to have all that power pushing into her? To fall to her knees and take him deep into her mouth?

"Did they fix the paint color in your office bathroom?" he asked, smooth and easy, clueless to her wild fantasies. Or maybe he wasn't clueless. His shorts were tented slightly, and his eyes were all heavy-lidded fire, scorching a path over her body. Still, he was offering her control. Keeping their pace slow and gradual, making sure she was okay.

She blinked hard, forced a few steadying breaths. "This week. But the website's giving me a headache. I need it running before I get home."

"I can help you."

It was such a simple offer, kind and generous. One minute he looked ready to devour her, the next he was being a thoughtful friend, their sexual tension returning to a simmer. More proof taking this step with him had been the right decision. "I forgot you were a tech genius, Rick Rosner."

"Are you asking me to strip for you, Isla Slade?"

She liked that he picked up on her joke right away—Rick Rosner's high IQ and odd stripping history their own private joke. She wanted more in-jokes with Eric, for them to glance at each other from across a crowded room, one smile or raised eyebrow filled with a novel's worth of communication. For now, she'd revel in their shared feelings. Being open and honest with each other for the first time. "Stripping in due time. Until then, I'd love the website help. Maybe we can work on it tonight."

"Count me in." But he stiffened slightly. A tiny shift, impossible to miss while she moved the ultrasound probe over his skin.

She studied his furrowed brow. "Does something hurt?"

He fidgeted on the table, adjusted his position slightly. "Is your dating profile still live?"

Oh. Jealousy. Insecurity. From this man the world called Brick Smash.

She focused on her hands moving as they should, tried to get the ground to settle below her feet, while the rest of her wanted to float away. "I'll be deleting it after this session."

His body softened in an instant. "Good," he said, gruff.

20

ERIC FLICKED between the two screens on his laptop, unsure which background option worked best for Isla's website. "Sticking with white is clean and classy, but the textured dark green is also cool. Gives off a nature vibe. Which do you like better?"

When Isla didn't reply, he glanced at her. She was beside him on his hotel room couch, her legs tucked under her. Instead of watching his screen, her eyes were locked on him, hazy as though lost in a dream.

"Yes?" she said, her voice rising in uncertainty.

He smiled, a rush of heat pushing at his ribs. They'd made solid progress building her website tonight, had figured out the general layout and pages needed. He loved brainstorming with Isla, watching her scrunch her nose when puzzling through a problem. He also loved that she'd been distracted at times, watching him with that hazy, blissed-out expression.

Sitting next to her hadn't been easy for him either—the delicate smell of eucalyptus teasing him, the soft brush of her body when she'd lean over him to point at his laptop screen.

Around her, he was on the constant edge of arousal, but he was determined to keep his wants on the backburner. Support her and her business any way he could.

Messing with her distracted state was a different story. "I knew you'd like the idea. We should get going before they close. I'll just be there for moral support, though. I won't get in the shark tank."

She froze. "Shark tank, what?"

"I'll take lots of pictures. You can put one up at your office."

"I don't do sharks."

"But you just said *yes*. I showed you the shark activity on my screen and asked if you wanted to dive in that tank, and you said yes."

Her gaze shot to his laptop, where her website-in-progress loomed. "You are such a liar."

She shoved his shoulder playfully, a teasing glint in her eye. Then she pinched his side. On most people, the cute move wouldn't have much of an effect. But Eric jumped. He was unbearably ticklish, a fact his niece and nephew lived to exploit.

Isla's eyes grew wide, shining with glee. "This is my lucky day." She dug in, going for his armpits, wiggling her fingers, making him laugh, until his control snapped.

"Not so lucky." He manhandled her, fended off her attack and caught her wrists, pinning her to the couch. He realized the predicament too late: how close they were, his thigh pressing between her legs, his growing hard-on straining against her hip. She made a small, needy sound that fucking *undid* him, and he rotated his hips, couldn't control the answering move. Both their smiles slipped, their chests rising faster as heat shot to his groin.

"So you're ticklish?" she said, her soft voice turning throaty.

Being ticklish was the furthest thing from his mind right

then. He needed to pull it together. Get his body under control. He forced his hips to still, but he couldn't hide how hard he was, flush against her. "If you tickle me again, you'll lose every time."

Or win. If she let him, he'd kiss his way down her body now, spread her open, taste her, lick her until she dissolved in pleasure. But tonight wasn't about giving into the sparking attraction between them. Only this morning Isla had decided to overlook his boxing and give him a chance. She needed time to adjust, figure out how to deal with her anxiety before things moved too quickly between them.

He released her and pushed up, adjusting himself as he stood. "You're distracted." And beautiful and sexy, and *damn* she smelled so good. "We should take a break." Or a cold shower...together—wet, soapy, naked. Another sharp pulse flooded his cock. He gritted his teeth, couldn't remember the last time he'd been this desperate for a woman. Even as a teen he'd had more control.

Music drifted through the wall, some old jazz from his neighbor's room. Music he loved.

Rubbing against Isla on the couch was a monumentally bad idea, but he couldn't seem to move far from her. Or quit fantasizing about her. And an urge struck. Unable to control the impulse, he turned to her and held out his hand. "May I have this dance?"

"Dance?" Her attention drifted to the wall, where the music was loudest. When she looked back at Eric, her cheeks were pink. "I took hip-hop as a kid, not fancy ballroom."

"My mother taught me how to dance. I'll lead you." Hold her the way he should, tenderly, not rutting against her hip like an animal. Prove she'd made the right choice by letting him in.

"Okay," she said quietly. Almost bashful.

He helped her up from the couch, led them to the carpeted

space by the large windows. Vegas lights shone below; jazz drifted around them. He held her close, one hand pressed to her lower back, the other linked with hers. Occasionally her steps faltered, but he adjusted his rhythm, made sure she caught up and swayed with him.

"We should be dressed fancy for this," she said. "In a tuxedo and ball gown."

He didn't love wearing suits. For Isla, he'd happily button up. "You'd have to choose mine for me. I don't do style well. Not like Preston."

"Considering I crimped my hair when I was young and wore a pink velour track suit on the regular, I probably shouldn't be your style consultant."

He laughed. "I need photographic evidence."

"Only if you share your worst style crimes, assuming you served time for bad taste." Her hand drifted over his upper back, tracing random patterns.

His body was back to defying him, but he didn't fight the burn this time. There was something special about waiting—the anticipation, the flare of desire sparking in his gut. Excitement in the delayed gratification. "I was charged and sentenced by Rosa. I wore this chunky fake gold chain every day, thought it was the height of cool. According to her it was *tacky as hell*. And I had a mullet."

She snorted, rested her head against his chest. "Oh, yeah. We're definitely swapping embarrassing photos. The mullet must be seen."

"What's the worst date you've ever been on?" He was eager for more from Isla. The bits and pieces of her history. Her worsts. Her bests. Every detail in between.

"A dude thought taking me to his ex's wedding to make her jealous would be smart."

"No."

"I ditched him when he went for the ass grab on the dance floor."

Eric's fingers twitched, wanting to do exactly that. Reach lower, fill his palms with Isla. He also loved this, dancing together, laughing, talking. Complete ease, like their afternoon shopping in the promenade, but better. "I took a woman to dinner who insisted on proving she could stick her toe in her mouth while at the table."

Isla tipped her head up, looking so fucking amused. "I assume there was no second date."

"Hell no." He spun Isla faster, a whirl that had her smile spreading wider. His sternum warmed, then the music died, but Eric didn't stop. He held her closer, hummed a Russian song, sang the words softly as he continued to dance.

Isla melted against him. "I'm sorry."

He had no clue why she'd be sorry. He couldn't be happier, holding her like this. "Are you apologizing for stepping on my feet?"

"Oh, you mean like this?" She stepped on both his feet, forcing him to carry her as they danced. He spun them faster. She laughed, then adjusted herself back onto the floor. "I'm sorry I'm making us wait. That I'm not ready for more yet."

"If we rush things and it sets you back or I lose you because of it, I'll never forgive myself. Waiting is testing my willpower. I won't lie about that, but it's worth it, and it's kind of fun. As long as I know where your heart's at, I'm in no rush."

She ran her nose over his collarbone. "We can't be like this in public, though. No touching or flirting."

No, they couldn't. And it sucked. "Or tickling," he added.

He could feel her smiling against his chest. "Or tickling. But jokes are still a must. I can't live without those."

Taking her cue, he said, "What's the best thing about living in Switzerland?"

She quit dancing and looked up at him. "Did I miss the segue into this conversation?"

He pulled her closer, forced her feet to move again. "Just answer the question, Slade."

"You're annoying, Kramarovsky. And I can't, since I've never lived there."

He turned them in a tighter circle. "Me neither, but I hear the flag is a big plus."

She unleashed one of her snorts—adorable and carefree. "You're hopeless."

Hopelessly into her, yeah. The coming days would be a challenge. He wanted to shower Isla with affection, show her how much he cared anywhere and everywhere. But he'd never jeopardize her job. "What if, when in public, we say the opposite of what we're thinking?"

She nuzzled deeper into him as he hummed and they swayed. "Like...I hate how cold and uncomfortable I feel dancing in your stiff arms?"

He grinned, more pleased than he should be by the twisted-up admission. He sang a few lines, thought about what he loved most about this moment: dancing in a hotel room with Isla, his laptop filled with their teamwork, Whit dozing on his bed. He thought about what the changes ahead truly meant for him, and how talking about poetry and studying with Isla had been such a novelty. Such a beautiful gift. "I hate that you don't get me at all," he said.

She stilled. So suddenly, he stumbled. But he caught them, swung her fast and loose, finishing with a dip that had her arching over his arm.

"Do you really feel that way? That I get you?" The question sounded timid, her beautiful face full of so much adoration, his heart squeezed.

He lifted her up, held her close. "I've never felt like this with anyone, Isla. Like I'm better with you. Like I'm dying—"

"To learn every detail about your life and figure out your most ticklish spot and which side of the bed you sleep on and if you prefer the beach or a pool and if you like horror movies and butter on your popcorn."

Yeah, they were completely in sync, both of them greedy to spend time together, learn every detail about each other. Their worsts and bests. He rubbed his hand up and down her back. "In answer to those questions: armpit, left, beach, no, yes. And I plan to spend many hours grilling you. For now, we should get back to work."

She sighed. "Probably a good idea. I promise not to get as distracted this time."

He kissed the top of her head. "I'll never complain about you staring at me. But next time, the shark tank is happening."

"Not in this lifetime, Mullet Boy."

"Don't test me, Velour Girl."

Laughing, they got back to work, sitting side-by-side, touching easily, giving Whit attention when he waddled over for a pat. Yeah, Isla understood him in a way no woman before had, but as the night wore on, and he helped her with her new business, he realized the inspiration to that admission was bigger than their common interests and attraction. It was the utter peace of being with someone who made you feel comfortable in your own skin. Wholeness you suddenly couldn't live without. If being with Isla felt this amazing now, he couldn't imagine the spell he'd fall under when they took their relationship to the next level.

21

Isla walked toward her hotel, sunglasses on, the chatter from milling tourists cheerful and uplifting. She'd never have imagined leaving a therapy session feeling this relaxed and happy, but there was no denying the utter freedom buoying her steps. She felt lighter than she had in years.

The hotel concierge had helped her find a lovely woman who kept walk-in appointments open for tourists. They'd had three sessions this week, filled with lengthy talks about her childhood and father and mother and everything developing with Eric. A flood of tears and release had accompanied each session, but so had a swell of inner strength, the building blocks of wellness. There would be setbacks, no doubt. She'd spent so long suppressing her fears, they were bound to pop up when least expected. Her father's health situation certainly wasn't doing her any favors.

For now, she felt as though she were a better version of herself. A woman who could offer Eric more. Be with him and know if she faltered, she had people—Heather, a therapist, a man who knew most of her issues—to go to for help. She was no longer in this alone, and Eric would be leaving boxing soon.

An itch of doubt surfaced. A warning that she should wait until he actually quit. Not get in deeper until he was free and clear of boxing. But she was tired of letting her mind rule her choices. All these years she'd been a victim of her anxiety. It was time to take charge. Be a hurricane. Maybe she'd change her relationship status with Eric tonight, from friends taking it slow to a man and woman insatiable for each other. Show up at his hotel door, wearing nothing under her robe. Or some sexy lingerie. Watch his face transform as he realized she was ready for everything with him.

She smiled to herself as she walked, loving the feeling of the sun warming her skin. Delicious fantasies warmed her body.

She pushed inside her hotel as a woman said, "Does anywhere here serve fried bologna sandwiches?"

Isla whipped off her sunglasses and did a little jump. She'd know that voice anywhere. "I can't believe you're here."

Heather spun around and beamed. "Of course I'm here."

No other explanation was needed. Heather was her best friend. They'd spoken every night since Isla had confessed the mess that was her life. Who else would drop everything and fly to Sin City to show her support...and eat a fried bologna sandwich.

They hugged and laughed. Heather pulled back and frowned. "Your eyes are puffy."

"Therapy session. There were tears, but it was good."

"I like the sound of that, and I love the madness of this place. Can't believe I've never been to Vegas. I'm only here for two days, but you need to show me everything, including the hunky boxer."

A non-hunky boxer joined them and crossed his arms. Isla's father regarded Heather. "This is a nice surprise."

"Then why aren't you smiling?"

"I am." He stared at her with his usual half-snarl.

Heather laughed. "I missed your face, Graham."

The corner of his lips twitched. "Nice to see you, too."

Throngs of tourists bustled around them, the doors in constant motion as people came and went. Where the busyness had irritated Isla at times while in this nutty town, today the action elevated her mood. Even while facing her stubborn-ass father.

"Did you have a good morning?" she asked him tentatively. He hadn't called her again to cover for him, but she was still on edge, waiting for a sign that he was unwell.

Instead of being annoyed with her prodding, he relaxed his stance and squeezed her arm. "Feeling great, Princess. We should all do dinner tonight. I like seeing what Heather orders to eat."

Heather pursed her lips. "I'm not sure if I should be offended."

A wheezy sound came from his damaged nose: the hint of a laugh. "You're impossible to offend."

"True. But I'm only in if the boxer joins us."

He frowned. "I am joining you."

"Not you, big man. The *other* boxer." Heather gave Isla a nudge and bawdy wink.

Isla cringed and snuck a look at her dad. She hadn't mentioned the Eric Development to him, wasn't sure how he'd react.

On cue, his gaze snapped to Isla. "Is something going on with you and Brick?"

"Maybe?" *Definitely* if spending every night together this week and flirting shamelessly counted as something. But she hadn't planned to tell her father about Eric until after the fight, when her dad wouldn't worry she'd spill his big secret to the man she was dating. A man who was his employer.

He clasped her arm and dragged her away from Heather. "How long has this been going on?"

"Nothing's going on yet." She poked her head around his thick body and gave Heather an apologetic smile. "Excuse us while my father behaves rudely."

"That's okay," Heather said. "My stomach will just eat itself while I wait for you." She pulled out her phone and strolled away.

Swinging Graham Slade didn't relent. "Don't lie to me, Isla."

Said the man who'd lied to his daughter's face *for two years*. "Eric and I like each other, but we're taking it slow. And before you say anything, I haven't said a word about your health. So don't go freaking out about that."

His wide nostrils flared, the wheezy sound more angry than amused this time. "You can't date him."

She shrugged out of his grip. "Why the hell not?"

Not only was she ready to test her boundaries with Eric, they'd had an amazing week together. Their physio work had been peppered with more laughter and teasing touches. They'd spent their nights in his hotel room, poring over her website construction, bouncing ideas off each other, or just reading while Whit rested his head on Isla's lap and they ordered room service. The sexual tension was ever-present, stretching as Eric would lean over her to pat Whit, or when she'd teasingly pinch Eric's side, pretending she was about to tickle the hulking boxer. Through it all, they were developing an incredible friendship.

"He's a fantastic guy," she told her dad.

"You started your own physio practice to avoid boxers. You tell me all the time how much you hate the sport. You can't date him." His voice rose as he spoke and red slashed his cheeks.

She'd expected him to worry that she'd inadvertently spill his secret, put his job in jeopardy. This anger came from a different place. Worry for Eric's focus likely. "Whatever's going on between us, it's not affecting his training. If anything, he's been more driven lately."

His workouts had grown more intense the past few days, his runs longer, his sparring more aggressive. The stakes on this match had risen for Eric—the massive life change a win would offer. A flush bank account to ease his transition to regular citizen. If he lost, he'd still quit. He'd said as much, and she'd seen his sadness and dissatisfaction with his current life, how much he loved books and learning and language. Studies he was meant to pursue. Facts she couldn't share with her father, but he couldn't deny how in the pocket Eric had been these days.

But he glared at her so hard, she felt like an opponent in his ring. "You will not date him."

Not a rebuttal on Eric's focus. Just pure, unfiltered anger, and Isla was at a loss. "You're the one who didn't want me internet dating. You even set me up with Preston."

His square jaw flexed. "You will not date Brick."

"You have no say in who I date. Besides, Eric's kind and smart and loving. I can't imagine what your issue is with him."

He gripped her upper arms fiercely, as though she might slip through his fingers. "He's your client. I'm pretty sure there's a rule about that. He's also a boxer, Isla. I don't want that for you. What your mother dealt with. What you *are* dealing with. I don't want this life for you."

Oh. Wow. That. An admission she'd never have imagined. Not in a million years. Tears threatened, another burst of emotion on an already emotional day. She'd thought she'd been cried out at today's therapy session. Apparently not.

She wished she could tell him he didn't have to worry, that Eric wouldn't be a boxer for much longer. She also understood his concern. If Eric hadn't offered her a future without him in the ring, she'd have been too scarred from her father's Parkinson's to make that leap of faith and risk her heart for Eric. Dealing with her panic attacks was one thing. A mountain she felt she would and *could* eventually climb. Dealing with another man whose health would likely deteriorate because he'd been too stubborn to see the consequences of his brutal sport?

No, she wouldn't have been okay with that.

She removed one of her father's big hands from her shoulder and kissed his palm. "I know what I'm doing, Dad. Eric is a short-term patient. We'll keep things quiet until after his fight. And as much as I fought falling for him, it was inevitable. He's incredible, and he's not you. You need to trust me on this."

Trust that she wouldn't set herself up for this life again.

He slumped and sighed. "I don't like it, but I guess I'm not surprised. You always liked the intellectual guys."

Heather came over and slid her arms around both their waists. "Can we continue this super-secret conversation at a restaurant? I'm starving. I'll even put in earbuds and pretend I'm not eavesdropping."

Isla's dad chuckled. "As entertaining as that would be, I have a meeting with Preston, then a training session with Brick." To Isla he said, "You can skip this afternoon's physio, if you want. Catch up with Heather. I'll see you both tonight."

He held Isla's eyes a moment longer, then he left. She couldn't tell what was going through his mind, but she was glad he knew about her and Eric. She also liked the idea of all of them out to dinner tonight and of an afternoon with Heather. Hopefully Eric would feel the same.

"Give me a sec," she told Heather as she pulled out her phone. According to Eric's schedule, he'd be in his room eating lunch while studying.

"It better be a second," Heather said. "I'm antsy and need to eat and explore." She fluffed her blonde hair and smiled at a cute guy walking in.

With Heather occupied, Isla focused on her phone.

Isla: **Can we cancel this afternoon's physio?**

Eric: **Everything okay?**

He was immediately concerned for her, not his lost session. Time and again, Eric earned her trust.

Isla: **Heather came for a surprise visit.**

Eric: **Does this mean I get to meet your best friend?**

Isla: **Dinner tonight. With my dad too...who actually knows we're doing whatever it is we're doing.**

Eric: **Shit.**

Isla bit her lip, unsure if that was an angry shit or a nervous shit. She also didn't like thinking about this much shitting.

Isla: **What's wrong?**

Eric: **Now I'm nervous to see him.**

She smiled at his worry. If Isla had to guess, her father wouldn't say much to Eric about their involvement. He'd keep their training professional, keep his golden boy focused on the tasks at hand. She wanted to put Eric at ease, though. Not just for him. She was frustrated with the snail's pace of their relationship. Nothing about their involvement had followed a typical get-to-know-you schedule. Working together twice a day, spending nights together the past week, had accelerated their emotional attachment. There was no game playing between them. No waiting to call or wondering if Eric was into her. All their chips were on the table, neither of them questioning the other's intent, and she was starting to resent leaving his room at night.

Heart racing, she typed her message.

Isla: **Will it make you less nervous if I tell you I plan to sneak into your room tonight, wearing nothing but my bathrobe?**

Dots bounced to indicate a reply. They disappeared. Reappeared.

Eric: **Don't rush this if you're not ready.**

Again, always putting her first.

Isla: **Not the sexy reply I was hoping for, Rick Rosner. And I'm ready. For you and everything that comes with that decision.**

More dots. There, then gone.

Eric: **My craving for you is ether. Seeping into me, bleeding out from me. Consuming me with insatiable hunger. Our story begins in a burst of flames. If you sneak in here, you better be sleeping over, *milaya*.**

Hello, rapacious desire. Nice to make your knee-buckling acquaintance.

Who else but Eric would woo her with seductive poetry, his creative mind one of the many reasons this decision felt so right. And *milaya*. She hadn't asked what the intimate word meant. She loved when the guttural syllables slipped past his lips and couldn't wait to get ready for tonight: dinner with her favorite people, an intoxicating evening showing Eric she was all in. Nervous but excited, she pocketed her phone.

22

"HANDS UP, you fucker. You're tripping over your fucking feet." DeAndre danced around the ring, his pads in Eric's face, saying *fuck* every chance he got. "You like being slapped on the fucking head?"

This was target practice. DeAndre moved his pads around for Eric to jab or cross or hook, being unpredictable, often swatting Eric's head. Timing. Speed. Reflexes. "Fuck, man. *Hands.* The circus will be here in twenty fucking minutes. Show me some fucking hands."

DeAndre made a "pop, pop, pop" sound as Eric's fists connected with his moving pads. Eric blocked, ducked, sidestepped. Tried to anticipate DeAndre's next move, while protecting himself. Breath, speed, pads, fists. The beauty of his body moving like he could predict the future.

Graham worked Eric differently than DeAndre. He focused more on the mental approach, getting Eric's mind ready and focused. DeAndre was aggressive, relentless. The yin to Graham's yang. Both trainers were integral and often fed off each other. This afternoon's session had Graham on the sidelines, shouting directions: *Watch DeAndre's upper body. How are his feet planted? Is he leaning to his left or right? Where will he hit next? Think before you act.*

Eric slid a look Graham's way, wondering if he was happy about him being with Isla. Or pissed off. There was no knowing with the man. He hadn't said a word since Eric had gotten Isla's texts today.

DeAndre slapped Eric in the head with another, "Put your fucking hands up."

"You're distracted," Graham yelled. "Get it together."

Eric was slightly distracted. Hard not to be when Isla teased him with promises of unwrapping her beauty tonight. And Graham just stood there, not a word to Eric about dating his daughter. Eric shook his head and dug in. *Train. Focus. Work hard. Win that damn match*. Those were the only thoughts he should entertain.

He danced around DeAndre, went at it for another ten minutes.

"Fucker," DeAndre mumbled as he snuck in another head slap. "And your time's up. Let the fucking circus fly."

On cue, a security guy at the door let waiting reporters into the training gym, their cameras up and ready. Eric was dripping, his lungs pumping hard. He held up his hands to go another round with DeAndre. The press liked him like this: grimacing, already sweating buckets, like he'd run a marathon. Anything for publicity. Even chopping wood like an asshole.

After the show and shots, Eric answered a few questions. Snarled *Brick Smash* and glowered at the cameras. He sucked back water, then showered. No longer reeking of sweat, he walked into the locker room, exhausted and sore, wearing nothing but a towel, only to be confronted with Graham's hard-knocks glare. "Hurt her and you deal with me. And you better keep your focus." He marched out.

Eric stood frozen, blinking at the empty room, his pulse back to racing. He was glad Graham had broached the topic, even if it was more of a blunt warning than a discussion. An ultimatum Eric could get behind. If he hurt Isla, he'd happily walk into Graham's big fists. Eric hoped she wasn't getting ahead of herself. That she was ready for the closeness that came with sex. It was her choice alone at this point. If she snuck into his room later, he wouldn't have the strength to turn her away.

He went up to his room, relaxed a bit with a book, took Whit for a walk, then got dressed for dinner. When going on first dates, Rosa often told him to wear his gray crewneck sweater. She said it was soft to touch and fitted enough to show off his assets. *Girl catnip* had been her words. Since he wasn't a style-addict like Preston, he took Rosa's advice. The gray sweater, dark jeans. A pile of nerves about the night ahead.

He left his room and walked down the hall to Isla's door. Took a deep breath, then knocked.

"I'll just be a sec," she called, giving him more time to fidget.

When she finally opened the door, he blew out a rough breath. She wore a blue-green dress, low cut. Her hair was loose with its slight wave, brushing her shoulders. Pink lips. Dark-lined eyes. Rosy cheeks and days of sex appeal.

"*J'ai eu un coup de foudre*," he murmured. French words, the romantic sounds perfect for Isla.

She looked at him like he was something fantastic. He could soak up that look all day.

"What does that mean?" she asked.

"That I have a crush on you." More specifically, that lightning could strike. Love at first sight, though there had been no love, let alone like, at their first meeting. Only frustration and irritation on his side. Now? There was no denying the intensity of his feelings.

She blushed and placed her hand on his arm, her eyelids falling slightly. A door down the hall slammed shut and she snatched her hand back. "That's an awful sweater. Looks horrible on you."

He stiffened. Then he remembered his suggestion, that they should say the opposite of what they were thinking when in public. He smirked. "I hate that birthmark on your neck."

Her fingers drifted up to her elegant neck, feathered over the spot he loved. Her heated gaze dipped down his body. "You might want to curb your calorie intake. You're looking flabby around the middle."

"Your lips are too full."

"Your intense eyes are unattractive."

He fought a laugh. "Your soft voice grates on my nerves."

She dragged her teeth over her enticing bottom lip. "When you speak in other languages, my eardrums hurt."

Now all he wanted to do was whisper to her in Russian and French, tell her how much he "hated" every beautiful thing about her. "We better go before this ends in a brawl."

"Excellent point." She closed her door and strutted ahead of him. "Wouldn't want to embarrass you by knocking you on your ass."

He took an eyeful of *her* ass from behind. "Are we picking your father up or is he meeting us?"

"He's meeting us in the lobby. Heather's staying on the other side of the hotel. He said he'd wait with her."

Eric met Isla's stride, walking with a slight distance between them. Close enough that their hands nearly brushed, the air between them moving with each swing of their arms, static charges vibrating with electricity. A delicate whiff of eucalyptus inflamed his senses.

"You smell awful," he said.

She made that cute snorting sound. "I wish those jeans didn't emphasize your weird thighs."

"Weird?"

"Lumpy."

He chuckled. "I'll have to up my exercises."

He pressed the elevator button. Loved feeling Isla's teasing energy next to him, both of them amused and happy. When the doors opened and revealed a blessedly empty elevator, his playful mood morphed into hunger.

Once inside, he quickly pulled her against his body. "You're driving me crazy."

"You look insanely sexy in that sweater."

Unable to wait, he leaned down and kissed her. A rough press of their lips as he hauled her closer. They moaned in unison—rasping sounds of starved impatience. She gripped his biceps, kept moving her fingers, whether to feel the softness of his sweater or the muscle below, he wasn't sure. Either way, he was thankful for his exhaustive workouts and strict diet. He fucking *loved* pressing his non-lumpy thigh between her legs.

The second the elevator stopped at the main floor they broke apart.

He wiped her lipstick from his lips. "Those sexy sounds you make are a real turn off."

Cheeks red, she fixed her hair. "You definitely didn't make me so wet I can barely walk."

He groaned and bit the inside of his cheek. That was not a visual he could handle before a family dinner. Time for a safer topic. "Did you and Heather have fun this afternoon?"

They walked off the elevator, both adjusting their clothes, trading heated looks.

"Heather did a marathon worth of selfies, and we found fried bologna sandwiches at this diner place and laughed our faces off at drunk tourists." She glanced over at him, licked her lips slowly, like she could still taste him. "It was a blast."

Although she was talking about her afternoon with Heather, the last words came out husky. And *fuck*, he wanted her. More than a quick kiss in an elevator. He wanted to tease and touch Isla in private, where he could confess a fraction of what he loved about her: her spark of vitality when she talked poetry, the quirk of her lips when she gave Whit a loving pat, the way the curves of her body filled out that short dress, the soft flutter of her eyelashes and her delicate nose and her slightly crooked middle finger, because he was that far gone. He ached to push into her, feel her contract around him, pulling him deeper into her body. He also wanted to spend time with her family, learn everything possible about this singular woman. So he thought about boxing and changing the twins' diapers and did his best to get his body under control.

When they spotted Graham and Heather in the lobby, she smiled at her favorite people. "Heather, this is—"

"The linguist you've been mooning over. Nice to finally meet the man who is *not* publicly dating his physiotherapist."

He laughed at Heather, who fit Isla's description to a tee: exuberant, confident, and blunt. "I'm lucky to be *working* with the best, and I'm thrilled to meet you." He was also thrilled she'd called him a linguist, not a boxer. He was touched Isla had described him like that to her best friend. He slid his attention to his trainer. "Nice to see you socially, Graham."

Graham grunted.

Isla punched her father in the arm. "Be nice or don't come."

"I was being nice."

"It's true," Heather said as she took Graham's arm. "When he's not being nice, his lips shrivel more."

They walked out of the hotel, joking and chatting, Graham

less verbose, but not overtly challenging. Eric had to restrain himself from taking Isla's hand.

The restaurant they walked to was lively without being garish, with a low ceiling and wood-panelled walls. "I have to pee," Isla told Eric, as their waiter came to take their order. "Order me the ribeye."

He liked ordering for her, as though they were on a proper date, even with Heather and Graham and their no-public-flirting rules. He did as she'd asked. Added, "Cooked well done," then ordered himself the salmon.

When she returned to the table, she immediately said, "I forgot to tell you how I like my steak."

He helped her with her chair. "I told the waiter well done. If I got it wrong, I'll go grab him." He was pretty sure he'd overheard her preference when he'd snooped on her date with Preston. A fact he could laugh about now.

She gave him that look again, the one that said: *you're fantastic*. "You know how I like my steak."

He leaned closer and whispered, "I know a lot about you, Isla Slade."

There was nothing sensual about his words, but he hoped she read into his tone: *I know how you taste. I can't wait to get you alone.*

The heat in her eyes replied in kind, making his stomach clench. Then he noticed Graham glaring at them. Eric tried not to laugh and gave Isla her space.

The rest of dinner was better than he could have expected, those nerves earlier tonight unnecessary. Conversation flowed easily. Heather was quick to put him at ease, even had Graham laughing at her antics.

Family was Eric's cornerstone, the core group of people who knew and loved him as he was. Not because of his career or status. Being with Isla and Graham and Heather, he felt that inner circle growing. A new friend in Heather with her teasing quips, approval in Graham's grudging acceptance—the protective father he didn't have. So much affection from Isla: soft looks sliding his way, small touches of his thigh hidden under the table, leaning into him when Heather had her laughing so hard tears leaked from her eyes.

With them, he was once again Eric Kramarovsky, a quiet Jewish boy who'd rather study than brawl. It was a wonderful glimpse of normalcy, the true success he'd been missing in his life. It was also a reminder he needed to win his upcoming match. Play his Brick Smash role a little longer. Train harder than he ever had, with one end goal: victory. That big check in his bank, for himself and his family. And for Isla.

They all piled into the hotel, full of good food and entertaining conversation.

Heather pulled Eric's head down and planted a kiss on his cheek. "I like you. Don't get hurt in the ring."

"Joe Bradley's the only one who'll get hurt." It was a Brick Smash line but spoken lightly, not in a menacing growl. For these last weeks, Eric needed to embody a portion of his alter ego, but not all of him. If people had seen him out smiling at dinner tonight, he didn't care. He'd be a brute for interviews and the media. With the people close to him, he was done acting like a fool.

But Isla glanced away from him, looking distant. He immediately regretted mentioning the upcoming match and the possibility of either fighter getting hurt. He'd have to be more mindful in the future.

Heather headed to the west elevator that led to her room. Eric stuffed his hands in his pockets as he trailed Isla and Graham to the east elevator. The ride up was quiet. Once on their floor, they reached Graham's door first.

"Sleep well, Dad," Isla said and kissed his cheek.

Graham nodded in reply.

Eric's door was next, then Isla's a few down. She stopped at Eric's room, looked up at him with parted lips and red-apple cheeks, no longer feeling distant, all the restrained touches between them seeming to pour from her eyes.

A throat cleared.

They glanced at Graham, who was still standing at his door.

Eric laughed. "Goodnight, Graham." To the protective man's daughter, he said quietly, "Visit later if you want. If not, I understand."

He wanted to lean down, capture her lips in a blistering kiss, but a heavyweight champ was giving him the evil eye, and they weren't in private. He slipped his extra keycard into her hand and left the ball in her court.

23

One Mississippi. Two Mississippi. Three my-body-is-an-inferno-of-want Mississippi.

How long was a woman supposed to wait before sneaking into a man's room? One hour? Two? Five?

Hour two was nearing, and Isla felt like her teenage self about to sneak out her window to visit Tommy Semper, the too-old-for-her crush who'd invited her to a house party. She'd followed her fragile sixteen-year-old heart that night, had showed up at the raucous gathering, only to catch Tommy with his tongue down Tanya Crowley's throat. Even worse, her father had been waiting in her room upon her return to rub salt *and a grounding* in her brokenhearted wound.

Her father may be down the hall now, but there'd be no grounding or reprimand tonight. She was an adult. Eric wanted her. She wanted him.

She may not have liked hearing Eric mention the Joe Bradley fight at the end of their night, but she hadn't hit full panic mode. When the first hints of rapid breathing had struck, she'd replayed a conversation with her therapist, how her fears were tightly woven with her mother's abandonment and dismissal. Isla had assumed boxing was the source of her anxiety. The brutality of the sport. This new insight changed her perspective, shone a brighter light on the shape of her issues. She hadn't panicked over the Bradley comment as roughly as she might have in the past. She was ready to risk more with Eric.

She tightened her bathrobe's sash, loved the sexy feel of the lingerie beneath. Like she was a seductive siren, not a physiotherapist who spent most of her days in yoga pants and runners. She and Heather had visited a fancy store before dinner, where Heather had picked out the cherry-red set of garters and lacy pieces, saying, "The man's face will melt off when he sees you in this."

Isla liked Eric's face where it was, but she was buzzing with nerves and excitement to see his reaction. She was already turned on, imagining his hands sliding up her thighs, plucking at her garters. The snap of lace against her skin. Her whole body clenched.

Tired of waiting, she opened her door slightly, poked her head out. A couple was walking from the elevator, their arms hooked around each other. They stumbled, smiling and laughing intimately, and stopped to kiss between two rooms. The man pressed the woman to the wall, pushed his hand up her shirt, kissed her hard while she snaked her leg around his thigh, dragging him closer. Isla nearly moaned.

If she was turned on before, she was about to combust now.

The man rolled his hips into the woman, hitched her leg higher while she grabbed his ass. Then he tore away and tugged her to a hotel door, fumbling with his keycard before they stumbled inside.

Isla tensed her abs, unsure she could make it the short walk to Eric's room without needing to stop and relieve the ache between her thighs. She hurried to his door, paused, and fluffed her hair. A swipe of his gifted keycard later, she walked into Eric's room.

And heard snorting.

Whit ran over to her, his stubby face pushing into her leg. She hadn't factored an excited dog into her seductions, and there was no avoiding the dog's enthusiastic demands. She crouched and rubbed his neck, practically falling over from Whit's exuberance.

"He likes you," Eric said. His voice was low and gravelly, coming from the direction of his room.

She looked up. One lamp was lit, casting his bare chest in seductive shadows. His shoulders somehow looked wider, his arms strong enough to lift cars. In nothing but tight briefs, his massive thighs framed the thick line of his cock. She fell unceremoniously on her butt.

Whit, of course, took advantage of her position and licked her arm and neck. She laughed, tried to fend off the slobbery onslaught.

Eric laughed, too. Then he whistled and sternly said, "Bed."

That one word had Isla wanting to obey Eric. Sprawl on his bed. Let him have his way with her. She stayed on her butt, but Whit obliged his master and trotted over to his dog bed, lying down with a grunty groan.

Eric walked closer to Isla until he was standing over her in all his manly glory. His gaze dragged from her face to her robe, slightly open now, a tease of red lace revealed. "You came."

She better come. That much she knew. She'd never felt so close to orgasm without being touched. Looking at Eric, the deep grooves of his muscles, the V dipping into his tight briefs, the large bulge that twitched and thickened ever-so-slightly, a soft breeze might send her over the edge.

He leaned down and helped her to her feet, hauling her close.

She clung to him. "My entrance was supposed to be sexier."

"You're the sexiest woman I've ever seen."

"I thought my neck was too long and my lips were too full."

"You're fucking beautiful," he said roughly.

Then he kissed her, not giving her a chance to tell him how gorgeous *he* was, that his thighs weren't lumpy and that his intense eyes were stunning, not awful. He coaxed her lips open, twirled his tongue with hers, wrapped his arms around her and took two handfuls of her ass, squeezing her through the bathrobe. His thigh met her center, rubbing where she ached for him.

Unlike their nights this week, Eric didn't pull back, ask if she was okay, suggest they slow down. He'd let her lead this whole time, going at her pace, ensuring she was okay. Now he was the one leading them, giving in to his desire, trusting she was ready for this next step.

She gripped his back, let her fingers sink into the muscled grooves, hoping he understood the hard pull of her hands. *Take me. Don't be gentle with me.* They kissed harder, moaned. When he pressed his thigh harder against her, she stiffened. Her core clenched. White-hot heat blinded her, so quickly she squeaked out a string of *oh gods*, convulsing with the release.

She clung to him, her body still shaking, unsure when she'd become a thirteen-year-old boy unable to control his orgasm. "I was kind of worked up before I snuck in."

His low laugh snaked through her. "You're about to get more worked up, *milaya*."

He hoisted her up by her ass, guided her legs around his waist, his erection so hard and *insistent* against her she was on the verge again.

He walked them to his bedroom, dropped her on his bed.

From this new vantage point, she drank in his sharp cheekbones, those intense eyes, darkened and hungry, the way his briefs looked ready to bust from the strain of containing him. She was so wet her pretty red lace panties felt drenched. Somehow her bathrobe was still on, the material suddenly suffocating and hot. Or maybe that overwhelming constriction was the ache in her chest—the strong clench of her heart, beating hard and fast, filling her veins with an intoxicating rhythm, a percussive symphony conducted by the man standing over her.

Even more rattling was her certainty. There was no hesitation on her end. No worry about opening up more fully to this man, an actual boxer. A soon to be *ex*-boxer, but still. One of her greatest fears, and the biggest surprise was her utter trust in him.

He hoisted her farther up the bed and joined her on the sheets, laying over her, one thick thigh between her legs, his huge forearms planted on either side of her head. Tenderly, he brushed her hair back. "You make me feel drunk." He brushed his lips over her ear. "Intoxicated"—he kissed the birthmark on her neck, the dip between her collarbones—"so fucking high on you."

He kissed her lips, slow and passionate, lighting her every nerve as she arched and moaned and clutched at his back. She was lost to the sensations, wrapped up in Eric's heat and affection. Her breathing grew shallow. Tight. Intensity so bright it threatened to choke her.

"touch steals words
but skin confesses
in goose bumps
and shivers"

"I need you," she whispered.

Their foreplay had been too long. Weeks of working together, talking, laughing, pining from the sidelines, while she'd discovered Eric's mind and kind heart: the Baby Whisperer who studied Latin and knew Japanese proverbs and hadn't rushed Isla when they'd admitted their affections.

"*Podría perderme en tus ojos*," he murmured. A language she couldn't pinpoint. The words or origin didn't matter. That look in his hungry eyes? She was done for.

He undid the sash at her waist, unwrapping her like she was a long-awaited gift, the slow movement sending shivers skating across her body. She squirmed for him to touch her harder, fill her up.

The man ignored her desperate moans, but a cocky smile curved the corner of his lips. "Patience," he murmured and traced the edges of lace around her breasts, scraped his thumb across her erect nipples.

Heat engulfed her. His hands were huge, callused and perfect. Still moving too damn *slow*. "I need..." She didn't know how to finish that sentence. Couldn't focus through the emotions burning through her.

"You'll get everything you need from me tonight, *milaya*. But I need this. Need to map every inch of you." He tugged her lacy bra down, groaned and took his sweet time, licked and sucked her breasts, like he'd never seen a naked woman before.

God, how could a man be this tender and commanding all at once? Taking what *he* needed, while making her feel like the center of his world.

Deftly, he rolled her over, straddled her from behind. "If I do anything that makes you uncomfortable, just tell me. I'll stop."

His weight held her down, but she didn't feel confined. Not with his promise and the care he'd always shown her. With

Eric, she felt precious. Like every touch and kiss and move was born of a deeper desire, the need to unlock her secrets. The same way she wanted to explore *his* body, imprint every scar and valley into her memory, for *her* greedy desires, then drown this amazing man in pleasure.

She shifted below him, tried to rub herself on the bed, find some relief. "The only thing that's making me uncomfortable is that we're not completely naked."

He chuckled. "Good things come to those who wait."

His cotton-clad erection settled into the crease of her ass, turning her on even more. Hot molten fire throbbing painfully. She wiggled again, to no avail. Gave up and pressed the side of her face to the mattress, closing her eyes, letting him take charge, but that unequivocal trust suddenly felt harder. This type of letting go wasn't just about sex for her. Her whole life she'd been thinking five steps ahead, anticipating the scenarios that would set her off at work or with her father, protecting herself while limiting herself at the same time. Being intimate with Eric meant giving up control.

He splayed his huge hands on her lower back, pressed down slightly as he squeezed her waist. The heavier his weight on her, the lighter she felt.

Eyes closed. Trust. Faith. Let go.

He glided his hands up, his hips rocking in the tiniest motions, rubbing his erection against her as he unhooked her bra's clasp. She relaxed into his caress, the soft scrape of his calloused hands. Reveled in his throaty moans and grunts—masculine sounds sending vibrations along her skin. *Eyes closed. Trust. Faith. Let go.* With him, she could do this. *Be* this. Take enjoyment for herself and open her heart.

He lifted her arms above her head, gathered her wrists in one hand, held them down as he lowered himself onto her, his hard chest to her back, his pelvis over her bottom. "Fuck, *milaya*."

Fuck was right. She'd never felt so possessed, revered. Worshiped in the most beautiful way, because they'd become friends before lovers, the comfort in their relationship building into more than she could have imagined. With his free hand, he brushed her hair to the side, kissed the shell of her ear, gave it a lick. Treated her jaw and the line of her neck to the same pleasure. Both shoulders and every space between.

And suddenly she wanted to cry. Why did she want to cry?

"Eric." She squirmed under him, terrified to voice what she was feeling.

He stilled. "You're trembling."

"You...I..." The words wouldn't come. She was dizzy with desire and overwhelmed with emotion.

His hot breath blew against her back. "I know," he whispered, his voice back to honey and gravel. "I feel the same."

He dragged his nose up her spine, followed with his tongue and lips. Not pushing for her to explain her stilted words or this too-tight feeling in her chest, how she wanted to shout her happiness and cry at once. He somehow understood without asking. Like he was mapping more than her body. Seeing through her skin to the beating center of her, giving her what she needed by taking control and letting her exist in this place of burning desire and blooming emotions, no questions asked.

He released her wrists, moved down her body, stopping to bite her ass. She laughed, a burst of joy mingling with her overwhelming feelings. When he lifted her garter and let it slap against her inner thigh, she gasped.

He smoothed his hand over the spot. "This lace is criminally sexy."

"You're criminally sexy." She opened her eyes, twisted her head to see the gorgeous man straddling her from behind. She wiggled her butt, tried to entice him to move faster, get naked. Relieve the need throbbing between her thighs.

Smirking, he took handfuls of her ass, squeezed, kissed each cheek, his fingers grazing the hot center of her. When he finally flipped her over, he didn't give her time to bask in his manly glory. His mouth found hers, a rough kiss as he removed her loosened bra. Then he was everywhere, moving faster —*thank God*—unhooking her garters, kissing her stomach, rolling down her stockings, cupping her between her thighs. *Finally*, he dragged her lace panties down, and his breath stuttered.

He stretched out beside her, still in his infuriating briefs, his huge hand splayed on her belly. The tips of his fingers drew circles through her soft curls, driving her mad. "I didn't know being with someone could feel this way," he said, his eyes flicking to hers. "I'm dying to make love to you, but I can't stop exploring your body." His Adam's apple bobbed, like he was suddenly uncertain. Vulnerable.

Her body was still hovering on a knife's edge of pleasure, her hips moving while his fingers teased her, but those blasted tears threatened again—happy tears. *How could a man be this incredible* tears. "Everything with you feels different."

She pressed her hand overs his, their fingers moving together as she guided his hand lower, to where she positively *ached*. His eyes drifted shut on a moan. She squeezed her thighs, forcing more pressure from his hand. Her hips bucked. Together, they trailed through her wetness. She almost wept from how desperately she wanted him.

She clamped her hand on his. "I need you naked and inside me." Moving with her, filling her up. "I'm done being patient."

"Then I guess I better obey." Fire in his smoke-gray eyes, he nipped her shoulder, then extricated his hand from under hers and left the bed.

Immediately, she felt bereft. Empty. Rushing heat still pulsed through her body, the clawing need to have him buried inside her flaring, but the emptiness went deeper. Seeped into her marrow. "You're taking too long."

He got a condom from his dresser and tossed it on the bed. "You're demanding."

"Get over here."

Amusement sparking, he dropped his boxers, and his cock sprang free. He was as thick as she'd imagined. Big. Curving up slightly toward his stomach. She was beyond hot, burning up from wanting him. Needed his skin sliding against hers, his heart beating next to hers. He kneeled on the bed, his heavy thighs nudging her legs apart. Instead of dragging him closer like she craved, she maneuvered to her knees, too. Had the sudden need to explore *him*, touch and kiss and learn his body.

She stroked the scar cleaving his right ribs, the bruise darkening his left pec. Sparring injuries, no doubt. Her heart gave a sharp squeeze, and a shot of fear mixed with the ten thousand emotions vying for dominance. "I'm scared," she whispered. Sudden nerves. Stupid anxiety.

"I know it looks big, but I'll go slow."

She laughed and dropped her forehead to his shoulder. "Thank you for that." For lightening her heavy.

His hands moved to her back, brushed up and down. "If you tell me to stop right now, we stop. No questions asked."

Another reason why she was falling hard and fast for this man. He was as honorable as they came, and he deserved her unequivocal trust. She leaned down, kissed the scar on his ribs, the bruise on his chest. "I don't want to stop." She brushed her fingers down his sides.

He shivered, his hands gripping her back harder. "That's fucking great news."

And he was fucking gorgeous. She reached between them,

fisted his length—silky and hot, hard and perfect. Air hissed through his teeth; his erection twitched in her hand. Too turned on to wait, she grabbed the condom and ripped the package—*magnum size*, of course—lined the plastic circle up with his tip, and trembled slightly. Feeling emotional again. Overwhelmed and excited.

As she rolled the condom down, his knuckles met her cheek, stroked softly. Eric murmured something in a language she couldn't decipher, and her chest squeezed. Burning tightened her throat. She lay down and reached for him, *desperate* for him. He followed her movement, eyes locked on her face as his hips lowered and her knees came up.

He was right there at her center, prodding her opening, the intensity on his face making her throat burn hotter, so intently and insistently she whispered, "I love you."

When? How? She was suddenly bursting with so much love.

He stilled. A sheen glossed his eyes. "I love you, *milaya*. I've never felt this before. Can't even describe it."

"I know. Me, too." A guy she'd disliked at first sight. A connection she'd fought so hard he'd been forced to woo her through another man.

All she saw now was *love, love, love.*

He pushed in slightly. They both groaned. And wow, he was big. A hint of pain followed his slow push, then the ache bloomed into a wave of pleasure that made her feel gloriously full. *Love. I love this man so much.* Tears burned the backs of her eyes. She lifted her knees higher, gave him better access to her body and heart until he slid all the way in.

He dropped his head forward, his body shuddering as his jaw pulsed. "Jesus, Isla."

All she could do was clench. Squeeze the solid length of him harder, drag his upper body closer. Taste his pulse point and read the emotion pumping his blood. He dropped some of his weight on her, the perfect amount. Enough to feel completely owned by this brilliant linguist. She ran her hands over the soft buzz of his shorn hair, reveled in his answering grunt. He sucked on her neck, bit her collarbone, eventually lacing their fingers together as he planted their hands above her head.

Eyes locked, they moved. Slightly faster. Connecting so deeply she felt her first tear slip out. Then another. He kissed her damp cheek, nibbled and sucked on her bottom lip. They rocked, the thick length of him moving in and out of her so thoroughly heat blasted through her. She arched her back, closed her eyes. Those sharp pulses gathered tighter, hotter. Building brighter. And *fuck*. She cried out, the strength of her orgasm blinding as she met him thrust for thrust, harder and faster, chasing every drop of her release. He wasn't far behind, his guttural grunts and Russian sounding words joining his shaking body.

Boneless and breathless, she placed her hands on his pecs, gave those crazy muscles a squeeze. "Your boobs are bigger than mine."

He laughed. His cheeks and neck were red from exertion. A hint of sweat glinted in his clavicle. She gave the spot a lick.

He made a satisfied male sound and kissed her nose. "I love you, Isla Slade."

"I thought I knew love. But I didn't. Not until you." He was still inside of her, their hips flush, that connection deeper than the merging of bodies. Eric had carved a place for himself in her heart so irrevocably she wasn't sure how it had beat without him in her life.

24

Eric's body had an internal clock constantly set to Crack of Dawn. He liked being up early, rising with the sun, fitting in studying before his training kicked in. This morning there would be no studying, unless cataloguing Isla's gorgeous features counted.

She lay facing him, one of her strong legs stacked between his, her hair a mess, her lips slightly parted. Her left arm rested on his hip, the other twisting awkwardly under her pillow.

A fierce sense of protectiveness fisted his gut.

He'd known he was falling for her. Spending so much time with her the past weeks had drilled that reality home. What he hadn't realized was how ass-over-heels in love he was with Isla Slade. Last night, before they'd made love, he'd gazed at her, unsure why his lungs had hurt. Her sexy lingerie had been discarded and she'd been a vision, but it hadn't been her glorious body stealing his breath. It had been her expressive eyes, the way he'd seen an image of himself reflecting back at him: the man he wanted to be. His true self, utterly seen.

He tugged her closer now, kissed her jaw and ear until she stirred.

"It's too early," she mumbled.

"I need you before my day starts."

"I need to shower and brush my teeth," she said into his neck.

He chuckled, loving her soft and pliable and sleepy. And naked. Hugging her close, he rolled them to the edge of the bed and lifted her as he stood, wrapping her legs around his waist. Her arms came around his neck effortlessly.

"Oooh." Her voice was groggy, but she adjusted her body, aligning herself so his morning erection rubbed where she wanted. All he could think was: *Fuck.*

Not eloquent. Isla had the power to drain his mind of everything but his desire for her. He'd planned to take her to the shower as she'd requested. He only mustered a few steps. He needed her now. Again. He pressed her into the wall, rolling his hips into her. They were both naked, insanely close. If he wasn't careful, he'd sink into her before he got a condom.

She moaned, kissed his neck. "That feels amazing, but wall sex doesn't work for me. The position's awkward, and I get too in my head."

She was the only thing in his head this morning, and her claim was a challenge if he'd ever heard one. "You haven't had wall sex with me." He palmed her ass harder. "Trust me to hold you."

A double entendre maybe. *Trust me to take care of you. I won't let you fall.*

She was taking a huge risk having visited last night, confessing her feelings while they'd made love, sleeping over, when she'd only just begun to face her mental health issues. He wouldn't falter. He lifted more of her weight, rubbed his length against her.

She moaned. "God. Okay, yeah. I guess being strong helps. We need a condom."

He needed a defibrillator to control the erratic beat of his heart.

He put her down briefly, returning with a condom so she could sheath him. He liked watching her line up the latex and roll it down, the way her teeth lodged into her bottom lip. He loved the little squeeze she gave him at the end, her eyes dilated with excitement. Need tightened his skin. He lifted her back up, almost shaking with the urge to be inside her.

She secured her legs around his waist again, but said, "Toothpaste."

He stilled. "What?"

"Morning breath. I need toothpaste."

She flattened her lips and jutted her cute chin toward the bathroom. He laughed. Couldn't get over how much he loved laughing with her. Loving on her. How completely themselves they were around each other.

With her hooked around him, he walked to the bathroom sink, where she squirted a small bit of toothpaste on her finger. Eyes shining with amusement, she sucked it off and swirled it around her mouth. "Your turn."

She squirted more toothpaste out and slipped her finger through his greedy lips. Instead of focusing on the toothpaste, he swirled his tongue around her finger, gave it a tiny bite. Her eyelids fell heavy and her hips shifted. He spun around, pressed her back to the bathroom wall, bent his knees just enough, found her entrance, and slid into the glory that was Isla.

"*Fuck.*"

"*Yes.*"

They groaned and spoke in unison, mint on their tongues,

Isla all he could see. All he could *feel.* Her tight heat squeezed his dick, obliterating his senses.

She knocked her head against the wall, clenched around him. "Your cock was made for me."

Isla Slade was made for him. He had no doubt about that.

He held her weight, shifting upward with each stroke—*so fucking good*—hitting her in the spot that coaxed a needy little cry from her parted lips. "Let me do the work," he told her as he picked up the speed. *Let me take care of you.* "Let go."

Her thighs clenched his waist tighter, then she loosened enough to rub her pelvis against him. She moaned. Fire shot up his spine. He fucking loved her like this, using his body for her pleasure. Taking from him.

She dug her fingers into the back of his neck and stiffened. "Holy shit," she said, "this view."

He slowed his strokes, turned his head to glimpse them in the bathroom mirror. His ass was clenched, her face flushed with excitement as she stared at their reflection. His balls tightened at the sight. Yeah, that was one hell of a view. She was one hell of a woman, trusting herself to experiment with him, making him feel like the best version of himself, in the bedroom and out.

He turned his focus back to her, pulling out slower and thrusting in hard, giving her a show. Driving himself crazy. He sucked on her neck and circled his hips, held her weight until he felt that telltale squeeze, her inner walls clamping down on him. She cried out. A blast of heat fisted his balls. He moved faster. So fast, he worried her back was banging the wall too hard, but he couldn't control the burn gripping him by the soles of his feet, barreling up his legs. He came so hard and rough he had to lean on her slightly, keeping her pinned to the wall until his senses returned.

Slowly, he eased her feet down.

She smiled up at him, her face blissed out. "You have a phenomenal ass."

Smirking, he gave *her* ass a playful squeeze. "Is wall sex on the yes list now?"

"It's on the *hell yes* list. And I'm apparently into mirror kink."

He dealt with the condom, then tugged her into the shower. "You look even better wet." He positioned her under the hot stream, ran his hands down her soaked hair.

She hummed contentedly. "You usually study in the morning, don't you?"

"I studied *you* this morning."

She took the bar of soap, got it lathered up. It smelled like mint, too. Mint in their mouths. Mint on their bodies. All they were missing was chocolate sauce. She worked her hands over his chest in small circles, massaging his stiff muscles, spending extra time where he hurt most, because she knew his body. Felt like she knew him down to his soul.

"I can walk Whit if you want," she said. "Give you time to sneak in a lesson or two before your run and our physio session." She moved her soapy hands to his abdomen.

His abs flexed. "Don't you have to work on that accounting program?"

"I do, but I can do it later. You should study."

He stood in the glass-walled shower, while Isla soaped his perpetually sore body, feeling luckier than he had any right to be. He was the caretaker in his family. The doer. The fixer. The one who sacrificed to make sure those he loved were happy and well. As it should be. Then Isla Slade walked into his life, said she loved him, and offered to put him first.

"*Scio me nihil scire*," he said.

Her slippery hands moved around his back, down to his ass, exploring. He let out a rough grunt, and his cock stirred.

Chocolate sauce *would* really be fun right now. And some whipped cream. Sadly, not with his diet. When he won this match, though. He'd treat himself to foods he hadn't eaten in years, feed Isla chocolate cake from his fork. Take more than one lick from her ice cream cone.

She tilted her head up, her expression bright with interest. "What did that mean?"

He wasn't sure he'd get the translation perfect, but he gave it a shot. "It's Latin. It means *I know that I know nothing.*"

She scrunched her nose. "I don't follow."

He took the soap from her, turned her around to wash her back, map her body in the brightness of the shower this time, every curve and crease lit for him to see. "With you, the rules I know about my life are out the window. My expectations for myself are changing. I'm seeing possibilities where they never existed before. Like someone told me a knocked-out opponent has the right to stand again. Regain his pride. Find his footing and fight back."

Steam filled the stall. The water pelted them both.

She rested the back of her head on his chest. "Am I the referee in this new knockout rule of yours?"

"No. You *are* the knockout rule. You're the loophole that allows me to get back up and fight, for myself this time."

She turned and wove her slippery arms around his neck. "You said you weren't quitting boxing for me."

"I love you, Isla. Really fucking love you, but I'm quitting for me. I just needed someone to believe in me before I could believe in myself. When I win this match, I'll be celebrating my freedom as much as my victory."

He'd been hungry before, intent on the money that came with beating Joe Bradley. The win was doubly important now. That cash would pave the way for a future he hadn't been brave enough to imagine on his own.

Isla traced patterns on his neck and ear. "You've done that for me, too. Gave me a reason to challenge the rules I set for myself."

Because they made each other better. "We'll celebrate tonight, a private party in my room. Toast to our own knockout rule. The chance to get back up and fight to be better."

She tipped her head back and laughed. He hadn't said anything funny. No stupid jokes this time. The move seemed to be pure happiness, and he'd been the one to put that smile on her face. A flood of contentment filled him, along with another shot of determination. Nothing and no one would stop him from getting this win.

25

Eric loved studying grammar. Where most people's eyes glazed over when they learned how many rules were woven into basic conversation, he got off on the intricacies of communication. How the smallest change in structure altered meaning.

He sat on his couch this morning, focused on Latin's past tense: the imperfect, the perfect, the pluperfect. Variations of each, translating sentences, checking his answers, getting some wrong, but getting most right, mainly thanks to Isla. She'd walked Whit every morning the past two weeks, giving Eric time to study. She'd also warmed his bed and body every night. She was his reward at the end of each grueling day. Just knowing they'd be having dinner together, making love, cuddling and talking poetry under the sheets, made his intensive training more bearable.

His studies were further along than he'd have expected, but this morning was his last session. His match was in a week. The only thing on his mind for the next seven days would be boxing and more boxing. Which meant he had to have a potentially uncomfortable conversation with Isla.

Twenty minutes later, his favorite person and animal walked in.

Isla unhooked Whit's leash and gave him a vigorous rub. "We almost got arrested. Didn't we, Walt Whitman?"

Whit squirmed and snorted under her attention, then he trotted to Eric, stubby tail flailing, like they hadn't seen each other in years.

Eric put down his pen and scratched Whit behind his ears. "Did Isla try to sell you on the dog black market again?"

Isla huffed. "Apparently it's illegal to feed pigeons in Vegas."

He gave Whit one last pat, then focused on Isla. His girlfriend. A sentiment that still winded him. Who'd have thought this match would have led him here. "Where were you feeding pigeons?"

"We weren't feeding them. Some other criminal mastermind scattered the breadcrumbs," she said, gesturing animatedly. "But Whit liked watching the birds, so we stopped and observed the pecking action. Until a rent-a-cop decided we were inciting a pigeon riot."

Only in Vegas. "How'd you escape with your life?"

"I used your name."

"It was that serious, was it?"

"I wasn't about to spend the next six months in lockup for a crime I didn't commit. And your name has clout. The cop was a fan. I also saw my father on my way back to your room. He's perfected his evil-eye routine."

Graham had been glaring extra hard lately. Especially at the hickey Isla had left on Eric's neck last week. "I like that he's protective of you."

"That makes one of us."

He chuckled, loving everything about this. Them. The easy

banter. Like he had an instant family of his own. Which made their next conversation all the harder. "Come sit for a sec."

She walked over and fell onto the couch beside him. "How go your studies?"

"Good, but I need to talk to you about something."

She leaned away from him and narrowed her eyes. "How many times do I have to tell you, I'm not into furry kink. If you want to attend an orgy dressed like a stuffed bunny, I'm out."

He laughed harder and grabbed her hips, manhandling her until she was on his lap. "Even if I'm dressed like a sexy wolf?"

"Especially then. But a pink, sparkly unicorn might do it for me."

"Halloween this year will be fun." He kissed her, soft but deep, and pressed his forehead to hers. "My match is in seven days."

Smile slipping, she cuddled closer. "I know."

"It's an intense time for me. I need my focus to be undivided."

She didn't speak, just held on to him, their foreheads connected.

"As much as I love having you stay with me every night," he went on, "I need to be on my own for this. No distractions. I get pretty intense in the days leading up to a fight, and I don't want to worry about hurting you by being rude or not giving you the attention you deserve. We'll still see each other during the physio sessions, but even then, I'll probably be less social. More in my head." She stiffened in his hold. He talked faster. "This isn't me pushing you away. It's just—"

"The boxer in you. Yeah, I know. I lived with one for most of my life. I know the drill. It's fine. I get it." But her chest was rising faster and she pushed at him, trying to move off his lap.

He eased her off. Felt sick watching what looked like another panic attack rise. He hated feeling helpless while she struggled with an invisible demon. He whistled for Whit, who waddled right over to Isla, mashed his face into her shins. She pressed her hand to her sternum, closed her eyes. She hadn't talked much about the new techniques her therapist had suggested, but as Whit nuzzled her and she did whatever it was she was doing, her breathing seemed to deepen. Her shoulders dropped slightly.

His racing heart wouldn't slow.

On her next inhale, she opened her eyes. "That wasn't too bad, as far as attacks go. I'm practically cured." She laughed thinly.

He wasn't fooled. The woman hated showing weakness, like her father. "Isla, I'm so sorry."

"It's not your fault. My issues go much deeper than boxing."

"But I'm the one causing you pain now."

She shook her head, let her hands sink into the wrinkly skin at Whit's neck. "When I was out with Preston and you spoke through him, you said love is hard, but anything hard is worthwhile." She looked at Eric. Her skin was still flushed, but her dark eyes were fierce. "You're worthwhile, Eric. And I'm fine with spending the week apart. I won't get offended if you're quiet during physio, and I won't sneak into your room at night. I'll miss you, but it's probably better for me to be around you less as your match nears. I won't watch the fight, though. I wish I could be there for you, but..." She dropped her gaze.

He moved closer to her on the couch, ran his fingers through her wavy hair. "I understand. I'd probably worry too much if you were there anyway. And I still hate that I'm the source of your attacks."

She turned her head, kissed the center of his palm. "'The door to the heart moves in both directions. Step forward or step back. The choice is yours.'" It was a poem, spoken softly against his skin.

"The heart is fickle and changes its mind?" he asked, suggesting his interpretation of the prose. A possible meaning he didn't like. Was she preparing him? Telling him she might change her mind? That enduring this week might make her realize he wasn't worth her pain after all?

"The heart can hold more than we give it credit for," she said and took his hand, kissing each of his fingers. "There's a door that will always swing inside of me, linking my past and present. For so long, I followed it backward. I allowed my past to control my direction. Now I'm moving forward, but that link will always be there. There's no protecting me from my issues. It's not your fault. I'm the one who chooses to walk forward, even though that door hits me in the ass sometimes as I go through."

She was so incredibly impressive. Smaller than him, but miles stronger. "*Mea levavot ihiyu meat midai kdei lehakhil et kol ha`ahava sheli elaikh*," he murmured.

Her face softened with affection. "Is that Hebrew?"

He nodded. "A hundred hearts would be too few to carry all my love for you."

There was his favorite look again. The one that said *you're fantastic*. "You can't say romantic things like that when I have to go seven days without kissing you."

The next week would be painful, no doubt. But he was accustomed to denying himself, and there was one loophole. "The seven days can start after this morning, *if* you're feeling up for being devoured right now." He ached to have his mouth on her, one more taste to get him through.

She fisted her hand in the front of his T-shirt, dragged him with her as she lay back on the couch. "This better be earth shattering to last seven days."

He nipped her ear. "I'll take that challenge. And when I win the fight, this will all be over. No more boxing to stress you out."

The win. Only one option. Seven days to prime his mind and body for that reality.

They didn't talk again. Not with words. He peeled off her clothes, used his tongue on her until she cried his name. She took her turn on her knees, wrapped her pretty pink lips around his cock and sucked. Stars. A blast of heat. It took all his willpower not to explode in her mouth. Then she straddled him on the couch, rode him, rolling her hips, taking him deep, both of them clutching at each other, desperate to make this last as long as possible.

He detonated too soon, a second before her, both of them milking every last bit of pleasure from each other.

"I love you," she whispered, hot and sweaty in his arms.

"Love you so much." He did. Still couldn't believe one woman could mean this much to him. Now it was time to focus.

ERIC WALKED through the casino toward the training gym. People stopped and pointed as usual, whispering to their friends. Others held up phones to snap his photo. A few guys asked him for autographs. More people recognized him lately, publicity for the big fight gaining momentum as the date neared. Where he'd normally stop and say a few words, sign an autograph or two, he used his Brick Smash image to his benefit and grunted, pushing past the gawkers.

No distractions this week. Press was limited to the weigh-in and a few select promotions, just enough to keep up his end of his shitty contract. The rest of the time all he'd think about was boxing. Graham had drilled into Eric, time and again, how clear his mind had to be going into a fight. His fists did half the work. His mind—focus, determination, belief in the win, visualization techniques—did the rest. Graham's head game and the psychology of boxing was a big part of why Eric had made it this far. Mental fortitude separated professionals from amateurs.

He walked into the training locker room, unloaded his clothes. Once he was changed, Graham came in. His coach didn't speak as he tied Eric's wraps and checked their stability. "You're good to go," Graham said afterward. "Get in the gym when you're ready."

He left and Eric rolled out his neck, bounced on his toes a few times, tossed a few jabs.

"Looking in fine form, my man." Preston walked in and slapped Eric's back. "How's my champ feeling?"

"Good." He didn't elaborate. He never talked much when he was in his zone. Graham knew the drill, hence their silent hand wrapping. Preston knew the drill, too, usually gave him space leading up to a fight.

Today the guy paced, wearing uncharacteristically creased slacks and shirt. "I hate to ask this, but I'm assuming you can't pay back any of those loans, right?"

Eric quit bouncing and jabbing. "You know my situation." This win was his ticket to paying his manager back, with interest. To never worrying about covering family emergencies again. This wasn't news to Preston. "Something happen?"

Preston slumped slightly. "An investment went south. It was supposed to be a sure thing, now I'm a little screwed at the moment. Anyway"—he waved a fidgety hand—"not your concern. Just focus on the fight. We both need it."

Eric didn't like the added pressure or seeing Preston in a tight spot. The guy spent money carelessly, lived beyond his means, even though his means were substantial. Eric might not agree with the excess, but he didn't want his manager to lose his shirt. "The win is ours," he told him.

Preston's fidgety hands settled. He nodded once, sharply. "That's my guy. I'll check on you later this week."

He left, and Eric rolled his neck again. Threw a few more jabs. Took a step toward the gym, but his phone rang.

"Goddamn it." He shoved his hand into his gym bag, pulled out his phone. Rosa again. He swore a few more times, then picked up. "I'm busy." He winced at his curtness, couldn't find an ounce of calm to channel.

"I know this is your broody week of focused silence," she said, coasting over his rudeness. "I wouldn't normally call—and please don't freak out, everything's fine—but Eliza's in the hospital. Something went around at school and she got sick. Looks like asthmatic bronchitis again."

"Jesus." He sat on the bench, dragged a hand down his face. He pictured beautiful little Eliza the last time she'd been really sick, so tiny in the hospital bed. "Is she okay?"

"She's fine, like I said. She will be, at least. And I'm not just saying that so you don't worry. We caught it early. Knew how to read the signs this time. But..."

Money. They needed to pay more bills, and he couldn't ask Preston for help this time. "We'll have a buffer between receiving the bill and when we have to pay," he said. "After my win, we'll be covered, so it doesn't matter."

"And if you don't win?"

"I *will* win, Rosa."

She sighed. "Maybe I'll look into financial aid on my end. Just in case."

"I said I'd cover it." He swallowed hard, forced a gentler tone. "I'll have the money in a week. Just please tell Eliza I love her. Give her a big hug and kiss from me."

"Of course I will. And..."

She paused so long he pressed the phone harder to his ear. "You still there?"

"Yeah." But her voice sounded tiny. "Just miss you."

"I miss you all."

They hung up and Eric rubbed the heels of his hands into his eyes, stress throbbing in his temples. He wished he were at home, reading to Eliza in the hospital, having tea parties with Mr. Squish-A-Lot and Mrs. Nutter and Mr. Green and Miss Candy, not worrying about her from across the country.

He clenched his jaw.

He needed to clear his mind. The match of his life—his *last* match—loomed so close. The only way to win was to push these problems aside. Not think about Eliza. Preston. Money. Any of it. He had a job to do, and Joe Bradley didn't give a shit that Eric's niece had been gifted with a weak set of lungs.

26

For the end of their physio session, Isla attached electrodes on either side of Eric's Achilles. The electric current helped stimulate blood flow and promote pain relief. Before their seven days of abstinence, they'd joke and talk and flirt during those quiet minutes. Use the time to their benefit. They were on day six of Eric's intensive training, the last day they'd see each other before his match, and neither of them said a word.

He was on his stomach, lying on the treatment table with the side of his face pressed to the pillow. His eyes were closed, his body tense when he should be relaxing into the treatment. She wanted to place her hand on his back, tell him to breathe. With how quiet and broody he'd been this week, she didn't dare.

He'd warned her he'd be distant and possibly rude. She wouldn't describe this week's behavior as rude exactly. But definitely cold. Based on what she knew about Eric, she'd go so far as to say he'd seemed upset—the downward tilt of his lips she'd noticed, the slight slump of his shoulders when he rested between exercises. She'd never witnessed him during the lead up to a fight. This could be normal for him. That fine line between too much pressure and just enough to bolster his training.

Her father had certainly been extra gruff the week of a fight. She didn't remember him seeming sad. *In the zone* was a better description. He'd march through the house, his face pursed and fists clenched, like he'd swivel around with a right hook to your face at any moment. She'd stayed away from him those days. Let the man be in his head, get ready for his fights.

She did the same with Eric.

She busied herself cleaning up the physio room, wiping down equipment. The machine beeped when it was done. She felt ready to beep. Be done with the world of boxing. Move on to the part where Eric studied on weekends, while she curled up beside him reading a book. No bloody matches on the horizon. Just them and a lot of sex. God, she really missed the sex.

Eric cleared his throat. He'd already removed the probes and was standing at the table, his expression unreadable. She'd been so in her head, she hadn't noticed him get up, and she wasn't sure what to say. He flexed his fingers, the thick tendons along his forearms straining.

She wanted to run to him, kiss him with all she had, make him promise to come out of the ring tomorrow whole and healthy. The closer his fight loomed, the more on edge she'd been. Therapy sessions had been a godsend, and she'd talked to Heather daily. Voicing her stress with others made her anxiety more manageable. She was jumpy and hadn't been sleeping great, but all in all, she was dealing with Eric's impending fight pretty damn well. Still, she wanted it done. Whether or not he won, they'd figure out their life, as he'd promised. But winning would be even better. A reward for how hard he'd worked these past weeks—his entire career—to get to this match. Go out with a bang.

She twitched, about to go to him, but he moved first, stalking over to her and sweeping her up into his arms. He hugged her fiercely. It wasn't even sexual. More like the comfort hug he'd given her when she'd been scared over her father's health. She squeezed him back, offering as much understanding as she could, but his limbs trembled slightly, like there was more going on with him than the stress of the match.

She shouldn't ask if something else was bothering him. He'd been clear about his needs during this time. "Are you okay?" she whispered anyway. She wasn't a robot. This was the man she loved, and he seemed to be hurting.

He hugged her tighter, stuck his nose in her hair and breathed deep. Then he was kissing her, desperately, passionately, moving hard and fast, their compassionate hug turning heated. He was suddenly turned on. There was no missing the erection jamming into her stomach. She was on fire. This abstinence nonsense was physically painful. It shouldn't be. She'd gone a heck of a lot longer without a man. This was what happened when you knew what you were missing.

She tugged at Eric's shirt, pushed her hands underneath the fabric, absorbed the heat of his skin. He slowed his lips before she got too far, pulled back, and stepped away. He didn't answer her question: *Are you okay?* At least, not in English. He said something in Russian, his penetrating eyes intense, and left before she could wish him good luck.

He'll be fine, Isla told herself on the way to the elevators. Eric was just an uber-focused athlete, doing mental gymnastics to prepare for the fight of his life. The sad desperation she'd sensed in that hug and kiss had been her projecting her worries onto him.

Yep, the man would be perfectly fine.

She rode the elevator up, tapped her heel while thumbing through her phone. There was an email from Mark Lawson, the Major League pitcher her client Álvaro had mentioned might be looking for a new therapist. She squealed in delight. She hadn't heard more about Álvaro's possible referral and the timing couldn't be better. Another big name for her client list, who might refer other athletes her way. Exactly the good news she needed today.

The basics of her website were up and running, thanks to Eric. She still had to go in and add some content, but he'd done the tough stuff. All she had to do was change details. That work would be the perfect distraction for the next day and half, until Eric's fight was over. Then they'd fly back to Chicago together, on Preston's fancy jet. Maybe have fun on those white leather couches in the back area. She'd finally force her father to rest, and she'd be able to share his illness with Eric. Eric would better understand some of the anxiety she'd been battling, why his choice to quit boxing meant more to her than he knew. They wouldn't have to date in secret any longer.

She wasn't sure how Eric's decision to quit boxing would affect her father's career. She was still hopeful her father would go public with his illness when they returned home, hoped there were boxers who'd still want to be trained by the legendary Swinging Graham Slade, regardless of his diagnosis. Only time would tell, and Eric needed to start thinking about himself.

The elevator opened on her floor. She walked off and eyed

her father's door up ahead. He'd be resting before his next training session with Eric. She should knock. Wish him well. Hug him just because she felt like hugging him. She put her phone in her purse and reached to knock, but she heard a bang and thud.

From her father's room.

"Dad," she called, knocking hard. "Dad! Are you okay?"

Nothing. She couldn't hear a damn thing except her wild knocking and the loud pound of her heart. "Dad, please. Open up."

Shit. Key. She had his emergency keycard, and this was an emergency if she'd ever seen one. She rifled through her purse, digging through a notepad, pen, eye drops, and other useless items. She found the keycard, but her hand shook too hard to use it on the first shot. Effort two had the green light flashing.

She pressed on the door handle, pushed the door open, and gasped.

Her father was on his knees, hunched forward, one hand braced against the hotel dresser. Then he turned his head toward her and she saw blood.

She rushed over and fell to her knees, reached for him, needed to see how bad the gash on his forehead was.

He flinched away. "Why are you here?" He looked slightly dazed. Also annoyed. His usual glare was extra-special sneery.

Something in her snapped, anger burning as bright as her worry. "I'm here because I heard a bang and found you on the floor with a massive cut on your stubborn head, which, by the way, is deep and needs stitches."

Maybe they could give the man a facelift while they were at it. Change his resting sneering face to a resting happy face. A trusting face that wasn't too proud to ask for help or admit when he was sick, and God, she was just so *mad* at him for being so difficult. Sad and scared and pissed off to see him like this, facing the brunt of his illness alone.

He touched his forehead again, looked at his red fingers. “Just fell is all. Smacked my head on the dresser going down. No big deal.”

The man was on his knees, bleeding from his head, blinking to regain his focus. But it was no big deal. “You need stitches.”

“Just gotta get up and wash my face.” He leaned on the dresser to stand. Took a moment to regain his balance, then sat on the bed, never once asking her for support. As usual.

Swinging Graham Slade was a boxer to the core. Hitting the floor didn’t matter. He had an intimate relationship with that hard fall, the blood and pain. It was in his nature to get up, force a brave *sneering* face.

Biting her tongue, she left him briefly. Returned with a wet cloth and dabbed at his forehead. The white cloth turned pink. He grunted, otherwise keeping quiet while she cleaned him up, but the wound wouldn’t quit bleeding. “You need stitches,” she said again.

“I have a training session to get to.”

“Head wounds bleed like crazy. Do you think Eric wants you bleeding all over the ring while he trains? Will that be good for his focus?”

Another grunt, angrier this time. His molars made a clacking sound as he mashed his teeth together. “Fine. We’ll go for stitches. My focus is off, so you’ll have to text Brick. Don’t say a word about why I fell. Tell him I tripped on something.”

For the first time, she fully supported his plan to lie. As stressful as the training change might be for Eric, the last thing he needed, the day before his big fight, was to learn his trainer had Parkinson’s.

"Keep this pressed to your head," she told her aggravating father.

She fished out her phone from her purse and went to the bathroom, needing privacy for this awkward text. She closed the toilet lid and sat on the seat.

Isla: **I have to take my father for stitches. He slipped on the wet floor in his bathroom and smacked his head.**

Although she hated lying to Eric, her racing heart slowed slightly. She craved this connection. A moment of concern from him, a brief balm for her haywire emotions.

Eric: **He's missing training?**

She frowned at his text, waited for another message to show up, one asking if Graham was okay. If *she* was okay. Nothing came.

Isla: **He'll miss this one.**

Eric: **I need him here.**

Isla: **He needs to see a doctor.**

Eric: **Fine. I'll see him later.**

Fine. Like a disgruntled teen's "whatever." So much for concern and comfort from the man she loved.

Isla: **I'll have your trainer back as soon as possible.**

Eric wouldn't know how scary this was for Isla. He didn't have a clue about Graham's illness. And he was stressed. Their kiss before he'd walked out of their physio session hadn't just been a loving farewell. His rough movements had been laced with desperation. Hints of distress. Still, his selfishness stung. He didn't care if she was upset or if her father was okay. He cared that his trainer was missing a session.

She closed her eyes and exhaled. He'd warned her he might be rude and challenging this week. It shouldn't be a surprise. The outcome of this fight impacted his entire life.

Three hours later, she was riding in a taxi with her father. They hadn't spoken much during the drive to the hospital, or while waiting for a doctor, or while *lying* to the doctor about why he'd fallen. His head was stitched up. His balance seemed fine. She still felt brittle and mad, tired of Swinging Graham Slade constantly fighting her help.

The taxi stopped at a light. The driver talked to someone on his Bluetooth in a language she didn't understand. Eric would likely recognize the words, but thinking about him made her edgier. Her father's usual wheezy breathing filled the backseat's silence, and when she glanced at his stern profile and the bandage on his forehead, exhaustion swamped her.

"say it
yell it
whisper it
sing it
scream it
whatever you do
set
it
free"

"I have panic attacks," she told her father.

He cut a look at her. "What?"

"I have panic attacks. Awful moments where it feels like I'm suffocating and can't breathe. Like I'm dying and can't do anything to stop it."

"Isla..." He frowned and his bandage wrinkled. "I don't understand. You've never said a thing. When did they start?"

She breathed deep, regretting it when she got a nostril full of the pine tree air freshener hanging from the driver's rearview mirror. "When I was a teenager."

"A teenager?" The words were loud, angry. Kind of reminded Isla of how she'd reacted when she learned her father had been diagnosed with Parkinson's for *two freaking years* before he told her. "Why didn't you tell me?" he demanded.

"I didn't tell anyone. I thought the attacks revolved around boxing—how scary it was for me back then, seeing you hurt, worrying you'd never get up from the mat. But the mind is more complicated than that. I mean, the violence of the sport was part of it, fear of losing you. But it was Mom leaving, too. Unresolved hurt over her loss from my life, dealing with her resentment of me."

He took her hand. A thin line of red seeped through the bandage on his forehead. "You should have told me."

Pot, meet kettle. Pride was a pitiful thing. "I should've, but I didn't. I actually didn't say anything to anyone until a few weeks ago. But I've been talking a lot lately, to Heather and Eric and a new therapist, and what's become startlingly clear is that my biggest roadblock to getting better has been that I'm too much like you."

He reared back. "I don't suffer from panic attacks."

"No, but you're bullheaded and obstinate, and you think you can handle your illness on your own. You don't want to burden others, and you think asking for help is weakness." She was talking about herself as much as him. Her throat burned as her voice quieted. "You're embarrassed for people to see you as anything but strong."

"Isla, I…" He rubbed his hands on his thighs. A louder wheeze escaped his broken nose. "You're not weak, Princess. You're a hurricane."

"A hurricane with mental health issues. You're a heavyweight champ with Parkinson's, and I can't keep pretending I'm not worried about you." A tear snuck out. She didn't bother wiping it off. "After Eric's fight, you need to stop pushing me away. I can't live like this, Dad. I can't live with you fighting this on your own. I need you to lean on me, so I can be there for you. I want us to fight this thing together."

Tears shimmered in his eyes. "I thought I was doing what was best for you."

"Because you're a stubborn fool, like your daughter. And"—she swallowed hard, remembering all the times he'd ignored his doctor's advice, returning to training and fights when he should've been resting—"maybe consider telling the press about your illness. Use your story to make a stand, force the World Boxing Association to make changes for better player safety."

He shut his eyes, looking more tired than she'd seen him in ages. "That's your fight, Princess. Your views, not mine. I'm not using my illness to drag boxing down. I love the sport. I have no regrets there. But being honest with you, letting you in?" He tugged her into his side, kissed the top of her head. "I'll try and change. We'll help each other, okay?"

"Yeah, okay." The best promise she could ask for. And she had to respect his stance on going public and attacking boxing. Their views on the sport would never align.

The taxi bumped over a pothole. He kissed her head again. "Eric—he's been good to you? Not making the anxiety worse?"

Eric hadn't been awesome this week, but his recent behavior was Brick Smash behavior, not Eric Kramarovsky behavior. Soon the former wouldn't exist. "He's been amazing."

Her father pulled back, looked her in the eye. "Even with my illness, seeing me like this, you're still willing to date a boxer?"

It was the same question he'd asked when he learned about her and Eric, but there was more heartache in his words this time. More sadness. Tomorrow, after the big fight, he'd learn

Eric was quitting. Unlike Swinging Graham Slade, Eric was choosing himself over the sport. Tomorrow, her father would know.

Today, she said, "I love him so much. He's my match."

Her father pressed his lips together, but he nodded. "Then I support you."

"And you'll quit acting like an overprotective tyrant, giving us the evil eye when we're together?"

He ran his tongue over his teeth. "How's your new office space doing? My guy said he got all the work done." Mr. Subject Changer.

She rolled her eyes. "It's all done and ready for next week's opening. And I'm serious about the dirty looks."

"You should teach me how to make those smoothies you used to whip together. With all that green stuff? I'll start making them when we get home."

She laughed at avoidance number two, too content to keep nagging him. Her father had promised to quit shutting her out. Her business was full steam ahead, with two Major League Baseball clients on her roster. She was in love with a (cunni) linguist who recited poetry in French and Russian and Hebrew. All she had to do was survive Eric's fight tomorrow night and her life would be better than she could have imagined.

27

Eric sat on the table in the arena's locker room, wraps secured, gloves on.

Graham got up in his face. "Keep your brain switched on. Don't rush your moves. Joe's too big to go hard at him. Pick him apart, wear him down."

"Let loose in round three. Yeah, I know." Graham had drilled in their plan, every day for six weeks.

"Keep him moving. Tire him out."

Eric grunted. They'd worked hard on his endurance: extra runs, swimming, skipping, endless sparring. He was as fit as he'd ever been. Physically, at least. Mentally, he needed to get his shit together.

He shouldn't have called to speak with Eliza yesterday. He'd tried to push his niece's sickness from his mind. Rosa would call if she got worse. No news was good news. But he'd caved, needing to hear Eliza's sweet voice for himself. Instead of making him feel better, her rattling cough had broken his heart. Then Isla's text had come in.

He'd been sitting on his bed, his head in his hands, when

he learned about Graham's fall, and he'd felt unhinged. Furious at everything undermining his focus. At himself for being rude and inconsiderate to Isla when she'd probably been upset about her dad. Her news had been one more setback. One more uncontrollable event. One more unplanned hiccup infecting his mind. Distractions he needed to quit reliving on the day of his fight.

He jumped off the table, bounced on his feet. Loosened his body and arms and neck.

Joe Bradley. The fight. The win. Nothing else mattered.

All this hard work and training culminated in this one night, to prove he was the stronger man, earn the right to his freedom. Pay Preston back, love Isla properly, offer his sister and mother financial security, give Eliza the biggest hug and maybe a dog. She'd like that. A pup of her own. Company if Whit was somewhere with Eric.

Joe Bradley. The fight. The win. He smacked his gloves together.

Graham grabbed Eric's mitts and stilled them, stern as ever. "Your mind is your secret weapon. Stay focused. You've got this."

Eric nodded. The hard bass of a hip hop tune thumped from the auditorium, followed by cheering: Joe Bradley making his entrance. Eric bounced on his toes some more, shadow boxed. Visualized his footwork, punching combinations. The song changed to the screamer music his PR team said suited his Brick Smash image. Whatever it took. This match was his.

Joe Bradley. The fight. The win.

Graham led the way and opened the auditorium doors.

Noise and energy blasted from the sold-out venue. Eric's adrenaline punched up, his vision swimming along the edges, while his central focus became razor sharp. *Joe Bradley. The fight. The win.* He followed Graham into the madness.

"If I could kiss Justin Timberlake," Heather said, "I'd happily join a nunnery and never touch another man." She was back in Chicago, video-linked with Isla through their phones while they watched *Friends with Benefits* on their computers—tonight's movie choice for their rom-com watch party.

Otherwise known as tonight's avoid-the-biggest-boxing-match-of-the-year party.

"I mean, JT is cute," Isla said. "But not *join a nunnery* cute." Not that she'd paid much attention to JT or the movie. Anxiety hadn't fully sunk its claws into her yet, but her hotel room felt slightly claustrophobic. Her ability to focus was abysmal.

Heather's blonde hair was in a messy knot on her head, as usual. She flicked a piece of popcorn at her phone's screen. "JT's hilarious. And talented. And there's something about him seeming like an average guy. But he's, like, way better than an average guy."

"An average guy with benefits."

Heather sighed. "I need one of those."

Isla had one of those. Well, not quite. There wasn't anything average about her hulking linguist, who whispered Russian endearments against her skin. A man who was possibly getting his face busted up right now. Yep, the walls felt painfully close.

She glanced at the clock. With the media preamble and televised circus, Eric would be twenty minutes into his match. Almost halfway, assuming there wasn't a knockout. The arena wasn't far. A block and a half down the strip, where the man she loved was facing off against the heavyweight champ of the world.

Clammy sweat developed on her brow. She swiped it off with her forearm, left her computer for a minute to gulp some water.

Heather's "Oh, shit" had her diving back to her bed.

"Oh shit...what?" Isla tried to calm her pulse. It wouldn't slow.

Heather's wide eyes filled the phone's screen. "Nothing. Nope. Not a thing. Just spilled some popcorn is all."

"It's the match, isn't it? You're watching it." After promising they'd boycott it together.

Heather bit her lip, looking so guilty it would have been funny if Isla wasn't a pile of nerves. "Maybe?"

"What happened? Is he okay?" She desperately needed to know. She didn't want to know.

"First tell me how you're feeling."

"I'm angry at my best friend, who said we were watching a rom-com so I wouldn't stress over my boyfriend's boxing match."

Heather swatted her hand at the screen. "Your internal Zen. Are you feeling okay enough to know, or will it set you off?"

Isla was about to shout a string of swear words at her phone and tell Heather where to shove her Zen, but she paused, took a deep breath. She was not awesome, that was for sure. No one would hire her to spread Christmas cheer, but she didn't feel like she was choking on air. She was worried and scared, but she also felt strong and lucky to have a friend like Heather. "I can take it. Just tell me if I need to get Whit from Eric's room for support."

"I don't think so. Eric went down, hit the mat hard, but he got back up."

Isla massaged her chest, hating the visual of her big, strong man taking a huge blow. Had he been hit in the kidneys? His ribs? His handsome face? There was no way she'd be able to watch a silly rom-com now. "Give me the play-by-play."

"You sure?"

Isla was surprisingly sure. Watching his match herself was a different story, but pretending it wasn't happening was a losing battle. "It's better than imagining the worst."

For the next twenty-odd minutes, Heather winced and cheered and told Isla when Eric took charge, forcing Joe into the ropes. When Joe snuck a hook to Eric's kidneys. As far as Isla could tell, the match sounded relatively even, but Eric had hit the mat that one time. Not good for his score, and Heather wasn't a boxing aficionado. Her descriptions wouldn't paint an accurate picture of the match.

Isla paced, wrung her hands, occasionally pressed her face close to her phone to ask Heather how bad Eric looked.

"Cut up and tired," Heather said this last time, worry in her voice.

Another visual that gutted Isla. Instead of falling apart, she focused on how compassionate Eric was, always following her lead, taking things slowly when she'd admitted her feelings. Putting her first. She reminded herself how supportive Heather had been, her father as well. Her team, always in her corner. For tonight, her anxiety hadn't won. For tonight, she was victorious.

"What happens when it's over and both guys are standing?" Heather asked. "How do they decide who wins?"

"Is it over?" *Please let it be over.*

"Last round."

And Eric was still standing. Not laid out on the mat or being rushed to the hospital. *Yet.*

"The judges keep scores each round," Isla said nervously. "They mark things like defense, clean punches, getting knocked down. Then they tally them for the winner." The answer was rote, details her father had taught her. All she could think was: *it's almost over. Eric's boxing career is almost finished. Please let him come out of it okay.*

She suddenly needed to see him. Be there for her man, even

from a distance. Even if he didn't know she was watching him. She found her remote and turned on her TV, flipped to the televised channel, heart beating in her throat. The first thing she saw was Eric jab Joe Bradley, a hard shot to the ribs, and she shouted, "*Yes!*"

"You're watching, aren't you?" Heather asked from the phone Isla had tossed on the bed.

"I had to." She resumed pacing, one arm wrapped around her stomach, her fist pressed to her mouth.

Eric's right eye and his lips were swollen. Joe wasn't as cut up, but they both looked tired and sweaty, their feet heavy as they danced around each other. Then Joe surged, a quick combination that had Eric's head whipping backward. Isla winced. Joe worked him into the ropes, landed a couple more body shots. But Eric lifted his arms. Pushed back and maneuvered off the ropes. Fought to regain control. Isla sucked in a harsh breath, her entire body tense.

Then the bell rang. The referee got in the middle of the men.

And it was done. *Over.*

Instead of feeling relieved, her stiff limbs felt ready to snap.

"Who won?" Heather asked.

From Heather's play-by-play and the bit Isla had seen, she wasn't sure the answer was Eric. She picked at her cuticles, anticipation making her queasy. "They'll announce it soon. Hopefully before my pacing drills a hole in the floor."

The network showed a shot of Eric in his corner, being tended to by her father: iron pressed to Eric's swelled right eye, blood wiped from his split lip. They cut to Joe, and Isla wanted to force the camera back. Those were her guys in that ring. Her favorite men in the world. What were those idiot cameramen thinking taking the focus off of them?

She paced. Couldn't watch the screen as it panned between

the judges and commentators. Then the announcer was out, his voice booming from the TV. "Your winner and still heavyweight champion of the world is...Joe Bradley!"

The crowd roared, but Isla's heart sank. Joe's people flooded the ring. They only showed a quick shot of Eric, the dejection and defeat in his eyes, and Isla started rushing.

"I have to go," she told Heather. Jeans. She needed to change out of her sweats, put on jeans. Get to Eric as quickly as possible.

"Go take care of him. Send him my love." They hung up.

Isla hoped her love would be enough to ease that defeated look on Eric's face. Competitive athletes took their losses hard. He'd be angry with himself, crushed about the cash he'd lost. She'd have to help him through this, discuss his options going forward. Figure out how to make his retirement work. All daunting prospects, and her gut twisted.

What if he changed his mind? Decided he needed to fight again, salvage his image? Earn money with his fists instead of his mind?

No. She firmed her jaw and caught her reflection in her room's full-length mirror. She had dark eyes, like her father's. She could mimic his glare, too. She was strong. Unyielding and persistent. She wouldn't let Eric falter. He'd been beyond frustrated with his life, playing the role of Brick Smash. This life change wasn't about money for him. It was about being true to himself.

There would be interviews after the fight. People wanting one last piece of him, before he trudged to his locker room to shower and lick his wounds. She'd be there for him when he was out.

28

ERIC PRESSED his hands to the shower wall, head bent forward, water pummeling his sore body. Images flew through his mind, each one making him angrier. Joe Bradley standing over him. Joe Bradley landing punches to his ribs. Joe Bradley calling him a dirty Russian, cabbage eater, and other slurs to get into his head.

Nothing new in the ring, but tonight, he'd thought about his mother, working herself half to death in that first vinegar factory, sending him to school with cabbage rolls, the sour smells, the taunts from kids. How helpless he'd felt back then. The way he'd felt helpless lately, with Eliza and his family's money problems. And suddenly he'd been more angry than focused.

Instead of going slow, wearing Bradley down like he'd been trained, his mind clung to one word: *attack*. An uppercut for the father who'd left them. A jab for the choices Eric had been forced to make. A right hook for Eliza's damaged lungs, for his mother's broken wrist and Rosa's struggles and Eric's shame at borrowing money time and again. Pissed off fighting. Not calculated moves and counter moves.

Graham had barked at him to get his head in the fight. DeAndre had said *fuck* ten thousand times. So many people he'd let down, himself most of all.

He dragged a hand down his wet face, over his swollen right eye. His mouth and right cheek weren't much better. He leaned into the pain and thought of Isla, at the center of everything. A woman who expected him to retire now, walk away with nothing—no pride, barely enough cash to live on, beyond paying the extra expenses and his mounting debts.

When he'd promised her he'd quit, he hadn't known Eliza would get sick again. Preston hadn't come to him yet, anxious, asking for money. And Eric hadn't allowed himself to contemplate this outcome. *Loser.*

He watched the water pummel the floor, swirl down the drain, mixing with the blood from his cuts. He breathed and welcomed the hot stab in his ribs, the throbbing in his head and face. He was bruised and battered and looked like hell, and he didn't want to leave the shower.

Eventually, he turned off the spray. Trudged to the locker room with his towel around his waist. He wasn't much of a drinker, but he needed something stiff tonight. A lot of that something stiff. He changed into sweatpants and a T-shirt, every shift and move making him wince. He paused to catch his breath, leaned on the locker.

Preston sauntered into the room, dressed in another of his fancy suits. "Tough match."

More like embarrassing match. "Sorry I let you down. I know you need the cash."

Preston crossed his arms and shrugged one shoulder. "Looks like I'll be one private jet lighter, among other things, but life goes on. Has the doctor been in?"

"Briefly. Told him I'm fine." Moving hurt, along with thinking and breathing, but he didn't have the patience to be prodded tonight. He'd borrowed money he couldn't pay back, and Preston was once again proving how decent he was, not holding guilt or the debt over Eric. "I'll get you the money. It won't be quick, but I'll pay you back."

He wasn't sure how. He pictured himself returning to training mode, growling *Brick Smash* in interviews. Telling Isla retirement wasn't realistic, trying desperately to convince her she was strong enough to date a boxer, when he'd promised her he was getting out. Something inside him shriveled, but he didn't know what else to do. He had no qualifications yet. His studies had only been a hobby. More schooling cost money and took time. Minimum wage at some job wouldn't cover Eliza's bills or Preston's loans.

"Speaking of paying me back," Preston said, "I have a lead on an endorsement deal. Not BDA and you'll hate the idea, but it's quick cash."

Eric hissed out a sore breath, hating where this was going. "What is it?"

"A barbecue chain that boasts massive meat platters. They want you dressed like a barbarian, gnawing on their meat, doing a few Brick Smash grunts." Preston spoke smoothly, his tone matter of fact, like the prospect didn't make Eric physically ill.

More aches added to his endless list, but maybe this humiliation was a solution. A way to ease into retirement. "How much are they offering?"

"Fifty grand, but I can get that number up."

It wasn't thirty million, but, aside from Preston's cut, most of the money would be Eric's. No cash would be lost to a setup like this Vegas show or to training and his wellness team if he actually quit boxing. He'd likely have enough to cover the medical bills and pay Preston what he owed. Plan for his future. His nausea shifted slightly into the stirrings of hope. "I'll do it."

"Really? I thought for sure you'd say no."

"I'll do it," he repeated and looked his manager in the eye. "I'm also retiring from boxing. It'll be my last Brick Smash gig." He'd stretch that money, live leanly and get a job while finishing school. Be a regular guy with a regular life, one that included keeping his word to Isla.

Preston frowned, then walked over and leaned on the lockers, facing him. "You want out?"

If Eric was honest with himself, he'd never wanted in. "It's time. It's not what I want anymore, but I need that cash. So, yeah—I'll do the commercial."

"If it's not what you want, I'll support you. You know I always have your back, but that plan can't work."

Eric moved to rub his eyes, then thought better of touching his swollen skin. "Why not?"

Preston's phone buzzed. He checked it, then shoved it back in his pocket. "Sorry. As per the endorsement, they don't want a retired guy for the ad. They want Brick Smash, intimidating-as-hell boxer. If you quit, they'll use someone else. If you lie about it and quit afterward, it'll look bad. They could sue."

Eric muttered, "Fuck," and pushed off the lockers, pacing. Every move shot pain to his broken ribs. He didn't care.

He couldn't keep boxing. He didn't want it, but he needed that money. Always the money. His choices were once again ripped away from him, but Eliza's health was more important than his wants. If she got sick again, he'd make sure she got the best care.

He quit pacing and faced Preston. "What if I fight one more match? No promises of more down the line. As long as I have one on the books, they'll hire me, right?"

Preston pocketed his hands, rocked on his heels.

"Theoretically, I don't see why not. No career is a guarantee. As long as you're still in it, they'll be on board."

So that was it. One more fight and a ridiculous commercial. He'd have to convince Isla this would be it. That she was strong enough to stay with him. She'd mentioned how much better she'd felt lately with the therapy and talking to Heather. She'd understand his choices were limited. Losing her wasn't an option when he'd already lost so much.

"Fine," he told Preston. "Book me another fight."

"Another fight?"

Eric's attention snapped to the locker room entrance, to Isla standing there looking like she'd been punched in the stomach.

ISLA MUST HAVE HEARD them wrong. Eric had promised he'd quit boxing. He'd spoken the vow when she'd hesitated to pursue their connection, unable to imagine a future with this remarkable man.

After I win this fight, I'll quit. You won't have to worry about dealing with the training and the fights. I'll just be a man, putting the woman he cares about first.

"Just one fight," he said now. "One match, so I can secure an endorsement deal."

The move made sense, but she'd been here before. Her father retiring, then returning to the ring. Her father never really seeing how his boxing affected those he loved. It was always one more fight. Then one more and one more, until he was lying on his hotel floor, a gash to his head, because Parkinson's had knocked him on his ass.

That could be Eric one day. He might look invincible now, big and strong and at the top of his fitness, *when* he hadn't been boxed to a pulp. This wasn't athleticism, though. This was science. Boxers exposed to repeated head trauma weren't likely to live long, healthy lives. Eric may not know about her father's illness, but he knew how this sport had torn her down time and again. He'd promised this would be the end for him, offering her what she'd needed to hear, sealing the deal to be with her. Had it all been an act?

"You promised you'd quit," she finally said, her breathing coming fast. "You knew I wouldn't date a boxer, and you promised. Was that all bullshit? Lies to get what you wanted?"

"I'm not sure what's going on here," Preston said slowly, his attention bouncing between Isla and Eric. "But if he promised you he'd quit, he meant it. He even told me he wanted out before you walked in."

Preston could be protecting his client, having Eric's back. Isla could barely think through her hammering pulse and the twisting in her stomach. She looked hard at Eric, focused on his intense eyes. Even through the swelling, his pleading bled through. Remorse and sadness in the depths of his gray gaze. No. His promise hadn't been an act. If he'd won, he'd have quit. Unfortunately, none of those good intentions changed Eric's broken promise.

Frustration and sadness winded her, along with a flood of guilt. She'd rushed here, desperate to help Eric deal with the blow of his loss. He stood slightly bowed, his bruised face pinched and his breaths shallow, like he was in pain. Her father had come home looking like that and worse, walking gingerly around the house. Wincing when he coughed or talked or chewed.

Instead of being there for Eric, all she'd done was accuse him of lying. "I should go," she said. She couldn't offer the comfort he needed now, not after what she'd overheard. But she could give him space. "You should rest. We'll talk tomorrow."

"No," Eric said, his voice strong. Then to Preston, "Isla and I need to talk alone."

Preston glanced between them again and nodded. "Call me later."

The second he left a sea of tension expanded between them. She felt nauseous, didn't want to have this conversation now. It was unfair to Eric. He deserved to wallow, get angry, or sad—whatever it was he did when he lost a fight. "Please, Eric. We'll talk tomorrow, after you've rested."

"Things happened," he said quickly, ignoring her suggestion. "Eliza got sick this week. She's fine, but she ended up in the hospital. I'll need to cover those bills, and I haven't told you, but I've been borrowing money from Preston. Cash to cover the cost of my mother's broken wrist and our busted furnace. Normally Preston wouldn't care when I pay him back, but an investment of his went south and he needs the cash."

She hated hearing Eliza had gotten sick. She felt every inch of Eric's desperation, her body aching to go to him, to offer him the hug he surely needed. She couldn't move.

"Isla, please." He moved closer, took her hands. "Please don't leave me. It's just one more match."

Preston was right. Eric Kramarovsky was the best man she knew. He'd never have promised to quit boxing if he hadn't believed in that outcome. He was also loyal to a fault. His role of caregiver in his family hadn't been a choice for him. It was duty, because he was that kind of guy. Even if his choices weren't the right ones for him personally, he'd never falter. She'd also bet he was as clueless as her father about how his fighting impacted those he loved.

She doubted Rosa and his mother liked watching him get slaughtered in the ring on their behalf. She'd bet her new business Rosa would've rather had her brother there in the flesh, as a support, instead of his money. Eric didn't know what it was like to be on that side of the boxing ring. The family. Second best to the sport. Watching the person they loved get hurt.

He didn't know that helplessness, and he didn't know why all the reasons in the world couldn't change Isla's mind.

In the taxi with her father, when he'd asked if she was willing to date a man who could end up like him, she'd believed Eric was quitting boxing. She'd told her father Eric was her match. *I love him.* The reply hadn't been a direct answer to his question, only a sentiment.

Nothing had changed on that front. She couldn't imagine finding a better man than Eric. If her dating app experience was anything to go by, she'd be lucky to find a man half as wonderful as her Baby Whisperer. But if she'd answered her father's question truthfully, the reply would have been *no. I'm not willing to watch another man I love deteriorate.*

This wasn't just one fight for Eric. He'd always feel responsible for his family. Health and home expenses would always pop up. He'd carry the burden of father and son and brother and uncle, even if it broke him. His loyalty was part of what Isla loved about him. What right did she have to ask him to change?

She suddenly felt incredibly selfish. This was Eric's life, not hers. His responsibilities. He had people who depended on him. She was just a woman in love.

Tears burning the backs of her eyes, she pressed her hands to his cheeks, softly, careful not to hurt his swollen face. "I love you, Eric. More than I thought possible. But there's no guarantee this will be your last fight." He opened his mouth to argue. She pressed to her tiptoes, kissed his lips gently. "You want it to be the last, but it's not a promise you can make."

His bruised face slackened. "But you've felt better, haven't you? The anxiety isn't like it was."

She did feel stronger, and Eric was the main reason she'd faced those demons. This wasn't about her panic attacks, though. This was about long-term health, and she couldn't tell him about her father. If Eric kept boxing, he'd want his trainer with him. As much as she hoped her father would come clean about his Parkinson's, she couldn't make that choice for him.

"My anxiety's better," she said, "but I've lived this life already. It isn't the future I want."

As hard as it was watching her father's health struggles, watching Eric deteriorate would be even harder.

Eric's nostrils flared on a ragged inhale.

A tear slipped down her face as she pressed to her tiptoes again, stole one last kiss, and walked out of Eric's life.

29

Álvaro Garza stood from Isla's treatment table and shook out his legs. "Feels good. Better than it has in ages."

Isla jotted down some notes on her clipboard. "Might have something to do with the fact that you're between seasons. Talk to me when you're in the thick of your games."

"How about I talk to you over drinks this weekend?"

Isla tried to laugh at Álvaro's usual pickup line. At least once a session, he hit on her. She didn't think he was actually interested. It had become a running joke: his asking, her turning him down with a snarky comeback. Over the past month, her snark had fled the building.

"This was our last scheduled appointment," she said as she led him to reception, ignoring his date request. "We should book next month's sessions." She sat at her desk and pulled up the appointment calendar on her computer. "I've left Tuesday and Thursday mornings clear for you." Because she didn't have many clients yet, but he didn't need to know that detail. Better to make Álvaro feel important.

When he didn't reply, she glanced up.

He leaned on her counter, looking more concerned than flirty. "You've been off lately."

"My treatment's been off?" Panic had her voice rising. She could not lose Álvaro as a client. While she'd been doing better than she'd expected for the first two months of her business, Phoenix Physiotherapy was still in its infancy. The books weren't showing a profit. She was barely able to pay herself.

"Not your treatment." He waved off her worry. "Your mood. You've been, I don't know, a bit flat."

Flat made sense, if flat meant sad and weary and heartbroken. Even now, she wanted to flop on the floor and cry like a frustrated child. Moan about how unfair it was to meet the best man, only to break up with him because he worked the worst job. Details Álvaro didn't need to know, but she had to say something. He often opened up to her about his personal life. Being honest was the best way to explain her recent lackluster personality.

"I broke up with someone a couple months ago," she admitted. *I stabbed myself in the heart with a rusty knife.* "It seems to be hitting me harder as time goes on, but it'll pass."

Álvaro nodded, then waggled his eyebrows. "You should date me. We'll go to a bar. Have some drinks. I'll help you forget your someone."

His cockiness reminded her of Preston, which reminded her of Vegas, which reminded her of Eric talking to her through his manager, saying the perfect words because he was the perfect man for her, and it felt like an anvil pressed on her chest. Two months. Two months and this pain had gotten worse, not better.

"I'm sure you're a blast," she told Álvaro, forcing lightness into her voice. "But you're a client, and I doubt your ego would fit into a bar." That was better. Their usual snarky banter.

He grinned and smacked the counter. "There's my girl."

She laughed, appreciative of their growing friendship. "I'm sorry about my mood. I promise to keep my personal life out of our sessions from now on."

"Don't apologize. I prefer getting to know my team, and I know what it's like being on the bad end of a breakup. Your work doesn't suffer, and I get to tease you more this way."

They scheduled his next appointments and he left with a smile, but Isla planted her forehead on her desk. Pathetic. She'd become a pathetic mess.

Leaving Eric had been her only choice. Since Vegas, she'd been to all her father's doctor's appointments. They'd found a new medication to help with his dizziness. He was doing well, but he'd shared more details about his health with her: his slight difficulty swallowing, which he'd been hiding, along with the extent of his fatigue. As promised, he no longer pushed her away. Between clients and paperwork and growing her business, she spent more time with him than she had in ages. He hadn't been willing to go public with his illness yet, or open up to Eric or the press, but their relationship was the best it had ever been.

The only downfall of their closeness was seeing more clearly how hard his illness was on him, physically and mentally. She couldn't date a boxer with firsthand knowledge of that challenging road. Not even a man she still loved desperately.

"Princess? You okay?"

She lifted her head, blinked at her father. "Sorry. I didn't hear you come in."

He stared at her, his usual sneer locked in place. "What's wrong?"

"Nothing. I'm fine."

"the greatest lie

i ever told is
i'm fine"

Ramona Estle sure hit the nail on the head with that blatant poem. Isla twitched her nose, making sure it hadn't grown.

Her father's jaw flexed as he watched her, a hard stare that went on so long she stood from her desk and rounded the counter. "Is everything okay?"

He frowned, then patted his pants pockets. "Came by to say hi, but I think I forgot my credit card at the grocery store. I'll see you later."

He left as quickly as he'd appeared. She stared after him, too emotionally drained to say goodbye.

Eric whipped the skipping rope over his head. Faster loops, faster jumps, double-unders to work his endurance. Air hissed through his nose. The balls of his feet touched the floor briefly, tasted air for a second, before connecting again. He was nothing but his body in these moments. Muscle moving. Blood flowing. Heart pumping. The second he finished his set, he was back to being a shell of a man who didn't know love could hurt this much.

Hardcore music pumped from the gym's speakers. Two guys grunted in the ring. Another handful worked out around it, their fists smacking the heavy bags and speed balls. Eric tossed the rope on the floor, grabbed his towel, and dragged it down his face. This had been his life the past two months. Workouts to train his body, unending cardio to bleach his mind of memories. Sore muscles afterward, including an aching heart.

He'd known he loved Isla. She'd snuck into the small circle of people who inhabited his life. He'd welcomed her intrusion like a starving man, took what he'd wanted, even with the barriers in their way. Now he suffered.

He hadn't known a person could leave a shadow behind. A forever memory that followed everywhere, reminding you food tasted better and poetry was lovelier and smiles were easier when she'd been around. At times, he wished they'd never met.

Graham stalked into the gym, so fast and angry, Eric stepped back.

"You." Graham jutted his chin toward Eric. "In the office. Now."

Graham swiveled on his heel, not waiting for Eric's reply, and silence cloaked the gym.

Someone behind him whistled. "Dude's gonna get thrashed."

Slowly, the sound of gloves hitting leather resumed. Eric's pulse rushed. Graham had never been a touchy-feely guy. The man rarely smiled. Even when he did it was more of a slight lip tilt. Eric was used to Graham's hard-knocks ways and steely looks. He appreciated his trainer's all-business approach, but as he walked into the office and got slammed full force by Graham's piercing glare, he knew something bad had happened.

"Is Isla okay?" Just saying her name felt like a fresh stab.

"No. She's not."

This wasn't a stab. This was acid in his gut. "What happened?" His voice came out as a croak. Was she hurt? Had something happened to her in her apartment? Driving to work? While out with another man? The acid in his gut sloshed.

Graham's glower deepened. "That's what you're gonna tell me. What the hell happened between you two?"

So, she wasn't hurt. Not physically, at least. "We broke up. But what do you mean she's not okay?"

"I know my girl. She's strong and willful and stubborn, and

sometimes a pain in my ass, and she has bouts of anxiety, but what she isn't is sad. Until now. All she's ever said is that you two didn't work out. She didn't say why, and I didn't pry. But I'm prying now. You've been as big of a mope as her lately. So I'll ask again—what the hell happened between you two?"

The office was small. Nothing but a messy desk, stray boxing equipment, and sparse walls with a few hanging photos, including one of Graham holding up his heavyweight belt. Eric sat in the too-hard chair opposite the metal desk, his forearms propped on his knees, feeling like the small space was closing in. Isla must be as sad as him about their irreconcilable differences. The awareness gutted him. "How's her anxiety been?"

Graham crossed his arms, not budging from his intimidating pose. "Fine lately. Now answer my question."

Eric was glad her anxiety had dissipated. She'd obviously made the best decision for herself, breaking up with him, even if it was tough on them both. "It's pretty simple, really. I told her I'd retire when I won the last fight, but I didn't win, and things got tougher at home. I needed that endorsement deal. So I'm still boxing and she doesn't want to be with a boxer."

A hard line in permanent ink. He rubbed his eyes.

"So quit the damn sport."

Eric snapped his attention to Graham. "What?"

His trainer flung his arms. "You quit boxing. You two love each other, so you quit and you be with her."

Oh, like it was that simple. "My family needs the money boxing provides. And why the hell would you suggest I quit? You never stopped, never backed down when it was your time. How am I any different than you?"

"You don't love the sport!" Graham's growly voice echoed off the walls. "Not anymore, at least. Not the way a fighter should."

Eric opened his mouth to argue, yell because he felt like

yelling, but Graham wasn't wrong. Eric didn't get off on the high of the crowd, the adrenaline of landing a solid punch. He felt good in those moments, and boxing strategy challenged and interested him, but if given the choice, he'd take a quiet night with a textbook over sweating it out in a ring any day.

"It's not that simple," he said. Eliza was healthy and happy these days. His mother's wrist had healed and she was back to work. They had heat in their house and food on the table. He may be miserable in his personal life, but seeing his family well took precedence. "I may not fight for the love of the sport like you did, but I fight for my family. Not the same drive, but it's a responsibility I don't take lightly. I do this for them, and I won't let them down."

Graham made a disgusted sound. His scowl shifted to the floor, his jaw bunched, like he was having an internal yelling match. Then he said, "I have Parkinson's."

Eric froze. "You what?"

"Parkinson's, for two years now, but the symptoms didn't give me trouble till last fall. That's why I asked Isla to come to Vegas. I told her right before that trip and told her she couldn't tell anyone. That's why I missed some sessions with you, and why I ended up with stitches in my forehead. It's also why you may *think* you're doing this for your family, but you're dead wrong."

Eric pressed his fist to his chest, tried to stem the sharp pain behind his ribs. Graham was a rock. A solid beast of a man. If he'd been ill, Eric hadn't noticed. The sneers and scowls and shouts to work harder hadn't changed. Or Eric had been too in his head, focused on his training and falling for Isla and the heartache afterward to open his eyes and see beyond his own nose. *Parkinson's.* He was sick for Graham. Hated to see this man, who'd become a fixture in his life—a man he'd grown to *love*, gruffness and all—shrink in any way.

And Isla. So much suddenly made more sense: her brash rudeness when they'd first met, the panic attacks he'd witnessed, and her final words to him: *My anxiety's better, but I've lived this life already. It isn't the future I want.*

Her anxiety had only been a portion of what had held her back from staying with Eric. The bulk had been this: firsthand anguish of loving a fighter who'd been cursed with a cruel disease.

Eric's body felt incredibly heavy. His head. His shoulders. His heart. Eyes stinging, he said, "I'm so sorry."

For Graham and for Isla.

The edges of Graham's frown softened slightly. "Then listen to me. I've fought Isla on going public with news of my diagnosis. She wants to use me as a mouthpiece, to go after the World Boxing Association, get them to make changes to better protect its athletes. What she doesn't understand is I may resent aspects of my health, but I wouldn't change my past. I loved boxing. Still do. If this is the result, so be it. But she was right to push me to quit lying. I plan to announce my illness. I'm still not sure how, and I don't want to shine a negative light on boxing, but I'm done lying to the world and putting my daughter second."

Eric hung his head, sad for Graham and feeling incredibly stuck.

Graham's big hand landed on Eric's shoulder. "This isn't the life for you. Your brain's too damn important. You're a natural-born athlete with enough drive and hunger to get the job done, but your heart isn't in it. It's with my daughter. If you don't quit now, while you're still young, starting over will only get harder."

"I have responsibilities. People who need me to take care of them."

Graham leaned in closer. "I used to think I was fighting for Isla. Then I found out my career gave her panic attacks. We see the world the way we want to see it. Warp our views to fit our own agendas." He released Eric's shoulder and stepped back. "I'm in talks with a fighter who wants me as a coach, even with the Parkinson's—Nikki Castle. She's good and hungry and has a ton of potential. DeAndre got an offer to head up Max Rietveld's team, which means I'll need a new assistant coach. You're smart and a great strategist, and you know how I work. The job's yours if you want it. If you decide to keep fighting instead, I'll still coach you too. But that would be a pretty fucking stupid choice."

In typical Swinging Graham Slade fashion, he marched out of the office, leaving Eric sitting on the hard chair, reeling from Graham's barrage of information. He kept picturing Graham in the future, tremors quaking his limbs, unable to land a punch or aim a fork toward his mouth or hug his daughter with strong arms. He pictured Isla caring for him, as she no doubt would, watching that powerful man deteriorate slowly, bit by bit.

The realities of boxing had never hit so close to home, and Eric hated not being there for Isla. He wanted to hold her, let her cry on his chest, take care of her while she took care of her father. The only way he could do that was by quitting boxing. Not eventually. Now. Prove to Isla he could be trusted. But he'd lose the endorsement deal. They'd insisted on adding his next match to the fine print, a clause stating Eric had to boast about the food chain when interviewed.

If he quit, he'd have Isla, but he'd be in the red again. Preston had managed to save his own financial ass, another client's big deal making him flush. But Eric still owed his manager money and assistant coaching would only help so much. What if Eliza got sick again?

His breathing came faster. The room spun slightly, like a sinkhole was spiraling around him. One wrong move and he'd tip into the unknown, drop into a freefall.

Was this how Isla's panic attacks felt? An invisible force dragging her under?

Somehow, he got to his feet, walked to his car, drove home. When he opened the front door, Whit ran at him, tongue lolling as he made his snorty sounds. Eric crouched and dug his hands into Whit's wrinkly skin. Let the pup's heat ground and settle him. He really was the best therapy.

"Asher has a favor to ask," Rosa said, standing inside the entrance. "For the twins' birthday next month."

Eric stood, brushed the fur from his hands onto his sweatpants. He was still processing Graham's diagnosis, working through all the possibilities tangling his mind. Distracted, he glanced at Rosa. "Why isn't he the one asking me?"

She folded her arms around her middle and rocked on her heels. "He wants you to be Brick Smash, entertain his friends with boxing stuff."

Irritation flared up his neck. That was the absolute last thing he needed to deal with right now. "I won't act like a dimwitted fool in this house. This is my space. My escape from the madness. The answer is *no*." After everything he'd done for them, how could she even ask?

She flinched. "You don't need to yell about it."

"You should know how much I hate playing that role."

"Hate it? You love boxing and marching around yelling *Brick Smash*."

He stared at her, dumbstruck. Was she really this clueless? Did she have no idea how much he'd grown to despise his image? Resent his career? Graham saw him to his core, why he boxed and what the ring had cost him. How could Rosa not know her own brother?

Just as quickly, the answer hooked him in the jaw.

This had been part of the role he'd played with his family.

Be the strong one. Don't show weakness. Support them at all costs. He'd never talked about how hard the responsibility was on him. He hadn't wanted them to worry.

Whit lay on his dog bed, eyeing them warily from the small living room. The dog didn't like raised voices. Eric didn't like his tone much either. "Can we sit a sec?"

Rosa nodded and followed him to their couch, tucked her leg under her as she faced him. "You've seemed sad lately," she said. "And angry."

Maybe he'd shown more weakness than he'd realized, more vulnerability. It was time he explained why. "When I was in Vegas, I worked with Graham Slade's daughter. And..." He pictured Isla's smile, the brightness in her dark eyes when discussing poetry, how she supported Eric's studying and made him laugh. Fighting the burn in his throat, he said, "I fell in love with her."

"Eric." Rosa's eyes brightened, pure joy beaming at him. Then her face sobered. "So why have you been a bear, moping around, barely talking?"

"She broke things off. She doesn't want to be with a boxer, and she's right. She shouldn't be with me. So when you say I love what I do, you're miles off. I'm good at what I do. Not the best, obviously, or I'd have won in Vegas. But I'm good enough to earn us money. To pay for broken furnaces and hospital bills with endorsement deals. And if I ever win big, I'll send you to school and the spa and hire a housekeeper and buy us a big house, and mom will never work again. That's why I box, Rosa. For all of you."

"You box for us." It was a statement, not a question, but the incredulity in her voice was odd.

"Only ever for you."

"You are such an idiot." Rosa shook her head slowly, then punched his arm.

"Why the hell did you do that?" He rubbed his arm. He'd certainly taught her how throw a jab.

"If you think we wanted you to box, you really are dense. My genius brother who speaks a trillion languages is a moron."

"Have you lost your mind?"

"I'm about to lose something." Red splotches mottled her cheeks. "Do you know Mom won't watch your fights anymore? She sits in her room and pretends to sleep. *I* watch the matches. I watch them, feeling sick every second of every round. Like, physically ill, waiting for the punch that will change everything and mess up your stupid, brilliant brain. Eliza cried during your last match. Asher got quiet and wouldn't talk for the rest of the night. I only pushed you to keep at it because I thought you loved it. You do so much for us I wanted to do that one thing for you—support the career I thought you loved. I didn't want you to be stuck in this boring life with us."

Eric was back in that sinkhole, unsure how to climb out, the walls spinning around him.

Nothing in his world was right. Graham's illness. Rosa's shock. He replayed Graham's rant, how he'd scoffed at Eric's fighting motivation. *I box for my family.* Apparently boxing hadn't lifted Eric's family up. Not if Rosa's revelation was true. Boxing certainly hadn't been good to Isla. And here Eric was, facing his sister, seeing her fears for the first time.

"I only ever wanted to make your life easier," he said. "Provide for you and Mom. And nothing about living here is boring to me. I love spending time with you and the kids."

"I let you do it," Rosa said quietly. "I actually want to work full-time, get out of the house, do something for myself. But every time I bring it up, you get angry, and I clam up. I think I've been afraid since Dad and after my divorce. Worried one wrong move would send you away, too. But I should have known better. I should have pushed harder for what I wanted, told you how hard boxing is on the family. So I'll tell you now: if you don't love it, it's the last thing I want you doing."

Simple discussions neither of them had broached. For a guy who studied language and communication, his observation skills were severely lacking.

When translating, if you switched the order of words in sentences, the meaning changed. Same words, different outcome. Remove context, and you could offend someone in seconds. He and Rosa had done exactly that, not paying attention, reading the wrong words between the lines.

He thought back to the choices he'd made. Not recently, but all his life, the driving force behind his determination, then his decision to finally quit boxing in Vegas, reversed so quickly, always falling back on his imagined family pressure. Getting it all wrong.

"I still owe Preston a ton of cash."

"But it's not your burden alone," Rosa said, patience returning to her voice. "I'm not a kid, Eric. I'm an adult and functioning member of this family. If we work together, instead of you trying to do everything on your own, we'll figure it out."

Such a simple statement, a rule you learn as a child: share, work together. When had she become the wiser of them? "I think about quitting boxing all the time, but I'm scared, I think. Like I'll be doing a tightrope walk without a safety net, one step from falling."

Rosa nudged his arm. "Then I'll be here to pick you up, the way you've picked me up a million times. Maybe it's my turn to take care of you for a change. And the timing is pretty great. My office just posted a full-time position, with salary and benefits. I'm pretty sure I could get it."

His instinct was to fight her on it, but there was brightness in her eyes he hadn't seen in a while. Pure excitement. He'd convinced himself she'd needed his financial support. That she'd be happier spending as much time with her kids as possible. In the end, he'd forced his views on her, so he could feel like he was the man of the house, standing in where their father had failed. "If that's what you want, I'll support you."

It was also time to start honoring himself. Quit boxing, like he'd considered umpteen times. Not after the next match. Not in a week. Not after he'd secured an endorsement deal. He was done today, *if* Preston could work his magic and get Eric out of the contract. Rosa securing that promotion would relieve some of their financial burden, and Eric would jump on Graham's assistant coaching job. Nothing was certain, but for the first time in ages, Eric didn't feel helpless. He had choices and hope.

Graham's trust in sharing his illness also gave Eric an idea. A way to help his coach shine a light on Parkinson's without undermining boxing, as he'd worried. If Eric played his cards right, this move might even be a way to get Isla back.

30

ISLA SIPPED her red wine while Heather cooked her famous buttermilk roast chicken—a succulent bird that always came out golden brown and perfectly juicy. As a food stylist, Heather spent her days shellacking food with non-edible sprays and varnishes to make them look magazine-ready. She also excelled at cooking actual tasty meals. Isla's apartment had never smelled so delicious, but she was still in a sad funk.

"Dinner will be ready in twenty," Heather called from the kitchen, "but you're not sufficiently tipsy. Get your sad butt in here."

Isla didn't want to move her sad butt. She had plenty of wine in her glass, and her couch had a comfy groove in the cushion, the exact shape of her ass. She'd been perfecting the ass-groove for the past three months, spending every night making her mopey little nest. Her apartment had also never been so clean. The books on her bookshelf were organized by color. All dust bunnies had been eradicated. Instead of following Heather's orders, Isla sunk deeper into the couch.

"You either get over here right now, or I dump this gorgeous bird in the trash."

So much for Fort Wallow. Isla huffed out a breath, leveraged herself off the couch, and trudged into her small galley kitchen, only to find Heather with a shot glass in her cleavage. It was filled with liquid. Isla didn't need to guess its contents. "I'm not doing Goldschläger boob shots."

Heather pushed out her full chest. "Oh, you definitely are."

"I don't give into peer pressure."

"Please. This isn't peer pressure. This is bribery. Do the shot, or the bird is toast."

Isla glanced longingly at her oven, inhaled the savory, roasted smells making her mouth water. Goldschläger it was.

She leaned down, suctioned her mouth around the shot glass in Heather's cleavage, and grimaced while shooting it back. "Oh my God, that will never not be gross."

She wiped her mouth and gave a body shiver, remembering the last time they did boob shots: the day her father had told her he had Parkinson's. The day she'd agreed to work with his boxer in Vegas. The day that had changed everything.

Isla sniffled, wiped her mouth again.

Heather cupped Isla's cheeks. "That was supposed to make you feel better, not worse."

"I miss him so much," she whispered. An unending ache.

"Oh, honey." Heather wrapped her arms around Isla. Her friend gave the best hugs. Well, second best. The Baby Whisperer had a black belt in hugging.

Heather rubbed her back. "I hate seeing you like this."

She hated being like this.

Isla's phone buzzed. She gave Heather a good squeeze, then found her cell by the sink. She frowned at the message.

Dad: **Turn the TV on to channel 9.**

Isla looked at Heather. "What station is channel 9?"

Heather shrugged. "News, I think?"

"My dad said to turn it on."

Curious, Isla returned to her living room and retrieved the remote from the crack beside her ass-groove. The TV blared to life, set to her usual Food Network station. An awesome distraction when sad and mopey.

"Maybe he did another infomercial," Heather said. "A thigh master for men."

"He better not have." Isla still shuddered when she thought of the toilet plunger infomercial he'd done when short on cash. During that delightful E-Z Plunger ad, they'd had him use a regular plunger in one scene on a clogged toilet, only for raw sewage to overflow and flood around his feet.

Isla found the channel and a reporter filled the screen. It was a news station, as Heather had assumed. The brunette was talking about a dog that had saved his sick owner by breaking out of the house and getting help. The story reminded her of Whit, the ugliest, best dog she'd ever known, and she sighed. This sad sack routine was getting tiresome. More wine might help. It would mellow her mood and eradicate the Goldschläger taste in her mouth.

She reached for her glass from the coffee table, but the reporter said something about Parkinson's. Glass of wine forgotten, Isla swiveled toward the screen.

"Most of us know Brick Kramarov as the recent contender for the heavyweight belt," the reporter said. "Today, he's here to talk about something near and dear to his heart and make an exclusive announcement for our viewers. Brick, tell us about your Parkinson's initiative."

Announcement? Parkinson's initiative?

Isla and Heather shared a quizzical look.

None of those words made sense, not with Eric at the center of the hubbub. But his handsome face filled the screen and Isla couldn't help herself. She moved, like a lovesick zombie, walking toward his back-lit face until she was kneeling on her area rug, a foot from her TV. She tried to absorb every gorgeous inch of him: the blond hair that was a bit longer, those slate-gray eyes, sharp cheekbones, strong nose, full lips that could undo her in seconds. God, she still loved him so much.

"I prefer to go by my real name," he told the reporter. "There's no point being Brick Smash when I'm retiring from boxing."

Isla leaned forward, like the shorter distance would explain the shocking comment coming from Eric's mouth. She whipped around and searched Heather's smiling face. "Did you know about this?"

"I'm as surprised as you."

Isla's father wouldn't be surprised, though. He'd texted because he'd known this was airing, which meant he'd been in cahoots with Eric, and Eric must know about her dad's Parkinson's. The reporter was asking Eric more questions, details about the retirement and what had prompted the decision. Isla focused on the screen, tried to understand how and when this all had happened.

Eric stared at the camera, his chin ticked up. "Boxing's been good to me. It allowed me to support the people I love, but I have other aspirations in life, other avenues I want to pursue. I've also recently learned some upsetting news that helped me see my path more clearly."

"Can you share that news with us, Eric?"

His strong jaw tightened briefly. "My long-time trainer, Graham Slade, has Parkinson's. It was devastating learning about his illness, for many reasons. It was also a wake-up call for me."

"Because you saw how dangerous a sport like boxing can be?"

He shook his head. “We all know the dangers. Boxers walk into the ring with clear eyes. Graham will tell you himself, he wouldn’t do anything differently in his life. Boxing will always be a tough, dangerous sport. It’s part of the draw and excitement, for most fighters and for the fans. But his admission reminded me that we need to live our best lives while we can, whether it’s facing fists in the ring or walking away from those golden handcuffs.”

“What does this mean for you going forward?”

“Well.” He shifted on his seat, seeming nervous now, the first sign of uncertainty Isla had noticed, and she felt nervous, too.

If Eric was retiring, everything could change for them. The likelihood of him getting sick like her dad would diminish greatly by quitting now, not *sixteen years* from now. She wouldn’t have to continue pretending she didn’t still love him desperately. But that was a big *if*. This could be a repeat of her father, retiring one minute, returning to boxing the next. And he might not even miss Isla the way she missed him. He hadn’t reached out to her about this massive change in his life.

Eric cleared his throat. “It means several things. First, I’m leaving boxing to focus on my language studies. I plan to become a Russian interpreter, so I can help people struggling to communicate. While I’m studying, I’ll be working as an assistant coach under Graham Slade for the talented Nikki Castle, a powerhouse who will turn women’s boxing on its head. Second, Graham Slade and I are holding a benefit to raise money for Parkinson’s research. In particular, we’re partnering with Weston Aldrich of Aldrich Pharma to fund a treatment that has shown potential. And third…” He trailed off, closing his eyes briefly as he dropped his gaze. He definitely seemed nervous.

She was an anxious mess.

His eyes snapped back up. "The third reason I quit boxing is because I fell in love with the most beautiful, smart, funny, strong woman I've ever met. Through her I learned love is a language I didn't understand—the nuance of smiles and touches. How much power every action holds. Through her I learned I deserved more. She's why I had the courage to make a change. I unfortunately lost her in the process of getting here, and I desperately want her back."

A knock sounded on Isla's door. The sound wasn't as loud as her pounding heart. No one had ever said such profoundly romantic things about her before, but of course Eric would: the brilliant linguist who'd turned her world upside down.

Another knock rang out.

She shot a look at her door. The interviewer was talking. Isla had missed what she'd said. Isla was still struggling to absorb all *Eric* had said.

Through him, her father had come out publicly about his illness. Not directing the focus toward the harm boxing caused. He was using his name to raise money for his disease. An illness that affected millions of people, most of them non-boxers. And Eric was retiring.

She still worried this was like her father all over again, one minute retired, the next announcing his return to the ring. But her father had never planned for his future during his retirement. He'd spent money and moped around and had created his own ass-groove in the couch. This was Eric making a public declaration about his studies and future plans: assistant coaching, fundraising, studying. He was telling the world he loved Isla, even though he hadn't used her name.

The interviewer was still talking, and when the camera panned back to Eric, the person at her door knocked again. Isla growled and hit *pause*, thankful for DVR. There was no way she'd miss Eric's interview. Not when he was fidgety and nervous about what he'd been about to say.

"Let me check who that is," she told Heather as she stood. Her head swam slightly from the boob-shot and wine and Eric's revelations. Seeing his face again, even on a TV screen, added an extra spin to her belly. When her focus cleared, she marched to the stupid door and the stupid person interrupting the moment.

One look through the peephole had her clutching her chest. "It's him." Not a stupid person. The smartest man she knew. Looming large in her hallway.

"The cunni-linguist?" Heather asked.

"Yeah," Isla whispered, scared any volume would send this mirage away.

Eric was *here*. At her apartment.

Heather released a giddy laugh. "He's totally here to get you back. The bird should be ready. I'll take it out of the oven and leave it for you two to enjoy."

Isla couldn't look away from the door. Everything was happening so fast she was struggling to keep up. Hand still pressed over her pounding heart, she faced Heather. "I should trust him, right? Believe he's done with boxing for good?"

Heather paused at the kitchen entrance. "I can't tell you what to do, but that man's making major life changes. I'm guessing the only reason he'd be this public about it is to prove himself to you. Either way, you need to open the door. I'll hide in the kitchen, then sneak out." She blew Isla a kiss and hightailed it into the kitchen.

Isla ran her shaky hands over her hair, glanced down at her yoga pants and tank top. Sad, mopey attire. There was no changing now. Taking a deep breath, she prepared to let Eric in.

Eric stood in front of Isla's door, reliving his awkward teen years in every nervous breath. He wiped his damp palms on his jeans. Tried to swallow through the dryness in his mouth.

He'd never been this anxious to speak to a woman. Maybe it was the stretch of time. He hadn't seen Isla in three months. They'd gone from seeing each other twice a day, with added sleepovers and room service dinner dates during their last few weeks together. Not the last week, when he'd been in training mode. But before then, she'd been part of his every day and night, and he couldn't believe how much he missed her. The intensity often flattened him with its ferocity.

If everything had gone to plan, she was behind this door, watching his taped interview. Graham had said she'd planned to be home, that he'd text her and tell her to turn the program on. There were no guarantees, though. She could be out or napping or hadn't bothered checking her phone. She might not have heard Eric's public declaration and his very important third reason for quitting boxing.

He raised his fist to knock again, but the door opened. The second he saw her, his stomach flipped.

"Hey," she said. One soft sound that hit him in his heart.

"Hey," was all he managed back.

Her dark eyes had a glow to them. So damn beautiful. Her gorgeous lips were slightly parted as she stared up at him with a look of...

He wasn't sure how to describe her expression. A cross between wonder and surprise and longing? He really hoped he saw longing.

She was in yoga pants and a light blue tank top. The thin fabric clung to her breasts and flat stomach. His mouth dried more, and he suddenly couldn't speak. He wasn't sure if he should get on his knees and beg her to take him back, or if he should follow his body's urge to kiss her until neither of them remembered the past three months.

Unsure what to do, he glanced past her, into her small apartment. All the time they'd spent together, they hadn't seen each other's homes. He was curious, wanted to catalogue every inch of her space, but he saw her dining table, which was set for two. He noticed the smells. Meat roasting in an oven. Fancy meal smells. Having-a-date smells. Eric's gut twisted.

He should have known a woman like Isla wouldn't stay single. When she'd first installed that dating app, it had pinged ceaselessly with matches, men who'd wanted to take her out. Of course he'd missed his chance. He'd screwed up and waited too long and now Isla was seeing someone else.

"I'm sorry," he muttered, stepping back. "You obviously have a date. I shouldn't have come." Shouldn't have made an ass of himself, when she'd clearly moved on.

He turned, needing to get away, get air. Figure out how to get over Isla, but she grabbed his arm. "Eric, wait."

For what? To be told they were done? He wasn't sure he could handle that right now. Along with nausea, the urge to break something flared. Destruction. The base human need to sink his fist into plaster. Embody his alter ego Brick Smash one final time. He was furious at himself for pushing Isla into another man's arms. For making selfish choices that had hurt them both. But he didn't have the strength to leave and lose this small connection to her.

Reluctantly, he turned.

She was right there, inches from him, those shiny dark eyes softened at the edges. "My plans are with Heather, not a man. There's been no man since you."

His breath rushed out of him. *Thank God.* But adrenaline still had his blood pumping and heart pounding. "I'm really glad to hear that."

I'm really glad you're still free to be mine.

She quirked her lips. "Would you have been jealous?"

"Extremely." He wouldn't pretend the idea of her with another man didn't break him.

She bit her lip, seeming pleased with his reaction. A good sign, and he wanted that lip between *his* teeth, her mouth on his, her taste filling him up. He wanted a lot from Isla Slade, but he said, "I'm so sorry about your father."

Sadness flickered across her face. "I wanted to tell you in Vegas. He wouldn't let me."

They were in the hallway. Nowhere romantic or private. Eric closed the distance between them anyway, couldn't handle not having his hands on her. He brushed his palms down her back. The tank top was as soft as it looked, worn and flimsy. He spread his hands on her back, tried to touch as much of her as possible. She placed the flat of her hands on his chest.

He liked her hands there a lot. "You don't need to apologize," he said. "I'm the one who needs to apologize. Losing you, Isla...it's been unbearable, and I did an interview, hoping you'd see it. But I guess you didn't, so I need you to know I've quit boxing and—"

She pressed her finger to his lips. "I saw it. Most of it, anyway. Until some big man started making a racket on my door."

She was teasing him. Teasing was good. Teasing meant flirting, which meant she might actually be giving him another chance. A different sensation swam through his stomach. Like he'd swallowed sunshine.

He walked forward, forcing her back a few steps until he had her against the hallway wall. "Then you know I've quit. No false promises this time."

Her chest rose faster. "But what about your family? The

medical bills and money you owe. And you signed an endorsement deal."

"Preston got me out of the endorsement contract. As far as debt goes, Rosa took a full-time job and Aldrich Pharma is paying me and a small team to coordinate the Parkinson's fundraiser with your dad. A one-time thing for now, but it'll help cover my family's expenses. There could also be more of that kind of work in the future. Weston, who runs the company, is smart and intense, but incredibly supportive. There's also the assistant coaching, and I've researched online courses, programs I'll take in my free time. It'll be a lot of work, and money will still be tight for a while, but this is what I want, Isla. Unfortunately, without you, it all feels empty."

She was his knockout rule. His loophole to true happiness.

Get up off the mat. Get her back. Get on with living a better life.

"I'm so proud of you." She hooked her fingers through his belt loops. "I love the idea of you coaching and especially translation work. You'll be brilliant at it, help so many people. And how's Eliza? And Whit? And is your mother's wrist better?"

"They're all good." Not as good as him, though. Seeing the concern and care on Isla's face proved how important this life change was for him. Isla was part of his definition of success—having the love of a smart, strong woman, who cared about him deeply. "I've missed you so much."

"I didn't know it could hurt this bad," she whispered, her eyes tearing up. "I didn't know I could love someone this much. I just...I can't go through this again."

Fuck. He knew exactly how she felt. The pain. The sadness. The worry. No more. "I'll never choose boxing over you again. Or over myself. And you were right about my family, how hard boxing has been on them. I was too blind to see it, but Rosa and

I had a long talk. We both misjudged a lot about each other. So I'm learning to work *with* my family instead of trying to take care of them on my own. And I want you, Isla. More than anything, I want us."

"You have me," she said, breathless. "I'm yours. And I can't believe you got my stubborn father to announce his illness. He's been—"

He kissed her, couldn't wait another second. She squeaked in surprise and leaned into him, desperate sounds escaping as she tugged him closer. *This.* He'd missed this so damn much. Her soft sounds and sweet taste. Their lips met and moved, trying to cover the distance of the past three months. He was out of breath in seconds, panting for her, sliding his tongue against hers, moaning at the contact.

"You two need to get a room."

He pressed his forehead to Isla's, chuckling. "Hey, Heather."

"You're welcome for cooking you dinner. Have a nice night."

He didn't look at Heather or watch her go. He only had eyes for one woman. "Can I come in?" he asked.

Isla's pink lips were swollen. She licked them, took his hand, and led him into her place. When he shut the door, he finally got to absorb Isla's home.

The small space was neat like it had been professionally cleaned, with food and sports magazines stacked evenly on her coffee table. A red shelf held textbooks and novels and pictures of her with her father, some seashells and rocks and other odds and ends. Eric hadn't imagined her as a rock and shell collector. He pictured them scouring a beach, searching the sand, kissing in the hot sun while waves lapped at their toes. A fantasy that would become reality one day.

A black-and-white shot of her father was framed on the wall. He remembered that magazine layout, a full spread of Swinging Graham Slade. Most photographs had shown him in the ring, his fist connecting with faces, spittle flying. Action shots. This one, though. It was special. His usual sneer filled the frame. Every scar and wrinkle and gnarly surface of his skin was visible. Shadow and light played across him, like a shot of the moon's textured surface. It was the photograph of a man who'd endured.

"If you want alone time with my apartment, I can leave for a bit."

Smiling, he strutted toward Isla, picked her up into his arms, bringing her to sit on the couch with him. He tugged her onto his lap. "You're not going anywhere. I need you to watch the end of my interview." He needed to see her face when she watched his best surprise.

She snuggled into him, kissed his neck, ran her fingers through his hair. "I'll watch whatever you want as long as you don't let go of me."

His body stirred and he held her closer. "No chance of that. I love you, *milaya*. Never stopped." Never would.

"What does *milaya* mean?"

"It's a Russian endearment that means *darling*." The word didn't begin to describe how he felt about Isla Slade. But her face transformed, softening into that look he'd missed like crazy. The one that said: *you're fantastic*.

"I like that," she said quietly. "Being your darling."

He fucking loved it and kissed her deeply because he could. "Just so you know, I didn't mention your name in the interview. It'll no doubt come out later, but I made sure the interviewer thought we got together after the fight."

The last thing he wanted was to hurt her or her business ever again.

She planted another kiss on his chest. "Thank you. And I bet the publicity will be good. Maybe I'll even be strong enough to take on boxing clients in the future."

He'd support her in whatever she chose. Holding her closer, he found the remote, rewound slightly, and pressed *play*, listening as he finished explaining his third reason for quitting boxing.

"...lost her in the process of getting here, and I desperately want her back."

Eric was used to seeing himself on TV, but not like this. His voice cracked at the end of his confession. He could see the tears in his eyes, remembered how scratchy his throat had felt when admitting how much he'd missed Isla. He looked like a lovesick sap, not a Neanderthal brute, and he'd never been prouder.

Isla tucked tighter into his body.

"I'm not sure there's a dry eye in Chicago," the reporter said, blinking rapidly. "And we at the station adore a good love story. So if your lost love is watching now, what would you say to her?"

"Although I study language, I'm not a poet. I can't put into words how loving and missing someone this deeply feels, so I asked an expert to help me out."

A split screen appeared, with Eric on one side and a young woman on the other side. She had long dark hair, wore thick-framed glasses, and was dressed in a masculine-cut suit.

Isla gasped. "That's Ramona Estle."

Eric laughed. "It is."

"Ramona Estle's on the screen. Next to you." She twisted on his lap and gripped his shirt. "You met Ramona Estle."

He laughed harder, kissed her adorable mouth. "Turn around or you'll miss the poem she wrote for us."

"Ramona Estle," she repeated, bouncing excitedly, then turned and glued her eyes to the TV screen.

"When Eric told me the woman he loved was a fan of my work," Ramona said, "I offered to write something special. A snapshot of love and pain, two opposing emotions that often coincide. I titled it: *Forgiveness*."

She lifted a single page and read.

"tears land on the page
bleed the ink
anger, they say
sadness, they accuse
hurt, they scream
but the page doesn't rip
it softens
and thins
i've got you, it says
i'll catch you, it promises
those words remain
there, unforgotten
but forever
blurred"

Isla sighed and wiped her eyes.

He held her tighter, his heart beating hard and fast. "I'll catch you," he said, repeating the sentiment of Ramona Estle's beautiful words. "Always." Never again would he lose sight of what he had and let Isla fall.

EPILOGUE

ISLA LIFTED HER TEENY, tiny teacup and pretended to sip the invisible liquid. "The tea is lovely, Eliza dear. The perfect temperature. Don't you agree, Miss Candy?" Isla's English accent was pathetically awful, but the pink stuffed bear beside her didn't seem to mind.

"Miss Candy agrees," Eliza said decidedly. "Want a scone with your tea, Uncle Eric?" Eliza held the empty plate toward him.

He grabbed an invisible pastry and made a show of eating it slowly and wiping at his mouth. "Tell Mrs. Nutter her scones are divine." His posh accent was perfect, of course. Isla couldn't get enough of seeing his huge legs folded so high his knees were at his armpits, his thick fingers delicately holding his teacup and saucer. That twinkle in his eyes was too sweet. "Isla, darling, pass me the butter, would you?"

She snorted and reached for the plate, but Whit scampered over with Asher hot on the dog's heels. The slobbery dog knocked into the table, sending Mrs. Nutter onto the floor and Mr. Green face-planting into his hot "tea."

"Asher! You ruined everything. You always ruin everything. And you're not allowed to run in the house. Mom! Asher's running in the house!" Eliza's cheeks were red with anger, tears shining in her eyes.

Instead of waiting for Rosa to settle things, Eric had his niece up in his arms, then upside down, hanging by her ankles. "Which way did your heathen brother go?"

"I'm upside down." She wiggled and laughed, no longer on the verge of crying. "I can't see!"

"You can hear him, though. Close your eyes and listen for Whit, then point in the right direction. We'll show Asher upside down girls have more fun because they don't run around the house."

Eliza squeezed her eyes shut, then flung her arm out. "That way!"

There wasn't far to go in the small home, but Eric extended the game, moving the wrong direction on purpose, making Eliza shake with laughter.

"He's going to make her pee," Rosa said as she eyed the destroyed tea party.

Isla picked up the fallen stuffed toys and righted them on their seats. "He loves Sundays."

Sunday was family day. Regardless of how much studying Eric had to do, he spent Sundays playing with his niece and nephew, helping his mother cook dinner, getting teased by his sister.

Rosa stared after her brother, smiling tenderly. "So do they." She gathered a couple of scattered cups. "So do I, but don't tell him I said so."

Isla didn't have a brother or sister to tease and love and torment in that special way siblings ragged on each other. She didn't have a mother like Eric's, who tutted over her kids and kissed their cheeks and told them how special they were. She did have this, though. Sundays with his family, where she was welcomed as one of their own.

Eric's mother called them to dinner, a raucous affair as usual. The twins talked loudly, vying for their uncle's attention. Eric's mother beamed at her son. Rosa called him out for dribbling sauce on his shirt, and he laughed so hard at one point, he nearly fell off his chair. Then he looked at Isla from across the table, with so much love and fondness in his eyes, *she* almost fell off her chair. Sundays really were the best.

He found her in the kitchen afterward helping his mother with the dishes. He slipped her cell into her back pocket. "Your father called. I think he was giving me that glare through the phone."

Always with that glare. "What did he want?"

Eric wrapped his arms around her from behind. "To tell you not to worry and he's feeling good, but he has a doctor's appointment tomorrow. He'd like you to meet him there."

Wonders would never cease. "I didn't even make him promise to tell me. Apparently you *can* teach an old dog new tricks."

"Whit might argue with you."

"Whit is a human, not a dog," she said. Eric hugged her tighter, effectively trapping her from drying the plate in her hands. She tried to wiggle out of his grip. "I'm helping your mother."

"Sorry, ma. I'm stealing her. See you Tuesday."

Tuesday was his day to pick up the kids from school. Although he'd moved in with Isla and was busy with his fundraising work and coaching and studying, he was here often, helping out when he could. His life was no longer ruled by scheduled workouts and strict diets, constant training. He still exercised and stayed ridiculously fit, but his priorities had shifted, and the shift looked good on him.

His mother said something in Russian, then took the plate from Isla. "Go with my boy. He will only break something."

"Yeah," he whispered in Isla's ear. "Go with me. Before I break something...like the zipper on my jeans."

He clutched her to his body, her back to his chest. And, oh yeah, something there might break. He walked with her suctioned to the front of his body while he nibbled at her ear.

"Let me go," she muttered, none too convincingly. "I can walk on my own."

"I can't." He picked her up and swung her over his shoulder, fireman style.

"Bye!" the kids called from the living room. They were watching TV, no longer fighting. For the moment.

Isla waved at them, while pounding on Eric's back. When he marched to the car without putting her down, she pinched his butt. "You can't drive like this."

"Sure, I can."

"You'll get a ticket."

"For being in love?"

She grinned. "For being too sexy."

He grunted and deposited her on the ground beside the passenger door, then adjusted himself in his jeans. "Buckle up. I'll be driving fast."

He wasn't lying. The drive was fast and a little reckless. *She* felt reckless.

Too happy for it to be safe.

Every time Isla told Eric she'd landed a new physio client, they celebrated with a home-cooked meal, ending with Eric's face between her legs and her crying out his name. Every time Eric aced a test or made headway on the Parkinson's fundraiser, they ended up panting, tangled in the sheets. If one of them had a good day, they spent the night reading and talking and making love. If one of them had a bad day, they spent the night reading and talking and *fucking*.

Recklessly happy was an understatement.

His big hand rested on her thigh as he drove, squeezing, inching higher. She was already wet, desperate for him. Needing to touch him, she palmed his growing bulge...because *fair was fair*. Air hissed through his teeth and he drove faster. By the time they parked and kissed and stumbled up to their apartment, she could barely see.

He kicked the door shut behind them, a trail of clothing littering the floor on their way to the bedroom, and she felt drunk. Warm and loose and dizzy with how much she loved Eric. She'd never tire of this, the silk-hard feel of his erection sliding against her hip. His big, strong body under her control. How in sync they were.

She straddled him on the bed, not taking him inside her, just rocking together, teasing. His eyelids got heavy. And, *God*, he was so hard between her thighs. Thick and heavy and all hers. When he palmed her breasts, she gripped her hands over his, moving with him. She'd never been this free with her body with men in her past, this comfortable in her own skin. Being with the right person had pumped up her confidence and enjoyment of sex, whether against a wall or on the floor or a bed.

He released her breasts, guided her up his solid body until she was straddling his face. Master Cunni-Linguist. She rocked and moaned, couldn't get enough of this man and his talented tongue until she dissolved in a shock of pleasure, shaking with her orgasm.

He gripped her hips, kept her under his control. Then she was on her back, all that male power pushing into her—hot thick heat filling her up. They gasped. He murmured words as he moved. Some nights he spoke to her in Italian, some nights

Hebrew. Tonight was a cascade of guttural Russian that drove her wild. But he moved languidly, their hips meeting, the long drag of him making her inner walls clench.

She put her palm on the words inked on his chest. The matching tattoo to the one on her ribs. Their poem, written by the one and only Ramona Estle.

Let the past blur.

Accept our faults.

Be each other's everything.

Even with their stresses—her father's health, his family's financial stability, her work-in-progress therapy business—Eric was her everything.

They lay together afterward, sated and pliable. "*Naite kurasu mo issho, waratte kurasu mo issho,*" he said against her head.

She recognized the sounds as Japanese but had zero clue what the words meant. "Did you just insult me, Rick Rosner?"

He laughed, adjusted on the bed so they were facing each other at eye level. He stroked her hair. "It's a Japanese proverb."

"If I'm a superficial flower again, not a substance-filled dumpling, I'll be changing the locks on the doors."

"A dumpling *and* a flower," he said and kissed her nose. "But no. It means our life's the same, whether we spend it laughing or crying."

She mulled over the translation. "Our outlook determines our life?"

He nodded. "The life we're dealt doesn't define us. How we choose to walk that life makes us happy or sad. A bit idealistic but choosing to walk this life with you makes me unbearably happy."

"Recklessly happy," she said.

"Yeah." He smiled and tucked her close. "Recklessly ever after."

THANK YOU FOR READING ISLA AND ERIC'S STORY!

Want to know what happens when a scorned woman accidentally keys the wrong man's car and ends up working for the surly man? Buy this falling-for-your-boss romantic comedy today: ***New Orleans Rush***

(Book 1 in the Showmen series)

NEW ORLEANS RUSH

You know that Carrie Underwood song? The one about her keying her cheating ex's car? Beatrice Baker totally did that, except she vandalized the wrong guy's Mustang.

Now she's stuck in New Orleans, working for Huxley Marlow—owner of said vandalized car—attempting to cover her debt.

And desperately trying not to fall for him. His vague nightly activities are highly suspect, and he's on the vexing side of demanding, but he's secretly kind and caring under all that gruffness.

Beatrice can't quit fantasizing about his adept hands and kissable lips. Even worse, his tortured past hits her right where it counts: in her heart. The last time she trusted a man, her bank account got drained and she almost got arrested. Surely this can't end *that* badly...right?

Thank you again for reading Isla and Eric's story. If you enjoyed it, please consider posting a review to help other readers who might be looking for a story just like this one.

And keep reading for a New Orleans Rush excerpt.

New Orleans Rush Excerpt

Seeing the world through rose-colored glasses was a cultivated skill. A sunny outlook could brighten partly cloudy skies and refract that brilliance into the world. Most days smiling through adversity was effortless. Tonight, Bea's positivity had fled the building.

"Hit me with another, sir." Her request came out faster than intended, each word knocking into each other.

The bartender in question cocked an eyebrow. "You sure that's a good idea? Looks like you enjoyed a few before coming here."

She squinted at the man's gelled hair and fancy bow tie. He seemed the unflappable sort, the type who could have survived her gray day with a sip of tea and self-deprecating chuckle.

Bea planted her elbows on the bar, briefly grimacing at the sticky surface. "I appreciate your concern, but that was my first drink. And if we switched bodies in one of those body-swapping movies, and you had to relive my last thirteen hours, you'd realize I could win the Guinness World Record for Worst Luck. Denying me another drink would be barbaric."

Except the alcohol *was* fogging up her usual rosy glasses. Or maybe it was the cold medicine she'd taken when she failed to find Advil in her purse.

The bartender cracked a smile. "Barbaric?"

"A crime against humanity."

He shook his head and reached for the vodka on the shelf. "Maybe don't inhale this one."

Another lemon drop in hand, she swiveled on her stool and scanned the room. The low lighting made her eyelids heavy, the red carpets and mahogany walls adding to the bar's sleepy warmth. It had a Rat Pack vibe, accentuated by the bow-tie-wearing servers and lampshade table lights. Jazzy music joined the hum of the crowd. A crowd as unfamiliar to her as the rest of New Orleans.

Move with me to the Mardi Gras City, Nick had begged. *We'll work the bar scene at night. You can paint all day. We'll live each minute like it's our last!*

Her boyfriend—now of the ex persuasion—had neglected to mention that four days into their adventure he'd change the rules, leaving Bea homeless and jobless in the birthplace of jazz. She also hadn't painted anything but artless amoebas the past month.

Sinking lower on her stool, she cupped her drink with both

hands. She didn't sip it right away, letting her tipsiness linger instead. Then a guy in a top hat and cape appeared.

Yep. That just happened.

She looked into her full glass, then back at the mirage, wondering if she was drunker than she'd realized. She *had* consumed her first drink faster than usual, and mixing cold medicine and alcohol wasn't the best idea. She squinted harder at the man. The top hat was still there, making its already tall owner stupendously taller. The cape was still there, too. Not just any cape. A midnight velvet cape with stars stitched through the material.

It was a galaxy far, far away. Right here. In a New Orleans bar.

The cape looked soft and plush. If Bea could rub her face in the fleecy fabric and roll into a cocooned bundle, she was sure she could sleep for a week and wake up in a different life. One that didn't resemble a fifty-car pileup.

The top hat man focused on her, as though sensing the longing in her stare. Or maybe he'd heard her say, "I'd love to nuzzle your cape."

A thought she'd accidentally unmuted.

He walked toward her like she was the only person in the jazzy room and stopped in front of her barstool. "You can touch it, if you'd like."

The fabric looked even softer up close, but the sensual timbre of his low voice had her sitting straighter. "If you're not referring to your cape, things might get ugly."

She wasn't above tossing her drink in his face.

His lips twitched. "I do mean the cape. Unless you'd like to try on my hat." He tipped up the felt brim.

She loosened her grip on her glass, pleased she wouldn't have to waste a perfectly good martini. But the way her day was going, the hat would probably give her lice. "I don't accept hats from strangers. Or capes."

"I believe that applies to candy, not capes."

"What if it carries an ancient spell and whisks me away to some dark castle where I'll be imprisoned and tortured until they learn I can't command the cape's magic?"

The edges of his eyes crinkled. "A valid point."

His languid gaze slid down her body and up again. He studied her so long she finally sipped her drink, then he extended his hand. "I'm Huxley."

The second her fingers—cold and damp from the chilled glass—slid into Huxley's large grasp, heat shot up her arm. The cape most definitely had hidden powers. "Bea," she said. "Fascinating to meet you."

The most fascinating moment of her gray day.

Aside from the subtle blond scruff highlighting dramatic cheekbones and his aquiline nose, Huxley wasn't traditionally handsome. Puckered skin overtook half an eyebrow, part of his right ear was missing, and a thick scar ran down his left cheek. His dirty-blond hair had a slight unruly curl, the ends licking at his neck.

Individually, his features weren't particularly attractive, but as a whole this man was ruggedly elegant. Like when you stepped back from a Monet and all the paint strokes blended into a masterpiece.

Until he said, "Bee, as in the insect?"

Now he was more of a disturbing Picasso painting than a Monet masterpiece. "As in *Beatrice Baker*, but make a bee joke and I might borrow your cape after all. See if I can use its dormant magic to turn you into a colon rectum."

He barked out a laugh. "Excuse me?"

She fixed him with her best menacing stare. "A colon rectum. It's an ugly beetle."

Frequently taunted with "bee" jokes as a kid, Bea had

studied insects and animals. The odder the name the better. Using the insults against bullies would often confuse them into silence. It had a different effect on Huxley, whose striking cheekbones rounded, his lips curving upward like he'd stumbled upon a four-leaf clover in a barren land.

She found herself leaning toward him. "Are you from New Orleans?"

"I am. But you're not."

She froze, worry weaving up her spine. He wouldn't know she'd just arrived from Chicago, unless he'd followed her here. Not impossible, but the one person who would have tailed her was even taller, with a slight paunch. Big Eddie could have sent someone else after her—an accomplice to intimidate and threaten. Except a gun for hire wouldn't waltz around, brazenly, wearing a cape and top hat, and Big Eddie had no clue where she was.

She relaxed on her seat. "How'd you know I'm not local?"

"Deductive reasoning."

"Because you're a clairvoyant with a photographic memory and can tell me every meal I've eaten the past week?"

Amusement lit his eyes. "My ways are much simpler than that."

"Do share."

He pointed at her lap. "The keychain on your purse is a dead giveaway."

Right. The Chicago Bulls tag. A gift from her ex-boyfriend on their third date. She didn't love basketball, but the keepsake had been sweet. It was now a sour memory. She removed it from her purse zipper and tossed it onto the bar. "Now I'll blend in."

Huxley's posture shifted, shrinking the distance between them. "A woman as beautiful as you doesn't blend."

Whoa.

Her pulse tapped up her neck, her rapid breaths chasing the erratic beat. She tried to decipher the odd color of his eyes, but the dim lighting made it tough, and a man bellowed Huxley's name from the back of the room, breaking the moment.

Huxley turned, and she gawked at the hollering man... because mustaches like his were extinct. That was a mustache wearing a face, the type of hairy handlebar that could serve as a playground for miniature children. A monkeybar-stache! She snickered at her internal joke and checked her drink again. It was still half-full, but her day no longer felt half-empty, thanks to the cape-wearing man before her.

"I'll be back," he said, all wonder eclipsing from his Monet face.

Once he joined the owner of the monkeybar-stache, Huxley glanced at her, but the mustache man's aggressive hand gestures drew his attention away. She sipped her drink and watched the odd interaction, wishing she could read lips.

When she finished her lemon drop, she turned and flagged the bartender. "One more, please."

He accepted her extended glass. "How 'bout we call this your last? You should head home after, sleep this Guinness Record Day off."

A brilliant idea, if she had a home, or a bed.

It hadn't taken much effort to stuff her clothing and paintbrushes back into her duffle bag this morning. She'd then loaded her yellow Beetle—the trusty automobile being the only mainstay in her life—and had sat in her parked car for an unhealthy length of time, replaying today's disaster.

"Here's the thing," Nick had said when she'd woken up this morning. "I've changed. I don't want to be in a committed relationship. It's best we know this now, before we get in too deep. It's been fun, and you're great, but it's time we moved on."

She had tugged at her ear, sure her hearing had failed her. "I'm sorry, but it sounds like you're breaking up with me?"

His answering nod had been all sympathetic puppy-dog. "It's for the best. I mean, I was getting coffee this morning, and a girl in line asked me out. I wanted to say yes, which means there's something missing between you and me. If we stay together, I might regret it and hurt you in the process. And you know I'm a stickler for honesty."

Getting dumped four days after following Nick to New Orleans had been humiliating. Listening to him admit he'd accepted the coffee girl's date *for tonight* had driven her mortification home. All because Nick believed in honesty. So much so, he reminded her the apartment he'd rented was in his name. He then graciously suggested she crash there until she found something new, no hint of irony in his voice.

Bea had stared at him. And stared. She hadn't screamed and cursed, because she wasn't a screamer or curser. She'd simply looked at the man who'd convinced her to quit her waitressing job, leave Chicago, drive across four states, upend her life for a dream, and she'd said *nada*.

The fact that he'd never blessed her when she'd sneezed should have been a red flag, along with his Kardashian-sized shoe collection. But Bea had wanted to escape and delve into her art and forget about her father, and the mess her sperm donor had made of her life. The matter of a certain loan shark threatening her bodily harm may have also expedited her departure.

Now here she was, the victim of another sabotaging man.

She dragged her newly filled martini glass closer, ignoring the pull of the caped man behind her. She was in no state to find any man intriguing. Not on a Guinness Record Dumping day. Sipping her lemon drop was no longer an option, either. She tried to suck that puppy back, but the straw jammed into her cheek. Huffing, she pushed it aside and downed the martini, finishing by wiping her wrist across her mouth. The room took a lazy spin.

She sat awhile, twirling the empty glass, waiting for her equilibrium to settle. The weight of her troubles hunched her shoulders. She still had no job. No place to live. The alcohol provided no insight, nor did the monotony of the spinning glass. She couldn't reverse time, so telling Nick where to shove his "*it's for the best*" face was off the table. Time to call it a night.

Tip left for the bartender, she hopped off the barstool. The walls did a tilt-a-whirl—a questionable sensation. She'd only had three drinks. Enough to make her mind feel loose, but not enough to turn the room into a merry-go-round. The cold medicine she'd used to Band-Aid her headache must be the culprit. The aching no longer plagued her, but the room's drowsy spin could pose a problem.

Bathroom. She just needed to make it to the bathroom, splash a little water on her face, and she'd be rain as right. Or right as rain. She'd shake this wooziness and figure out a plan. Translation: she'd sleep in her car tonight and hope to wake up in one of those body-swapping movies.

Maybe she could become Emma Stone. That girl had a sassy spine, no qualms about mouthing off to deserving men. They both had the red hair, freckle thing going on. Emma's boobs were smaller, so wearing fitted tops wouldn't make Bea feel like a Hooters waitress trolling for tips. But Bea had an hourglass figure with a daylight saving's hour padding out her rear, which she loved. Come to think of it, Bea liked her body just fine. It was her life and backbone that were in need of swapping.

So lost in her hypothetical switcharoo, she didn't recall walking to the bathroom or flushing the toilet or even leaving the stall. She hoped she hadn't sat directly on the seat.

Beside her, a black woman with peroxide blond curls reapplied red lipstick. She cut a look Bea's way and whistled. "Someone's had a rough night."

Bea sighed at her bleary reflection. "I made a bad decision."

One that shouldn't derail her life. Nick's name *did* rhyme with prick, but she was in New Orleans. A colorful city with men in capes and monkeybar-staches. The perfect place to replenish her drained creative juices. She didn't need Nick the Prick to start fresh. To prove her capability, she fumbled for the watermelon lip gloss in her purse and managed to paint on a layer. Everything in the world could be made better by watermelon gloss.

The woman curled her top lip and wiped some excess red from her tooth. "You're preaching to the choir. My bad decision is named Miles, and he has a special ringtone."

She pocketed her makeup and pulled out her phone. A few swipes of her thumb later, Carrie Underwood's "Before He Cheats" blared from her rhinestone-covered cell. Bea bobbed her head as Carrie sang about keying her cheating boyfriend's car and smashing his headlights.

When the chorus ended, the woman shoved her cell into her purse. "That, girlfriend, is how you remind yourself to avoid bad decisions. Miles calls every few days. He leaves a voicemail apologizing, and I don't call back. I could block his number, but I like remembering I'm no man's doormat." Her pointed look was as fierce as her leopard-print dress.

Bea was still wearing the pink pedal pushers and turquoise polka dot blouse she'd pulled on this morning. The outfit exuded more bubble gum cheer than Hot Tamale attitude, but she'd always been a Double Bubble gal. She also wasn't sure Nick had earned a Carrie Underwood ring tone. Definitely a Taylor Swift lyric jab or two, but Carrie could be pushing it. They had, after all, broken up prior to his date tonight, but accepting the date *before* his "it's for the best" speech made the situation suspect.

Still, she didn't want to key his 1978 Mustang Cobra, which he loved more than his shoe collection. Life was too short for revenge.

With a wink, the woman left the bathroom. Bea followed. A little too fast. One hand on the wall, she closed her eyes as the tilt-a-whirl whirled again. Eyes open were preferable. Air was also in order. She tried to strut outside with Hot Tamale attitude, but it likely resembled a dizzy stumble. She made it outside and sucked back air like a drowning swimmer breaching the water's surface.

Her first breath cleared a layer of fuzz from her head. The second restored clarity to her blurry vision. She wished it hadn't. There, across the street, was none other than Nick, walking hand-in-hand with his date.

The bar wasn't far from his apartment, something she should have considered before setting up camp inside, and her uncharacteristic anger returned to a simmer. She didn't love Nick. Moving to New Orleans and leaving her past had been as much for her as for him. But she'd trusted the man wouldn't leave her high and dry...for another woman. After four days.

Because he was honest.

She contemplated stomping across the street and telling him to screw off. She detested confrontation more than she hated green lollipops, but calling him a spiny lumpsucker or tufted titmouse would leave her with a modicum of satisfaction.

Then she noticed his black Mustang. Half a block down, his treasured automobile sat parked at the curb. A gift from the Carrie Underwood gods. Nick was walking the opposite way, and Bea's attention lasered in on his vehicle. She wasn't a malicious girl. Her back was basically made of Teflon, all resentment and stress sliding to its demise. Yet she was ogling Nick the Prick's muscle car with devious intent, and she barely recognized herself.

She'd worked since she was old enough to deliver papers. She'd then cut lawns and babysat and eventually waitressed. She'd dabbled in house painting—anything to add color to the world and money to her pocket, all while pursuing her art in private. Growing up, she'd been the levelheaded one who had kept the electricity on and heat flowing. She prided herself on being the only member of the Baker clan to never procure a mug shot.

See? Totally levelheaded.

Which meant her next action could only be blamed on Nick's "honesty" and the brilliant Carrie Underwood. She'd also revised her cheating theory: dating a woman the same calendar day of a breakup was definitely considered running around.

She walked to the side of his Mustang.

If he wants honesty, he'll get honesty.

She lifted her car keys from her purse.

I honestly think you're a fungus beetle.

Fisting the keys, her mind drifted to her father. To the feeble shrug of Franklyn Baker's shoulders when he'd admitted to gambling away her life savings, and how she'd caught nothing but a mouthful of flies in reaction. Her wicked grin faded. Her keys bit into her palm.

I am no man's doormat.

ALSO BY KELLY SISKIND

STANDALONES

Chasing Crazy: "...this is one of the best New Adult contemporary romances I've read to date." ~ *USA Today* Bestselling author K.A. Tucker

INTERCONNECTED STANDALONES

Showmen Series

New Orleans Rush: "The romance in New Orleans Rush will leave you smiling and filled with optimism." ~ *USA Today* Bestselling author Helen Hoang

Don't Go Stealing My Heart: "This book sparkles and sizzles with Siskind's trademark humor and heat. Don't go missing this one!" ~ Jen DeLuca, author of *Well Met*

The Beat Match: "The perfect balance of sensual, sweet, and sassy, while also delivering a satisfying, sometimes tear-inducing and heartfelt love story." ~ Bookgasms Book Blog

The Knockout Rule: "There's only one way to review this...by yelling it from the rooftops about how awesome it is!" ~ Red Reader

---

Over the Top Series

My Perfect Mistake: "This has easily earned itself a place on my all-time favorites shelf." ~ The Sisterhood of the Traveling Book Boyfriends

A Fine Mess: "Delicious, sizzling chemistry that leapt off the page!" ~ *USA Today* Bestselling Author Jennifer Blackwood

Hooked on Trouble: "...experience the romance, the sexy times, the heartbreak, and the swoons...you can thank me later!!" ~ The Book Hookup

---

One Wild Wish Series

He's Going Down: "An intoxicating romance that lingers like a great Merlot and leaves you with one hell of a book hangover!" ~ author Scarlett Cole

Off-Limits Crush: "...with loads of flirty and witty banter. Siskind knows how to write characters that have off-the-charts chemistry." ~ RT Book Reviews

36 Hour Date: "Kelly has blended a mystery into this compelling love story in a way that keeps the reader flipping pages. I couldn't put it down!" ~ *USA Today* Bestselling Author Ellis Leigh

ACKNOWLEDGMENTS

I've never considered myself a poet, but I absolutely loved stretching my poetry muscles when writing this book. Channeling the fictional Ramona Estle was fun and challenging and added another dimension to this novel I hadn't expected. My main inspiration for her poems was Rupi Kaur's powerful work. She's miles better than me at spinning words into thoughtful wisdoms, and I highly recommend reading her books or following her Instagram account.

Huge thank you to Sue Underhill for your insight on all things physiotherapy. You helped me fine-tune the language and exercises Isla used, giving me the confidence to polish those scenes. Any errors are of my own making. My critique partners on this book were my lifelines. J.R. Yates and Jamie Howard, I'd be lost without your insights. Huge thank you to my beta readers and proofreaders: Shelly Hastings Suhr, Michelle Pike, Jen DeLuca, Nena Drury, and Lisa Bardonski. Thank you to Brianna Lebrecht for your awesome copyediting skills.

My cover designer, Mary Ann Smith, knocked this design

out of the park, as per usual. You continue to astound me with your talent and always bring my visions to life perfectly.

To all the readers and bookstagrammers and bloggers who take the time to read my work and help spread the word about my novels: I wouldn't be able to do this without you. Thank you to the moon and back.

ABOUT THE AUTHOR

A small-town girl at heart, Kelly moved from the city to enjoy the charm of northern Ontario. When she's not out hiking with her husband or home devouring books, you can find her, notepad in hand, scribbling down one of the many plot bunnies bouncing around in her head. Her novels have been published internationally.

For giveaways and early peeks at new work, join Kelly' newsletter: www.kellysiskind.com

If you like to laugh and chat about books, join Kelly in her Facebook group, KELLY'S GANG.

Connect with Kelly on social media:

twitter.com/KellySiskind

facebook.com/authorKellySiskind/

instagram.com/kellysiskind/

CPSIA information can be obtained
at www.ICGtesting.com
Printed in the USA
LVHW050814230221
679709LV00007B/83

9 781988 937168